MW00480013

CHRISTMAS PARANORMAL COZY MYSTERIES - VOLUME 1

Copyright © 2022 by K.E. O'Connor

ISBN: 978-1-915378-48-4

Written by: K.E. O'Connor

# Christmas Paranormal Cozy Mysteries

Volume 1

K.E. O'Connor

K.E. O'Connor Books

# Every Witch Way but Yule

## K.E. O'Connor

# Chapter 1

I dabbed the gold tinsel as it danced in the chilled evening air. I hadn't felt this playful in a long time, but there was something about Christmas that brought out the kitten in me.

Zandra Crypt, my always wonderful witch, inspected a market stall festooned with scented candles. She turned to me and pulled down the red scarf covering her mouth. "Too girly for Tempest?"

"She's more of a build-your-own hex kind of witch than a scented candle witch." I forced myself away from the enticing tinsel draped around the candy cane stall and joined her, being careful not to get jostled by the crowds.

It was the final week before Christmas, and Crimson Cove bustled with visitors as they enjoyed the daily festive market and shopped for last-minute Christmas gifts. Or, in Zandra's case, finally getting around to buying any at all.

"You're right. Unless I find one that smells of sarcasm and sass, she won't be interested." Zandra sniffed at another candle. "I want to get her something she'll use."

"You should invite her to come and stay. She'd love the horse skull parade. Then she can pick her own gift."

"Tempest's too busy with Cloven Hoof this time of year. She's got back-to-back parties throughout

2

the festive season. Tonight, she's hosting a coven of powerful witches. The theme is brimstone and fire."

"Sounds fun." I hopped over a pile of snow banked against one stall. "She's missing out. I've seen dozens of horse skull parades, and they never disappoint." I was a fan of the ancient rituals that seeped into mainstream celebrations unnoticed. There was something deliciously primal and powerful about the old ways.

Zandra shrugged. "I don't see what the big deal is about some mangy old skull on a pole being carried through town and shoved in your face."

I hopped onto her shoulder and dabbed the end of my cold booping snooter against her cheek, making her gasp. "Respect the old ways. This custom has existed for thousands of years. It's a powerful ceremony. It'll strengthen everyone's magic and ensure happiness for those who touch the skull and allow it entry into their home, or gift it food."

"Yeah, yeah. I get it. The horse skull gets fat and happy, and so do we. I'm more interested in the dinner we'll have with Vorana and Sage after. She's been showing me the recipes." Zandra patted her stomach, which had grown nicely round since our landlady started feeding us so well. I could now make excellent biscuits on Zandra's perfect belly.

"Vorana loves to spoil us."

"I'll put up with the parade, so long as we get fed. And it's not raining. Or snowing." Zandra cast a critical glance at the leaden sky.

"I can't guarantee that. It's been snowing on and off for weeks. We'll wrap up warm and still have fun."

Zandra ambled past more festive stalls, inspecting potential gift ideas.

"When will you head to Willow Tree Falls? You are intending to see your family this year?" I said.

"Sure. Dad wants us there for New Year's Eve. Does that work for you?"

"Wherever you go, I'm happy to follow." As a witch's familiar, it was my honor and duty to be by her side.

"Then it's sorted. Freaky horse skull parade, Christmas with friends, then New Year's celebrations with the family. How about Sammy? He's welcome to join us. I know he doesn't have a bond with anyone, so I don't want him to get lonely while you're away."

"I'll invite him, but he's already got plans with Sorcha." Sorcha Creer took in all the unloved cat familiars and gave them a home and a hearth in her wonderful café, Bites and Delights.

Zandra stopped to examine some hand-knitted scarves. "How about this for Tempest? She's always chasing demons in the dead of night. She could do with something to keep her warm."

"Too colorful. Stick to her favorite color, black. Besides, she has the adorably smelly Wiggles to huff his pongy breath over her when she gets the chills."

We were sauntering past the busy broomstick stall, when a broad-faced, smiling man stepped in our path. "Good evening, ladies. May I interest you in a new stick? Ten percent discount on orders placed this evening. You won't find a better broomstick."

"No, thanks. I don't fly much," Zandra said. "It makes me sick."

"And I have no need for a broomstick." I lifted a paw and waved a little magic at him.

"Come and look. You may change your mind. I make them myself. Finest quality wood." He attempted to usher Zandra closer to the stall, but she didn't move.

"We're good."

"Then how about a gift for a loved one? Every witch needs a perfect broomstick."

I cast my gaze over what he had on offer. There was an array of broomsticks, and they all looked well made and sturdy for the amplest of witch's buttocks.

"I see your fine familiar has an eye for quality. I'm Paxton Starstride, owner of Imperial Broomsticks. If you don't see what you want on display, tell me your specifications, and I'll make it. Anything you desire is within my capability. This business has been passed down through many generations of my family, and we all have a talent for woodworking."

Zandra shrugged, not looking impressed. "I'm glad you've found your calling. But really, I don't need a broomstick. Not for anyone."

As Paxton attempted to convince Zandra she was making a mistake, I hopped off her shoulder and wandered among the customers.

"I don't know what happened to it. I've looked everywhere. Under every item of furniture, behind every door, in every closet. It's gone!" A tall, thin witch with a shock of messy red hair inspected a broomstick, turning it over in her hands, her lips pursed.

"I'm the same. I figured I'd misplaced it. I've been so busy getting things ready for Christmas." A smaller, apple-shaped witch with blonde curls and a thin mouth made a sweeping motion with the broomstick she held. "We need to get them put away, so the spirits don't take them."

I hopped onto the counter. "Greetings! I couldn't help but overhear. You've both lost your broomsticks?"

The witch with the red hair startled and looked around, before noticing me. "What business is it of yours?"

"I'm curious. I don't like to think of a witch without her broomstick."

Her forehead wrinkled, then she turned to her friend. "I must complete the closing ceremony to stop those

5

pesky spirits from bothering us. And I'll need something to fly home on. I need a broomstick."

"These are so expensive, though," the other witch said. "Although this one has an excellent swooshing motion."

"There's a ten percent discount if you order this evening." A hunchbacked, pale-faced man wearing a large mistletoe pin on the lapel of his black suit scuttled closer. His arms were twig thin and his cheeks hollow.

"Even with the discount, these aren't cheap. Can you do us a better deal? I'll pay in cash," the red-haired witch said.

"I'll speak to Paxton. Don't go anywhere." The guy scuttled off, one leg dragging slightly behind him.

"Dolores! Look at the price on this!" The blonde witch held a huge black ash broomstick with threads of gold crisscrossing the handle.

Dolores shook her head. "I don't know how he can charge so much. Broomsticks literally grow on trees."

The two women cackled laughter.

Paxton strode over with his limping assistant beside him. He flapped a hand at a waiting customer. "Godric, attend to that charming lady. Be quick about it."

Godric tripped over his feet in his haste to serve, his shoulders stooped and his gaze down.

Paxton shook his head. "The young man is loyal, but he's not got any sales instinct. Still, you must always love a trier." He wasn't speaking to anyone in particular, but I nodded, anyway.

"Hey, let's get out of here while we can." Zandra scooped me up and settled me back on her shoulder. "I didn't think I'd get away without buying a broomstick. He sure is pushy."

"The sticks are excellent quality," I said, as we headed away from the stall and toward the enticing smell of cinnamon and sugar from the crepe stand.

"If I was into broomsticks, I'd agree. But since I prefer driving, and you can click your paws and translocate, who needs a broomstick wedged between their thighs? And don't get me started on the updraft."

"I overheard some witches saying their broomsticks were missing. The timing couldn't be worse."

Zandra chuckled and wriggled her fingers in the air. "You're thinking the spirits stole them because they didn't look after their magical rides properly?"

"It happens all the time when a witch is negligent of her broomstick."

"Juno! That's an urban legend. Why would evil spirits steal a witch's broomstick?"

I huffed into her ear. "You never studied."

She shrugged. "I studied. Some. And Vorana insists I read at least a book a month."

"She doesn't mean magazines."

"Hey! I have spell books. And I'm working through all the books Adrienne left me."

I curled my tail around her neck. "Well, if you were into your broomsticks and had appropriately studied, you'd know you could do a lot with a pile of powerful witches' broomsticks and some dark intentions."

"Then I'm glad I don't own one. It would definitely have gone missing by now. You know what I'm like with my keys. I'd always lose the wretched thing."

"Hey! Having fun?"

I turned to see Finn striding toward us. He wasn't wearing his usual head-to-toe white Angel Force uniform, though. He was dressed as a jolly Santa Claus, complete with hat and fake beard.

"That's an interesting look." Zandra grinned at him. "You're not working?"

"This is work." He tweaked the beard. "You should see the others. We're all dressing up for Christmas week."

"Because..."

"Cythera wants us to look approachable. We're getting lots of visitors because of the market, and she doesn't want those unfamiliar with us to feel uncomfortable asking for help."

"And dressing as a fake Santa is reassuring?" I asked.

"It's hard to tell." He popped a roasted chestnut into his mouth from the bag he held before offering them to Zandra. "I'm just smiling and keeping the crowds under control. It seems to work."

Zandra nodded. "No riots over the candy canes so far."

"You see! I'm doing a great job." Finn looked around. "Although, I've also been assigned broom patrol. We've had six complaints in the last few days about people having their broomsticks stolen."

"Stolen! I've heard about them vanishing. You think it was theft?" I asked.

"That's what people are claiming. I doubt they've been stolen, though. It's just the usual Christmas chaos. People running around, trying to get everything done last minute, and they've forgotten where they put their broomsticks."

"You're sure?" Worry trickled through me and made my toe beans tingle. A couple of broomsticks going missing could be a coincidence, but not six. Witches valued their broomsticks. They never left them lying around to be misused.

"I'm sure. But it gets worse. I'm having to go to the local school to talk to the kids."

"About what?" Zandra strolled along with Finn, inspecting more of the festive stalls.

"Some poor kid had a nightmare about an evil Santa. Now, they're all having the same dream." Finn munched on another chestnut. "Apparently, this creepy Santa sneaks into their rooms, whacks them with a stick, and shoves them into a sack."

"They're all having the same nightmare?" I said.

"Nah. I reckon most of them are making it up to get attention," Finn said. "Maybe one of them had the nightmare, and the rest joined in because it sounded cool. Anyway, Cythera clearly hates me, because she's got me going into the school assemblies every morning to reassure the children there's no such thing as an evil Santa."

"Technically, there is. But he won't bother the children. He can't."

Finn arched an eyebrow. "Why is that, Juno?"

I lifted my chin. "Because he's locked up."

"Oh, that's right." Finn chuckled. "Angel Force put Evil Santa behind bars last year for lewd conduct in a public place. I remember now."

My whiskers twitched. "His incarceration had nothing to do with Angel Force. You'd never be able to take down such a powerful being."

Raised voices had us looking at the snow globe stall. Two guys fought over what looked to be the last golden globe.

"Uh-oh. Duty calls." Finn adjusted his beard as he strode off. "I'll catch up with you another time, and you can tell me all about Evil Santa."

Zandra watched the two guys tussle. "Christmas. It can bring out the worst in people."

"Especially when you don't forward plan and have to rush to get all your gifts bought and wrapped in time."

She rolled her eyes to the snow-laden heavens. "I'm almost done."

"Exactly how many gifts have you purchased?"

"Two or three. And I'm not buying for everyone. Dad said he wants nothing."

"You've got to get him something."

"He told me visiting at the New Year was enough of a gift." She looked a little shamefaced.

"Zandra Crypt. Don't be a Grinch. Get your father a gift."

She huffed out a breath. "He's so hard to buy for."

"And what will you get your mother?"

Zandra groaned. "I have no clue. What do you get a ghoul for Christmas?"

"A chiller full of the finest innards?"

"Gross. But not a bad idea. Maybe Sorcha's got something I can buy off her."

Since the snow globe tussle was dying down, we kept wandering, checking the stalls and debating over what to buy people.

My gaze skittered around, and I shivered. I couldn't put my paw on it, but something felt off in Crimson Cove. There was a darkness lurking under the tinsel and fairy lights. Why were all the broomsticks going missing? And why were children having nightmares about an evil Santa?

I knew without a shadow of a doubt, only the good Santa was left, and he was all about family, friendship, and kindness. There was no room for dark deeds during the festive season.

"Ooooh! I've found you the perfect Christmas gift." Zandra darted to a stall called Pampered Pets. She lifted a fairy onesie and held it out. "It's your size! We have to get it. You'll look amazing."

"I'd rather chew off my tail."

Zandra laughed as she set down the costume. "Not even a set of adorable wings?"

"I'll wear the wings if you get the reindeer antlers to wear."

"I'm almost tempted by that deal." She smirked and turned back to the stall. "What about these? Catnip mice. Way better than the disgusting little corpses you leave on my pillow."

"But not so satisfying to kill." I lost myself in the delights of Pampered Pets, testing the toys and sniffing the treats. I hadn't forgotten the strangeness flickering through town like a guttering candle in a draughty church, but I'd circle back to it after we'd had all the festive fun we could handle.

# Chapter 2

"Are you sure this is a good idea?" Sammy, my fluffy, sometimes adorably timid sweetheart, hurried along beside me, his tabby fur dotted with snowflakes. "It's already snowing. And Sorcha said a blizzard is predicted."

"We won't be long. I just want to check something out," I said.

"The cold doesn't bother me." Archie, my favorite drooling hellhound, ambled beside us, chuffing out hot breaths to melt the snow and heat the ground beneath our paws. "And since Remus has become obsessed with buying me coats, I'm always too warm. He even suggested I get a pair of snow boots."

"I could do with some snow boots," Sammy said. "My paws are frozen. I'm a fair-weather cat."

"Archie, huff hot breath over Sammy," I said. "You'll have to put snow boots on your gift list for this year."

"I already know what I'm getting." Sammy staggered sideways as Archie enthusiastically huffed at him. "Sorcha has promised us each a turkey. Imagine that! I'll get an enormous bird all to myself. And she's stuffing it with treats, too."

"When you've devoured your turkey, you're welcome to join me and Zandra," I said. "We're having Christmas with Vorana and Sage."

"I'd love that. Maybe in the evening? Sorcha is opening the café on Christmas Day, so if anyone hasn't got company, they can join us. She's fully booked! We're having food, party games, and singing carols."

"That's sad," Archie said. "No one should be alone at Christmas."

"That's just it. They won't be, thanks to Sorcha," Sammy said. "I'm looking forward to it. Hey, maybe you could all come to the café. The games sound fun. There'll be pass the ham hock, guess the number of wishbones in a jar, and who goes there."

"It's a good idea," I said. "We could drop by after we've eaten. Archie, will you go?"

"I'll try, but Remus is having a party at his mansion," Archie said. "All the vampires will be there. As usual, I'm the guest of honor."

"It'll be a rare-steak Christmas for you, then," I said.

"I can have what I like, but I'll stick with steak. You can't go wrong with a juicy hunk of warm meat. And after Christmas, Remus is taking me on a cruise designed especially for familiars."

"A cruise for familiars?" I said. "Sounds fun."

"I read about it in one of his magazines, and the next thing I know, he books it. He's the best vampire in the world." Archie sighed. "There's an enormous swimming pool with giant slides, back-to-back movies featuring my favorite familiars, all the entertainment you can imagine, an all-day buffet, then a gourmet dinner at night. And I get to wear a bow tie for the posh dinners."

"Don't cruises usually take you somewhere sunny?" Sammy said. "How will Remus handle that?"

"We're going to Alaska. Super cold and not much sun. It's all figured out." Archie wagged his tail.

I was thrilled Archie had found his happily ever after with Remus. It was no less than he deserved.

"What about you, Juno?" Sammy said. "What's on your Christmas wish list?"

"My needs are simple. A whole dressed salmon and unlimited snuggles with Zandra will make the day perfect."

"Sounds great." Sammy glanced at the darkening sky again. "The snow is falling faster. Are you sure we can't do this another day?"

"I promise, once we find where Paxton is staying, we'll be in and out in ten minutes." I stepped up the pace, not keen on getting soaked by the snow that plopped around us in chunky, freezing clumps.

"Why are we investigating this guy again?" Archie said.

"Finn told me six witches' broomsticks were stolen this week."

"By the evil spirits?" Sammy glanced over his shoulder. "Those pesky beasts are always on the lookout for broomsticks at this time of year."

"That's what I told Finn, but he was unconcerned. Just like Zandra, he thinks evil broomstick-stealing spirits are urban legends."

"So, you think Paxton is in charge of the light-fingered spirits?" Archie said.

"No. And I don't think it's spirits taking the broomsticks. We have a flesh and blood thief on our paws."

"Paxton?" Sammy said.

"It's too much of a coincidence he arrives in Crimson Cove and then all the broomsticks go missing. And he'll make a killing selling new broomsticks to desperate witches."

"He's stealing them and then selling them back to desperate customers?" Sammy said.

"I don't think Paxton is that bold or foolish," I said. "I inspected his stall, and he makes magnificent broomsticks. I suspect he's hidden the stolen sticks, so the witches have no choice but to purchase from him."

Archie grumbled out a bark. "I'll give him a good shake and tell him it's wrong. Where's his Christmas spirit?"

"Hidden in his deep pockets," Sammy said. "New broomsticks aren't cheap."

I slowed as we reached the local inn. "The market stall holders all stay here. This is where we'll find Paxton."

We headed in and over to the receptionist, who stood behind the desk next to an enormous, brightly decorated Christmas tree with tiny sparkling silver webs glistening from the branches. Soft Christmas music piped from an invisible speaker, giving the place a cheery vibe.

He greeted us with a smile. "Checking in?"

"Checking in on a guest," I said. "Is Paxton Starstride in his room?"

"Let me see." The receptionist scanned a book in front of him. "We don't have anyone here by that name. Perhaps he hasn't arrived yet. Were you meeting him here?"

"He's the broomstick seller at the Christmas market," I said. "Aren't all the stall owners staying here?"

"Most of them. They get a discount. But we have no Paxton Starstride in residence. Perhaps he's renting a private room in town."

I wrinkled my booping snooter. I'd assumed it would be easy to track Paxton.

"How about the woods?" Archie said. "Since this guy makes brooms, he'll need access to magical sticks."

"Excellent idea," I said. "And there are rentals in the woods."

After saying goodbye to the receptionist, we headed outside again.

Sammy shivered and cast a gloomy eye at the sky. "We should try the woods another day. Come back in the morning."

"It's just a little snow," I said. "We'll find where Paxton is staying and have a discreet snoop to see if he's hiding piles of witches' broomsticks. If we catch him, we solve the mystery. We'll make sure the brooms are returned to their witches, and they can safely store them. We don't want Crimson Cove full of evil spirits looking for untethered broomsticks. It'll ruin Christmas."

"I suppose," Sammy said. "Let's be quick, though. And after this, we need food. The cold makes me hungry."

"I'm always hungry," Archie said. "Count me in. It's almost time for my second dinner. Or should that be supper? It's time for food, anyway."

We dashed through the steadily falling snow. I didn't love the white stuff, but it went perfectly with my beautiful fur.

A few minutes later, we entered the woods and followed a well-trodden path. There were neat brown signs pointing toward the rental cabins.

The cabins came in all shapes and sizes, from simple wooden shacks, to deluxe, detached residences with several floors, hot tubs, and heated swimming pools.

"Did Paxton strike you as a swanky guy who splurged his cash, or tightfisted?" Sammy said.

"He was dressed well, and he sells quality products. I say we look at the midrange rentals and go up from there," I said.

We checked a couple of nicely presented cabins, but they were empty. The third one had a warm light in the front room. I knocked on the door.

A small female elf opened it. "Oh, how adorable. Are you here to sing carols?"

"We could give it a go," Archie said. "Remus says I have an amazing singing voice. A cross between a werewolf and a screech owl."

"That's a compliment?" Sammy glanced up at Archie.

"Of course. He only ever says nice things about me. Listen."

I thumped a paw on Archie's muzzle to stop the inevitable, painful noise. "Another time. Greetings. We're not here to sing carols. We're looking for Paxton Starstride."

She pouted. "I want carols."

"Do you know Paxton? He usually wears a suit. Dark hair. In his fifties. Possibly carrying broomsticks. Have you seen him using any of the cabins?"

The elf wrinkled her nose as she crossed her arms over her chest. "I'll tell you what I know, in exchange for a carol."

Pesky elf! "Archie, would you do the honors?"

He thumped his tail on the ground, opened his mouth, and howled. Mingled with the howls were festive words such as Santa, crackers, and tinsel, but he mainly howled about food.

The elf squeaked her delight and jigged along, while Sammy and I clamped our paws over our ears.

When the last howl filtered through the trees, Archie grinned at us.

"Perfect. You're a good boy." I petted his side. "Now, Paxton. Where can we find him?"

The elf shrugged. "I've not seen him. But I've not been here much. A few of the cabins further along are occupied. Try there."

After giving her a grudging thanks, we headed off. There was no answer at the next two cabins, but a man wearing only a small towel and a smile opened the third door.

"Oh! You're not who I expected."

"Greetings. It looks like you have a Merry Christmas planned," I said.

The guy's cheeks flushed. "You'd better believe it. A few days with my favorite honey and all the candy canes a man can handle. Bliss."

"We won't hold you up. We're looking for Paxton Starstride. He's renting a cabin here." I gave the man Paxton's description.

"Doesn't ring a bell. Some creepy little dude scuttled past a few times, though. Thin, hunched over, and dressed in a black suit. I thought he was an undertaker."

"That sounds like Godric. Paxton's assistant," I said.

"If you say so. I think he's got the cabin a few doors down. It's the one with the big wreath hung out the front."

I thanked the man for his time, then we headed along the path. The snow was coming down heavily, and I struggled to see through the blanket of white frostiness. Maybe Sammy was right, and we should postpone this trip. Still, the trees offered some protection, and we wouldn't be long. If the weather got too bad, I'd translocate us home.

A flash of dazzling magic made me pause.

"What was that?" Sammy was crouched, his ears lowered.

"It came from that cabin." Archie loped away to investigate.

I hustled Sammy along, and we quickly followed him. As we trotted toward the cabin, a deep, low bell rung. I tilted my head. Crimson Cove church didn't have a bell.

"That was a powerful spell." Archie looked over his shoulder. "Something wrong, Juno?"

I hurried to join him with Sammy. "Did you hear that bell?"

They shook their heads.

"Maybe I imagined it. Let's go see who cast that spell."

We dashed up the wooden steps and onto the porch. The cabin was sweetly rustic, with a wraparound wooden porch, cedar roof, and small windows with clapboards. There was a large green wreath with a red ribbon on the door.

As I nudged the door with my booping snooter, it opened.

Archie barged in, almost sending me flying. "Huh! Even I know that's a fire risk, and I set light to everything."

I sidled around him with Sammy and stopped. In the middle of the room was an enormous, smoldering yule log. And poking out from underneath it was a foot.

# Chapter 3

I dashed to the smoldering yule log. I hadn't been mistaken. There was a foot poking out from underneath it. And it was attached to a body. "Help me roll this thing."

Archie slammed into the yule log with his shoulder. Wood splintered, and the giant log rolled away.

"It's Paxton!" I leaped onto his chest and checked for signs of life. There was no pulse, and he wasn't breathing, although his body was warm.

"Did that log fall on him? How did it get in here?" Sammy stood by Paxton's feet, his eyes wide.

"No idea." Paxton's face had several red lines slashed across it. He had more on the back of his hands, too, suggesting he'd defended himself from his attacker. "Archie, get the yule log outside. It's smoking and might burst into flames. If it does, it'll take this place with it."

He hunkered down and bit the log, then backed up, spitting out splinters. "Boy! It's heavy."

"Sammy, help Archie. I'll stay with Paxton."

Sammy's tail quivered, then he nodded and dashed over to join Archie. Archie tried shoving it with his shoulder again, but even his hellhound strength couldn't defeat the log.

Between the two of them, they conjured a spell to float the log through the front door and into the snow. It was a squeeze to get it through the doorway.

I remained on Paxton's chest as I took in the room. There were bundles of sticks scattered around, and the air smelled hot, as if fire lurked in the shadows, waiting to burst to life.

Archie bounded back in, stopping to shake the snow off his fur. Sammy joined us, flicking his paws and shivering.

I hopped off Paxton's chest. "This has only just happened. That flash of magic must have been thrown during the fight between Paxton and his killer."

Archie growled, and his hackles rose. "You think the killer is still here?"

"We need to search the place. Check every room, look under every bed, and in any space someone could hide."

"I'll come with you," Sammy said.

"We should split up. It'll be quicker that way." I rubbed my face against his. Sammy was adorable, but didn't have the biggest heroic streak, and needed a little motivation before springing into action. But when he did, it was always impressive.

It took less than five minutes to search the cabin. There were two bedrooms, two bathrooms, the living room where we'd discovered Paxton, and the kitchen. There was no one hiding in any of the rooms.

We met back in the living room.

"It looks like two guys lived here," Sammy said. "I don't see any ladies' cosmetics or clothing lying around."

"Paxton must share with his assistant. But where is Godric? I'm surprised he's out when the weather is so bad." I briefly inspected both bedrooms again. They were tidy and well put together for guests' comfort, but there was no hint where Paxton's assistant might be.

"Do you think the blast of magic came from Paxton or his killer?" Sammy said as I returned to the living room.

"Possibly Paxton. Although he'd need potent magic to transport that yule log," Archie said. "Even I struggled to move it."

"Given the work he did, Paxton would have had an affinity with trees. Maybe he summoned the log," I said.

"To use against his attacker?" Sammy said.

"It's a possibility." I sniffed around Paxton again. There was a tiny piece of stick poking out of the corner of his mouth. I wedged a paw between his lips and eased his mouth wider. Stuffed inside were even more sticks. "Why do that to him?"

Archie wandered over. He carried a bundle of sticks in his mouth. "They're tempting. And these sticks are tasty. Maybe he needed to chew on something. I've been resisting the piles ever since we came in."

"You're not resisting them now, are you?" I flicked my tail at him. "Spit those out. You could be chewing on evidence."

Archie's eyes widened, and he spat out the sticks. "I didn't think. There is magic in them, though. Powerful stuff. But it's been distorted by something I don't recognize."

I gently prodded a stick poking out of Paxton's mouth. There was a faint tang of magic on that, too.

Another look around the room showed six carefully placed piles of sticks. They could have been used to evoke magic to kill Paxton. Unfortunately, Archie had stomped his way through them, obscuring any pattern.

"Someone really wanted this guy dead." Sammy's tongue swooped around his whiskers. "He looks like he's been whipped in the face, choked with sticks, crushed by the yule log, and his hands are burned, too."

I inspected Paxton's hands and discovered fresh red marks and blisters. "Could these be from a spell he used? Something beyond his capability, so he injured himself?"

"If he didn't translocate that log in here, his killer did. Paxton would have been desperate to avoid being whacked by it," Sammy said.

I sniffed Paxton's hands. There was a faint smell of burning. Sammy joined me a few seconds later, and this time, he was chewing on something. When he caught me watching, he swallowed and looked away.

"What are you eating?"

"Um ... there are mini sausage rolls on the table. I noticed them when we came in. I'm surprised you didn't smell them."

I held back a smile. "And you couldn't resist?"

"I had little time for lunch. I needed to make sure I wasn't late for our mission. There's plenty. You should try one. They're tasty."

"They're delicious." Archie stood by a low coffee table, his mouth full.

"Less eating, and more focusing on the murder scene." I shook my head, although I appreciated the faint hint of sausage meat and stuffing in the air. "We need to get Angel Force here. This was no accident."

"I can run to town. Let them know what's going on." Archie gulped down the rest of the sausage rolls.

I glanced outside. A blizzard swirled around the cabin, fat white blobs of snow spinning about, the daylight almost gone. "Let's find a snow globe and let them know what happened. Angels can fly through bad weather."

We split up again and went in search of a globe. The cabin must have one, but a search of every room showed no way of communicating with the outside world.

"It's set up as one of those rural retreats," Archie said as we met back in the living room. "Remus took me on one. You leave behind all forms of communication so you can be at one with nature and forget modern world stresses."

"As charming as that is, it's inconvenient when a body turns up and you need to tell the angels you've stumbled onto a crime scene," I said.

There was a muted thump from somewhere in the cabin, and my gaze flashed to the others. "Did you both hear that?"

Sammy was already crouched low, his eyes wide, while Archie growled.

"How could someone have hidden from us?" Sammy said. "We searched everywhere."

There was another thump to confirm my suspicions we weren't alone. "That came from outside. Out the back. Follow me." I dashed out of the living room and through the small kitchen. I reached the back door, placed my paws around the handle, and pulled. It swung open onto a snowy back porch.

Godric was in the middle of the yard, on his knees, and covered in snow.

"That's the killer!" Archie said. "I'll get him."

"Hold on. It's Paxton's assistant," I said. "Godric, are you okay?"

He said nothing, just swayed from side to side.

As reluctant as I was to head into a blizzard, there was something wrong with that young man.

"I could throw a snowball," Archie said. "I've been practicing making them with my paws. That would get his attention."

"Better not. One gust of wind, and that unfortunate guy will be face first in the snow," I said. "Godric, I'm Juno. I'm here with friends. Are you hurt?"

A soft groan reached my ears.

"I'm coming for you." I braced myself and stepped off the porch.

My companions joined me, not once complaining about the snow that froze toe beans and whiskers.

I trotted down the steps and dashed to Godric. There was a large red lump on his forehead, and blood trickled from a deep cut on his head, dripping dark red spots in the snow.

When his gaze met mine, he flinched, but then he swayed again on his knees.

"What happened to you?" I asked.

He lifted his hands, his palms blistered as if heat had damaged them. "I tried to stop her. She attacked Paxton. Came out of nowhere."

"Who? You saw who killed Paxton?"

"He's dead?" A strangled sob left his lips. "Yes. I know that. I saw him crushed by the log, but I didn't want to believe it. I tried to help, but she was so fast."

"Paxton didn't survive the attack," I said. "It looks like you almost didn't, either."

"I couldn't let her get away after what she did, but I had no choice."

"Come inside. We'll treat your injuries, and you can tell us everything." I rested a calming paw on his frozen knee.

Godric went to stand, but his legs buckled, and he passed out.

# Chapter 4

"Is he dead?" Archie leaned over Godric and sniffed.

"No, he's breathing, but he's badly injured. Archie, drag him inside. Be careful not to shake him around too much. He could have other injuries. We need to get out of these freezing conditions and warm him up." I hurried onto the porch with Sammy as Archie lifted Godric as if he weighed nothing and heaved him inside the cabin.

I shut the door and followed Archie as he dragged Godric into the living room. "Take him into a bedroom. If he wakes and sees his boss dead on the floor, he'll faint again."

Archie did as instructed and dropped Godric onto a bed in the nearest room.

Godric shivered, even though he was unconscious. His clothes were soaked, as was his hair.

Now I could see the extent of his head wound, I realized he was lucky to have survived the blow.

"Archie, get the fire lit in the main room. And Sammy, find blankets. We need to get Godric warm. He's in shock."

As my wonderful companions got to work, I sat next to Godric, rested a paw against his head injury, and pulsed out healing magic.

My power was behaving. It wasn't always the case, so I was glad I could be of service to Godric.

"The fire is roaring." Archie trotted back into the bedroom, wagging his tail. "How's he doing?"

"Not good. I hate to ask you to go out in this weather, but we need Angel Force here. They'll have to speak to Godric about what happened as soon as possible, in case he doesn't survive."

"I don't mind going. The cold doesn't bother me. If I get chilly, I'll just blast out flames."

"I'm more worried about you getting lost in the blizzard. Follow your nose, don't get distracted, and head straight to town. Got it?"

"I never get lost. Well, I do sometimes. Remus wants me to wear a tracking collar, but I'm not sure. He said they come in different colors. I could go for—"

"Let's discuss the use of collars on familiars another time. Godric needs you to run fast and smooth." I rubbed my face on his front leg. "Archie, we're counting on you."

"Oh! Of course. I'll be back soon." He blasted out of the room, and the front door slammed back and hit the wall.

Sammy trotted in a moment later, dragging a brown blanket behind him.

I helped arrange it over Godric and then covered him with the bed sheets. Sammy found several more blankets, and soon, Godric was snuggled in them.

The whole time, I'd been pulsing healing magic into him, and was getting tired from giving so much, but he needed it. "Godric's magic feels strange. It wavers. It's as if he has no control over his own magic."

"Because of his injury?" Sammy sat on the other side of Godric's head. "When Sorcha accidentally burns herself on the stove, her magic gets fizzy and strange. Mine does too, when I'm stressed."

"It must be that. He feels weak, as if any second, he'll die." I gently sniffed his pale face. "It's like when a familiar bond is abruptly cut. Suddenly, they're tethered to nothing, and their purpose has been ripped away from them."

Sammy ducked his head. "I understand that. When Rachel died, I lost hope. I stopped caring about anything. I wanted my life to end."

I reached over and gently rested a paw on Sammy's head. "It's a terrible thing to go through. Maybe it's shock. Godric saw what happened to Paxton. If they were close, he'd have been devastated."

"That's assuming they liked each other," Sammy said. "Not everyone likes their boss."

I considered that option. I hopped onto Godric's chest and placed both paws on his face, so I had easier access to heal him. Something hard rubbed against my soft belly, and a peek under the covers revealed he still wore his mistletoe pin.

"What's that?" Sammy said.

"Mistletoe."

"He's hoping for romance?"

I shifted my position, so the pin didn't dig in. "Possibly. Although in ancient times, they believed the plant had healing properties."

"I thought the berries were poisonous."

"They are. But many poisons, in tiny doses, also have beneficial properties."

The front door crashed open. Archie ran full speed into the bedroom and skidded to a halt before shaking snow everywhere.

I cringed as cold splatters rained around me. "Archie!"

He wagged his tail, his tongue lolling out. "I got Finn! He didn't believe me when I said we'd found a body. But then I told him about Godric and what you were doing to keep him alive. And I told him the dead guy's name, and how we found him crushed under a log. He said I had to stop talking and show him where you were. That's what I did. I did good, right?"

"Thank you, Archie. You completed the perfect mission. Always such a good boy."

Finn appeared in the bedroom doorway. He was dressed in a bright green and red elf's outfit and wore a pair of pointed ears. Snow speckled his sandy brown hair. "Hey, Juno. Sammy. I wondered if Archie was joking with me."

"No joke. Nice ears," I said.

Finn's cheeks flushed. "They're all in the name of public duty. I hate to think about what Cythera has in store for me tomorrow. This is Godric?" He moved to the bed.

"Yes. I don't know him, but I saw him working with Paxton Starstride at the Christmas market. We found Godric outside, badly injured. He's stable now, but I'm concerned about his magic."

"Did he tell you what happened? I looked at the other guy on my way in. He definitely won't be giving a statement." Finn took out a notepad and pen and flipped the pad open.

"Not much before he passed out. He said he tried to stop the attacker, but she did this to him." I pointed at the diminishing head wound.

"We're looking for a woman?"

"It sounds like it."

"You stay with him. I'll have a proper look at the crime scene." Finn left the room.

"It was hard to find an angel," Archie said. "I didn't recognize most of them because they're wearing costumes."

"You did an excellent job to locate Finn. He's the best angel we have in Crimson Cove." Because he was part demon, which gave him an edge over the officious, slow-moving nature of other angels.

Archie sniffed Godric. "He smells weird. Like burned wood. Just like Paxton."

"Maybe he tried to move the yule log to save Paxton," Sammy said.

"It could be the reason his hands got so burned," I said. "If Godric's magic is unstable, he'll find it hard to cast spells."

Finn returned a moment later. "I've called in reinforcements, but it could take a while for them to get here. Several people were hurt during an incident on the ice rink. Never take a juvenile snap dragon near ice. It doesn't end well. I took a look out the back, but it's still snowing hard, so any tracks have vanished. Did you see anything when you were outside?"

"No, and the snow was coming down fast when we discovered Godric," I said. "There was no sign of who attacked Paxton."

"Well, there was the enormous smoking yule log," Sammy said. "That's a clue."

"I saw it outside. That was the murder weapon?" Finn arched an eyebrow.

"It was on top of Paxton when we got here," I said.

"Interesting. What were you all doing out this way, anyway?" Finn stood at the end of the bed and looked down at Godric.

I settled on Godric's chest and tucked my tail around my paws. "I was concerned about the missing broomsticks. Angel Force aren't doing anything about it, and I needed to ensure nothing untoward was happening to them."

Finn wrinkled his nose. "The mislaid broomsticks are on my list of things to do, but Christmas is a busy time, so a few missing broomsticks will never be a top priority."

"They should be. Six witches missing their brooms at such an important time of year is a problem."

"And you decided to solve that problem?"

"I decided to make your life easier."

"Thanks, Juno. You have my undying gratitude." Finn shook his head. "You reckon Paxton had something to do with the broomsticks going missing?"

"It makes sense. He was doing a roaring trade at the Christmas market. Most of those witches wouldn't have visited his stall if it weren't for their broomsticks vanishing. I heard a couple of them complaining about the prices, but they had no choice but to buy from Paxton if they wanted a broom over the holidays."

Finn furrowed his forehead. "So you think Paxton stole the broomsticks to make more sales?"

"Why not?"

"Where are the stolen brooms?"

"You mean the ones in the closet in the other bedroom?" Archie looked up from licking his soggy tail.

Finn turned to stare at him. "The broomsticks are really here?"

"When we got here, we looked for the killer. We searched everywhere. I checked that closet, and there were loads of broomsticks in there. Most of them are damaged, though. No one can use them to fly."

I jumped off Godric's chest and marched out of the bedroom.

Finn followed me. He opened the closet and discovered ten broomsticks inside. All had pieces missing. Either the handles had chunks carved from them, or the main broom was damaged.

"Huh! You were right. These could be the missing broomsticks. Although I've not had ten complaints," Finn said.

"Maybe there are more witches yet to come forward. Or they think they've misplaced their broomstick and don't realize it's been stolen."

Finn inspected each broomstick. "It'll be easy to trace the owners. Every witch knows her broomstick inside out. Most of these are damaged beyond repair, though, so they won't be happy when I return them."

"He must have damaged them to ensure the witches had no choice but to buy new," I said.

Finn pulled out the last broomstick and set it against the wall. "It's a motive for murder. Witches are protective of their sticks. If one of them learned what Paxton was doing, they could have confronted him."

"Then crushed him as punishment," I said. "That motive has legs."

"Hey, get in here," Sammy called out. "Godric's awake."

We dashed back into the bedroom.

Godric was slowly blinking and staring at the ceiling.

Finn removed his elf hat and ears and leaned over him. "Take it easy. There's nothing to worry about. You're safe. I'm Finn. I work for the local branch of Angel Force. And you are?"

Godric drew in a shaky breath as his gaze focused on Finn. "Godric Gander. What's going on? How did I get here? I don't remember going to bed."

I hopped onto the bed. "Greetings. I'm Juno. My furry companions are Sammy and Archie. We found you in the snow. We brought you inside, and I've been healing you. Your magic is troubled. Do you have any other injuries that need healing?"

"No. I mean, I don't think so." He lifted a thin hand and touched his forehead. "Did I faint?"

"You did. Due to shock and your head injury," I said.

"How did you get that head wound?" Finn had his notepad in his hand again, his pen poised to write the killer's name.

"I'm not sure. It happened so fast. One second, I was chasing someone, and the next there was this blinding pain in my head."

"What else do you remember?" Finn said.

"Could you help me sit up?"

I shuffled out of the way as Finn eased Godric up and positioned pillows behind him so he was comfortable.

"Thanks. I'm feeling a bit sick." Godric's lips were blue, and he clutched the blanket against his sparrow chest.

"It may take a few days to feel better," I said.

"You could have a concussion," Finn said. "I'll take you to the hospital and get you checked over."

"Sure. I want to help, though. I don't want to forget anything that could be useful." Godric swallowed, his gaze shifting to the doorway. "Paxton, he is dead, isn't he?"

"He is," Finn said. "And we want to find his killer. Could you tell me why you're here?"

"Me, too." Godric's pale blue gaze lowered to his shaking, clasped hands. "We're here for the Christmas market. Paxton owns Imperial Broomsticks. Or rather, he used to."

"We saw you at the market," I said. "I visited the stall with my witch. You were busy."

"We have been since we got here. Everyone wants a new broomstick for Christmas."

I was tempted to say, especially because you've been stealing them from people, but I held my tongue.

"Did you see the attack on Paxton?" Finn said.

"Not really. I was in my room. I heard this bang and then Paxton shouted. He sounded surprised, or maybe angry. I hurried out to see what was going on."

"What did you see?" Finn said.

"Paxton under a log. Smoke was coming off it." Godric pressed his lips together. "I couldn't believe it."

"Did you see the flash of magic?" I said.

"Oh! Yes. It happened at the same time as the bang."

"Did you help Paxton?" Finn said.

Godric's bottom jaw wobbled. "I'm not great with magic. I'm a muddle of abilities and none of them are stable. I tried to lift the log with a spell, but I only made things worse by rocking it from side to side. Although, I think I was already too late. Paxton wasn't moving. I tried to push it but injured my hands." He lifted his palms. Although they were pink, the blisters had gone.

"You mentioned you chased the attacker," I said.

"I ran outside. Mainly to get help, but also to see if Paxton's attacker was still around. A woman was at the edge of the tree line. She was running. I yelled at her to stop."

"And did she?" Finn said.

"Unfortunately. She turned around, marched toward me, and hit me with a spell. I tried to get out of the way, but I slipped in the snow. Her magic smacked me in the head and knocked me over."

"Did you recognize her?" I said.

"No, but it was snowing hard, so I couldn't see clearly. It was definitely a woman, though. She was dressed in black and wore a hat. And she was powerful. Her spell rattled my bones. I tried to fight back, but I had no idea what spell I threw at her." His eyes flooded with tears. "I thought she'd kill me. After what she did to Paxton, I was scared I was next."

"But she left you alone?" Finn said.

"She must have. The next thing I remember is this cat and her friends yelling at me. Then I fainted."

"You're fortunate to be alive," Finn said. "The attack sounds ruthless."

Godric dabbed his damp cheeks with the backs of his hands. "I still can't believe what she did to Paxton. Why do that?"

"Perhaps she was unhappy about a recent deal she made with him?" I said.

"Why? Everyone loves Imperial Broomsticks. We're one of the best in the business."

"Perhaps it was a rival business owner who wanted Paxton out of the way?" Sammy said.

Godric shook his head, then winced and touched his injured forehead again.

"There must be money in high-quality broomsticks," I said.

"True. Paxton does well. But I don't think he had rivals who wanted him out of the way so they could get his market share." He sucked in a breath. "I meant he did well. The business was successful."

"What about a wife or partner?" Finn said. "Any troubles at home?"

"Paxton never married. His work kept him busy," Godric said. "He told me when you find a job you love, you never work again in your whole life. His passion was broomsticks."

"And you were happy to work for him?" I made my question sound innocent, but since Godric was on the scene when the murder happened, we couldn't discount him.

"Paxton is a great boss. Always joking. Sure, he works me hard. Well, he was a great boss, and he worked me hard. I didn't mind. I enjoy my job." The color drained from Godric's face. "Sorry. I don't feel so good."

"You rest," Finn said. "I'll have another look around, and then we'll get you to the hospital."

Archie stayed with Godric, and the rest of us left the room. Finn gently eased the door shut and beckoned us away.

"What do you think?" I whispered.

"I think this is another thing to go on my to-do list," Finn said. "Right at the top."

"About Godric. It was just the two of them here. Did he kill Paxton?"

Finn pressed his lips together. "Once his injuries have healed, I'll get his magic tested. But he doesn't seem powerful. More troubled than anything else."

I nodded. "I don't see a motive for Godric wanting Paxton dead. He's just lost his job because his boss has died."

"Unless he inherits the business," Sammy said.

"Good thinking." I nuzzled Sammy. "Finn?"

"I'll look into it." He glanced into the living room. "Anything odd strike you about this scene?"

"It's a mess," Sammy said. "Some of that is my fault, though. Sorry, I ate some mini sausage rolls. I hope they weren't clues."

Finn grinned. "I don't think a sausage roll was the murder weapon."

"You mean the sticks?" I said. "Six bundles were arranged around Paxton's body. And, of course, the murder weapon itself. Crushed by a giant log won't often go on the report as the cause of death."

"It seems ritualistic. Someone used old magic. And I didn't sense old power on Godric," Finn said.

"Neither did I," I said.

"So, we hunt for a mysterious woman dressed in black," Finn said. "I'll dig into Paxton's past, see if anything pops. Godric, too. And I'll need more angels to sweep the scene. Are you all good to stay here for now and help?"

"If you need us, we're here," I said.

Archie and Sammy nodded.

As Finn went to get the investigation underway, I sat by the door and took in the scene again. There was more to this murder than met the eye. I was missing a lot of puzzle pieces, but I was determined to find them.

It was time to investigate.

# Chapter 5

"We shouldn't touch them." Sammy stood beside me in front of the stunningly decorated Christmas tree in Sorcha's café. It occupied one corner by the window, the top brushing the ceiling. Gold, red, and green decorations hung from the pine branches.

"They're asking to be batted with a paw." A slow-moving gold bauble teased me with its gentle motion as the café door swung shut, causing a breeze.

"Sorcha's already yelled at Elijah for breaking her favorite ornament." Even though Sammy was telling me not to touch the tree, he had a paw raised, his pupils dilated.

Bites and Delights was buzzing this evening. Despite the blizzard, residents still came to the pre-Christmas samples evening. For a small fee, guests could try all the nibbles they could handle, so long as they provided feedback so Sorcha could perfect her Christmas treats.

Witches rubbed shoulders with warlocks over the brandy butter crepes. Goblins sampled puff pastry delights with pixies. And even a few gremlins had turned up, and they were usually too busy at Christmas creating chaos to take a break. It was all testament to Sorcha's amazing food.

"Hey, get over here and leave the tree alone." Zandra held a plate of goodies as she gestured at me with her free hand. "There are fishy treats for you. Sorcha needs to know what works best for cat familiars."

All thoughts of batting the bauble faded, and I dashed over to join Zandra and her friends, Sammy close behind me. Vorana had Sage with her, and when Sorcha wasn't dashing around making sure her customers were happy, she dropped in and out of the conversation to make sure she didn't miss the gossip.

"You've got a winning event on your hands." Vorana raised a slice of iced fruit cake dusted with edible gold.

Sorcha looked around, a smile on her face, just a hint of fang on show. "I know most of them are here for the food, but they also want the gossip. Everyone's talking about the broomstick seller being killed."

"What's the latest?" Vorana hand-fed a piece of roast turkey to Sage, who had stayed in her papoose strapped against Vorana's chest, rather than in her usual wheeled carriage.

"Juno is in charge of this one," Zandra said. "I've been hearing about how she found Paxton."

"With some help from my friends," I said. "I went to have a friendly chat with Paxton about why witches' broomsticks were going missing. When we got to his cabin, we were too late to save him."

Sammy nodded. "He'd been flattened. We just missed seeing it happen."

"You're so brave." Sorcha petted his head.

"You really think Paxton was scamming people?" Vorana said.

"It would appear so," I said. "Archie found ten damaged broomsticks in the cabin Paxton rented. Finn took them and plans to identify the owners."

"From what I've heard about Paxton, he wasn't popular with his customers." Sorcha sipped her cranberry punch, her gaze darting around to make sure everyone was enjoying themselves. "People say he was pushy. Paxton hated taking no for an answer."

"He was eager to make a sale when we met him," Zandra said. "Even though I told him I didn't use a broomstick, he wasn't put off."

"Paxton took a risk, stealing witches' brooms," Vorana said. "It's no wonder he ended up dead."

I sampled a delicious sliver of salmon from Zandra's plate. "Whoever killed him was determined to succeed. Although Paxton fought back. He had defensive injuries on his hands, and scratch marks or whip marks on his face as if his attacker had beaten him into submission."

Sorcha grimaced. "Surely, if it was a witch getting revenge for her broomstick being stolen, she'd have blasted him with a spell."

"Unless he stopped her," Zandra said. "Maybe she confronted him and demanded her broomstick back, and Paxton attacked, so she had no choice but to use whatever weapon was close by."

"Why use a log to crush him?" Vorana said.

"Finn thinks it was a witch who uses old magic," I said.

"Maybe a hedge witch?" Vorana fed Sage more food. "What do you think, sweetie?"

"I think the treats are slow in coming, although they're excellent, Sorcha. Anyone who steals a witch's broomstick deserves everything they get. Paxton was an idiot for scamming witches."

"Where's your Christmas spirit? No one deserves to be crushed under a log." Vorana tickled Sage's chin.

Sage grumbled, but started to purr.

"Not only that, but there were sticks shoved into Paxton's mouth," I said.

"Before or after he died?" Sorcha said.

"I'm uncertain. But this witch was determined to make him pay."

"Any suspects yet?" Sorcha pointed someone toward the washrooms.

"It's being looked into," I said. "I don't know much about Paxton, but he's not married, and his assistant, Godric, said he wasn't involved with anyone. Godric couldn't think of any serious business rivals or problems with family. It sounds like Paxton lived for his work."

"He lived to con people," Sage grumbled.

"What about this assistant?" Zandra said. "The way you described him, I didn't get any killer vibes."

"You mean Godric Gander?" Sorcha dashed away and grabbed a few empty plates before returning.

"That's him. He was found at the scene, badly injured. I'm waiting to hear from Finn to see how he's doing," I said.

"Godric couldn't have done it," Sorcha said. "He's been coming here every day since the Christmas market started. He's such a sweet guy. Really nervous, though. And clumsy. The first day he got his order, his hands shook so much he dropped it. I gave him a replacement on the house. Poor guy. Some people live on their nerves. It can't be good for him."

"He was in a bad way when we found him," I said. "He'd been whacked on the head by a spell and injured his hands helping Paxton."

"Godric tackled the killer?" Vorana said.

"He did what he could."

"Did Godric get a good look at them?"

"No. All he could tell us was it was a woman dressed in black."

"That's not so helpful," Vorana said.

"We found ten broomsticks at the cabin," I said. "But there have only been six reports submitted to Angel Force about missing broomsticks. Maybe one of the witches who hasn't come forward took matters into her own hands."

Zandra scratched me between my ears. "That's a lot of suspects to get through. Godric really saw nothing that could narrow it down?"

"No. The blizzard had started, and he was in shock after discovering Paxton."

"I'll send him a care package and make sure he's doing okay," Sorcha said.

I twitched my whiskers in approval. Sorcha always looked out for the waifs and strays in Crimson Cove, whether they had four legs or two.

"Hey, ladies." Finn strode over, brushing snow off his elf costume. "It's wild out there. Although at least the crazy weather is keeping people inside."

"Still on duty?" Sorcha tweaked one of his elf ears.

"I got the late shift tonight. But I need a break and food. And I can never resist your treats, Sorcha."

"Help yourself. On one condition. Well, two. I need feedback on what you like, and we want to know everything about the murder."

Finn grinned as he grabbed a plate and filled it with cheesy tarts, thin slices of cheese, grapes, and candied apple. "I figured you would. Although I shouldn't share information about an ongoing investigation. It could get me in trouble."

"You can share with me," I said. "After all, I'm assisting in this investigation. If our friends overhear our private conversation, there's nothing we can do about it."

"Is that so?" Finn looked around the eager-eyed group. "Fine. Just keep this to yourselves."

They all mimed zipping their lips.

Finn chose a candied apple from his plate of goodies and spent a few seconds sucking it.

"Stop teasing! Tell us what you know." Sorcha thumped his arm.

"It's not much. I'm working solo on this, since Bertoli has already gone home for the holidays."

"I'm not sad to hear that," Zandra said. "One less Christmas scrooge humbugging around town is perfect."

Finn shrugged as he munched on his grapes. Since he worked with Bertoli every day, he knew what an uptight angel he was.

"How's Godric doing?" I said.

"He's staying in the hospital overnight. The doctor is worried about his head injury. They had to sedate him because he couldn't relax."

"He definitely needs a care package," Sorcha said. "As soon as this evening is over, I'll make something up and send it to the hospital."

"I asked him a few questions, but got shooed out by the doctors. They said I was stressing Godric. I hung around for a while, but they wouldn't let me see him again."

"Did you test his magic? Is he powerful enough to have killed Paxton?" I said.

"That won't happen tonight," Finn said. "I'll see how he's doing tomorrow. I should get more answers then. Maybe once he's had a good night's sleep, he'll remember more. Give us clues to the killer."

"We've been hearing it was a witch out for revenge because her broomstick was stolen," Sorcha said.

"Let's not get ahead of ourselves," Finn said. "Although it's likely, there's a connection between the stolen brooms and this murder. I've been digging into Paxton's background, but nothing concerning has shown up. He's been in the broomstick business for thirty years. He took over from his father when he retired."

"Any reports or complaints about him overcharging?" I said.

"Nothing like that."

"What about reports of broomsticks being stolen when Paxton's in the area? Perhaps there's a link between his business and these thefts."

"It's an idea, but not one I can follow up on my own," Finn said. "There are half a dozen open cases Cythera wants closed before Christmas, and there are few angels around. Those who are, are patrolling Crimson Cove to keep order."

"A murder must come before monitoring Christmas high spirits," I said.

"It does. And Cythera is happy for me to focus on the case, but running a search like you suggested would take time I don't have."

"Recruit someone else," I said. "Zandra can help."

She shook her head. "Normally, I'm happy to lend a hand, but animal control is in the same position. We're down fifty percent on our usual crew, and Barney is going away tomorrow to the annual conference. He's giving that speech he's been stressing about."

"For now, I'm focused on finding Paxton's killer," Finn said. "If he's linked to other thefts, I'll figure that out at a later date."

"What if it was a witch he'd conned somewhere else?" I said. "If she just figured it out, she could have come after him. It doesn't have to be someone local."

Finn grimaced. "Yeah, that's a point. But I'm sticking with the immediate suspects. I've identified twenty customers who bought a broomstick from Paxton since he started selling at the Christmas market."

"You've spoken to them all?" I said. "Anyone's alibi not check out?"

"All but two. I've left messages for them, but they haven't gotten back to me," Finn said.

"Which is suspicious," Vorana said. "Who are they? People who live in Crimson Cove?"

"No, visitors. Dolores Veil and Vera Paddlesack."

Sorcha wrinkled her nose. "Those two! They come to Crimson Cove every year."

"You don't think much of them?" I said.

43

"They're troublemakers. Every store they visit or stall they go to, there's a problem. They bring the Christmas Grinch spirit with them and tip it over everything festive. They enjoy making people miserable."

"What do they complain about?" Zandra said.

"Overpriced items, things being the wrong color, or out of stock. Anything, really. When I offered to order in a book they requested, they said they didn't want it," Vorana said.

"When they visit my cafe, they complain about the food being too Christmassy, there's too much cinnamon in everything, and why can't they get a summer salad? They love to whine."

"I saw them at the market looking at Paxton's stock," I said. "And you're right, they were talking about how overpriced the broomsticks were."

"That sounds like them," Vorana said. "They even had the cheek to say my store was boring because all I sold was books."

"They have a point there," Zandra said.

Vorana arched an eyebrow. "Books are perfect."

"So long as you haven't gotten me books for Christmas, that's all I care about."

Her expression grew stricken. "You really hate books that much?"

"She's joking," I said. "Zandra is grateful for every gift she receives."

Zandra looked embarrassed, realizing she'd stuck her foot in it. "Sure. After all, it's the thought that counts."

Vorana looked no happier. I'd seen her bundling books and wrapping them, and there was definitely a book-shaped gift under the tree for Zandra.

"So, we have two troublemaking witches who love to cause problems and aren't returning your messages," I said to Finn.

"That's about it."

"Then we've found two prime suspects to grill. Shall we?"

# Chapter 6

The next morning brought a chilly but sunny day. The blizzard from the previous evening had blown itself out, leaving a glorious winter wonderland of frost and glittering snow.

I was admiring the view from our basement window as Zandra got ready for work.

"Sorry I can't come with you to help with this murder. With Barney going away, we're all covering for him. And Oleander is being a jerk and making out he's the boss because he's been at animal control longer than me."

"Oleander couldn't organize a bun fight in a bakery. Make sure he doesn't bully you, or he'll have me to answer to."

"He can try. But we both know I have no time for bullies." She pulled on her thick-soled winter walking boots.

"I'll be fine looking into this mystery without you. It'll give me something to do, since I'm almost done with my Christmas shopping."

"What have you got me?"

"It's a surprise."

"Please don't let it be anything covered in fur."

I turned from the window. "Um ... you don't like fur?"

"No! Nothing rodent for Christmas." Zandra grabbed her jacket and hunted for her keys.

"Does vole count as rodent in your book?"

"Juno!"

I raised a paw. "You'll love your gift."

She hesitated by the stairs. "You could always come to work with me."

"I said I'd help Finn figure out what happened to Paxton. And since I found the body, I feel involved."

"I get that. It's hardly a Christmas treat for you, though, poking about in a murder."

"Ensuring justice is done is always a reward."

She half smiled as she discovered her keys on the chest of drawers. "Let me know how things go. And stay out of trouble."

"I never get in trouble."

Zandra scooped me up and rested her forehead against mine. "Trouble finds you. Well, it finds both of us. And be careful of those witches. If they figure out you're tracking them, they might come after you."

"If they do, they'll regret it." I slashed a murder mitten through the air.

"No fighting. Isn't this the season of goodwill?"

"It's the season of making sure killers don't get away with it. What Paxton did was wrong, but he didn't deserve to be killed. And it was a violent death. He suffered before he died."

Zandra huffed out a breath, which ruffled my fur. "Maybe I can work a half day and join you and Finn this afternoon."

"The animals need you. This is a busy time of year."

"It's always a busy time of year at animal control. I'll be glad when the day comes when our services are no longer needed, and all animals have safe and loving homes."

"Sadly, that's a long way off. You stay safe, too. No chasing baby dragons or anything that bites."

After a minute of delicious snuggles, Zandra set me down, bundled up against the cold, and we left the basement.

I was happy for her to work with the unloved and troubled critters in Crimson Cove rather than help me hunt a killer. If I knew my witch was safe, it was one less thing to worry about.

"Oh, my cauldron!" Zandra snort laughed as she opened the front door. "What is Finn wearing?"

Finn waited outside, marching on the spot and swinging his arms. Gone was his normal white uniform. It had been replaced with a glorious, multi-colored tutu, pink tights, and a pale pink bodysuit that left little to the imagination. Every time he moved, he shimmered.

He raised his hands to the sky. "When I got to the office this morning, Cythera had these laid out for us."

"Is she wearing one?" I admired his sparkling tutu.

"Of course."

"You're a Christmas fairy?" Zandra giggled as she inspected the bodysuit.

"I even come with sugar plums. Would you like one?" He pulled a bag from a hidden pocket on the back of the tutu.

Zandra took one and popped it into her mouth. "Few people could pull off this look, but it suits you. It shows you work out."

I circled Finn. "Every muscle. You work every muscle."

"Nah. I was just born this gorgeous." He raised his arms above his head and pirouetted. "I like it. When I put on the tights, I wasn't sure, but you get a great range of movement in them. Watch me lunge."

We averted our eyes as Finn lunged in the snow, revealing many intriguing bulges.

"Enough lunging! We have work to do," I said.

Finn lunged his way back to us, a grin on his stupidly handsome face. "Angel Force is getting positive feedback about the costumes. Cythera has been collecting data, and noted our average approval rating has gone up five points since we started wearing them."

"Uh-oh. Does that mean you'll have a new costume every day?" Zandra said. "Not just at Christmas."

Finn's smile faded. "I'm not sure I could handle that. But I'm keeping the tutu. And the tights. The bodysuit cuts in, though."

"If it's getting people in a festive mood, keep wearing it," Zandra said.

He shrugged. "Cythera argued the outfits get suspects to lower their guard when we discuss Paxton's murder. I'm not so sure, but when Cythera thinks she's right, there's no point fighting her."

I side-eyed Zandra. "I know someone like that."

She checked the time. "I've got to get to work and make sure Oleander isn't being too much of a douche. Glenda almost punched him yesterday because he kept teasing her. You have a good day. Remember what I said, Juno. Stay safe."

"You, too." I watched her go, then turned to my favorite sugarplum angel. "Who's first?"

"Dolores. She's staying at the inn."

"Then let's go. We should be in time for breakfast." I hopped onto Finn's shoulder to avoid getting frozen toe beans.

He didn't complain as I settled around his neck. He even drifted out a little demon energy to keep me warm.

"Did you find anything useful in Dolores's background check?" I said.

"Not much. The system was on a go-slow last night. It was still processing when I got in this morning. The weather is messing things up."

"Your system is already on Christmas break. Just like everybody else."

"Most likely. I got the basics, though. And what Sorcha and Vorana said about her is right. Every year, since she's come here, she's filed a complaint with Angel Force. One year it was about littering, another year it was a complaint about being overcharged at a restaurant, and another it was about the music being too loud at a private party."

"Some people are born professional complainers. What about her criminal record?"

"Still waiting to see if she's got one. But if you're a master criminal, you keep a low profile, rather than get yourself known as a complainer."

Our short walk took us to the Serpent Inn. They'd decorated the outside in beautiful glittering lights, and there were two small, elegantly decorated Christmas trees set on either side of the entrance.

Finn pushed open the door, and we entered a warm, cinnamon-scented lobby. He headed to the reception area, where a smiling elf greeted us. "I'm here to speak to Dolores Veil. Could you let her know I'm here?"

"She's having breakfast." Although her smile remained in place, it looked strained.

"Let me guess, she's unhappy about something?" I said.

The elf clasped her hands together, two red dots of color highlighting her cheekbones. "We always want to make our guests happy, but sometimes, they make it hard."

"Is the coffee not hot enough? The bread stale? Bacon too crispy?"

"Well, some of that. I assure you, we offer an excellent service to our guests."

"We're not here about Dolores's complaints," Finn said. "We know Serpent Inn is amazing. Mind if we head through to the dining room? We won't be long."

"Of course. And help yourself to a complimentary breakfast. It's a pleasure to have a member of Angel Force with us. Especially when you're dressed so gloriously." The dots of color turned a deep red, and it ran down the elf's neck as she enjoyed the view.

Finn adjusted his tutu. "Thanks."

"You should wear this costume more often if it gets you free stuff," I whispered in his ear as he headed to the dining room.

"Not sure it's worth the trouble. This thing chafes. Although the food here is amazing."

"They'd better have smoked salmon," I said. "I only got dried food this morning."

"We're here to work, not eat."

"We can do both. I'm excellent at multitasking."

We stopped at the entrance to the dining room. There were a dozen people eating, all couples or families, apart from one thin, red-headed woman who sat alone. Her expression looked pinched as she inspected the cooked breakfast in front of her and then looked in the pot of coffee and shook her head.

"That's Dolores," I said. "Grab my salmon, and we'll go over."

"I guess I could do with a coffee." Finn ambled to the breakfast buffet. He piled smoked salmon on a plate, poured himself a coffee, and couldn't resist the cranberry muffins. With full plates, we headed to Dolores.

"Mrs. Veil?" Finn said.

She looked up, her expression set to surly. "It's Ms."

"Of course. I'm Finn from the local branch of Angel Force, and this is Juno, my partner."

Dolores's gaze flicked to me. "They're recruiting cats now?"

"We work freelance. They couldn't afford to pay us on a full-time basis," I said. "Excellence never comes cheap."

"May we join you?" Finn was all charm and genuine smiles.

It didn't work on Dolores as her gaze cut around the room. "There are other empty tables."

"We have questions about Paxton Starstride," Finn said. "It won't take long."

"The broomstick seller?" She stopped inspecting her breakfast. "What about him?"

Finn gestured to the empty chair opposite Dolores.

"Fine. Take a seat."

"Thank you." Finn set down our plates and his coffee and settled himself in.

I hopped onto the table and discreetly ate some salmon. I could never focus when my stomach was empty.

"Are you aware Paxton is dead?" Finn said.

"I heard something about it. Although I don't listen to gossip."

"Unfortunately, the gossip is true. An investigation of the scene suggests his death wasn't from natural causes."

Dolores's eyebrows flashed up. "Paxton was killed?"

"We believe so. We're talking to anyone who had contact with him in the last few days to discover why it happened." Finn pulled out his notepad and checked his scribblings. "I believe you had an appointment with Paxton regarding a new broomstick? It was in his diary."

"Oh, well, yes, I did. It was a week ago, just after the Christmas market opened. I saw nothing, though. No one hanging about and causing trouble, if that's what you want to know." She stabbed a sausage and bit off the end.

"Where did you meet Paxton to talk about broomsticks?"

"At his stall."

"Your current broomstick isn't working?" I asked.

Dolores bit into her sausage again. "It works fine, but it went missing. I checked into this dump, left the broomstick in my room, and then went out with my friend to look around, see what was new. When I got back, my broomstick was gone. I was furious. I argued with that stupid manager for hours, but he wouldn't listen. He said no one had been in my room since I'd checked in, and there was no way any of his staff took it."

"You think someone from the Serpent Inn stole your broomstick?" Finn made a note on his pad.

"Who else? I intend to make a complaint about this grot hole. They don't deserve to stay open if they can't keep their customers' precious items safe." Dolores inhaled a big breath and wheezed it out before slurping down coffee.

"After your broomstick went missing, you met Paxton to order a new one?" Finn said.

"Why else would I meet him? I needed my broomstick to get home easily. I've been to Crimson Cove Christmas market plenty of times, so I knew Paxton had a stall. I arranged to see him when I realized I wasn't getting my broomstick back from the thieves who run this place."

"It's convenient timing, don't you think?" I said.

She stabbed another sausage. "What do you mean?"

"Well, there was a broomstick seller at the market at the same time your broomstick vanishes."

Dolores took a piece of bacon off her plate and bit into it. "You've lost me."

"Before we get to that, Juno, were you happy with the order you placed with Paxton?" Finn said.

Dolores sniffed. "I wasn't unhappy. I got a good price, and I'd been thinking about getting an upgrade. The timing wasn't great, though. Christmas is an expensive time of year, and they don't like to bargain around here."

"You didn't seem happy about the prices when I saw you," I said.

She stiffened in her seat. "You never saw me. What are you talking about?"

"I overheard a conversation you had with your friend about Paxton's prices."

"Oh! Sure. You were the nosy cat asking questions. That was nothing. You never buy anything direct from his stall. That stuff is overpriced. It's for the tourists and those who don't know what they're doing. I drove a hard bargain with Paxton." She fluffed her red hair, leaving a smear of bacon grease on her cheek. "He had a crush on me. He's a charming man. Respectful. Well, he was charming. Being dead, all that charm will be of no use now. What happened to him?"

"We're still investigating," Finn said. "Getting back to Juno's point, we believe Paxton was conning his customers."

Her brows lowered, making her look even grumpier. "Conning them how?"

He drew in a breath. "Paxton was stealing broomsticks, so customers had no choice but to buy a new one from him."

Dolores dropped the bacon she held. "That thieving, deceitful liar! How dare he take my broomstick and force me to buy a shoddy replacement. I never liked him. A sales jerk and too slimy for his own good."

"You just said you thought he was charming," I said.

She shoved back her seat. "If he wasn't dead, I'd strangle him. That weasel!"

Several diners looked over as Dolores ranted.

"Since you were in contact with Paxton shortly before his murder," Finn said, his affable tone gone, "I need your alibi. Paxton died yesterday, around four in the afternoon."

She stared at him, then snorted. "Me! You can't think I'm a suspect."

Finn glanced at me. "We need to track Paxton's movements leading up to his death. You may have seen something useful when you were with him. Maybe someone watching him. Or you overheard an argument."

"I already said I didn't. I can't help." Dolores grabbed her napkin and wrung it in her hands.

"You could, by telling us where you were yesterday afternoon. Just to rule you out, of course," I said.

She tossed down the crumpled napkin. "I was with my friend, Vera. We always do the Christmas markets together. Yesterday was late night opening, so we looked around, got something to eat, and then went back to shopping. We were out until about nine o'clock."

"Even though there was a blizzard?" I said. "You must be hardened in your cause to find the perfect gift."

"We ducked into a few places when it got really bad. It wasn't a problem. Ask Vera. I was with her, so I couldn't have killed that cheat. I'd like to, though."

Finn made a note of the information on his pad. "When you've finished your breakfast, come to Angel Force. I collected several broomsticks from Paxton's accommodation. Yours could be among them."

Dolores's expression softened. "I'm getting my broom back?"

"Once it's no longer evidence in a murder investigation. But I should warn you, they were all damaged beyond repair."

She huffed out a breath. "I don't know why I bother coming here. It's never fun. I'm done with this overcooked excuse for a breakfast. I want my broomstick. Now!"

"Of course. I'll take you to the station." Finn stood. "Coming with us, Juno?"

I'd had enough of mealymouthed Dolores and her ability to find fault in everything. "I'm going to the hospital to see how Godric is doing."

Finn nodded at me, his smile resigned as he escorted Dolores out of the dining room. She complained with every step.

I polished off my salmon and then hopped down. Now I had the measure of Dolores, I'd ask Godric if he could identify her as the witch who'd attacked him.

If that avenue of investigation took me to a snowy dead end, maybe he'd remembered something that would lead me to the right person.

# Chapter 7

The Christmas market was in full swing as I headed to the small medical center on the edge of Crimson Cove.

I lifted my booping snooter and inhaled the tempting aromas of roasting meats and sugary delights. I was more of a savory fan, but I indulged in everything during the holidays.

And the Christmas market allowed me to do just that. Every stall was brightly decorated for the season to tempt buyers, and every other stall offered delicious, drool-worthy treats.

My stomach grumbled, and I took a step toward the roasted meats stall. They were doing a deal on a roast turkey and stuffing club sandwich. No! I must stay mission focused. There was a killer in the area, and she needed to be stopped. The tasty meats would have to wait. Finn could reward me with an extra-large helping of whatever I desired once I'd solved this murder for him.

I set my gaze forward and trotted past the distractions. Never let it be said a magical cat on a mission couldn't be relied upon.

I entered the neat, white building. It was all on one level and comprised of a dozen beds. Magic could heal most minor injuries, but the more serious cases, like Godric's concussion, needed monitoring. Especially if the magic user wasn't adept with healing spells. As seemed to be the case with Godric.

I'd never met an individual with such a trembling, fragile hold over their ability. Perhaps he'd never received proper training. Although some magic users had a tendency toward excellence, much like my wonderful witch, the majority needed schooling to ensure they could control their powers.

I waited until the nurse left her desk before venturing out. I hopped onto the desk to check which room Godric was in. A quick dash along the corridor, and I slipped through the open door and into his room.

There was a tiny Christmas tree set on the window ledge, and a single string of tinsel hanging over a watercolor of Crimson Cove. It was a discreet nod to the season.

Godric lay on the bed, flat on his back, his eyes open.

"Greetings! How are you feeling on this most merry of days?" I trotted over and hopped onto the end of his bed.

He lifted his head and flinched. There were deep circles under his eyes and lines of tiredness were etched either side of his mouth. "I've been better. Who are you? Have we met before?"

"I'm the hospital therapy cat. You can call me Jenny."

"Therapy cat? What's that?" He stayed on his back, his head dropping onto the pillow.

"It's been proven animals in a hospital setting calm patients and speed their recovery. You're my first visit of the day. Congratulations."

"What will you do to make me feel better?" Godric blinked several times. "I'm sure I know you from somewhere."

"No, I'm the therapy cat. If you'd like to, you may pet me. You'll find it soothing. I prefer the head, back of the neck, and base of the tail. Never attempt to pet my stomach."

"Um ... sure. If the doctor thinks it'll work. I've not been feeling good since being admitted. They keep saying I'll feel better soon, but nothing helps."

"Being around me is always helpful. You're guaranteed to feel calmer."

He blew out a breath. "I need that. I haven't had the best time recently."

I shuffled up the bed until I was within petting distance. "Remember, start with the head and then see how we get along."

Godric tentatively reached out a shaking hand and rested one finger on my head. "You have soft fur. Like velvet."

"I do. I regularly groom."

He gingerly stroked the top of my head. The tremble from his hands shivered down my spine to the base of my tail.

"If you tell me what happened to you, it'll help. Often, releasing a traumatic experience encourages healing."

"How do you know I've had a traumatic experience?" Godric tilted his head. "You know, you look like the cat who came to the cabin after Paxton died."

"That wasn't me." I needed Godric to think I was a neutral listening ear.

"Do you have a sister? Or a twin? There was definitely a pretty white cat at the cabin."

"That's impossible. I'm unique. You must have imagined me. It looks like you had a nasty bump to the head. That could make you confused. Pet me." I arched my back.

Godric frowned, then shrugged. "Maybe."

I let him relax for a moment, before continuing my gentle questioning. "You said your friend died. You witnessed that?"

Godric grimaced. "Yeah. I keep replaying what happened."

"I'm sorry to hear that. What do you remember?"

He gulped. "Paxton was attacked. Someone came in through the back of the cabin we're renting and crushed him with a giant yule log."

"Shocking! Why a yule log?"

"Paxton bought it at the Christmas market. We celebrate the season every year by blessing a piece of wood and giving thanks to the magic that serves the business." Godric's chest rose. "Paxton owned Imperial Broomsticks."

"I've heard of your operation."

"You won't find a better broomstick. Paxton had a talent for making exceptional broomsticks. He could turn his hand to any design." Godric swallowed loudly, and his hand shook against my side.

"So, the yule log?"

"Right. We had the log out the back and planned on bringing it inside, blessing it, and then lighting it to ensure good fortune for the following year."

"But instead, it crushed Paxton."

Godric's breath came out almost as shaky as his hand. "Part of me is grateful I didn't see it all. I was getting ready in my room when I heard thudding, and then Paxton cried out. By the time I got there, he was under the log. Not that I'd have been able to save him if I'd been any quicker. My magic's not up to much."

"What magic do you possess?"

"I'm part house-elf, I know that. Everything else is a mystery. I was a foundling, so I know nothing about my biological family. I got shipped between homes until I was old enough to fend for myself." His bottom lip jutted out for a second, a resigned look on his face.

"That must have been hard."

Godric looked away. "It could have been a better childhood. Still, it could have been a lot worse. I didn't do so bad."

I flopped onto my side. This felt like a belly exposing moment. "As part house-elf, you must enjoy serving and orderliness."

Godric's face brightened. "Oh, yes. I like everything to be in its place. I enjoy making sure the broomsticks are properly ordered and marked up, so it's easy for people to find what they need." His eyes flooded with tears, which trickled down his hollow cheeks. "I don't know what'll happen to Paxton's business now he's dead. Or to me."

"There's no one to take over and keep you on?"

"Few people want to take a chance on a guy like me. Paxton saw beyond my limitations and helped me."

"What do you consider your limitations?" I shuffled forward, hoping he'd get the hint and scratch my belly to make himself feel better.

"Look at me! I'm sick. I've been unwell for a while, and the doctors can't figure out why. I'm disintegrating before my eyes."

I sat up and studied him. He did look poorly, and it wasn't just from the shock of witnessing a murder. "You've been tested to see what's wrong?"

"There's not a test that hasn't been done. And I've tried all the suggested spells, tinctures, potions, and lotions. Nothing works. I'm getting weaker. That's hardly appealing to an employer. They need someone they can rely on, not a weakling who needs a day off at short notice because he can't get out of bed."

"Paxton understood that about you?"

"He was always great with me. He said we'd start on a trial basis, do a couple of months, and see how it went."

"I'm assuming it went well?"

"I'd worked with Paxton for three years. It's the best job I've ever had. Well, it's the only job I've ever had. And now ... I don't know what I'll do." Godric hid his face in his hands.

I gave him a moment to collect himself as sobs racked his body and his shoulders heaved.

"Is there anything you can remember about the person who killed Paxton?" I said. "It would make you feel better if we caught them. Was she a tall, thin witch with a shock of messy red hair?" Perhaps a little detail about our witchy suspect would jog his memory.

Godric grabbed a tissue from the bedside cabinet and dabbed his eyes and nose. "I don't know. I didn't see much. She attacked during the blizzard. All I know is she was female and dressed in black. Her magic was powerful, though. She was fearless. When she realized she was being chased, she turned and whacked me with a spell. It made me feel awful."

"Angel Force will find her." I snuggled next to Godric to give him some warmth. He appeared chilled to the bone with his continual shaking. "And I don't like to upset you further, but you should know there's a rumor going around that Paxton cheated his customers. He stole from them. Would you know anything about that?"

Godric's mouth dropped open, and his skin dulled to corpse ash gray.

"Hark, the herald angels sing, glory to the newborn witch."

Four carol singers entered the room, dressed in bright shades of red and green. They smiled and nodded at us as they continued their carol.

I studied Godric as the carolers performed. He struggled to compose himself and kept glancing at me. He knew what Paxton had been up to. Maybe he'd even helped steal the broomsticks.

The carolers ended their tune and were about to begin a new one, but I stopped them. "Thank you. You sound amazing. Unfortunately, this patient needs rest."

"Music is healing," a singer wrapped in gold tinsel said. "Doctor's orders."

"Godric hates music," I said. "It's stressing him out. I fear he could projectile vomit at any second."

The carol singers shuffled away, grumbling to themselves. I heard them start in the next room and receive a warmer reception.

"So, Godric, did you know what Paxton was doing? Was that how he ran his business?"

He gulped. "For a therapy cat, you're not therapeutic. I'm more stressed than I was before you came in."

"Take a deep breath and pet me. You'll feel much better. But I need an answer to my questions."

He was quiet for a moment. He didn't pet me.

"It's better to get these things off your chest. Unburden at Christmas." I leaned close and lowered my voice. "You don't want any broomstick-stealing spirits to whisk you away for being sneaky and concealing the truth."

His jaw wobbled, and his eyes grew wide. "I always cautioned Paxton about stealing. I said he was tempting fate by having so many broomsticks lying around."

"Broomsticks that he made, or the ones he stole from potential customers?" Now we were getting somewhere.

"Both!" The word came out on a soggy exhale. "I always buy protection spells this time of year. We kept dozens of broomsticks in stock to sell at the Christmas markets. Every morning, I'd make sure the protection spells were still stable."

"That was good of you. Did Paxton tell you to do that?"

"No, he wasn't concerned about dark spirits taking his broomsticks. I don't think he believed it happened."

"It happens. It's been going on for centuries. I've witnessed it a time or two. They leave a mess behind. Blood often gets spilled."

His gaze ran over me. "You've been around a long time?"

"I've lived through many interesting years. Some dull ones, too. Did you know Paxton was stealing to drum up business?"

Godric slowly rubbed his hands together, the dry skin rasping. "I was his lookout. Paxton would get to a place a couple of days before we started selling, and we'd walk around. He'd pick out houses that looked easy to get into. We'd watch until the owner left, and then he'd go in and grab the broomstick."

"How long has this been going on?"

"All the time I've worked for Paxton. And he had big plans this year. After Christmas, he wanted to go on a world cruise. January is a quiet time for Imperial Broomsticks, so he decided to close for a month and enjoy himself."

"You never suggested what he was doing was wrong?"

Godric inspected his hands. "Paxton hired me because I did what I was told. Don't get me wrong, I had no problem with that. Being half house elf, I love to please." His fingers went to the mistletoe pin attached to his lapel, and he tugged at it.

"That must be a favorite of yours," I said. "I saw you wearing it while you were working."

"It was a gift from Paxton. He was sympathetic about my health problems and gave me the pin not long after we started working together. There's healing magic attached to it. Although, I'm still going downhill. I never complained to Paxton, though. I wear the pin to show how much I appreciated the gift. I've not been given many gifts."

My heart went out to this sad half elf who lived such a sheltered, subservient life, devoid of the love of a warm, supportive family.

"You could take over Imperial Broomsticks," I said. "You must know how it operates. Of course, you won't want to continue the stealing."

A smile wavered across his face. "I couldn't handle the stress of running a company. I'm happy to take orders and do the day-to-day stuff. Paxton was the big ideas man. He was the face of Imperial."

"You should think about it. You're more capable than you realize."

"That's nice of you to say, but I know my limitations, and I'm not embarrassed about them." Godric yawned. "Sorry. I'm so tired. I can barely keep my eyes open."

I'd gotten all I could from him, so I stood and stretched. "I'll leave you to it. I hope you feel better after sharing with your therapy cat."

"I feel ... exhausted. Is that a side effect of sharing?"

"I'm certain of it. Have a good sleep. Things can only look up." I hopped off the bed and trotted to the door. I turned and looked at Godric. I needed to be certain he wasn't an excellent liar.

His head turned as he realized I was staring at him. "Was there something else?"

"Just this." I raised a paw and shot out a mid-level knockback spell. It wouldn't kill, but it would take power to block.

Godric did nothing. He must have seen the spell coming at him, since I ensured it moved slowly.

It thudded into his chest, and he slumped back with a groan. "That's not therapy, that's torture."

"My apologies. I was testing a theory. Merry Christmas!" I hurried out of the room and along the corridor. "The patient in room eight needs your attention," I said to the nurse at the desk.

Her forehead wrinkled. "How did you get in here?"

"Just visiting. Now, I'm just leaving." I dashed away as she yelled after me.

Godric had barely any magic which ruled him out as a suspect.

My focus had to be on any disgruntled witch who'd been cheated by Paxton and decided to get revenge.

It was either Dolores, or the missing Vera Paddlesack.

# Chapter 8

Temptation had gotten the better of me, and after my visit to Godric, I'd spent two joyful hours overindulging on Christmas market treats.

My belly and heart were full, and I'd enjoyed a long nap back home. I'd been tempted to stay there all day, but I was back on the street with another mission to complete.

Although I'd told Zandra her Christmas gift was in paw, I was unsure what to get my wonderful witch. I knew what I *wanted* to get her, which was why the delicious smell of a warm, fat mouse had led me along an alleyway behind Sorcha's café. It was the perfect furry gift to place on Zandra's pillow on Christmas morning. It should bring her endless amounts of joy once she got past the squealing and complaining about why I'd gotten her a rodent gift.

I shook my head to dismiss the unnerving catlike thoughts. Being in the body of a cat for over thirty years had changed me. When I'd first been transformed, I'd never had thoughts like this. But the longer I had four paws, a tail, and this magnificent white coat, the urge to be more catlike grew. Perhaps, one day, the memories of my former life and magnificence would be gone, and I'd be content to remain in this form forever.

I shuddered. There were benefits to being a magical familiar, and I hadn't regretted a single day I'd joined with Zandra to be hers, but I missed the old days. The unlimited power, the servants, the feeling of exquisite delight as my subjects bowed to me.

A deep, chilled breath of air slapped sense back into me, and I forced myself to stop hunting. No mice at Christmas. I must remember that. Focus on gifts like chocolate and a warm scarf.

I wrinkled my booping snooter. They were such dull gifts. How could Zandra want something like that over a unique, furry present?

After ambling around the Christmas market some more, soaking up the festive atmosphere, I couldn't help but be drawn to Imperial Broomsticks. It was empty. No warm lights or friendly smiles from the pushy Paxton. I hoped Godric would take to heart my suggestion to take over. Despite his lack of confidence, he was capable. Perhaps I could take him under my paw and educate him.

I shook my head as I trotted past the festive wreaths and Christmas baubles stall. No, I had too much going on. Supporting Zandra, helping Angel Force to not fall apart, keeping Finn on the straight and narrow so his demon side didn't take over. I also had my wonderful relationship with Sammy that needed attention now and again, and my magical misfits to care for. My plate was full. Godric would have to find his own way.

A purr of delight rumbled out of me as I spotted a welcome form striding through the snow toward Vorana's house. It was Zandra. And she was with Finn. It wouldn't be long until dinner was served, and I could always make room for one of Vorana's delicious meals.

I trotted as fast as the snow and ice would allow and caught up with them as they reached the porch. "Greetings. I have news."

"Hey! I was wondering where you were." Zandra scooped me up, wiped the snow off my paws, and kissed my head. "Good day?"

"Excellent day."

"I can see you've been enjoying yourself." Finn swiped a finger down my furry chest. It came away with a small smear of roast beef relish.

I was glad of my fur, so they wouldn't see me blush. "Hunting for a killer works up an appetite. And I always like to support local businesses. Shall we go inside before we freeze?"

Zandra chuckled as she hoisted me onto her shoulder. "I suppose that means you're not hungry?"

"When am I never hungry?"

"You sound like me," Finn said. "Every time it gets cold, my appetite increases threefold."

"Me, too," Zandra said. "I've been craving hot chocolate and double-dipped caramel cookies all day."

I licked my paw. "I'm in the mood for salmon."

"Surprise, surprise."

"Anything exciting happen at animal control?" I asked.

"I had licenses to check and some follow-up visits, but everyone behaved." Zandra set me down so she could take off her boots and coat. "Even Oleander wasn't a major jerk."

"It's a Christmas miracle," I said. "How about you, Finn? All the visitors keeping in line?"

"Sure are. It's the costumes. They love them. If anyone gets angry, I turn up in my tutu and dance around, and they forget what they were mad about."

"We're in the kitchen," Vorana called out. "Food's almost ready."

We eagerly headed to the kitchen. Vorana stood at the stove, her spoon dipped in a large, steaming casserole of meaty deliciousness.

Sage was settled at the table in her chair. She nodded a greeting at us all, and I hopped up in the chair beside her.

Once we'd gotten ourselves settled in, Vorana dished up a delicious chicken and roast parsnip delight, then sat in her usual seat. "I know you're more of a fish fan, Juno, but give this a try. It's a new recipe."

"Everything you cook is delicious." I inhaled the rich stew and sighed. Vorana was the best landlady.

"Juno's not hungry. She cleared out the fish stall at the Christmas market," Finn said.

"I did not! I tried a few samples of salmon roulade, but I know restraint. And I had a break from feasting before my nap, so I'd have room for dinner."

"You could have brought me some fish, instead of hogging it all," Sage grumbled.

"You could always get yourself some if you need a fishy feast," I said.

"My wheels hate the snow."

"Then float."

She harrumphed and stuck her booping snooter in her food.

Finn chuckled. "There are some great stalls this year."

"The market gets bigger every year." Vorana cut into a parsnip. "I considered having a book stall, but I'm not sure I need it. Visitors often drop by the store once they've been around the market." She looked pointedly at Zandra. "Books make excellent Christmas gifts."

Zandra grinned as she chewed on her food.

"Did Dolores behave when you took her to inspect the broomsticks?" I said to Finn.

"Oooh! Yes. Let's get an update on the murder," Vorana said. "Have you caught anyone yet?"

"We're working on it," Finn said. "Dolores was angry after learning about Paxton stealing her broomstick. She identified hers in the pile we collected from the cabin. It was beyond repair, though. I didn't leave her smiling."

"What about her alibi?" I said. "Perhaps she already knew about Paxton's theft and deceived us."

"There's still no sign of Vera Paddlesack. I've left more messages and asked around town, but no one has seen her, so I can't confirm Dolores's alibi."

"Maybe you're looking at the wrong witch for this murder if Vera has vanished," Zandra said.

"Could they be in on it together?" Vorana leaned across the table and cut Sage's chicken into tiny pieces. "Eat up, sweetie."

"I'm going as fast as I can," Sage grumbled. "You try chewing quickly when you've got hardly any teeth."

"I know what to get you for Christmas," I said.

"What?"

"A set of false teeth."

She ignored the joke. Sage was in a caustic mood this evening. Maybe she was unhappy about being left out of the murder investigation, but with Vorana busy at work, Sage liked to stay with her, so I hadn't included her. I should reconsider. Despite Sage's surly attitude, she had a tender heart, and it was easily bruised.

"Until we find Vera and confirm Dolores's alibi, and also Vera's alibi as a result, they stay my prime suspects," Finn said.

I turned my attention from Sage. "I visited Godric after our delightful breakfast encounter with Dolores. He was awake and had a lot to say."

Finn leaned forward in his seat. "That's interesting. I dropped by the hospital this afternoon, but the doctor said Godric had had a stressful morning and was sleeping it off. Apparently, some unknown cat got into his room. Would you know anything about that?"

"Juno! I hope you didn't terrify him into answering your questions," Zandra said.

"I'm the least terrifying magical familiar you'll ever encounter."

Sage snorted.

"You can be kind of terrifying," Finn said.

"Not in this case. I may have told Godric I was the official hospital therapy cat to get him to open up, though. That's not scary. That's kind."

Finn chuckled. "No wonder he needed rest."

"It was a gentle interrogation. Godric retold the story of Paxton's attack, and it tallied with the information we already had. He remembered nothing new about the attacker, though. He stuck to his story that she was dressed in black."

"Which is unhelpful," Finn said. "An ID on the attacker would be perfect. Did anything Godric say concern you? He's got no alibi."

"If anything, the opposite. He has a mysterious illness that makes him feeble. Paxton was understanding and helped him. He even gave him a healing pin."

"Does he know what's wrong with him?" Vorana said. "Magic can improve most illnesses."

"According to Godric, he's unique. He's tried everything, but his body is breaking down."

"That's tragic," Vorana said. "Surely, the doctors will look into it now he's in the hospital."

"They're on the case," I said. "But the state Godric's in, and with his limited magic, it would have been impossible for him to crush Paxton with that log."

"I agree," Finn said. "Although I still need to test his magic to be on the safe side."

"I did that for you." I chewed on a tender piece of chicken, reveling in the rich gravy that accompanied it.

Zandra set down her knife and fork. "What did you do?"

"I needed to ensure Godric had told the truth. So, as I left his room, I zapped him with a knockback spell. It was nothing. It wouldn't have harmed a fly."

"Did it harm Godric?" Finn said.

"No, nothing terminal. I gave him an opportunity to repel the spell, block it, or disperse it. He just lay on the bed and let it whack him."

"Juno! Godric sounds sick and is recovering from a head injury, and you slam him with a knockback spell. You're lucky he's still breathing," Zandra said.

"I knew what I was doing. And it proved he has no power. The poor creature can't even defend himself."

"At least we can rule him off the suspect list," Finn said. "I'll have to fudge the official report, though. Cythera won't like you zapping suspects."

"Whatever you write up, I'll agree with it," I said.

"What's the next step?" Vorana said. "Christmas is almost here, and we don't want a killer on the streets. It'll dampen everyone's mood if they're peeking around their curtains and wondering if they're safe."

"Simple," I said. "Tomorrow, we find the missing witch and get answers from her."

<hr />

I'd gotten up early the next morning and recruited Sammy for covert snooping in the hopes of finding Vera Paddlesack.

His breath plumed out as we trotted along the snowy streets, which were silent, apart from a few hungry birds.

We'd deliberately come out early, to avoid the crowds and ensure we could ask the stallholders if they'd seen Vera before they got too busy. Since Vera liked to complain, she must be known to them.

We started at the baubles stall. "Greetings. We're looking for a customer. A small, apple-shaped witch with blonde curls and a thin mouth. She's often with another witch. Tall and thin with messy red hair."

The stall owner, a pink-haired gremlin with a big smile, glanced down at us. "Sure. I know who you're talking about. The blonde one demanded a fifty percent refund on a wreath she'd bought from me. Apparently, the decorations fell off when she took it out of its box. When I checked it, someone had ripped them out. But she complained so long and so loudly, I gave her the money back to get rid of her. She was scaring away customers."

"How unpleasant to have to deal with that," I said. "Have you seen her around recently?"

"No. She's usually with that other witch, though. They're always moaning about something."

We thanked her for her time and continued along the stalls. We got the same response from everyone. Vera was known, and no one liked her. She'd tried to get discounts or refunds from everyone she'd purchased from.

"I'm not sure this is getting us anywhere." Sammy stamped his paws in the snow. "Should we take a break and warm up?"

We stopped at the candy cane and cookie stall. "This is the last one. If we don't get any information here, we'll grab breakfast and figure out what to do next."

The stall owner, a pleasingly plump witch, marched out with an armful of bagged cookies. "Morning! I'm not open for another few minutes, but feel free to browse. If you see anything you like, let me know."

"Greetings, and thank you. We're looking for someone. Vera Paddlesack." I gave her Vera's description.

"Oh, her. I know who you mean. I'm glad she's found something else to occupy her time. She's turned complaining into a full-time profession. Everyone hid when she stopped to check their stall."

"Do you know where she is?" I said.

"Sure. My friend, Simone, runs the ice sculpting contest in the woods. It's a new thing we're trying this year, and it's proving popular. Although, it's exclusive. They don't let just anyone in. You can view the sculptures for an hour a day at dusk, though. Have you seen what people are creating? So beautiful." She placed the cookies down and lined them up.

"I haven't been there." I glanced at Sammy. "What does that have to do with Vera?"

"That's where you'll find her."

I twitched my tail and nodded thanks. It was time to inspect some ice sculptures.

# Chapter 9

"It's supposed to be around here." I paced back and forth along the path. "This is where the stall owner said to come."

"She also said they don't let just anyone in, and you can only view the sculptures at dusk." Sammy's glum tone revealed his hatred of snow.

"We're not just anyone."

He wriggled his whiskers. "Of course. You're special."

"So are you."

Sammy had his booping snooter up, inhaling the frigid air. "I'm sensing more than just forest magic."

I paused, and my ears trembled. "I remember something about magic users who sculpt ice. In the past, they used their sculptures to assist them."

"Like frozen familiars?"

"Yes. But easier to break. Maybe that's why they don't want to be seen." There were ancient tales of ice art coming to life and rampaging through villages, freezing and destroying everything it touched.

"They're precious about their art?" he said.

"Perhaps. Or they want to protect it. Let's keep looking. There must be an opening."

We sniffed around and tested different areas of the woods for another hour. The air was freezing, though, and even I was prepared to admit defeat if we didn't get through soon.

Sammy beckoned me over with his head. "Here! There's resistance in the air. Walk along this part of the path. It feels odd. Kinda sticky."

Although I could navigate the route, it felt unpleasant, and a sticky residue stuck to my fur. "This must be the spot. We get through this, and we'll find Vera."

"This is why she joined the ice sculpting contest," Sammy said. "She's lying low behind this magic and waiting for the heat to die down. Then she'll slip away when no one is paying attention."

I nodded, but my focus was on the faint shimmering barrier Sammy had located. "Lend me some of your magic. If we do a reveal spell, it should show us what we're dealing with."

Sammy was happy to press his paws against the invisible barrier, and we spent a few moments testing its strength. With a few adjustments to the spell and a little concentration, we had it.

"On three. If we blast out a concentrated disintegration spell, that'll do it," I said.

It took several goes, but we were finally through. A world of incredible ice art greeted us.

There were two dozen people focused on their sculptures. Some wielded wands, while others waved their hands in the air as they carved into ice blocks. Their creations were astonishing. I spied dragons, giant ogres, even two ice werewolves in the mix.

"There's Vera." I trotted over to a small blonde witch with a scowl on her face as she inspected the carved Gorgon she worked on.

Sammy gently tugged my tail. "We should be careful. She must have skills to be able to form ice creatures. That suggests she's powerful."

"We'll tread carefully. Let's try a little sugar, see if we can get her to open up." I diverted and headed to the small coffee stand. I arranged for a deluxe hot chocolate with sprinkles and squirty cream to be sent to Vera, on us.

She looked surprised when she received her order, and her gaze shot over to us, her eyes narrowed.

I raised a paw. "That's our in. Vera will be curious to know why we bought her a drink."

"She doesn't look happy with her treat," Sammy said. "Maybe she's lactose intolerant. And we need to keep an eye on that wand she's waving around. We don't want her blasting us with spells."

"You watch the wand. I'll ask the questions." We sauntered over and stopped close to Vera. "Greetings. I'm Juno, and this is Sammy. We wanted to congratulate you on your excellent Gorgon. You must be an experienced sculptor."

"I've dabbled."

"I have a fondness for Gorgons. I've met many over the years. They're so misunderstood. They're fierce protectors of things they value."

She shrugged. "If you say so. I just like the snake hair."

"You're Vera Paddlesack, aren't you?" I said.

Her gaze skittered over me. "Maybe. What do you want?"

I kept admiring the ice sculpture. "You're a hard lady to track down."

"Why do I need tracking?" She set down the hot chocolate.

"There's been an incident in Crimson Cove. You may have heard about it."

"Incident?"

"Paxton Starstride, the owner of Imperial Broomsticks, is dead."

Vera's wand hand tensed. "And? Why are you telling me this?"

"We're asking everyone who met Paxton before he died if they saw or heard anything unusual."

"I can't help with that." Vera gestured at the Gorgon. "I need to get on before the ice loses its structure. I'm determined to win."

"Did you bring a broomstick to Crimson Cove?"

She hesitated, half turned toward the ice. "Yes. What do you know about that?"

"Has it gone missing?"

Vera pursed her lips. "Did you take it?"

I glanced at Sammy. I felt the same concern that was reflected in his gaze. Vera was being twitchy and suspicious. Was she twitchy because she was hiding something, or because she didn't appreciate being questioned by two stunning cats?

"We've discovered something unfortunate about how Paxton ran his business. He stole broomsticks and then played the charming salesman to convince the desperate witches to buy from him."

Vera's mouth fell open. "This has to be a joke."

"He stole ten broomsticks while in Crimson Cove."

She sucked air in between her teeth. "That cheating scumbag. I bought an overpriced broomstick from him because he took mine. I had that stick for ten years."

"When did yours go missing?"

Anger flared in Vera's eyes. "The day after I arrived. Of all the sneaky, underhanded things to do."

"You weren't the only one to think that."

"Hold on. You said Paxton was dead. Since you're asking questions, do you think he was murdered?"

"He was," I said. "Someone wanted to make him sorry for what he'd done. We're looking into customers who recently purchased from him. Especially those who had their broomstick stolen."

Vera smirked. "Oh! I get it. Me and Dolores are suspects. I hate to burst your bubble, fluffy, but I had nothing to do with it. Until you told me, I didn't know Paxton was stealing broomsticks."

"Did you meet with him to discuss your new broomstick requirements?" I said.

"Sure. I had to get a new one. And of course, he was there with his snake oil smile, convincing me his broomsticks were the best in town. Not that I had much choice, since he was the only guy selling them. He'd better not have sold me a second-hand stick."

"Had you ever met with Paxton before coming to Crimson Cove?" I said.

"No reason to. I didn't buy my last broomstick from him, if that's what you're asking."

"Paxton died two days ago, around four in the afternoon. Where were you at that time?"

Caution trickled across her face. "You really think it could be me?"

"We have to eliminate anyone who met Paxton just before his death," I said. "You must see how having your broomstick stolen by the man who then sold you a new one would give you a motive."

"Yeah, yeah, I see that. You still have Dolores on the suspect list, though. Anyone else?"

"We have several suspects."

"Take me off the list. I was at the Christmas market. I've got receipts with timestamps to prove it. Unless Paxton was killed in front of everyone at the market, it wasn't me. Where was he killed?"

"In his cabin. Crushed under a giant yule log."

She whistled out air. "Impressively gross. And inventive. But sadly, still not me."

"Were you with anyone while you shopped?"

"No. I'd been with Dolores earlier that day, but she went off to do her own thing, and I had other stalls I wanted to browse. The stall holders will remember me. One of them mentioned this ice contest, and I forced her to tell me how to get in. It's a big cash prize on offer, and it's got my name on it. I've been here ever since."

"You're certain you were on your own?" Sammy said.

"Just me and my bags of shopping. Why does that matter?"

I glanced at Sammy. It mattered because we'd just discovered Dolores lied about her alibi.

After asking a few more questions and getting nowhere, we left Vera to her sculpting and dashed back to town.

"Dolores has no alibi," I said.

"You think Dolores killed Paxton and assumed Vera would cover for her? Or she hoped Vera had left town, so we wouldn't be able to ask her if they were together?"

"Either option works. We need to ask Dolores why she lied. And I see the perfect snowman to help with that mission." Finn was up ahead, dressed in a fluffy snowman suit with a red bowtie and black buttons on the front of his white costume. "Snowman Finn! We need you."

He turned and raised a hand. "I was coming to find you later. I've got an update for you."

"So have we. We found Vera. Dolores lied about her alibi. They weren't together at the time of Paxton's murder."

"Interesting. And I found out Dolores changed her name. Five years ago, she was arrested and charged with violent behavior. Someone got on her wrong side, and she reacted badly. She served time for it. When she got out, she changed her name from Dolores Bracken to Dolores Veil."

"She's your killer!" Sammy said. "She's got a temper, faked her alibi, and she has a perfect motive for wanting Paxton dead."

"I'll bring her in," Finn said. "You go wait inside Angel Force. It's freezing. Even my toes are cold inside this ridiculous outfit."

"I thought you liked the costumes," I said.

"Even I have limits. And at least the tutu allowed for a full range of movement. I've fallen over twice in this thing. I won't be long. Dolores is at the Christmas market again. I'll grab her and bring her in for a chat."

"And charge her with murder," Sammy said.

Finn nodded. "If all goes to plan."

Ten minutes later, we were defrosted, having draped ourselves over a heater in Angel Force.

I was giving myself a quick groom when Finn marched in with an unhappy Dolores beside him.

"I'll put in a complaint about this. This is angel harassment. You've already questioned me, and I told you the truth. I have nothing left to say."

"We have follow-up questions." Finn nodded at an empty interview room, and we headed in and joined him and Dolores.

"You again." Dolores glowered at me. "And who's this?"

"I'm Sammy. Juno's assistant."

"He's more than an assistant. I couldn't manage without him," I said.

Dolores shrugged.

"Take a seat," Finn said.

After grumbling, Dolores pulled out a chair and dropped into it. "I'm losing shopping time. They sometimes do flash sales at this time of the day. I don't want to miss any bargains."

"You'll be losing a lot more than that," I said.

She jerked back in her seat. "What's that mean?"

"Let's do this the right way." Finn ran through the formal interview procedures and recorded Dolores's details. "When I first questioned you, you told me you were with Vera Paddlesack at the Christmas market when Paxton was killed."

Her gaze fixed on Finn, and she gave a small nod. "That's right. It's what we always do when we visit Crimson Cove."

"Vera says otherwise. She said you were together earlier in the day, but then parted ways. Where did you go?"

Dolores opened her mouth, then shut it. "I was with Vera. She made a mistake. She's going through the change, and it's messing with her brain. Her short-term memory is terrible. Let me speak to her and sort this out."

"Vera was clear. She said she wasn't with you," I said.

Dolores's top lip curled back. "Small-minded harridan. I'd have helped her if she needed it."

"Is that an admission of guilt?" I said.

"No! It's me realizing I can't rely on Vera. Not that I ever could. She's flaky. And she steals my chocolate when she thinks I won't notice."

"Dolores, you have no alibi for the time of Paxton's murder, and you have an excellent motive for wanting him dead." Finn leaned forward in his seat and rested his hands on the table. "You were open about how angry you were that he cheated you."

She stayed quiet, her gaze dipping to the floor. "I'm not a killer."

Finn glanced at me. "We've learned you changed your name. It made it difficult to find your criminal record, but it's extensive. You were sixteen when you were first cautioned for fighting. Every other year, you got caught doing something you shouldn't. All those charges relate to your inability to control your temper."

"People are idiots. They make me angry."

"Like Paxton did?" I said. "He stole your broomstick, you figured out what he'd done, felt cheated, and went after him."

Her head whipped up. "It wasn't me." The table shook.

"Everyone will understand why you felt angry, but you should have reported Paxton to us, not taken matters into your own hands," Finn said.

"I didn't! Of course, I was angry when I learned he cheated me, but he was dead by then. Maybe, just maybe, I'd have spoken to him if I'd found out before he died. I'd have insisted I get my money and my broomstick back." Dolores jerked her head at Finn. "You've seen my criminal history. I'm not a killer."

"You're prone to violence. You use your magic and fists when you're unhappy."

"Everyone wants to do that! They're just not brave enough."

The table rocked again as Dolores's magic trickled out of her.

"Let's keep this calm," Finn said. "Dolores, you're in a lot of trouble. If you confess, we may be lenient."

There was a brief tap on the door, and Cythera appeared. Her wings fluttered behind her, her shoulders were tense. "Finn, why aren't you outside with the others? The horse skull parade starts in a few hours, and the crowd is already restless. I don't want trouble. You know how swiftly these celebrations get out of hand."

"I'll join them soon," Finn said. "This is Dolores Veil. We're questioning her in connection to Paxton's murder."

Cythera's nostrils flared as she stared at me. "The fluffies are asking questions, too?"

"Yes! We're valuable fluffies," I said. "You should remember our names."

Her gaze skimmed over my head as if she couldn't believe I'd just spoken. "You have enough proof to charge Dolores with murder?"

Finn glanced at Dolores. "I'll be back in a minute." He hurried out of the room and closed the door.

Dolores tipped back her head and sighed. "The angels are making a mistake. Sure, I have a temper, but the last time I attacked someone, it was bad. I felt out of control. That scared me. I knew then I had to change."

"That was the time you got imprisoned?" I glanced at Sammy. She was opening up. Perhaps she'd confess.

"Yeah. It wasn't fun inside, but there was a shrink. We all got half an hour with him once a week. At first, I thought it was a joke, but then I started talking and realized my mistakes. He helped me see there was a different way to live. A different way to think about the world." Dolores blew out a breath. "That doesn't mean I don't get angry, but I have coping mechanisms. I meditate, journal, deep breathe. It's not perfect, but I've never felt the desire to hurt anyone again. Even when I learned about Paxton stealing from me."

"You did say you'd strangle him," I said.

She waved a hand in the air. "I didn't mean it."

Was Dolores being truthful? Had she changed her ways? I was uncertain.

"Where were you when Paxton died?" I said. "If there's one person who can vouch for you, you're in the clear."

Her forehead furrowed. "I was at the inn. My feet were sore, and I had a headache. Vera kept going on about some ice contest, but it sounded dull. She said she'd do more shopping, then go look at that. I didn't want to, so headed to my room."

"Someone saw you? The receptionist?"

"Don't think so. I saw no one. No one can vouch for me." She licked her lips. "This is bad, isn't it?"

The door opened, and Cythera and Finn walked in. From the expression on Finn's face, he didn't have amazing news for Dolores.

"I've heard enough to convince me to charge you with Paxton Starstride's murder," Cythera said.

Dolores shoved back her chair. "I'm innocent! I didn't do it."

"We can't have a killer loose on the streets when there are so many people in Crimson Cove. This is a safe town, and it must remain so. Finn, charge her and put her in a cell until we can arrange transportation."

"Wait! I have information." Dolores stepped back, one hand raised. "There's something you need to know about Vera. I'm not the only one with a motive. Vera dated Paxton, and he dumped her."

"Did this happen recently?" Cythera said.

"Well, no. About five years ago. But she can hold a grudge."

Cythera flicked the comment away. "That's ancient history."

"Why won't you believe me?"

"Because you have no alibi, a violent past, and hated the victim. Finn! Deal with her."

Dolores raised her hand and slammed a spell at Cythera's chest.

Cythera shielded herself using her wings, although the spell knocked her into the wall. "Seize her! We have our killer."

I coiled, ready to lunge at Dolores, but Finn was on her before she could throw out more spells.

He wrapped her in his huge wings, preventing her from moving. "Dolores Veil, you're charged with the murder of Paxton Starstride." He hustled her out of the room, and all I could hear were muffled complaints from under his feathers.

Cythera brushed herself down and examined her wings. "That's enough excitement for one day. What with murderous witches, and all those strange little horse skulls being jigged around by overexcited people, I'm ready for a break." She glanced at us, shook her head as if surprised to see us, then strode out.

Sammy's fur was puffed out, and his eyes were wide. "I didn't expect that to happen. We really caught the killer?"

"We did." Finn appeared in the doorway. "Dolores is screaming blue murder. She's showing her true colors, and they ain't pretty."

"Maybe we have, and maybe we haven't," I said.

Finn's smile slipped. "Juno! We got her."

"Dolores seemed genuine when she said she was innocent. She's improved herself. She got help when she was in prison."

"All the best killers seem genuine when they're asked if they did it. That's how they get away with it for so long," he said.

"We should look into her alibi some more. Dolores told us she went to the inn because she had a headache. Maybe someone saw her there."

Finn leaned against the doorway. "Why make this more complicated? Forget about murder. It's almost Christmas. Sometimes, a case is simple. We get the evidence and find the killer. There aren't always twists, turns, or a double cross."

"You didn't look happy when Cythera ordered you to charge Dolores," I said. "Do you have doubts?"

His mouth twisted to the side. "I have a slight concern, but we've got everything we need. I'm doing the paperwork, then heading out to the horse skull parade. You should do the same."

"I refuse to do paperwork," I said.

Finn chuckled. "Leave that to me. Go find Zandra and take the day off. I'll be patrolling later, but I intend to let my feathers down, grab mulled wine, and munch on roasted chestnuts during the parade. Let your fur down, you two. We won!"

I loved fun as much as Finn, but not if a killer went free, or an innocent witch, no matter how surly, got charged with a crime she didn't commit.

# Chapter 10

Finn wouldn't be deterred from the plan to charge Dolores. I'd hung around the office with Sammy until lunchtime, but got shooed out by Cythera, who was flapping around and stressing about the horse skull parade.

We'd grabbed snacks from a busy street vendor, and tucked ourselves on a window ledge to avoid getting trodden on.

The horse skull parade always conjured interest. Visitors and locals lined the streets, ready to welcome the horse skull.

The atmosphere sparkled with excitement, and children dashed around with their own homemade horse skulls on sticks. There were even some adults who'd fashioned their own skull headgear.

Sammy looked around the crowd. "Dolores is guilty. Case closed. And she wouldn't have attacked Cythera if she was innocent."

"Desperate people do desperate things. Maybe Dolores thought she could surprise her and escape." I resisted the urge to bat some streamers that floated past. "Or it was an extreme reaction because she felt trapped and scared because of Cythera's snap judgment over her future."

"Or it shows Dolores still has a problem with her temper," Sammy said. "Like Finn said, these mysteries don't always have to be complicated."

"They don't, but they usually are." I ducked as a group of rampaging children with horse skull sticks got too close. "Cythera jumped the gun. It's because she's stressed about this event. She can only focus on a single task at a time. Anything else, and she gets flustered and unable to cope."

"I'm not much of a multitasker, either," Sammy said.

"Let's keep an open mind."

He glanced at me. "Which means you want to keep investigating?"

"Which means I want to make sure the right person is charged with this murder. If an innocent witch goes to jail for this crime, justice won't be served."

We hopped off the window ledge and walked around, the crowd getting denser and the atmosphere buzzing as everyone waited for the parade to start.

I kept an eye out for Zandra as I mulled over Paxton's murder.

We'd completed a circuit of the main street and were wandering up it again. Sammy kept quiet, knowing it was best not to interrupt me when I was deep in thought. I had all the pieces to this mystery but didn't have them in the right order.

I was certain I'd met Paxton's killer. And I knew their motive, too. But somehow, it had gotten lost.

The fact Angel Force was happy to charge Dolores and move on so quickly agitated me. Dolores was a far from perfect witch, but what was happening to her was wrong.

"Finn must have done his paperwork. Look, he's with that group of children," Sammy said.

I gritted my teeth. "Which means Dolores's time is almost up." I trotted over to the group.

The children surrounding Finn looked concerned. Several clutched small horse skulls or horse-shaped toys, while others had balloons.

"None of you have anything to worry about," Finn was saying as we approached.

"I keep getting the same nightmare." A small boy of around eight waggled his horse skull in the air. "This scary looking guy with a black sack grabs me and takes me away."

"Me, too," a girl around the same age said. "He's horrible. He's got horns and a tail. Scary."

All the children nodded.

"It's a bad dream," Finn said. "Even I have bad dreams, sometimes."

"Do you dream about this scary, horned man?" the same girl said.

"No. But I sometimes dream about my teeth falling out. That's scary."

The children seemed unimpressed.

"I keep hearing a bell." The smallest child in the group held no toy. Her little hands were gripped tightly as she picked a thumbnail.

"You're hearing a bell?" I said. "What does it sound like?"

All eyes swiveled to me.

"Hey, Juno. This is the group of children I've been helping with their nightmares," Finn said. "They've come to watch the parade."

I nodded as I approached the smallest child. "The bell. What sound does it make?"

"Ding dong?"

"Was it high-pitched or low-pitched?"

"Oh! Really low. It makes my tummy feel odd."

"Has anyone else heard this bell?"

There were several nods.

A tickle of worry ran along my spine. I didn't want to get ahead of myself, but a low, booming bell was rarely a good sign. "Hearing a bell in your dreams can mean several things."

"I heard it's a portent," Sammy said.

"What's that?" one child said.

"A sign something is coming."

"Something good?"

Sammy winced. "I mean, it's possible."

"The sound of a low bell is a sign death is approaching," I said.

The children gasped.

"Not necessarily," Finn said swiftly. "The sound of a bell can simply be that. It doesn't have to have a meaning."

"It does, though," the boy with a red balloon said. "Does that mean we'll die if we've heard the bell?"

"No!" Finn said. "Absolutely not. No one is dying. Isn't that right, Juno?"

I wouldn't lie to these children. "Everyone dies. But a deep bell sound means trouble. Although the death it's predicting doesn't need to be literal. It could be the death of an old career and the start of a new job."

"I don't work," the smallest child said.

"Or a new school. Maybe the ending of one friendship and the beginning of another."

"You see! There's nothing to worry about." Finn's smile was too big. "And you can trust Juno. She knows her ancient history. She's lived through a lot of it."

I ignored his jibe. "Of course, there are the low ringing bells of the underworld. And jabba wookie bells."

"I read about him! He's the creature with all the fur and big teeth. He lets people know before he strikes." The boy with the balloon waggled it so fast, I thought it might burst.

"There are no jabba wookies in Crimson Cove." Finn shot me a stern look. "That's a myth."

"They're real. My dad says so," another child said.

"I don't want to be eaten by the jabba wookie. Is that what's coming for us?" The smallest child started to cry.

"I'll fight it. I'll thump it with my balloon. Bam, bam, bam. If that don't work, I'll pop my balloon in his face, and scare him. He won't hurt us." He put his arm around the crying child's shoulders.

"That's right. You protect your sister. And Angel Force will protect everyone. Now, that's enough talk of bells and scary creatures. You must all be excited because the horse skull is almost here." Finn looked up. "And I see the start of the parade. Everyone take your places. Get to the front, so you can see."

"Will the horse skull protect us?" the little girl who'd been crying said. "Even though he's scary and bony, he's our friend, isn't he?"

"He is," I said. "He brings good luck to everyone he sees, and leaves treats, but only if you watch him travel all the way along the street and turn the corner. Don't take your eyes off him. And be on your best behavior. He can be grouchy if he's been on his hooves all day."

The child's eyes were wide as she was hustled away by her brother to watch the parade.

Finn put his hands on his hips and stared down at me. "Not the maternal type, Juno?"

"I'm maternal with my own. But I don't hide the truth. What's the point in concealing how mysterious this world is? It won't serve anyone when they're confronted with an ancient terror."

"Some of those children were shaking when you talked about the jabba wookie," Finn said. "Be gentler the next time you speak with them."

"I'll leave the children to you."

He arched an eyebrow. "How about we watch the parade? See if old horsey wants to bring us luck?"

"Dolores could do with some of that luck. Has she been charged?"

Finn pursed his lips. "The paperwork is done. I'm waiting for it to be signed off by Cythera. She won't be back in the office until the parade has ended."

"So Dolores has a few hours of respite?"

"She's comfortable in her cell." Finn pinched his chin between his finger and thumb. "Juno, the more I think about this, the more I realize it had to be her. There's no one else."

The crowd surged forward, and there were excited shouts as the parade reached us. Tiny fireworks exploded from the front float, and the air grew alive with glitter and sparkles.

"I have to concentrate on the parade. We can talk about this later, but I think you're wasting your time pursuing other suspects. Go find Zandra and party with the horse skulls."

Finn dashed off to monitor the crowd, and I hopped onto another window ledge with Sammy.

"There's Sorcha on the other side of the street," Sammy said. "Let's go over there."

I nodded, and was about to hop down, when I spotted Vera in the crowd, munching on a giant chocolate crepe. "I'll join you in a minute."

"Juno! Let's have fun. Life doesn't always have to be about murder and mayhem."

"I am having fun. I'll find you soon." I dodged through the crowd, over to Vera. I had to stamp on her foot several times to get her attention.

She looked down, and a large dollop of chocolate sauce dripped off her crepe, almost hitting me on the head. "What do you want?"

"Greetings. I thought you'd like an update on Dolores."

"Did she do it?" Vera's eyes glittered. "I always knew she had a mean streak. You know, she's served time?"

"I do. And thank you for not sharing that the last time we spoke."

She shrugged. "What you gonna do? I enjoyed hanging out with her until I realized what a sneak she was."

"Dolores told us something interesting about your relationship with Paxton," I said. "Again, it was something you failed to mention."

"Oh, yeah. What's that?"

"That you and Paxton were involved, and he ended things with you. That must have made you angry."

She smirked and stuffed more crepe into her mouth. "Hogwash. Dolores must be desperate if she pulled that out of the bag."

"It's untrue?"

Vera gulped down her food and swiped the back of her hand across her mouth. "Yeah, okay. I went on a few dates with Paxton."

"You knew him before meeting at the Christmas market?"

"Sort of. It wasn't a relationship, though. I met him years ago in another town, while he was selling his broomsticks. I thought he was cute, so I asked him out."

"And the relationship progressed from there?"

"We went out a few times, had fun, but he was always on the move, going from one town to the next for work. I wasn't prepared to do long distance and only see him when he wanted to." She finished her food. "And he didn't end things, I did. There were no hard feelings."

"While that's good to hear, it proved you lied," I said. "What else have you lied about?"

"Nothing. And Dolores is officially unfriended since she tried to drop me in it to clear her name. She has a wicked temper on her. I'm not surprised she snapped and killed Paxton."

"We'll be double-checking your alibi, to be on the safe side."

"Knock yourself out, fluff ball. I've got nothing to hide. And you should charge Dolores. She deserves it."

I gently shook my head. Some friend she was.

"I'm done being questioned." Vera kicked out at me. "I'm here for a good time, not to be interrogated by some know-it-all familiar."

I hissed at her and backed away. Although there were several motives floating around, was I making too much of this? Dolores had been caught in a lie, she had a violent criminal past, and she had a motive. Others did, too, but with no alibi, Dolores looked like she'd go down for this crime.

After almost being squished by merry revelers who weren't looking where they were going, I dodged through the crowd, hunting for Sammy. I should find Zandra, forget this mystery, and move on.

I slowed and jumped onto a high stone wall to get a better view. There was a brief gap in the crowd, and on the opposite side of the road, heading away from the parade, I spotted Godric.

He must have made a remarkable recovery to have been released from the hospital. The last time I saw him, he was shaking, crying, and could barely lift his head from the pillow. Now, he strode with purpose and carried two sturdy broomsticks.

I watched for a moment, and my gaze cut to Vera. She was stalking him!

I hopped through the crowd and dashed over to her. "Hey, what's going on?"

She glared at me. "You won't take a hint, will you?"

"Why are you tailing Godric?"

"I want my money back. He'll give it to me."

"I'll come with you. I'd like to talk to Godric, too." And ensure Vera didn't terrify him so badly he relapsed.

"Suit yourself. If you can keep up." Vera broke into a jog, and I followed.

From the evil look on her face, there was no way I'd let her confront Godric alone. If I did, we could have a second murder on our paws.

# Chapter 11

"For a runt, he can move fast. I keep losing him." Vera stomped through the snow in sturdy black boots.

I slid her a narrowed-eyed glare. "Be kind. Godric's been through a lot."

"We all have problems. Was that toad in on the broomstick-stealing racket, too? If he was, I'll snap him like a twig."

"You won't touch him." I trotted beside her, the pace brisk as Godric headed toward the woods.

"He took something precious from me. That deserves punishment."

"Godric wasn't the mastermind behind those thefts."

"I don't care." Vera swung her arms as she plowed through the snow.

I couldn't dissuade her not to confront Godric, but I could minimize the damage she caused.

As we entered the woods, the snow piles grew smaller. I slowed and looked at either side of the woodland path. Small piles of sticks were heaped up.

"Keep up if you're coming with me," Vera shot over her shoulder. "I don't carry deadweight."

I sniffed each bundle, and an icicle of concern stabbed into me. Old magic was attached to them. Magic that should no longer be free.

I continued along the path behind Vera and discovered more piles of sticks. A quiver ran from my booping snooter to my tail tip. This magic was even older than me. I'd felt it before. But it couldn't be free again.

Vera must have sensed something powerful circling us like a starving black unicorn. She stopped and turned her head from side to side.

I caught up with her and rested a paw on her foot. "We must proceed with caution."

"I'm not afraid of Godric. He can't hurt me." The words quivered out of her. "There's something out here that isn't sitting right in my gut, though. You feel it?"

"I do. There's something else in these woods. See those piles of sticks?"

Vera glanced at them. "They're nothing. Just kids messing around."

A low clanging bell chimed, and there was a faint rattle of chains in the distance.

My fur stood on end, and my toe beans tingled.

"What was that?" Vera whispered. "Godric?"

"Something old, and very dangerous."

Vera gulped and took a step back. "Will it hurt us?"

"It's possible, if he doesn't get what he wants. But it can't be him." My heart galloped as I peered through the spindly, dead looking trees.

"He? He who?"

"Someone you don't want to meet. And if Godric comes up against what's lurking in the woods, he won't survive."

"I almost feel sorry for him. Well, I would if he wasn't a cheat."

Did Vera have a thread of goodness inside her, after all? "Are you intending to save him?"

She sniffed. "Godric deserves what's coming to him. He was in cahoots with Paxton. This is fate teaching him a lesson."

It wasn't fate. It was an ancient being with no kindness, just a dark soul and a determination to terrify. "Vera, I need a favor. Go back to town and find as many angels as you can and a witch called Zandra Crypt. Ask anyone. They all know her."

"Why should I help you?" Her wide gaze kept shifting, her hands in fists by her sides, looking for the thing that made our spines shudder.

"If you don't, the world will change forever. This magic we're feeling doesn't play nice. I've met it before, and only just survived."

Vera glanced down at me. "You're saying that because you don't want me to confront Godric."

"I'm saying it, so we all get to live and the world isn't blotted out with this darkness. You feel it!"

"No! I must shake the truth out of Godric. Whatever trick this is, I'm not falling for it." She drew back her shoulders and continued along the path, but her steps were hesitant.

I followed, my senses on high alert for impending trouble.

Vera slowed and ducked behind a tree. "There! He's in front of us."

I peered around the tree. Godric stood over a stack of broomsticks. There must have been twenty in the pile. His hands were raised and jagged flickers of red and black magic pulsed from his palms. He stayed like that for several minutes, but the spell wouldn't take.

He lowered his hands, shook them, and tried again.

The deep, bone-chilling foreboding remained with me as we watched Godric.

"What's the idiot doing?" Vera whispered.

"Go back and get the angels and Zandra. We have little time."

"Stop making me nervous. I'm done with this. I'm getting my money and teaching him a lesson." Vera strode from behind the tree and marched over to Godric. "Hey! I want a word with you."

There was a split second of surprise on his face when he realized he wasn't alone, before he hunched and focused on the broomsticks.

"Didn't you hear me? You're the sniveling loser that worked with Paxton. You helped him steal my broomstick."

I held my breath as I waited to see what would happen.

"Go back to town," Godric muttered.

"Is it here? Have you got my broomstick in this pile?" Vera jabbed a finger at the broomsticks that glimmered with whatever magic Godric flooded them with. "I'm putting in a complaint about you. Imperial Broomsticks is over. No one will buy so much as an enchanted twig from you once they know who you really are."

"Please, excuse me. I'm busy." Godric turned his back on Vera.

She caught him by the shoulder and yanked him around. "Don't ignore me."

"You need to go." Godric didn't fight back, simply hung limply in her grip.

"Not until you tell me what happened to my broomstick." Vera shook him.

He raised his head. "You're not a nice person."

"And you're a weak-willed, pathetic loser. I know what I'd rather be." She was about to shake Godric again, but then paused. "What's wrong with your eyes? They're a different color."

Godric rested his hands on top of Vera's. "Let me go."

"Something is off with you. I knew it the first time we met. What are you doing in these woods?"

Godric sighed and straightened his spine. "I gave you a chance. Don't say I'm not compassionate." A large bundle of thin brown sticks appeared in his hand, and he swatted Vera across the face.

Magic cracked in the air, and the bell rang again.

Vera shrieked, dropped her hold on Godric, and fell to her knees.

My gaze remained on Godric, shaken to my core as he stood over Vera, brandishing the whipping sticks.

"Run!" I shot out from behind the tree. "Get back to town. Get help!"

Godric looked up, his arm raised. Recognition flickered in his eyes, but also a question. And those eyes were no longer a pale, insipid blue. They were rimmed with red, the center black.

Vera staggered to her feet and raced away, clutching her face.

Godric stared at me, a sick, cold smile on his face. A smile that turned my stomach and made my toe beans sweat, despite the snow.

I stepped closer, not letting the fear roiling in my stomach get the better of me. "I should have known. All the clues were there. The piles of sticks, the whip marks on Paxton's body, the nightmares the children had, the stolen broomsticks, the bell. You've been here all this time."

"Have I?" Godric struggled to remain upright, his shoulders naturally rounding in his broken body. "And what do those clues tell you, little cat?"

"They tell me an evil Santa has come to town. Krampus, we meet again."

# Chapter 12

Godric, or rather, Krampus, nodded slowly. "We have met before, haven't we? You were a different creature the last time I encountered you. State your name, and step out of that disguise."

"You looked different, too. You had horns, pointed teeth, and a tail. Not a hunchback and a body that shook every time you used it." My instinct told me to get away from this monster, but I couldn't let Krampus loose in Crimson Cove. There'd be nothing left if I did.

He huffed out a breath, his bleak gaze tinged with curiosity. "If I'm correct, you didn't have white fur and four paws. Is it really you? The demigoddess who imprisoned me all those years ago?"

"These days, I go by the name Juno." It had been so long since my last encounter with Krampus, the years had blurred, but I'd never forget imprisoning him in a cold tomb. He shouldn't be free to inflict trauma on innocent people.

"Show me your true face."

"I like this face." I kept my panic under control. Krampus was here, and I'd deal with him, just like I did the last time. "Why don't you show me yours?"

He dropped the sticks, his body shook, and the Godric Gander disguise vanished, his clothing ripping.

The true Krampus stood in front of me. Twelve-inch horns jutted from his forehead. He'd grown several feet, his feet had become cloven hooves, and a long, thin tail whipped behind him.

"Godric was never real? You created him to form an attachment to Paxton?"

He smirked. "Not quite. Paxton adored me, though. Well, he adored bullying me. It gave him a thrill."

"You needed Paxton, didn't you?" My gaze was on the broomsticks. "You identified someone happy to bend the rules to get what he wanted. You used Paxton's greedy streak to ensure you could access powerful broomsticks. Did your imprisonment at my hand weaken you so much you needed to borrow power to survive?"

Flames flickered from the top of his head. "I have power."

"You needed time to regain your strength once you'd escaped your prison, so you formed an attachment to Paxton, got him to trust you as his obedient sidekick, and bided your time."

His top lip curled, revealing an impressive set of sharp teeth. "I feed on children's fear and nightmares. They make me strong." That same low, spine-chilling bell rang again, signaling Krampus was in town.

"Of course. You've been terrifying our children. Sneaking into their dreams and growing fat on their fear. But it wasn't enough. You needed more. You must have been planning this for a long time."

Krampus grabbed the bundle of whipping sticks and swirled them around his head. "I have everything I want. I've been denied for too long, thanks to your interference. Why did you lock me up?"

"You were killing children. Feeding off their fears was no longer enough for you. Once you'd tasted innocence, you were too dangerous to be allowed to run free."

"There is always evil in this world. It shouldn't be suppressed."

"I accept there needs to be a balance, and I allowed you to roam the nights before Christmas every year to slake your thirst. But when I learned of the murders, you had to be stopped."

"You had no right! We all have a mission to complete. You interfered with mine." The whipping sticks twirled faster as Krampus's anger grew.

"You can have as many missions as you like, providing they don't hurt others." I paced in front of him, my tail swishing. "You made a mistake when you came into my territory and took my children."

He growled. "You demigoddesses are all the same. You think you rule over us all, but you're nothing special."

"I was special enough to trap you."

Krampus bared his teeth, then sneered. "Not for eternity, like you promised, as you sealed the tomb door."

Defeat flickered through me. "How did you get out?"

"I had time to try different methods. And not everyone dislikes my work. Naughty children must be punished."

"Not by killing them," I said. "Put coal in their stocking or give them a nightmare. Don't drink their blood!"

"Some naughty children won't listen. They must be used to set an example for others. I imagine no child misbehaved the following year for fear they'd end up the same."

I hissed at him. "Those children were under my care."

"And you punished me because of it. You felt guilty for your failure, so you attacked me. But I always come back. I have to be here to right the wrongs children create."

I held in my anger. The abuse of my subjects always stayed with me. "Why has it taken you so long to act? You've been in disguise as Godric for three years, working with Paxton. You can't have been that severely weakened."

Krampus tossed aside his whipping sticks, and his tail thrashed. "That's no concern of yours. I will make this work."

Although Krampus had revealed his true form, he was still hunched. There was something wrong with him. The Krampus I'd known was full of surety in his power. It wasn't just my influence and imprisonment that caused this change.

"You're injured," I said. "That's why you need these broomsticks."

He waved a clawed hand at me. "You know nothing."

"You were hoping you'd get stronger, but something went wrong. This is your last, desperate act to regain your strength. You need broomstick magic to open Hell and get healed." I settled on the ground. That was it. Krampus had received an injury so great, he couldn't punish the children. He needed a blast of primal power from the underworld to get back to his full, former, twisted self.

"If you hadn't interfered, I'd be healed by now. Christmas is so close. I must be ready." He rubbed his hands together. "There are so many bad children to deal with."

"Then you shouldn't have murdered Paxton. Did he figure out your deceit, so you silenced him? Did he glimpse your true face?"

Krampus chuckled out a tortured laugh. "You see? You really don't know all of my plans."

I twitched my booping snooter. I was missing something.

Krampus studied me for a second. "We've known each other a long time, and have always been on opposite sides, but I sense a duality in you."

"I don't follow."

"We should stop being enemies and join together. We would be glorious if we united."

"Unite in Hell, you mean. No thanks. My pale ears burn in extreme heat."

He chuckled again. "If you stopped fighting me, you'd see I'm not all bad."

"You're known as Evil Santa." I glimpsed movement among the trees but hid my relief as I spotted Finn. Zandra was beside him. I'd been uncertain if Vera would get help, or simply flee to save her hide. I walked in front of Krampus to keep his attention on me. "When Paxton was killed, you played up the weakling card so effectively, we discounted you straightaway."

"That was always my plan," he said. "I knew it wouldn't take much digging before you discovered disgruntled witches missing their broomsticks, and you'd focus on them as your suspects. I'm disappointed you didn't charge the one who just assaulted me. She's unpleasant. I expect she was a naughty child. Her companion is almost as bad."

"You almost got away with it. Dolores is sitting in a cell."

He shrugged. "It's hardly my fault she lied and tricked you. They both deserve to be punished. I could lend you my whipping sticks."

I shook my head. "It must have been hard, playing the role of obedient assistant, hoping every day you'd get stronger, but the reverse happened."

Krampus waggled a finger in the air. "Not true. I'd never tolerate being so malformed for so long." He spun toward the pile of broomsticks, raised his hands, and poured magic into them. "Open! I command you. Reveal Hell's Gate. Welcome in your brother."

The explosion of power dazzled me, but Krampus still wasn't strong enough to open Hell.

He lowered his hands and roared out his anger, the sound of chains rattling and bells thudding all around us.

"Hell doesn't want you," I said. "Come with me. You can confess, and the angels will find you a comfy cell. Something you'll never break out of."

He raked his claws against the mistletoe pin attached to his lapel. "Hell needs me. It's my home, yet I cannot open the gate."

I stared at the mistletoe pin, then laughed.

"You find this funny?" He blasted a spell at me.

I dodged out of its way. "You really haven't been in disguise as Godric for long, have you?"

Krampus smirked and did a slow clap. "Well done, Juno! You figured it out."

"Oh! That's clever. You've simply disguised yourself to look like him so you'd have access to the broomstick magic. The real Godric is somewhere else, isn't he? Or have you killed him, too?"

"I'm not a cold-blooded killer, despite what you think. When I met Paxton and Godric, I couldn't believe my luck. Godric was so biddable."

"So, you watched them and waited for a time to strike?"

"I needed to ensure the pairing would work. I tracked them for weeks, learning Godric's behavior and schooling myself on how to be subservient and ignore Paxton's idiocy. Although, I liked his dark streak. He took pleasure in stealing witches' broomsticks and selling them his products. He'd often chuckle as he counted his money. Greedy little man. Another one who was naughty as a child."

"And when you finally took over as Godric, you had to make sure everything was perfect. Including taking his mistletoe pin."

"What of it? The sad little sap always wore it. I heard him say to Paxton how grateful he was for the gift. It's a bit of dried plant. Barely important."

"It wasn't a gift, and it is important." I paced again. "Paxton was a wicked man. He manipulated Godric's illness. He gave him that pin and said it would help him heal, but it did the opposite. Godric was getting sicker. And when you took it, you felt the same ill effects. Godric's mistletoe pin is the reason you can't open the Hell Gate."

Krampus's head jerked back, and he looked down at the pin. "This? It's such an insignificant little thing."

"It's a tainted pin. Paxton used it to keep Godric compliant. It's doing the same to you."

Krampus growled and curled his hand around the pin.

I thrust out a spell and zapped him off his feet. "Now!"

Angels poured from the woods, Zandra running with them. She dashed to me and scooped me into her arms, kissing the top of my head and holding me tight.

I snuggled against her chest, happy to let Angel Force restrain Krampus and prevent him from taking off the pin and unleashing a deadly power. "Did you hear enough?"

"We heard it all. That's Evil Santa, and he's been disguised as Godric?"

"It is."

"And he's here to open the gate to Hell?" Zandra's wide eyes went to Krampus. "That would have destroyed Crimson Cove."

"It would have been a terrible result for anyone within a five-hundred-mile radius. Krampus is starving." I wriggled onto her shoulder.

"How did you know who he was?"

"I didn't. Not until I found him casting magic over those broomsticks. Then I connected the clues that showed me Krampus was in town."

Zandra pressed a comforting hand against my side. "The angels will want to talk to you, but how about we sneak off and take a break? I want to hear everything. And I need to make sure you're okay. He didn't hurt you, did he?"

I pressed my cold booping snooter to her cheek. "We can rest soon. First, we need to find the real Godric."

❦❦❦❦❦ ❦❦❦❦❦

I bounced on my paws, holding my breath as I snuck toward Zandra's bed. I placed a small cardboard box on her pillow and stepped back, waiting for her to rouse.

I glanced out the window to see a brilliantly snowy day. The snow had pelted down all night, to leave a winter wonderland on Christmas morning.

Two days had passed since I'd discovered Evil Santa hiding in Crimson Cove, and the last forty-eight hours had been a blur of activity to get things back to normal in time for Christmas.

Angel Force had interviewed me, and I'd made sure to brush over my interesting history with Krampus, since it would raise too many questions. Krampus had been charged and sent to a secure unit for powerful supernaturals while he awaited trial. And everyone had wanted to talk to me about how I'd discovered an evil Santa Claus in town and saved the day.

And, of course, I'd been happy to share that news. And although it had been fun to be the center of attention, receive gifts of thanks and strange doodles from the children who no longer had nightmares, what I really wanted, was for life to return to normal, and for everyone to focus on the joy of Christmas.

And, of course, I'd still needed to find the perfect gift for Zandra. It had taken careful thought.

"Please don't tell me there's a corpse in that box." Zandra had one eye cracked open and was glaring at the box.

"Merry Christmas!" I rested my forehead against hers. "Don't scream, but there is a mouse in the box. It's made of sugar. You're welcome."

Zandra slid up the bed, caught me in her arms, and hugged me. "Just what I always wanted. A corpse-free Christmas. Would you like your gift?"

"I always love gifts. What have you got me?" I wriggled against her, enjoying her bed warmed body.

"A year's subscription to Mouse U Like. You can order a rodent each month, and it'll be delivered in a secure, cool box. You won't need to hunt anymore."

It was a welcome gift, since I didn't enjoy hunting during the colder months. I draped my paws over her shoulders. "It's a wonderful gift from my most wonderful witch."

"Hey, we've got turkey for breakfast. And your guest has arrived," Sage yelled down from the top of the basements stairs.

"Godric's early," I said.

Zandra scrambled out of bed. She grabbed the nearest clean clothes, tugged them on, smoothed her hair, and we went upstairs.

I welcomed the heady whiff of turkey, and was happy to see Vorana at the stove, pouring juices over the bird as we entered the kitchen. She wore a delightful apron with a horse skull parade image embroidered on the front in gold and green.

We exchanged season's greetings, but my attention was on Godric. His transformation was incredible.

He grinned as he saw me studying him and shifted from foot to foot. "Hey, Juno. I wanted to get here early to see if I could help. You know us house-elves love having jobs to do."

"No help needed," Vorana said. "You're a guest. And after everything you've been through, you need a proper rest."

"I've been resting since Juno and Zandra found me." He smoothed a hand over his thick, dark hair. "I feel like a new man."

Vorana turned away from the stove and hustled Godric to a seat. "You're doing nothing all day, other than eating, and knowing you're in a safe place among new friends."

His cheeks flushed red, but his smile was genuine. "I can't thank you all enough. When Krampus broke into the cabin, he came for me first. I thought I was dead. I tried to get away, but he was too fast and strong for me to beat him. He stuffed me into a sack, trapping me in limbo."

"And that's what's so magical about Krampus's sack. Once you're inside, you can't get out. He could have taken you anywhere," I said.

"But he hid you in plain sight." Vorana squeezed his shoulder.

"Krampus had little option, since we were right outside when he attacked, I said. I expect he planned to sneak back and deal with Godric when he wasn't being noticed, or stuck in a hospital bed feeling like death warmed up."

"If Juno hadn't known to look for that sack, you'd still be in the cabin." Zandra petted my head. "How did you know that was Krampus's sack? It looked like a plain, boring sack when we searched the cabin."

"Luck and good judgment." I settled in a chair and nodded at Sage, who wore a delightful glittering red bowtie.

Zandra looked like she didn't believe me, but didn't press. "You're looking so much better, Godric."

"Because I'm not wearing that poisoned pin. I'm back to my old self." Godric shook his head. "I can't believe Paxton did that to me. I thought we were friends."

Vorana set cranberry and apple tartlets on everyone's plate and then joined us at the table. Sage and I got tiny pieces of butter-boiled cod.

"Paxton needed someone who wouldn't challenge him when he stole from the witches," I said. "He needed you quiet, obedient, and preoccupied with your failing health."

"He had me fooled. I'd been sick just before starting my job. He manipulated my fear of remaining ill, and preyed upon my lack of family or connections, knowing I had no one to turn to for advice. He was a bad man."

"Paxton sounds almost as terrible as Krampus," Vorana said. "Still, he didn't deserve to die."

Godric pressed his lips together, then nodded. "What he did was wrong, but that was a harsh punishment."

"What will you do now?" Zandra sliced her tartlet in half and took a bite.

"Start again. I have nowhere to call home, since I was always on the road with Paxton. And I have no family or friends. I only have a blank slate." Godric's smile faded, and he toyed with his food.

"It's not much, but if you're interested, I've got a friend who owns a bookstore a few towns over. She's looking for an assistant," Vorana said.

Godric's eyes filled with tears. "You'd help me get a job? Why? You don't even know me."

Vorana smiled. "Everyone needs a chance to start again. You've had a rough go of things. And I find being around books so calming."

"Or boring," Zandra muttered.

I gently dug a claw into her knee, knowing what bookish gift awaited her under the tree.

Zandra lifted her shoulders, then winked at me.

"I love reading. That sounds perfect. When can I start?" Godric said.

Vorana chuckled. "I'll call her in a couple of days. You'll be in town until then?"

"Absolutely!" His smile returned, and he tucked into his food.

As we sat around laughing, joking, and having a wonderful time, Christmas joy flickered through me like a kiss from a wish fairy.

Crimson Cove was safe from Krampus. With the teamwork and diligence of my magical misfit companions, and a small amount of fluffy genius on my part, a holiday disaster had been avoided. My best witch was by my side, and my friends felt loved and happy. It would be a Merry Christmas for all who deserved it.

Even the naughty children.

# Fir Trees and Fatalities

K.E. O'Connor

# Chapter 1

"Who'd have thought something as creepy as spider webbing would look so beautiful?" Monty, my leopard familiar friend, lounged at the base of the twenty-foot Christmas tree erected in the center of Witch Haven, my eclectic village home.

I twirled down the tree on a thin strand of web and landed beside him on my eight legs. I jabbed him with a limb. "Webbing isn't creepy. It has many uses. We don't just spin webs to catch food. And many spiders prefer to live on their webs rather than in a home, like I do with Indigo. Even then, I spin a web to sleep on. They're strong and comfy."

Monty's huge amber eyes widened, and he thumped an enormous paw over his nose. "Sorry! Of course, your webbing isn't creepy. And it sparkles."

I skittered around him in the snow. "Spider webbing has been used for centuries to offer beauty to all. Those who can't afford the tinsel and sparkle get a treat when they open their curtains and see our magical webbing covering the trees."

Monty nodded, his expression sincere. He was an adorable leopard, but prone to opening his mouth and blurting out whatever wandered through his brain. It got him in trouble. "You should decorate all the trees in Witch Haven."

I glanced at my spider shifter companions, who twirled and spun above our heads. "There's not enough of us to do that anymore. The spider shifter community is small, and our numbers suffer because people fear us and still squash us under shoes and newspapers."

"We should punish them for that." Monty growled. "You always make Christmas so special with your stunning webs."

I twirled a strand of webbing around him, pushing out a dash of magic that brought it to life and made it glitter. "We add the finishing touches to everyone's hard work."

The villagers always made Witch Haven come alive with color, magic, and surprises at this festive time of year. The snowflakes sparkled, lights twinkled, ghost stories were told around open fires, there were cheerful carols, acts of charity, and wishes sent to the Christmas Fairy to ensure a bountiful new year.

"I'm not doing any more. It's stupid. You can't make me." Dylan Martinez, a small, plump, teenage spider shifter, hurled himself off the tree and thumped onto the ground, sending up a snowy plume. He waggled his front legs in the air.

"You promised you'd stay. Ten more minutes and we can go home." Dylan's mother, Ana Maria, whirled down from the tree and landed lightly next to her surly son.

"It's boring. Why do we have to waste our webbing on decorating someone else's tree? And you never said how big this thing was. I thought we'd be done in an hour. We've been here all day."

"This is the ceremony tree. It's important." Ana Maria waggled her head from side to side. She glanced at me and then looked away.

She'd been having trouble with Dylan since she'd dragged him to help decorate the tree. All I'd heard him do was complain. I could understand it wasn't a fun occupation for a young spider shifter, but this was his punishment. He'd been caught sneaking out after his curfew, so Ana Maria insisted he stay home or remain by her side.

"Those two seem unhappy," Monty said. "I can't hear them, but I see they're fighting."

"Mother and son trouble," I said. "Dylan is going through those tricky teenage years."

Monty made a grumbling growl of sympathy. "We all have to go through them. Did I tell you about the time Olympus turned me into a leopard soft toy because I misbehaved when I was younger?"

"Wasn't that because you pushed him into the lake full of mermaids and he almost died?"

"No, that was another time. It was when I accidentally interrupted his annual appraisal. I had to tell him about this amazing moose carcass I'd found partially buried in a swamp. It still had antlers. I'd brought it with me and threw it on the desk for him to see."

"You hauled a rotting carcass inside the Magic Council?" I snickered. "Those official little oinks must have lost their minds."

"No one seemed impressed. I couldn't understand why not." Monty shrugged and slumped onto his belly. "After that, Olympus was always turning me into a soft toy. There was this time, when..."

I smiled, half listening to Monty pour out his difficult early years with Olympus Duke, the magic user he'd joined with to become his familiar.

We all had the occasional struggle with our magic users. I had a wonderful witch companion, Indigo Ash, but our relationship wasn't always perfect. She was dating Olympus, so I spent lots of time with Monty, and he always had entertaining tales of his adventures and the problems he caused Olympus.

A quick glance at Ana Maria and Dylan showed an intense, but quiet, conversation going on. I didn't intrude. We all knew how complicated it was to handle a youngster.

My gaze drifted toward the main village street. Christmas was almost upon Witch Haven. All the stores had their windows brimming with decorations, and residents were coming together this evening around this beautiful Christmas tree to hold the lighting ceremony.

The ceremony was a magical time of year, inviting in positivity and light, and it was a chance for people to say goodbye to the past. They used the light from the tree candles to illuminate a new path. It wasn't only beautiful, but the tree was full of magic and old power.

"I'm not coming to the stupid ceremony," Dylan yelled. "You can't make me."

"We'll all be here. You'll have fun. There'll be games and food. Wait!" Ana Maria chased after Dylan as he scuttled away.

"I don't need to speak spider to see they've got issues," Monty said, breaking off from his breathless account of the time he dropped an angry skunk on Olympus's head. "Should we help?"

"They'll sort things out. Dylan is struggling to find a balance between responsibility and freedom."

"Hilda, how much more web should we put at the top of the tree?" Pierre, the spider shifter in charge of coordinating the volunteers, twirled down to join us. "It's looking top-heavy, and I want to make sure there's room for all the candles. We don't want our webbing to catch fire."

"It's looking beautiful." I examined the tree for a moment. "Perhaps a little more to the right, to balance things out. And we could do with filler webbing at the bottom."

"I'll get everyone on it." Pierre dashed away and whipped out orders in his usual official fashion.

"I wish I could shoot out webbing like you. Then I could make decorations and add them to the tree." Monty jumped to his paws. "I've got an idea! I'll go to the store and get pots of glitter and card. I'll work in Olympus's office, so nothing gets soggy in the snow. I can cut out shapes and paint them with glitter."

"That's thoughtful of you. But only if you have the time." I hid a smile. Olympus would hate his office getting covered in Monty's overenthusiastic distribution of glitter, but I didn't have the heart to tell him that. Monty was so eager to get involved. There wasn't a bad bone in this leopard, just lots of overexuberant ones.

"Hilda! There you are. I've been looking all over for you." Nugget, the black cat familiar I lived with, bounded across the hard-packed snow. Sweeping over his head was the other familiar I shared a home with. Russell the crow. He cawed out a greeting and circled around us.

"Is something the matter?" I hurried over to meet them, leaving Monty pouncing on the snow.

"We have a problem," Nugget said. "A massive one."

"Is the house still unimpressed with the decorations? If it's thrown the tree into the snow again, I won't be happy." I lived in a huge old house Indigo inherited from her stepmother. It was a glorious, haunted place. But those old ghosts had stubborn streaks. They'd disapproved of the traditional gold and green decorations we'd put up, and had rudely thrown the tree out the front door in the middle of the night.

"It's not the house. It likes the new color scheme."

"I hope Indigo and Olympus aren't arguing over Christmas gifts again. That's all we heard last night over dinner. It put me off my flies."

"They're not arguing. Well, there's some bickering about how many gifts to get each other, or whether to save the money and use it to go away somewhere."

"That's not a bad idea," I said. "It's been a while since we've had a break from Witch Haven."

Russell cawed out his agreement as he landed in the snow and fluttered his inky black wings into place.

"Hey, you two." Monty bounded over and attempted to lick their heads.

Nugget hissed at him and slashed out a paw. "Keep your drool away from me."

Russell didn't mind getting licked, and he affectionately pecked Monty's side as they greeted each other and bounced around in the snow.

"If it's not the house misbehaving, and Olympus and Indigo are okay, what's the issue?" I looked back at the tree. I needed to get it finished.

"The reindeer have vanished," Nugget said.

I turned back. "Vanished as in, gone for a walk, or gone missing?"

"All their stalls are empty. And they've been empty for ages. It's a nightmare."

As much as I adored Nugget, he had a tiny tendency to overreact. He was the kind of cat whose bowl was bone dry and had never seen a drop of water.

"They could have gone out to have fun before the big day. You know what those reindeer are like. I expect they've gotten their noses stuck in troughs of ale, and we'll find them staggering around a field singing rude versions of Christmas carols. That happened a few years ago. Santa almost had a heart attack when he discovered his drunken reindeer. Christmas was almost canceled."

Nugget made a noise of disgust in the back of his throat as if he was about to hack up a hairball. "All the stall doors are open, and they didn't leave a note. They've bolted."

"Hilda, I need advice on where to hang the next length of webbing," Pierre called from the top of the tree. "Could you come up and sort things? And there's a disagreement over the candleholders."

Nugget yanked on one of my legs. "The reindeer! This is important. We must find them."

My legs twitched, and I turned in a rapid circle. "I need to help finish the tree. You know the spider shifters love to fight. I'm here to keep the peace."

"They don't need you. You must help me find the missing reindeer."

"The tree magic needs to be balanced so everyone can be filled with light and love when the ceremony begins. We don't want anyone to feel let down." Our webbing acted as a conduit to ensure everyone's wishes were heard. Mess that up and trouble followed.

Nugget's tail swished through the snow. "I can't do this alone, and Russell won't focus on anything for more than a few seconds. He's such a birdbrain."

Russell jabbed at Nugget with his shiny black beak.

"Why the urgency? I'll help you look later if they haven't returned. I'm sure they've not gone far, though. Where have you looked?"

"All over Witch Haven. Someone has scooped them up and taken them."

"Father Christmas," Monty said. "He'll need them soon. Have you checked with the big guy?"

"He doesn't get them until Christmas Eve. And he knows better than to take them any earlier than that. We have an agreement." Nugget's tail swishing grew intense. "It'll be dark soon, and the reindeer are slippery. It'll be harder to find them once the light has gone."

"They'll come back. They know the tree lighting ceremony is tonight, and they love Christmas. They won't want to miss it."

"And they enjoy pulling the charity sleigh," Monty said. "They look so proud when they get their harnesses on and strut around the village, collecting donations."

"I'm not so sure they do," Nugget said. "There were grumbles last year over pay."

"Pay! But it's for charity," Monty said. "That can't be right."

"Reindeers are ruthlessly corporate. They do nothing out of the goodness of their hearts," I said.

Russell stamped his feet on the snow and shook out his feathers.

Nugget leaned in close. "From the rumors I've heard, the reindeer demanded a twenty percent pay rise, or they wouldn't be pulling the sleigh again."

"Did they get it?" I said.

"Hilda! What do you want done with this webbing?" Pierre held out a globule of misshapen, shiny webbing.

I waggled a limb at him. "I'll be up in a minute."

"Of course they didn't get the raise. It was an extortion attempt," Nugget said. "This is their revenge. They're showing they have all the power. Sure, they turned up and played nice, made certain everyone knew how valuable they were, then they scarpered."

Pierre kept calling to me, and Nugget kept snapping about the greedy reindeer. I danced one way, then the other.

We only had a few hours until the village square would be heaving with excited magic users. "I can't help you look for the reindeer. Not right now."

Nugget huffed out a breath. "Then it'll be your fault."

I paused, one limb on the base of the tree. "What'll be my fault?"

"When we end up in harnesses."

"Harnesses?" Monty tilted his head. "Why?"

"When Indigo heard the reindeer had gone missing, she suggested all of us pull the charity sleigh instead. You really want to be shackled like a dumb reindeer and drenched in tinsel on Christmas Day?"

# Chapter 2

"It looks incredible." Ginger Aspire, head of the spider shifter community, stood beside me in his spider form. He gazed at the beautiful Christmas tree being covered in lit candles, as magic users stepped forward, declared their intent and hope for the coming year, and placed a candle on the branches.

"Your spiders did an amazing job," I said. "This wouldn't have happened without their help."

The bright ginger tuft on his head quivered. "It's always a pleasure. It's important we show people spiders provide beauty. We're not terrifying, hairy, fanged creatures that bite you in your sleep."

"Most of us aren't." My gaze was on Dylan, who was being dragged around by his put-upon mother as she forced him to have fun.

Ginger's attention also turned to the feuding family. "I heard you had a few issues with young Dylan."

"He mainly behaved. And I hold no ill will against him for playing up. We all remember our unfortunate teenage years when we thought we knew it all. Back then, we had no concept of fear."

"Certainly. I had plenty of adventures," Ginger said. "I don't miss those days, though. Teenage boy hormones are the worst, especially when mingled with the trials of being a shifter. I've spoken to Ana Maria about Dylan, but it's difficult for her. She's a single parent, and her work is hectic. She also lost her bonded magic user not so long ago. She's pulled in too many directions, so it's making home life hard."

I understood how Ana Maria felt. After Nugget's dramatic revelation that we may have to pull the charity sleigh, I was concerned. I should have made more effort to help find the reindeer, but I'd been determined to ensure the tree lighting ceremony went without a hitch, so had made that my priority. Nugget probably wouldn't speak to me for a week as punishment.

"Dylan will come good," I said. "He's surrounded by support in your community, and we're all happy to give him advice."

"Don't think I haven't tried," Ginger said. "I thought Dylan might enjoy having a mentor and suggested he spent a few days with me. He laughed in my face and said he had no intention of learning from a boring bureaucrat who went to tedious meetings and played by the rule book." He danced around on his long limbs. "Being a leader involves a certain amount of bureaucracy, but we must have order. Spider shifters weave along a thin line. It can't always be excitement."

"You do an amazing job keeping the shifters safe and happy. And someone has to attend all those Magic Council meetings to learn the new regulations. I couldn't do it." I smiled at Ginger to reassure him. "Dylan will figure things out. He'll make missteps along the way, and give his mother a few gray hairs, but he has the makings of a fine young man."

"I'm sure you're right." Ginger seemed appeased, and settled in to watch the tree lighting ceremony continue.

I sighed. My world comprised of two families, neither of which I'd been born into. I had the spider shifters, who held a small, but established base close to Witch Haven, and then I had Indigo, Nugget, and Russell. I included Monty and Olympus in my immediate family, too.

And they were all here to take part in the ceremony. As were Indigo's friends and their familiars, which included a hellhound, more cats, and an army of huge, glowing-eyed scarecrows.

No one missed the tree lighting ceremony, and I was pleased to see our newest resident, Spike Buchanan, at the edge of the crowd, looking nervous, with an unlit candle in his hand. He was a former biker with shaggy red hair and several impressive tattoos chasing around his burly arms, which he often displayed. Tonight, he wore a black biker jacket with a red star on the back, and a thick, dark sweater underneath.

Spike moved to the village a month ago. He'd rumbled in on an ancient, throaty bike, and declared he was turning over a new leaf and planned to retire from his nefarious biker gang shenanigans.

I always kept an eye on new residents to make sure Indigo remained safe from harm. The village embraced those who were troubled, so long as they didn't bring any trouble with them.

Shrill giggles caught my attention. A small group of mistletoe witches with striking dark eye and lip makeup shimmered as they danced around the Christmas tree. They were always busy this time of year, blasting out their mysterious mistletoe magic.

Mistletoe had a poor reputation because the berries were toxic, but I preferred to dwell on the romantic notion of mistletoe bringing lovers together. And, of course, in small doses, mistletoe healed some ailments.

Although mistletoe witches had naughty, playful sides, they generally used their magic for good, so I was happy to see them dancing around and making people laugh as they sparkled and glistened.

"Do you know who that is?" Ginger pointed a long black leg at a group on the other side of the Christmas tree.

There were six men, dressed similarly in dark denim and leather jackets. They all had the same emblem on the back of their jackets. A red lightning bolt.

"I don't know all their names, but the one with the beard is Billy Worgan. He's the leader of the Burned Oak gang."

Ginger hissed softly. "I've heard of them. Bad news, aren't they?"

"They can be trouble. I've been watching them since they pulled up in Witch Haven. So far, they've been making noise, but haven't started anything."

"Let's hope they're just passing through," Ginger said. "We want peace and goodwill at Christmas, not biker fights and bloodshed."

"They're welcome to stay, so long as they behave."

"Your witch is up," Ginger said.

I hurried over as Indigo stepped forward and lit her candle from the orange candle that sat beside the tree. Russell soared down and landed on her shoulder, while I ran up her leg, across her torso, and sat on her other shoulder, occupying my favorite place.

Nugget weaved around Indigo's legs as she slowly approached the tree.

Love, companionship, and magic united us. The bond between us had never been stronger.

"You guys having fun?" she whispered.

"Yes. The ceremony is going well," I said.

"The tree looks great. You and the spider shifters did an incredible job." Indigo's voice was low, magic gently pulsing out of her as she stopped in front of the tree and held out the candle.

We were silent, allowing our magic to swirl around, mingling with the soft fall of snow in the breeze.

Our magic bond pulsed strongly, and I sent love and respect to Indigo, Russell, and Nugget. Our lives weren't always easy, but when we were together, we could achieve anything.

Indigo sent her silent wish through the candle and bowed her head over it. "Blessed be." She placed the lit candle into an empty holder.

"Blessed be," we all repeated.

We merged into the crowd as the next magic user stepped forward.

"The reindeer are still missing," Nugget muttered to me.

"It's weird how they've vanished," Indigo said. "If the reindeer are a no-show, you'll all look incredible pulling the sleigh."

"We won't fit into that thing!" Nugget said. "How is Russell supposed to fit a harness with his wings?"

"We'll figure out an adaptation." Indigo stroked Russell. "And if you're supersized, you'll barely notice you're pulling a sleigh."

A wonderful thing about being bonded with Indigo was that she gave us the power to turn into magnificently huge creatures. It was a handy skill to have when we went into battle or wanted to give someone a good scare.

It would be handier still if I ended up having a harness around me and pulling a heavy wooden sleigh through the snow.

"I don't want to parade through the village like an exhibition," Nugget said. "People will stare and laugh at us."

"Everyone will cheer you on," Indigo said. "You'll be our saviors. And it'll mean the charity collection won't be canceled. We're supporting the gremlin reform school this year. Odessa has a soft spot for that place and campaigned to get the donations sent there."

"We'll do it," I said.

"You don't get to agree on my behalf," Nugget grumbled.

Indigo lifted Nugget and leaned her head against his side. "Stop being a grinch. And, if you take part, there'll be an extra treat in your Christmas stocking."

Nugget's tail twitched. "Are we talking food treat or toy?"

"Maybe both if you stop complaining."

He grumbled some more. "I'll think about it. No promises, though."

I chuckled as I danced on Indigo's shoulder. Nugget was a grouchy, blustery old thing, but there was a heart of gold buried beneath that thick fur.

The last of the candles were lit and placed on the tree. Everyone stepped back as they flickered, and a wave of magic encased the webbing we'd intricately cast, causing it to swirl and glow.

Everyone oohed and aahed at the beautiful sight of our shimmering webbing. Sitting on top of the tree was a stunning, iridescent spider. It was a nod to our ancestors, who started the tradition of weaving webbing around trees at Christmas.

"You've outdone yourself." Indigo kissed the top of my head. "Every year, I think the tree can't get any prettier, but this one takes my breath away."

"It's not so bad," Nugget said. "Now we're done with all the traditions, let's eat."

The crowd slowly separated, some groups heading off to look at the games and entertainment, others going to the food stalls, or standing with friends and chatting, talking about all the things they had to do before Christmas Day.

My spider senses tingled, and I tensed. What had alerted me to potential trouble?

The Burned Oak gang lumbered around, looking menacing, but they weren't causing problems. The small group of mistletoe witches surrounded the coconut shy and hurled balls with abandon, filling the air with girlish giggles. No trouble there.

I couldn't see Dylan or Ana Maria, so I assumed she'd dragged him home because he was being surly.

My gaze went to the shadows stretching beyond the candlelight. There it was. A dark shape. A person.

I hopped off Indigo's shoulder and squinted into the gloom. We had individuals in Witch Haven who preferred to spend their time alone. Our cemetery guardian was one, but I'd seen Silvaria jigging to the music just before the ceremony began.

"Hilda, you ready to eat?" Indigo called.

I glanced at her and nodded, then focused back on the stranger. It was a man, early thirties, with a mop of messy dark curls. He kept his head down, but he was watching Spike, I was sure of it.

"Come on. We don't want to miss out," Indigo said.

Russell soared over my head, obscuring my view as he cawed and encouraged me to join them. When my view cleared of feathers, the shadowy man had vanished.

I skittered back to Indigo and leaped onto her shoulder.

"Everything good?"

I looked back at the spot where the man had stood. Witch Haven drew in complicated characters. It was the ancient magic that flowed through the village that appealed to so many.

I shouldn't be suspicious of someone who liked to celebrate alone. "Everything is perfect."

She grinned at me. "Then let's go feast."

I rubbed my distended stomach and shifted in my web in the corner of the living room. The rich food after the tree lighting ceremony had been amazing, but I was used to a simpler diet of insects and the occasional skin flake. All the butter and oil disagreed with me.

My stomach growled again, signaling I needed to move and digest more of this meal. I spun out a thin string of webbing and whirled to the floor.

Indigo always left a window cracked, so it was easy to get outside if I needed to. I slid through the tiny gap and dropped onto the frozen ground.

The world sparkled. There was a full moon overhead, which made the snow glisten. Witch Haven late at night under a blanket of snow was beautiful.

I wandered away from the house, drawing in deep, icy breaths, and my stomach instantly felt better. I'd need to pace myself over the next few days. We had dinners or celebration lunches planned everywhere, and I didn't want to spoil things by getting a stomachache.

Rather than circling the plot, I wandered back to the center of the village. I never had any fear when being out alone. Witch Haven was generally a safe place. Sure, we had the occasional murder or magical issue to solve, but if I ever ran into difficulties, I had my powers. I'd been a spider familiar for many years and had learned a trick or two from the powerful witches I spent time with.

My path took me toward the glowing Christmas tree. The candles still flickered, magic keeping them alight and ensuring the decorations didn't catch fire.

I stopped, the icy ground barely noticeable as cold grabbed my heart and squeezed.

There were two long, jean-clad legs poking out from underneath the tree.

# Chapter 3

I dashed over, slipping in the snow in my haste to get to the tree. "Hello! Are you hurt? Can you hear me?"

The lack of response wasn't encouraging.

I scuttled up the muscular body and slowed. It was Spike Buchanan. His eyes were open, and he stared sightlessly at the tree branches, his lips tinged dark blue from being out in the cold. There was a light covering of snow over his legs.

Despite these unwelcome signs suggesting life no longer lingered, I rested against the pulse point in his neck.

There was nothing. He was gone.

I took a few steps back. This wasn't the first body I'd seen, but it was never pleasant to discover a corpse.

My practical nature kicked in, and I spent a moment observing. There was no sign of trauma or injuries on his head, and no blood polluting the snow. It would have been obvious if he'd bled out.

I kept calm as I inspected the scene, so as not to miss anything. I hadn't known Spike well, but he'd always been respectful when we'd spoken.

Why was he out so late? Could he have been meeting someone? Perhaps the meeting took a dark turn, and he was attacked.

I slowed when I reached his head again. There was a small red mark that looked almost like a burn, and tiny pinpricks on his throat. Several of the marks were in one area. I inched closer and inspected them. A shiver ran through me, and it wasn't caused by the snowy conditions. These were spider bites.

Not all, but many spider shifters, had venomous bites. Some venom was toxic enough to kill, but some simply made their victims weak or sick.

But why would a spider shifter bite Spike? They were a reclusive bunch and preferred to mingle with their own kind, only coming out for public events, such as the tree lighting ceremony.

I wasn't even sure Spike had had dealings with the spider shifters. But I knew my spider bites, and Spike had been bitten.

I rapid-tapped my legs on the snow. I had to get the authorities involved. Olympus was at Indigo's house. I'd go home and alert him to my discovery. As I turned to scuttle away, someone called my name. I looked up and discovered Ginger speed marching toward me.

He glanced at the body, not surprised it was there. "Hilda! What are you doing here?"

"You've seen Spike?"

Ginger jiggled his two front legs at me. "I have."

"Have you been to the Magic Council? Is someone on their way?"

He waggled his abdomen from side to side. "Not yet. I went to the colony and told them what happened."

"You saw the bites on Spike's neck? A spider did them, don't you think?"

Ginger continued to shift around, and my senses tingled. Ginger hadn't done this, had he? What reason would he have for killing Spike?

"I was uncertain what they were, so came back for another look." He skittered in front of the body, unable to keep still. "Don't worry. I've got everything under control."

"I have to be worried. If a spider shifter bit Spike, we must figure out who did it and why. I'll go get Olympus."

Ginger dashed in front of me. "Wait! I'm not certain a spider bite caused this death. We don't need the Magic Council jumping to conclusions and accusing an innocent spider."

I tilted my head. "What else could have made those marks?"

"I don't know, but none of my spiders are vicious. And we don't interfere with other magical beings. It's easier that way. So many people are fearful of us." Ginger heaved out a sigh. "It gets tiring being the object of terror."

I nodded. I'd lost count of the times I'd startled people with a speedy shuttle or a sudden drop on a web when they weren't expecting me. It wasn't their fault. It was their primitive brains reacting, but it was never fun when someone batted you away or screamed so loudly your ears rang for days.

"Please, Hilda, I have the greatest respect for you, but this is a matter for the spider shifters to deal with. We don't want outside interference."

My gaze returned to Spike. "Do you accept a spider bite killed him?"

Ginger paused. "It could be the cause of death, but I'm yet to be convinced. I'll make sure there's a thorough investigation. Whoever did this won't get away with it."

I hesitated. I liked Ginger. He was a responsible, fair leader, but I couldn't understand why he was so reluctant to involve the professionals.

He must have sensed my uncertainty because he crept closer, keeping low as a sign of deference. "You're a clever spider, and one of the oldest I've ever been around. You have knowledge and power, and you understand how we do things in our community. If Spike was bitten by a spider and died because of it, we have a right to deal with this."

I knew my spider lore, seemingly better than he did. "It means you have a right to be kept informed about the investigation, but not to take over."

Ginger's dark eyes glistened. "I know you have a friend in the Magic Council who you believe will help, but you know what they're like. They'll get the idea in their head that one of my spiders did this. The community will be torn apart. We're small in number, and we struggle to thrive. This will only make things worse."

I understood his dilemma, but this death couldn't be kept a secret. "Let's inspect the bites again. There's a red mark, too. That could be a side effect of the venom."

Ginger turned to face Spike, his legs quivering. "If that'll set your mind at rest. When I was out looking for ... looking for somewhere quiet to walk, this was the last thing I thought I'd find."

"That was why you were out so late?" What had he been about to say? Had Ginger really been looking for some quiet, or had he been looking for someone? Someone he thought was guilty of murder.

"My mind sometimes won't quieten enough to sleep, so I often walk. It helps." He gestured to the body.

I walked back to Spike with Ginger beside me. I stopped by the small, red bites on Spike's neck. "Look at these. Tell me honestly, what do you see?"

Ginger barely glanced at the holes. "What about fairies? They have small, sharp teeth."

"But lots of them. These are fine holes set the same spacing apart. Just like we make with our fangs." I waggled my fangs in the air.

"Or ... a snake."

"We don't get snakes around here, especially when it's freezing cold. And surely, if it was a snake, the impressions would be deeper and further apart."

Ginger waved his two front legs again. "You're determined to block me, whatever suggestion I make."

"It's not that. I hate to think of any spider shifter doing this, but we must consider the possibility. It's what the Magic Council will think. Did Spike have anything to do with your colony? Anyone he had a problem with or argued with recently?"

"We barely knew the man. I'd seen him around, but he'd not been living here long. Why would he interfere with colony business? I doubt he was even aware of our existence."

"Maybe he made an error when meeting one of your spider shifters, and said something he shouldn't," I said. "You should ask the others if they had anything to do with him. Maybe there was a disagreement you haven't heard about."

"My colony keeps nothing from me. I'd know if there was a problem. It's not that. Besides, if any of my spiders have an issue with someone, they leave them alone. They don't sneak up and bite them."

I studied the body again. A spider made those bites. It would have been simple for them to creep up on Spike and sink their fangs into his neck. By the time he realized what was happening, it would have been too late.

There were several bites close together, suggesting whoever did this bit Spike more than once.

That was odd. Once a spider sank in his fangs, the victim knew about it. They'd squash you or swat you away. Why hadn't Spike done that?

A quick look around revealed no spider corpse, so whoever had done this survived.

"Are any of your spiders missing?" I said. "Is that why you were out? You were looking for them?"

"I already said I was looking for somewhere quiet to walk. There's no law against that."

Ginger was lying. He knew one of his spiders had done this, and he intended to cover for them.

He gently sighed. "Hilda, let's not make too much of this situation. Besides, we don't even know when Spike died. Looking at his lips and those ice burns, he's been out here for a while. His body is practically frozen."

"Which won't be helpful when figuring out exactly when he died," I said. "Cold and heat mess with determining the time of death."

"How would you know that?"

"My witch dates Olympus Duke, and he always investigates the more serious crimes. They occasionally have morbid discussions about murder over breakfast."

Ginger sidled around the body. "I feel uncomfortable dealing with the Magic Council. They always poke their nose in where it isn't wanted."

He clearly thought this was one such occasion.

I walked over and rested a front leg on Ginger's side. "I know you're uneasy with them looking into this, but they'll work with you. They'll be sympathetic and treat the spider community with respect."

"You say that as if you believe it."

"The Magic Council isn't so bad. And I'll be around to keep things under control. Olympus is one of the good ones. Let him lead this investigation."

"I can't agree to that." Ginger's breath plumed out as he looked at Spike. "I'll allow Magic Council involvement, but if a spider made this bite, then this is a spider shifter matter, and we'll take the lead on the investigation."

I could have debated this point with Ginger for hours, but he wouldn't budge. At least he'd made an allowance by permitting Magic Council involvement. "I'll support you with that."

"I'll stay with the body. You go get assistance."

"I won't be long." I dashed through the snow, sliding left and right in my haste to get back to the house.

After such a wonderful day, the last thing Witch Haven needed was a murder. Let's hope this was resolved swiftly and didn't taint the Christmas joy.

When I got back, I squashed myself through the gap in the window, scattering snow on the floor as I spun down on a string of webbing. I bounced up the stairs two at a time and slid through the gap underneath Indigo's bedroom door. I leaped onto the bed, dashed up the covers, and sat on her cheek. I had to tap her face several times before she roused.

"What is it?" she mumbled. "You'd better not be asking for food. You ate several times your body weight at the tree lighting ceremony."

"Unless this is about those missing reindeer, go away." Nugget was curled in a tight ball at the bottom of the bed.

"It's not food or reindeer related. I have bad news. I went for a walk and found Spike Buchanan dead under the tree."

Indigo's eyes shot open. She struggled up in bed and lifted me off her cheek, settling me on her palm. "Say that again."

Nugget's head was raised, his eyes not blinking as he stared at me.

"Spike is dead. Something bit him."

Indigo shoved Olympus's shoulder. "Hey! Get up."

He grunted and rolled over. "I'm not snoring."

She shoved him again. "Wake up. Hilda found a body."

Olympus switched on the lamp. "A body? Who? Where? Are you sure you didn't dream it?"

"No dream. Spike Buchanan is dead under the tree in the center of the village."

"That's some gift to unwrap," Nugget muttered.

"Get up and get dressed. We'd better look before Witch Haven wakes and chaos begins. You, too, Nugget." Indigo was rolling out of bed and reaching for her clothes as she spoke.

After much grumbling, Nugget did a full body stretch and hopped onto the floor. "This had better not be a joke."

"No joke," I said.

"You said Spike was bitten." Indigo tugged on her boots.

"I think so. I couldn't get a good look at the body, so there could be other injuries. I didn't want to interfere and contaminate evidence by poking around too much."

"Good work, Hilda. You did the right thing by coming to me." Olympus gently tapped my head. "Monty, up! We have a body to deal with."

Monty, who'd been dead to the world in his over-sized leopard bed in the corner of the room, leaped up and growled. "Ready for action. I just need to pee."

We headed down the stairs as a group, and I discovered Russell waiting outside. He must have realized something was wrong when he saw me dashing across the snow.

He cawed out his concern, then sailed above us as we raced away from the house and back to the center of the village.

"I'll take a look, get the scene secured, and then call in backup," Olympus said. "These conditions won't make it easy to work fast, but hopefully, we can get the body moved before the rest of the village wakes."

I slowed as I neared the tree and frowned. Ginger and Spike were gone.

# Chapter 4

Nugget turned on me and hissed. "I don't know what game you're playing, but I'm not participating. There's no body!"

Monty spun in a circle. "Where is it? Is it a zombie? A ghoul? Is it playing hide and go seek? Are we at the wrong tree?"

I dashed over to where I'd last seen Spike. "He was here! And you can see, there's an indentation where he fell."

As I looked across the snow, there were drag marks heading away from the tree. Ginger must have transformed and dragged the body away.

Concern whacked into me like an ice snowball. Ginger would only move Spike if he had something to conceal.

"Hilda is right." Indigo inspected the scene. "There was something in the snow. A big something. A person-sized something."

"And it was taken that way." Olympus pointed toward the trees. It was the direction you traveled to visit the spider shifter colony.

Nugget grumbled notes of unhappiness as he sniffed around. "At least the body didn't get up and walk away. I don't want a zombie infestation for Christmas."

I skittered around, uncertain what to do. The spider shifters were my family, and I felt an affinity to them, but I wouldn't lie to Indigo. "There was someone else here. When I was inspecting Spike's body, Ginger Aspire showed up."

"And you're only telling us this now?" Nugget said.

"Ginger said he'd wait with the body while I got help. I didn't think he'd take Spike away."

Monty wrinkled his nose. "To eat?"

I rubbed my legs together to create a hissing rasp of displeasure. "We do not eat dead bodies."

"You eat dead flies. And skin flakes," Nugget said. "That's like eating the dead, only it'd take you forever to get through an entire corpse."

Indigo raised a hand. "Let's focus. What was Ginger doing out at this time of night? And what were you doing out, too?"

"My earlier overindulgences got the better of me. I couldn't sleep, so I took a walk." I stared at the spot where Spike had been lying. "I think Ginger found the body first. When I arrived, he'd gone to tell the rest of the spider shifters."

"Why do that, rather than come to the Magic Council?" Olympus said.

I scraped a leg through the snow. "Ginger was worried about something."

"Oh! I get it. A spider made the bites," Nugget said. "That's why Ginger is so interested in his corpse."

I huffed out a breath. "I believe they were done by a spider. Ginger tried to convince me otherwise, but the wounds on Spike's neck couldn't have been made by any other creature."

"You think it was one of his spider shifters?" Olympus said. "Or even Ginger? You could have discovered the body just after he'd killed Spike. Maybe he was going to get help to conceal what he'd done, but you stopped him."

"Let's not get ahead of ourselves," Indigo said. "Why would Ginger kill Spike?"

"Why would any of the spider shifters kill Spike?" I said. "He's new to the village. No one knows much about him. And Ginger said none of his spiders had anything to do with Spike."

"Spider shifters are reclusive," Nugget said. "They're rarely sociable."

"But somehow, a spider crossed paths with Spike, and now he's dead." Olympus stood from his crouched position. "I need to get more people from the Magic Council involved in this."

I jumped onto Indigo's shoulder. "We need to be careful how we handle this. The spider shifter community is fragile, and they're protective of their own. They'll close ranks and stop talking if too many people get involved."

Indigo nodded. "Let's figure out what's going on first, before we make any accusations. We'll stay here and look around, and you, Monty, and Olympus speak to the spiders. Ask why he took the body. But be sympathetic. Ginger is obviously panicked. He's worried about his colony."

"He has a right to be if one of them is a killer and he's protecting them," Olympus said.

Indigo caught hold of his hand. "Go gently. Ask questions, but make sure they know you're on their side."

Olympus twisted his mouth from side to side. "I could go in first, lay the groundwork. And this scene is worthless, since the body's been taken and any evidence is being concealed by the snow."

"Does that mean we don't have to stay here and freeze our butts off?" Nugget said.

"We'll look around to make sure we've missed nothing, but there's no point in any of you staying here," Olympus said. "After that, I'll visit the spider shifters and ensure we're working on the same page. And I'll ask Ginger why he thought it was acceptable to mess up a crime scene. I could charge him for that."

"But you won't," Indigo said. "He just made a mistake."

"Because he's the killer," Nugget muttered.

"He's not. Ginger will have an explanation for why he did this." Although I couldn't figure out what it might be.

Indigo glanced at me and winked. "Let's get to work, before my toes turn into popsicles."

Twenty minutes later, after photographs had been taken and nothing useful was found to show what happened to Spike, Indigo, Nugget, and Russell, headed home, while I tracked through the snow with Olympus and Monty to the spider shifter colony.

Monty was happy to let me ride on his back, and I was grateful for that. I may have supernatural powers, but even I felt the cold.

"If you've no objection, I'll take the lead when asking questions," I said to Olympus. "The spider shifters have a particular way of doing things, and you don't want to get it wrong and anger them."

"I'm aware of their traditional ways," Olympus said. "It's not my first encounter with a spider shifter."

"Of course. You're well versed in all things shifter."

Monty chuckled. "Remember that time you met your first werewolf alpha? He almost bit your head off because you said the wrong greeting."

Olympus grumbled and tugged his coat collar up. "I don't remember that."

"And there was the time you met a goblin prince and did the wrong greeting bow. He swung his axe so close to your head, you almost lost an ear."

"That was a misunderstanding," Olympus said.

"Oh, sure! You've come a long way since then," Monty said. "I'm proud of you."

Olympus rubbed his hands together, a sour look on his face. "Perhaps you should lead, Hilda. Just until I develop a rapport with Ginger."

"That's an excellent idea," I said.

Monty chuffed out a laugh as he bounded through the snow.

It was easy to find the spider shifter colony, since the drag marks led us there. Ginger must have been in a hurry to move Spike. Which made me even more worried about his involvement in this murder.

We reached a small, concealed cave entrance. The spiders spent most of their time underground during the day, making use of ancient tunnels that ran through a rocky enclave on the outskirts of Witch Haven.

"I've never been in here." Olympus hesitated at the entrance.

"Expect the opposite of what you're thinking," I said. "They may be spider shifters, but they enjoy a life of luxury."

"So long as it's warm, that's all I care about," Monty said. "My paws are freezing."

I tapped several times at the entrance. The vibrations would rumble along the corridor, so the spiders knew we were entering.

Our arrival shouldn't surprise them. After all, Ginger had just stolen a corpse and brought it home. That kind of behavior would always require follow-up.

I edged past what looked like a solid lump of rock, but there was a thin passageway behind it that turned abruptly right. Once we were past the tight entrance, the passage opened, and the flooring turned from rough stone to polished wood. The rocky walls were smoothed and painted in a calming green. Warm air blew along the corridor, and lights were strung across the wall.

"This is cozy," Monty said.

"You've seen nothing yet." I'd visited the shifter home many times, and enjoyed a number of feasts here, so I knew to expect antique furnishings, plush cushions, and plenty of small, warm, snug spaces to burrow into.

I turned left, toward the main entrance hall, and detected vibrations under my legs. The spiders were awake. Ginger must have gathered them so they could discuss what to do about Spike.

As I entered the hall, I took a second to admire the pretty fairy lights intertwined with tinsel and the baubles dancing in the air, secured by pale strands of webbing.

I tapped my legs on the floor several times to announce my arrival. I turned the corner and found Ginger standing over Spike's body. He was alone, but there'd been others in the room just seconds ago.

Ginger crouched and rubbed his legs together. "Why bring him here? I told you, the spiders will deal with this."

I approached with caution. "Ginger, you agreed to wait with Spike's body. Why take him?"

Olympus cleared his throat. "I can hear Hilda, but not you, Ginger. May I use magic so we can communicate?"

Few magic users could hear us. My bond with Indigo and the other familiars, Monty included, meant they could hear me, but otherwise, I needed to touch someone to form a link.

Ginger rasped his hairy legs together again. "If you must."

"Go ahead," I said.

Olympus cast a spell that flickered through the air and landed on us. "Thank you. Please, go on."

"I changed my mind. There was no point in leaving Spike out there." Ginger waggled his front legs at me. "You're betraying your own kind by bringing the Magic Council here."

"Ooooh! They have floor cushions." Monty bounded off to sniff around the floor coverings.

"I'm here to help." Olympus speared Monty with a terse glare before focusing on Ginger. "I'm Olympus Duke. I'm head of—"

"I know who you are, Mr. Duke. And although I appreciate your interest in this case, it's not your concern. This is a spider matter."

"Of course, you'll be concerned because of the marks on Spike's body." Olympus's tone was respectful but firm. "I want to work with you so we can figure out what happened."

"I know how the Magic Council operates. You'll see those marks and assume the worst. My spiders had nothing to do with this. I won't have an innocent spider punished."

"Neither will I. I want us to work together to find out who did this."

"You can trust Olympus," I said. "We all want the same thing."

Ginger moved slowly around Spike's body. "Very well. You may examine him. But when I ask you to leave, you go. And if I sense you're making assumptions, this ends."

Olympus nodded. "I appreciate you letting me look. I'm just here to gather the facts."

I glanced at Monty to see him rolling among the plush, oversized cushions. At least he was keeping out of the way and not accidentally squashing spider shifters under his huge paws.

Olympus spent several minutes inspecting the marks on Spike's neck and taking notes and pictures.

"He's got frostbite." Olympus looked up at me. "His fingertips and lips are already blackened."

"The tree lighting festivities ended around midnight," I said. "I found Spike just after three in the morning, so he could have been laying out there for at least two hours."

"It's possible he was killed not long after the event ended," Olympus said. "Two hours would be more than enough time for frostbite to set in. Did all your spiders attend the tree lighting ceremony?" He glanced up at Ginger.

"We were all involved in one way or another. Most helped to decorate the tree, then we stayed to enjoy the celebrations." Ginger remained crouched close to Spike. "One or two of the older spiders stayed home because it was cold. They kept an eye on the youngsters."

"Everyone was back here by midnight?"

"To my knowledge. But I'd have to check. I can't imagine any of them would want to stay out later, though. By the end of the event, it was bitterly cold."

Olympus nodded slowly as he continued looking at the body.

"Those marks could have been made after Spike died," Ginger said. "They may look like bites, but they could have happened when he fell. Perhaps he was stabbed in the neck with twigs as he rolled around, or from pine needles from the tree."

"To find out for certain what killed him, I'll need to have tests run," Olympus said. "It would be easier if we had the body at the Magic Council."

"It wasn't Dylan!" Ana Maria rushed into the room. She skidded to a halt. "Oh! I didn't know you had company. I'll go."

"Wait! What do you mean?" I hurried over to her.

Ana Maria was backing out of the doorway. "Nothing. Forget about it. I'll leave you to your meeting."

Ginger joined us, the hairs on his abdomen sticking out. "Of course it wasn't Dylan. Why say that?"

Olympus marched over, Monty by his side. "Your son's called Dylan, isn't he? Do you think he bit Spike?"

Ana Maria gasped. "You can hear me?"

Ginger waggled one leg in the air. "He cast a spell. It doesn't matter. Ana Maria, go back to bed."

Her shiny gaze flickered around the group, her legs moving as if they had a mind of their own.

"You're worried about Dylan," I said. "Could he be involved in this death?"

Ana Maria shook, each leg quivering. "No! He's a good boy. But the other spider shifters are trash-talking him. He's not involved, he's just wayward. All teenage boys go through it. I know he's innocent. Besides, he's sick! He wouldn't do this."

I exchanged a glance with Olympus and Monty, who had a cushion in his mouth and sucked one corner. We needed to speak to Dylan and find out what he knew about biting Spike.

# Chapter 5

When Dylan was finally dragged out of bed, he'd shifted into human form. He wore khaki pajamas, with one leg bunched around his knee. His dark hair was messy, and teenage acne dotted his chin and cheeks.

We'd covered Spike's body with a throw from a couch, so Dylan wouldn't see the corpse. But you didn't need to look too closely to see the outline of a body.

"You can see the boy isn't well," Ginger said. "He needs rest, not interrogation."

"Sorry you're not feeling good, Dylan. We'll make this quick, and then we can eliminate you from the investigation," Olympus said.

"What investigation?" Dylan swiped the back of his hand across his sweating top lip.

"I told you he isn't involved." Ana Maria was perched on Dylan's shoulder, still in spider form. "The Magic Council is here because they need to know what happened to Spike."

Dylan slid her a glare. "Why are they asking me?"

Ana Maria tapped his cheek with a leg. "Other people are talking about you. They've been saying bad things."

Dylan folded his arms across his chest. "Everyone here hates me."

"No one hates you," Ginger said on a soft sigh tinged with irritation. "You're a part of our family."

149

Dylan sniffed and looked over his shoulder. "I want to go back to bed."

"Of course you can. Dylan is innocent. He's just a child," Ana Maria said.

"I'm almost sixteen! I can leave home whenever I like. You can't stop me."

Dylan hadn't asked who Spike was or what had happened to him. Was that because he already knew the answer?

Ana Maria jigged on his shoulder. "No more talk about moving out. Answer the questions this nice man has, then you can go to bed. I'll make you a warm, milky drink. See if that helps you feel better."

"I don't want a stupid drink. And I don't have to answer any dumb questions."

"You don't have to say anything to me," Olympus said, "but I'd appreciate it if you'd help us. We need to figure out what happened to Spike Buchanan."

Dylan shrugged, but stayed where he was.

"Did your mother tell you where Spike was found?"

"Sure. I know."

"I didn't tell him any details," Ana Maria said. "Who have you been talking to? It had better not be that Hitchcock girl. You know I don't like her. She's a terrible influence on you."

"No! Stop. You're embarrassing. Other spiders were talking about it. I overheard them. It's no big deal."

I glanced at Ginger. He must have shared the news so the spider shifters could figure out what to do. "Let's start with you telling us where you were this evening."

"I got dragged to that boring tree thing," Dylan said. "We all had to go."

"And how long did you stay there?"

"I kept trying to get away, but she dragged me around and made me play games for babies." Dylan jerked his head at his mother. "I kept saying I was too old for the stupid kids' games, but she wouldn't listen. No one ever listens to me."

"What time did you leave?" Olympus said.

"It wasn't long after the final candle was lit," Ana Maria said.

"If you could let Spike answer the questions, I'd appreciate it."

Ana Maria didn't look happy at being reprimanded by Olympus, but she remained silent.

"Dylan? What time did you leave?" he asked again.

"Whatever she said. I wasn't paying attention."

"And what happened after you left the event?" Olympus said.

"We came here." Dylan's hands went to his stomach. "I don't feel good. I might hurl."

"It could be the rich food from the celebration," I said. "It was why I was out so late and discovered Spike. I thought the fresh air would settle my stomach."

"You found Spike's body?" A spark of interest flashed in Dylan's eyes.

"I did." I pressed on, hoping he'd talk to me. "What did you do when you came back here?"

"Nothing. Hung around, then went to bed cause I felt gross. I still feel gross."

"It was a busy day for all of us," Ana Maria said. "Hilda, you know Dylan helped to decorate the tree, so I didn't want him out too late. He gets tired."

"Stop being embarrassing," he grumbled. "I can stay out as late as I like. You treat me like I'm a baby."

"Your curfew is eleven o'clock, and that's when it's not a school night. Any later than that, and you're grumpy the next day."

Dylan seemed grumpy all the time, regardless of the amount of sleep he had. But it was typical teenage behavior, so I didn't hold it against him.

"Did you go out again?" Olympus said to Dylan.

"He knows better than that," Ana Maria said.

Olympus arched an eyebrow at her.

She raised a leg. "Sorry. But my son had nothing to do with this. And I would like to get him back in bed. All these questions won't help his recovery."

"Just a few more. Did you know Spike well?" I said.

Dylan shrugged. "I'd seen him around."

"Did you ever speak to him, or spend time with him?" Olympus said.

Dylan looked away. "I didn't kill him."

"When was the last time you saw him?" I said.

"I don't remember. He might have been at the tree lighting ceremony. It's not like I watched him, or nothing. Why are you quizzing me? There are other spiders meaner than me. Ask them if they did the guy in."

"We'll get around to that," Olympus said.

"Why do you think a spider shifter might have killed Spike?" I said to Dylan.

He threw up his hands. "That's why you're here, isn't it? You want someone in the colony to take the blame. Maybe it was you. Everyone knows you're freaky old and have a bond with that scary witch. She tainted you with her twisted power, so you killed Spike."

"Dylan! You know Hilda's history, and how long she has served the Ash witches. We all respect her. Apologize."

He muttered to himself, his head lowered.

"Sorry," Ana Maria said to me. "Dylan didn't mean it. He's under a lot of stress. And he's unwell..."

"You checked Dylan's room and saw he was in bed?" Olympus said. "Spike died between midnight and three in the morning."

"He's a good boy. He'd never sneak out. He knows how much I worry about him." She brushed something off Dylan's collar, causing him to sigh.

Ana Maria hadn't answered the question, so it was possible Dylan snuck out while no one noticed.

Although Dylan was surly and unhelpful, I couldn't figure out his motive for killing Spike. Perhaps it was the actions of an impetuous youngster. It couldn't be rivalry. Dylan was a teenage boy, and Spike was a grown man who'd been turning over a new leaf.

"Think carefully, Dylan," Olympus said. "Any information you have about Spike could be helpful. When did you last see him?"

Dylan heaved a sigh. "Properly? I dunno. Maybe at the inn."

"Was that before the tree lighting ceremony began?" I said.

"No, a few nights ago."

"Dylan! You're not old enough to go into bars alone. Who were you with?" Ana Maria said. "Not the Hitchcock girl? I hope you weren't trying to impress her."

"No! Stop it! No one you know," he muttered. "I wasn't causing trouble, and I wasn't trying to get a drink. They never serve me. I've asked."

"Cornelia Norwood's inn?" Olympus said.

"Where else? It's boring in there, anyway. I didn't stay long. Just hung out for a while until she shooed me away. Stupid old bag. She hates me."

"Cornelia is an upstanding member of the community." Ana Maria swatted the back of his head. "But if she ever serves you, I'll demand the place is closed."

"Stop!" Dylan said. "You're always picking on me. Most of them are nice in there. They don't treat me like a baby, or laugh at me like you do."

"I never laugh at you. I just don't want you drinking underage and getting in trouble."

"Like I'd ever get away with that with you all breathing down my neck."

Ginger chuckled. "We all did it when we were younger, tried to get served a witch's brew or a goblin bomb when underage."

"That doesn't mean my son should."

Olympus nodded. "Of course. I'll be checking into it. But I trust Cornelia not to break any rules."

"Check all you like. I did nothing wrong."

"Was Spike with anyone when you saw him?" Olympus said.

"I don't remember. He talked to a few people, but he was drinking alone."

"You didn't see him argue with anyone, or get into a fight?"

"I wasn't paying him much attention." Dylan tugged at the hem of his pajama top. "You're making out like I was obsessed with the guy."

"I didn't mean to imply that. Any information we can get leading up to Spike's death could help us figure out how he died and why," Olympus said.

"You already think you know how he died. One of us bit him." Dylan's cheeks grew pinker and his forehead sweatier. "And you must think it was me, since I'm the only one you're grilling."

Olympus lifted his shoulders slightly. "Even if what you saw doesn't seem useful to you, it could be valuable to us."

Dylan shrugged again. "Whatever. I'm innocent. Why are people always out to get me?" He scuffed a bare foot along the floor.

"No one wants to get you. But your mother is concerned about you. We need to know if you've seen anything. Anything at all," Olympus said.

"I already told you where I was. This has nothing to do with me. Can I go to bed now?" He glanced at his mother, and although he'd looked away fast, I hadn't missed the tears making his eyes shiny and his eyelashes stick together.

Dylan was struggling. His skin was clammy, and his hair stuck to his forehead in damp clumps.

"That's everything. Go back to bed and rest. Make sure you eat plain food for a day or two to settle your stomach," I said.

Ana Maria took Dylan out of the room, still perched on his shoulder as she muttered to him.

"I'd like to speak to the rest of your colony," Olympus said to Ginger.

"No. It's late. And I've already told you, none of my spider shifters were involved. I've been courteous by allowing you to speak to Dylan, but it's time you went," Ginger said.

Olympus didn't move. Monty stopped messing with the floor cushions, sensing trouble.

"A spider made those bites on Spike's neck. This is the only spider shifter colony within a two-hundred-mile radius of Witch Haven. Unless we've got a rogue spider lurking in the shadows, the killer lives here," Olympus said.

Ginger skittered closer, rubbing his fangs together. "And as I've made clear, the marks on Spike's neck could have been made several ways. It's typical of the Magic Council to jump to the wrong conclusion."

"No one is doing that here." I stepped in between the two men as tensions rose. "But you must admit, those marks look like spider bites. If we can discount the spider shifters, we can move on to other possibilities."

"Look at the other possibilities first and leave my innocent spiders out of it." Ginger continued to rub his fangs together in a show of aggression.

"We need to take the body," Olympus said after a few seconds of silence. "Without doing a thorough examination and running tests, there's little we can do to figure out what happened, and I'll have no choice but to think one of your spider shifters is guilty."

Ginger slammed his front legs on the ground, and a second later, the air was alive with large spiders whirling on strands of webbing. They thumped onto the floor in their supersized forms, their legs huge and hairy, and their fangs dripping with venom.

Monty yelped, tucked his tail beneath him, and hid behind Olympus's legs.

"Leave," Ginger said. "If any spider of mine was involved, it's a matter for this community to handle. We don't tolerate outside interference."

"It doesn't need to be this way." As tempted as I was to morph into my supersized form, it would only agitate matters, so I stayed small and kept my cool. "We need to collect the evidence and get the facts. We need access to Spike's body."

"You've seen it! And as I suspected, you made the wrong assumptions. Olympus has gotten it into his head that a spider bit Spike, so that's the only avenue he'll follow."

"I won't." Magic shimmered in Olympus's palms. "But given the nature of the injury, it'll be one avenue I pursue."

Ginger thumped his legs down again, and the army of supersized spiders advanced on us.

"Remain calm." Their venom wouldn't hurt me, but too many bites would kill Olympus and Monty.

"I've been patient with you," Ginger said. "Look elsewhere for your killer. Dylan didn't do it. No one here did."

"Give us the body, and we'll leave," Olympus said.

"I can't do that."

"Because when we run our tests, they'll prove one of your spiders is a killer?"

The spiders rubbed their fangs together, creating an ominous, vibrating hiss that filled the stone chamber and echoed around us.

I scuttled up Olympus's leg and onto his shoulder. "Could we run the tests here? If they won't let us take the body, we could get samples and examine them elsewhere."

"That's not good enough. The body has already been contaminated because it was moved. Which is also a crime." Olympus glared at Ginger. "You're not making this easy. Your actions suggest you know one of your spiders was involved. Or maybe you were."

I hopped off Olympus's shoulder and dashed to Ginger. "Make this one concession. Let us have the body, and we'll leave you and the rest of the spiders alone."

"You can't guarantee that." Ginger looked at his army of spiders. "If there's the faintest belief one of my spiders did this, you'll be back."

"Of course we will," Olympus said. "If you're protecting a killer, we won't allow them to remain free."

Dylan raced back into the room, followed by Ana Maria. "Stop fighting! I know who did it. It was Billy."

# Chapter 6

"Dylan, don't tell lies." Ana Maria dashed around her son, admonishing him.

He ignored her. "It was him. Billy's been following Spike ever since he got here. He was always prodding him and trying to start a fight."

"Is this true, Dylan?" Ginger strode over to him.

Dylan backed away. "Yeah. He was always going at him."

"How did Spike respond?" I said.

Dylan's gaze flashed around the room, his eyes wide. "They argued. And a couple of times, it got intense. If anyone killed Spike, it was Billy."

"Billy Worgan from the Burned Oak gang? It's possible they knew each other," Olympus said. "Rival gangs often hold vicious grudges against each other."

"Was there anything in particular they argued about?" I kept watch on the giant spiders, but none of them moved, all waiting for an order from Ginger.

"I dunno. I couldn't always hear, but they often yelled about some girl."

"Did you get her name?" Olympus said.

Dylan shrugged and shook his head.

I scuttled over to Dylan and touched his leg. "I thought you didn't know Spike well. How did you see him get into these fights if you spent no time together?"

He stared at his feet. "I dunno."

"Spike had only been living in the village for a month. I've not noticed any arguments. Were you friends?"

"Dylan, what aren't you telling us?" Ginger said. "You won't get in trouble."

"It's nothing. It don't matter. I just know what I saw."

"The whole truth," Ginger said. "Were you friends with Spike? Did you fight with Billy, too?"

"No! But I wanted to help Spike." Dylan's cheeks flamed red. "He was cool. I... I wanted to be like him."

"Dylan! Spike was a terrible role model." Ana Maria skittered around her son. "He was involved in a ruthless biker gang before he came here. And from the rumors I've heard, he had a criminal record."

"So what? I liked his bike."

"I'm never letting you go on a motorbike. Those things are lethal."

Dylan rolled his eyes. "That's why I never said nothing. I knew you'd stop me. You're no fun."

"Racing around on a motorbike and emulating someone as shady as Spike, spider rest his poor soul, is something I'd never support."

"You're making my case for me," Dylan muttered. "I kept my mouth shut to avoid the hassle."

"You've been following Spike since he moved to Witch Haven?" I said.

Dylan glowered at me. "You make me sound like a creeper. I'm not. I saw him arrive, and he had on that cool leather jacket with the symbol. I even talked to him a few times about bikes and stuff. He listened and asked me questions about what I wanted to do when I was older. He even let me sit on his bike."

"If he wasn't dead, I'd be having words with him," Ana Maria muttered.

Dylan groaned. "I knew you wouldn't get it. But he saw me. He didn't talk over me and tell me what I should think and feel. He let me be me."

"And you wanted to be just like him," I said. Poor Dylan. He had few role models to look up to, so he'd clung to the cool, leather jacket-wearing former biker for inspiration.

"Everyone around here is boring. We have rules to follow and lessons to learn. I just want to have fun. I don't wanna be told what to do and what time to go to bed. I'm an adult."

Ana Maria drew in a breath to keep arguing with her son, but Olympus got there first.

"Did you see Billy attack Spike?"

"I saw nothing. At least, not last night."

"You don't know for certain Billy killed Spike? You're guessing?"

"Who else would it be? The guy was spoiling for a fight. Billy must have found Spike after the tree ceremony and gone at him."

I'd noticed Spike and Billy at the event. It was possible they'd clashed horns later in the evening. Both men had been drinking, and tempers could have flared.

"Thank you for being honest with us, Dylan." Ginger led him back to the door with Ana Maria. "Get to bed. You'll feel better in the morning."

Dylan looked at us, gave another surly shrug, and left again with Ana Maria.

Ginger turned and approached us. "You've gotten everything you're going to get. I insist you leave."

Olympus gestured to the watching spiders. "I have questions for everyone else."

Ginger's fangs lifted, and a drop of venom appeared. "I'll question my spiders and learn where they were. But I assure you, no one here did it. Especially not Dylan. He's dumb and headstrong, but he's just a child."

"A child who knows a lot about the victim," Olympus said.

Ginger sucked in a sharp breath. "Maybe so, but that doesn't mean he hurt him."

Olympus sighed and looked around the room filled with agitated spiders.

I was glad when he nodded. We were pushing our luck by staying a second longer.

"I'd appreciate it if you checked with everyone to see where they were. Let me know if you find any anomalies," Olympus said.

"Of course." Ginger lowered his fangs. "I don't want to block your investigation, but my colony doesn't appreciate unwelcome intervention, no matter how serious the situation."

"Understood. But we will need Spike's body," Olympus said.

"If you must, send someone here to run your tests. We'll keep him and contact any family to make arrangements for his funeral."

Olympus opened his mouth to protest, but I stepped forward. "The body comes with us. You owe me, Ginger. You have a debt to repay for the time I saved your life at the Battle of Fiery Lake."

"That was a lifetime ago!" Ginger's front legs waggled with irritation.

"It's still a debt. I've never called it in, and I never expected I'd have to, but you leave me no option. You swore if ever I needed a favor, to call in that debt. No matter what it was, you'd do it."

Ginger looked at Spike's body, then at me. He extended one front leg. "You may take the body. But that is the debt repaid. We owe each other nothing."

I touched his leg. "I agree. Thank you."

He studied me for a second. "That was a big sacrifice to make. I would have given you much more. I hope it's worth it."

"Solving a murder and getting justice will make the sacrifice worth it." I hopped onto Olympus's shoulder and huffed in his ear. "The spiders are at the breaking point. We don't want to be here when they snap."

"I'll translocate us to the office. Monty."

Monty slid out from behind him and cowered at his feet.

After a few more words with Ginger, we sidled around the spiders. Olympus touched Spike's body and laid a hand on Monty. The world tipped sideways, and we appeared in Olympus's small office in the center of Witch Haven.

Monty flopped onto his belly. "I had a panic attack. When those hairy, gross spiders descended from the ceiling, it was a living nightmare."

I hopped off Olympus's shoulder while he moved Spike into a room at the back of the building, then returned to the office and closed the door. He carried a mug of coffee in one hand.

"I should have checked overhead when we entered," I said. "I heard others with Ginger before we arrived. I've gotten soft and lost my edge since living with Indigo and the rest of you."

"You still have your edge, Hilda." Olympus dropped into his seat and rubbed a hand over his face. "You handled Ginger and the rest of the spider shifters better than me."

"I have plenty of experience with them."

"One day, you'll have to tell the story of the Battle of Fiery Lake and how you saved Ginger." Olympus gently petted my head. "I appreciate the deal you made. We wouldn't have gotten Spike any other way, especially since my mighty leopard familiar forgot how to fight."

"Hey! I have a spider phobia. Hilda, you're not included in that. I don't think you're scary. Mostly not. When you get big, you're kind of terrifying, though."

"Which is always my aim when I supersize," I said. "And you're welcome, Olympus. I consider you a friend, and I always help my friends. If the spider shifters are involved, they can't get away with it. I'm loyal to the spiders, but also to my family."

Monty whacked a paw on top of me, my legs bowing under his hefty paw. "We love you too, Hilda."

"You should get home and tell Indigo what's going on," Olympus said.

"I'll stay with you."

"There's no need. I've got people to contact and paperwork to fill in. It'll take a while."

"I'm staying. The spider shifter community must be handled carefully. One false step will set back their already limited cooperation."

Olympus stifled a yawn. "I'd protest if I had the energy, but the assistance is welcome. How about I get going on the forms while you nap? As soon as the village wakes, we'll visit Cornelia Norwood, see if anyone saw anything strange relating to Spike and Billy."

"You can sleep in my bed if you like," Monty said. "It's super comfy."

"I'll take a cell bed. I don't want you rolling over and squashing me." I was tired, though I suspected any sleep I caught would be full of bodies under glowing trees and accusations of murder.

---

A few hours later, the paperwork was done. Spike's body had been sent for tests and an autopsy, and I'd rested.

After a breakfast of bacon scraps from Olympus's take-out roll, we were on our way to the inn.

Monty skidded around in the snow, throwing up enormous clouds as he danced along and flicked his tail from side to side.

"That cat never runs out of energy," Olympus muttered as I perched on his shoulder.

"He's good for you. He shakes things up."

"I like my world calm, not shaken."

I chuckled. "Then you're dating the wrong witch."

He grinned, and his expression softened. "I wouldn't have it any other way."

Although the inn was closed to customers, the front door was open, and Cornelia was taking supplies out of the back of a van. She was a striking-looking witch with an eye patch and a messy scar that ran down one side of her face.

"Hey! Don't tell me the job has finally broken you and you've turned to day drinking?" She set down the box she carried and wiped her hands on the front of her black jeans.

"Morning, Cornelia. I have a few questions if you've got the time," Olympus said.

Cornelia nodded. She petted Monty and smiled at me.

"Have you heard about the body found under the tree?"

"Oh, yeah. Bad news. Not exactly the Christmas gift anyone wants to find. You want to talk about Spike?"

"Yes. He used to drink in here?"

"He did. Follow me inside. I gotta get this order sorted, and then I've got a Christmas lunch coming in. Fifty witches! It'll be a riot." Cornelia tickled Monty under the chin. "I've got dried jerky behind the counter if you want some."

Monty squeaked out his joy, then bounded off to help himself.

"So, what do you need to know?" Cornelia said as she walked inside.

"Spike Buchanan was a regular here?" Olympus followed her into a low-ceilinged, open-plan space that smelled of ale and roasting meat. Dried hops were strung from the dark beams, and a hearty fire roared in the grate.

"He came in most days. Usually had a couple of drinks in the evening." Cornelia slid behind the bar with a sealed box in her hands.

"When was the last time he was in here?" Olympus stopped by the scratched oak bar.

"The evening of the tree lighting ceremony. He came in for a few drinks and then left just before the ceremony began. He said he was looking forward to taking part."

"Was Spike with anyone? Did he talk to anyone in particular?"

"He was a sociable guy, and chatty with most people. It was busy, so I didn't notice everyone he spoke to, though." Cornelia pulled crackers out of the box.

I hopped onto her hand so we could communicate without Olympus having to cast another spell. "What about Dylan Martinez?"

Cornelia arched an eyebrow, not flinching as I danced up her arm. "Him! I'm always chasing him out of here. He sneaks in when my back is turned and tries to get customers to buy him drinks."

"When was the last time he did that?" Olympus said.

Cornelia rested a hand on one hip. "Grab the last of those boxes from out front, and I'll tell you everything I know."

Olympus heaved in the boxes and thumped them down.

She grinned at him. "You're well trained. I didn't think you'd go for that. The last time I chased Dylan out of here was three days ago. Poor kid. If he was old enough to hire, I'd give him a job, since this is his favorite place to hang out."

"Does he hang out with anyone in particular when he's here?" I said.

"He usually sneaks in alone. Occasionally, he has a friend with him. Another young spider shifter. Pretty girl. Wears lots of black eye makeup. I don't know the kid's name. The spiders keep to themselves." Cornelia drew a shot of whisky and knocked it back. "You sure you don't want one?"

Olympus raised a hand and shook his head. "All good, thanks. Who did they ask to buy them drinks?"

"Anyone who looked friendly. But my customers know if they don't want to get banned, they ignore all begging requests from underage drinkers. I run a respectable place, and I'm not losing my license because someone's trying to grow up too fast."

"Did you ever see Dylan talk to Spike?" I said.

"Sure. He was always hanging around Spike and asking questions. I even told him not to bother him once, but Spike said he didn't mind. Well, that was until they argued."

"What was the argument about?"

"I'm not sure. Maybe Dylan pushed his luck or got too cocky. Spike was usually a chilled-out guy, but I overheard him tell the kid to go away." Cornelia shrugged. "Maybe he got bored with being quizzed. Dylan was always asking about his life in the gang. Spike had left that behind. He was trying something new by moving here."

"Did Dylan retaliate when he was told to take a hike?" I said.

"He threw a drink over Spike. He got shoved over for his trouble and told to grow up. It wasn't pretty. Still, no punches got thrown. Dylan scuttled out, drenched in a pint of beer. He stopped bothering Spike after that. Sad little kid, really. He should have known better than to keep hassling Spike."

I tap danced along the bar. Dylan had concealed this fight from us. Why?

"What about Billy Worgan?" Olympus said. "Had he been causing Spike any trouble?"

Her nose wrinkled. "That guy causes trouble for everyone. He doesn't come in here much after I made it clear I don't tolerate troublemakers. And I heard his gang make home brew and hang out in the woods drinking and messing around. They're basically a bunch of overgrown kids, just with more muscles and noisier bikes." Cornelia kept unloading boxes. "Why the interest in Dylan and Billy? You think they did something to Spike?"

"It's a line of inquiry," Olympus said. "Billy wasn't giving Spike grief or hassling him?"

"Billy and his gang sometimes lurk outside, but they rarely come in. I couldn't tell you if he had a beef with Spike." The door to the inn crashed open, and a delivery driver rolled in more boxes on a trolley. "If there's nothing else, I need to get on. I've had a couple of my staff call in sick with a stomach bug, so I'm doing the work of three people."

"There's something going around," I said. "I wasn't feeling good after the tree lighting ceremony."

Cornelia grinned. "I feel you. We may have magic, but that doesn't mean we don't get a stomachache when we eat too many cinnamon cream Christmas crepes. I hope you figure out what happened to Spike. He was a good guy."

We thanked her for her time, collected Monty, who was snuffling crumbs from under the tables, and headed outside.

Olympus stood with his hands clenched. "Dylan lied to us."

"Don't be too quick to act on that information," I said from my perch on his shoulder. "It doesn't make him guilty."

"I have to act. We now have Dylan's motive."

As much as I didn't want to agree, I couldn't ignore the facts. Dylan was our prime suspect.

# Chapter 7

Olympus strode away from the inn, Monty beside him.

"Dylan could have lied about a problem between Spike and Billy, to distract us from investigating him too closely," Olympus said.

"Or, since Dylan was such a Spike fan, he saw things other people missed," I said. "Like Billy taunting Spike. You said yourself, there's often rivalry between gangs."

Olympus headed toward his office. "I need to bring Dylan in for questioning. And he could be a flight risk. He could already have left Witch Haven."

"He's not a flight risk! When we saw him, all he wanted to do was go to bed. He was unwell and scared. And I trust Ginger. He'll do what's right."

"He didn't do the right thing when he ran off with Spike's body and messed with a crime scene." Olympus unlocked his office door. "I'm still undecided whether to charge him over that."

"If you drag the head of the spider shifter community in and charge him with a crime, you'll get nowhere when you ask more questions. The spiders will scatter. There'll be no one left to talk to."

Olympus grumbled under his breath as he collected the post off the floor and switched on the kettle. "I need to speak to Ginger. He'll understand Dylan has to be questioned now this new information has come to light."

169

Monty leaped onto his bed and turned around several times before settling. "All that jerky has made me tired. Wake me up when anything exciting happens."

Olympus tutted out his annoyance, grumbling about what a useless familiar he had. Monty didn't hear. He was already snoring.

"You make coffee. I'll speak to Ginger and ensure he knows the situation," I said. "If we keep him in the loop, the spider shifters will be less suspicious of us."

"I doubt that'll make much of a difference." Olympus stifled a yawn.

"You're undercaffeinated and exhausted. You're more likely to snap than have a useful conversation with Ginger. We're all on edge. I'm happy to make the call."

"Thanks, Hilda. I could do with five minutes downtime before we carry on."

I made a quick call to Ginger using Olympus's desk phone and gave him an update about the situation. Although he wasn't happy, he agreed to watch Dylan and ensure he went nowhere.

I scuttled around Olympus's desk as I waited for him to return from the small kitchen at the back of the building.

I didn't think Dylan would flee, but maybe he was faking his illness to buy himself time to come up with a plan. I wanted to think the best of the young spider shifter, but perhaps he'd made a mistake. He'd been angry with Spike because he'd humiliated him in a bar full of people he wanted to impress, so he snuck up and bit him. Dylan simply hadn't thought through the consequences of his actions.

Olympus returned with a large steaming mug of coffee in one hand. "I pulled Billy Worgan's file while I was out the back. He's got quite a story." He flipped open the pages and scanned through them. "He's been in court for assault and robbery, and he's been cautioned numerous times for aggressive behavior. That's just the first two pages."

"He sounds charming."

"Billy's a thug and a bully. And he gets off on intimidating people."

"You've had dealings with him?"

"My colleagues have. He never stays in Witch Haven long enough to be much of a problem for me, but I always get pinged when he's in the area, so I know to look out for him."

"Any information in there about how he knew Spike?"

"Nothing specific." Olympus flicked through a few pages as he sipped his coffee. "But most gangs aren't friendly to each other. It wouldn't surprise me if those two haven't had a rumble without it being noticed." He leaned back in his seat and rolled his shoulders. "We should find out where Billy is staying."

"Cornelia said his gang lurks about in the woods. They could have rented a cabin. They're not popular this time of year, because they don't all have heating. It would be a cheap place to hang out and not get noticed."

"While getting drunk on home brew and planning their next illegal scheme. Good idea."

Fifteen minutes later, and after a check-in with Indigo to give her an update, we were headed toward Witch Haven woods. The woods were magical, and it was never sensible to wander around them if you didn't know what scurried about in the branches.

But the daytime was usually safe. And the woods were beautiful at this time of year. Although the branches were bare, a light frost covered them, and there were bright red berries on the holly bushes, giving the woods a festive feel.

I rode on Olympus's shoulder, with Monty following behind, frolicking in the snow. We headed along the well-worn path toward the basic wooden cabins used by those who enjoyed getting back to nature.

There were empty bottles of booze scattered about, and food packets littered both sides of the path.

"Someone is here." Olympus grabbed the litter and dumped it in a waste container. "And they have no manners or respect for their environment."

We rounded a bend and discovered six parked motorbikes. They were Harleys and had the same lightning bolt emblem painted on the sides that I'd seen on the bikers' jackets.

"This must be the place," Olympus said.

"Let's wake Billy and see what he has to tell us," I said. "If we catch him while he's in bed, we'll have the upper hand."

Olympus strode up the steps of the cabin and thumped on the door. "This is the Magic Council. We're looking for Billy Worgan."

No one stirred on the other side of the door.

"Open up." He thumped again.

"They might be more receptive when they discover an enormous spider as the greeting party. I can get through the smallest gap."

"That's breaking and entering." Olympus stepped back and rubbed his chin.

"I'm breaking nothing. And these cabins are owned by the people of Witch Haven. So, technically, this is my place. You can't break into your own home."

"Doubt that would stand up in court. How about I turn my back while you quietly break in? The less I see, the less I can report." Olympus twisted on his heel.

I scuttled off his shoulder, down his leg, and slid under the gap at the bottom of the door.

The place looked like a frat party gone wrong. Food was spilled on the floor and trodden into the boards. There were dirty plates littering every surface, along with mugs, glass beer bottles, and old wine bottles. The pungent stench of unwashed bodies lingered.

There were three slumbering figures slouched on various pieces of furniture in the living area. I scuttled past them and peeked into the bedrooms. There were two guys on single beds in one room, and Billy occupied the next room. He was still clothed, his boots on, and he lay on his back, his mouth open as he snored.

I took a moment to center myself. It was easier to go supersize when I had Indigo close by, but we had a strong bond, and I tugged on it to make my transformation work. I took a few deep breaths, imagined myself being six feet tall with impressively long hairy legs and fangs that dripped venom, closed my eyes, and allowed the magic to swirl around me.

Billy grunted, as if sensing something was happening as he slumbered, but he was too out of it to do anything. Perhaps it was the booze. I could smell it seeping from his pores, leaving a sour, tangy flavor in the air.

My limbs expanded, my body swelled, and I transformed. I stretched my limbs and waggled them. Then I tiptoed back to the front door and opened it.

Olympus's eyes widened for a second, then he nodded. "Monty, stay out here and keep watch."

He wagged his tail. "Got it. I'll scream if I see an adorable snowman. No, wait. Astonishing snowman. No, that's not right, either. An Adonis snowman. Yeah, one of those."

Olympus sighed. "Any trouble, Hilda?"

"No. They're here. All asleep. Billy's alone," I whispered.

Olympus stepped into the room, his nose wrinkling as he inhaled the stench of sweaty, hungover men.

I led him into the bedroom and presented Billy.

Olympus closed the door, then kicked Billy's booted foot. "Hey, I have questions for you."

Billy jerked upright, his gaze unfocused as his head whipped from side to side. "What the heck?"

"Billy Worgan?" Olympus pulled out his credentials and flashed them at him.

Disgust crossed Billy's face. "What do you want? You can't be here. Private property."

"Your front door was open, so we let ourselves in," Olympus said.

Billy's gaze went to me, and he did a double take, froze for a second, then scuttled back, whacking his head on the wall behind him.

"She's impressive, isn't she?" Olympus said. "This is my associate, Hilda. She's here to encourage you to answer questions."

"Get that thing away from me." Billy grabbed a pillow and hurled it at me. It hit the floor.

"Hilda won't jump on you, so long as you cooperate."

"You can't threaten me with an enormous, freakin' spider. I've done nothing wrong."

He sounded like Dylan, sullen, offhand, and his tone suggested the world was out to get him.

"We'll make this quick, since I see you're busy," Olympus said. "Spike Buchanan is dead, and we want to know if you had anything to do with it."

"I don't know that idiot." Billy's gaze remained on me as he swiped a hand down his face and tugged on his straggly beard.

"You know him. You were both at the tree lighting ceremony."

Billy shrugged. "So what? There were loads of people there. Doesn't mean I wanted them all dead."

"What did you do after the ceremony ended?"

"Came here. Witch Haven was dead, so we made our own fun."

"Was that before or after you killed Spike?"

"Hey! Don't pin this on me." Billy rubbed the back of his head where he'd slammed it against the wall. "Fine, I hated the guy, but I didn't kill him. I'm glad he's dead, but it wasn't me."

"Can anyone vouch for your whereabouts?" Olympus said.

Billy huffed out a breath. "What time are we talking?"

"Between midnight and three in the morning."

A smug look crossed his bed-creased face. "Easy. I wasn't here. I had business out of town. After the tree thing was done, I hung out with the guys and had a few drinks, then left with Grinder. We were gone until five in the morning."

"Grinder will verify that?" Olympus said. "If so, I'll speak to him now. Get this cleared up."

"Bad luck. He's already left."

"I didn't think bikers were early birds."

"Sometimes, the business can't wait. He'll be back later. You can ask him then. He'll vouch for me." Billy rolled an empty whisky bottle out from under his covers and sniffed it.

"What was your problem with Spike?" Olympus said.

"He was a jerk who thought he was better than me." Billy shrugged. "But before you get ideas about motive, I think most people are jerks, and I don't kill them."

"You like to use your fists, though."

"Some people don't listen to sense, so they need it beaten into them." He inched to the edge of his bed. "Like I said, I wasn't a fan of Spike's, but I killed no one. And I've got an alibi. You got nothing on me."

Billy may have an alibi, but it was a poor one. Any of his gang would say they were with him to protect him. And he had a motive for wanting Spike dead. Perhaps there'd been a fight over territory or gang members. Fights easily got out of hand, and the violence could have escalated to a terminal conclusion.

Although the lack of obvious marks on Spike's body suggested the fight hadn't been physical. Magic could have killed him just as easily.

Billy pulled himself upright, although he kept a watchful eye on me. "I've answered your questions, so unless you want me to wake the gang to help move you along, you can get out. This is your only warning."

Olympus glanced at me and nodded.

I nodded back, surprised Billy had been this helpful. Maybe my presence had something to do with it.

"If you remember anything else about Spike, let us know," Olympus said.

"Yeah, that's never gonna happen."

I scuttled closer, and Billy flinched and grabbed another pillow. I was only reminding him who was in charge. I wouldn't bite him. Well, I might, if he got disrespectful, but sometimes a shot of fear got people talking.

"It's okay, Hilda. We've got everything we need," Olympus said.

We left the cabin and checked in with Monty to make sure no adorable snowmen had snuck up on us.

Once we'd walked away from danger, I shrank to my usual size and jumped onto Olympus's shoulder. "Billy's a credible suspect. And that alibi wasn't great."

"It was convenient the only person who could vouch for him at the time of Spike's murder wasn't around." Olympus hurried along the path, picking up the occasional piece of trash he'd missed on our way in.

"I'm glad Billy's a suspect. I don't want Dylan involved in Spike's death. He's got his whole life ahead of him. It would be a tragedy for that to be taken."

"I don't disagree. But I'm still suspicious of that young spider. I'm certain the autopsy will show those marks on Spike's neck were made by a spider bite."

"Even if they were, we're not all full of venom. And sometimes, even if we give small bites, they tickle rather than kill."

Olympus gave me some serious side-eye. "Yeah, never test that theory on me."

I chuckled as I bounced along on his shoulder. "I'd never bite you. Well, unless you get Indigo a terrible Christmas present and make her angry. If she ordered me to nip you, I'd have no option but to obey."

"That's sorted. She gave me a list of what she wants, so I don't get it wrong." His breath plumed out of him. "But I want this case solved. I need a break, so I can enjoy some down time with the family."

"You're not in charge of finding the missing reindeer, too?"

Olympus pulled up fast. "The missing what?"

"The reindeer have gone missing. I thought you knew. Nugget's been stressing about it because Indigo suggested we pull the charity sleigh instead. I mean, not you, but the familiars. Monty knows about it."

Monty had his head buried in a snow drift, so he could only wag his tail in agreement.

"That's all I need! A delegation from the Magic Council is making a trip to see the sleigh drive this year. When did this happen?"

"I don't have the details. Check with Nugget."

Olympus groaned. "If anyone from the Magic Council has heard about this, there'll be a dozen messages waiting for me. They get so stressed about this kind of thing. You coming with me? I need to fix this."

"No. I'll catch up with you later. Good luck with the reindeer." I hopped off Olympus's shoulder, and he stamped away with Monty beside him. The leopard waved cheerfully with one paw as he licked snow off his nose.

I turned and ambled across the snow. Dylan was innocent, but I needed to find proof. It was time to focus on Billy and see how shady this biker gang leader was.

# Chapter 8

My legs hurt from all the walking I'd done. I'd been out in Witch Haven all day, asking around to see if I could find the elusive Grinder and confirm Billy's alibi. I'd returned to the cabin several times but had been ignored or chased away. There was no sign of Grinder anywhere.

Maybe Billy had made him up. He was buying time and hoping he could slip out of the village with his gang before we found enough evidence to charge him with Spike's murder.

I shook out my chilled limbs. I was overdue a break and in need of an early dinner. I'd missed lunch because I'd been so busy trying to find Grinder. My stomach growled, and I rubbed my fangs together.

"Hey! Where have you been hiding?" Nugget stomped toward me. "I've been looking everywhere for you."

"I've been busy searching for clues and suspects. Olympus needs to speak to you about the reindeer."

"He found me, and he freaked out about them. Thanks for dumping that on my back. The guy is such a stress head."

I smiled. Olympus was just like Nugget in that respect. "I was about to get food. Want to join me?"

"We're too busy for food. Besides, how can you eat at a time like this?"

I looked up and spotted Russell soaring over our heads, and gave him a wave. "What's keeping you so busy? Last-minute Christmas shopping?"

He hissed at me. "I've been looking for those vile reindeer."

"They still haven't shown up? With Olympus on the case, I figured you'd have it sorted."

"Yeah, right. Having the Magic Council involved will make life so much easier. They're probably forming a joint working party while we speak." Nugget swished his tail from side to side.

"They're not that bad. At least, Olympus isn't." I stopped outside the apothecary shop. The windows didn't get cleaned regularly. Would there be any tasty treats lying on the ledge?

Alas, I saw nothing yummy. I ate conventional food, too, but there was nothing better than a nice, juicy fly. But they were sadly in short supply this time of year. I hoped to get a few candied flies in my stocking on Christmas morning.

"What are you looking at?" Nugget said. "You won't find the reindeer in there."

"I'm not looking for the reindeer. They're not my priority."

"Make them your priority." He jabbed me in the head with a cold paw. "Indigo has arranged for us to do sleigh practice later. You've got to be there."

"Isn't that a waste of time? The reindeer will be back." I ambled to the next store and looked in the window for flies.

"And if they don't get back in time? We'll become the laughingstock of Witch Haven if we mess up."

"How hard is it to pull a sleigh?" I said.

Russell swooped over my head, emitting harsh caws.

"As Russell just cawed, hard!" Nugget dodged in front of me as I continued my search for food. "Have you ever tried to pull a huge sleigh through the snow?"

"Well, no." I trotted to Fandango's bakery and stared in the window. "Do you want to split a sandwich?"

"No! No eating until we find the reindeer."

"That could take days. We'd starve."

"It had better not. The charity sleigh pull happens on Christmas Eve. That's tomorrow."

"Is it?" I'd been so involved in the investigation, I'd lost track of time.

"We must get those reindeer back and make sure they're behaving themselves. My reputation is at stake if this goes wrong and I'm forced to tinsel up and prance around."

Russell cawed out a laugh and dodged Nugget's attempt to grab him as he soared over our heads.

I looked longingly at the bakery window. I couldn't eat a whole sandwich, and it seemed wasteful to discard so much food. "Russell, could you go for a sandwich?"

He cawed an agreement as he swooped past.

Nugget swatted me on the head. "You can't miss the sleigh practice."

"I'm solving a murder. That has to take priority." I waggled a leg at the bakery owner, Albert Black, and pointed at a sandwich. He waved back and nodded.

"Haven't you solved that, yet? It can't be difficult."

"I'm working on it. These things take time. Suspects need to be questioned, motives checked, alibis confirmed. It's harder than it looks. I understand why Olympus gets so stressed."

"You're making it complicated, so you don't have to be a part of the charity sleigh pull. Well, think again. You're doing it." Nugget hopped onto the window ledge and shook snow off his paws. "Monty will be up front with me, and you'll be in the back with Russell. We haven't figured out what to do about his wings, but that seems the most logical setup. You and Russell are a similar size when you both supersize."

"Whatever works for you. But I know the reindeer will come back and be merrily pulling the sleigh when the time comes."

He grumbled under his breath. "You have more confidence than me. Those reindeer are out of control. I don't know why the big guy in the red suit puts up with them."

Albert brought out my sandwich. "I'll put this on Indigo's tab, shall I?"

I touched my leg against his hand. "Yes, please." Before I took a bite, Nugget grabbed a huge mouthful and tore off a strip. "Hey! You said you didn't have time to eat."

"That ham smells too good to ignore."

I pulled the rest of the sandwich away, cut it in half, and presented one piece to Russell.

Nugget frowned as we ate and tapped one paw on the window ledge.

"You could always help me," I said. "I'll find the killer sooner if I have an assistant."

"Help you! We're too busy to help. We have a Christmas crisis to deal with." Nugget snagged another mouthful of ham. "Be on the green in an hour for practice. No excuses."

I kept my mouth full of food so I couldn't respond.

"Come on, Russell. We need to keep searching for the reindeer."

I shook my head as they raced away. I still didn't understand why Nugget was so stressed about this. Even if we had to pull the sleigh, it would be fun. We'd be the most terrifying version of reindeer the village had ever seen.

Once I'd eaten my fill, I tucked the remains of the sandwich in one corner for some lucky rodent or cat to find.

I was about to head off and do another circuit to look for Grinder when my spider senses tingled.

My gaze darted around. There was that guy again. The one who'd lurked in the shadows at the tree lighting ceremony. He wasn't doing much, keeping himself discreet as he looked around.

I scuttled toward him, then froze as his gaze locked onto me. He blinked several times, then turned and strode away.

Not this time! I didn't like strangers in Witch Haven, especially not after a murder had been committed and the killer was still on the loose.

I chased after him, leaping across the frozen ground. The stranger headed away from the main street, toward the woods. I tapped into my magic and ballooned in size as I raced along.

The guy looked over his shoulder and yelped as he saw me chasing him. But eight legs were always better than two, and within seconds I was within leaping distance.

I coiled, sprung, and landed on his back, sending him toppling into the snow. He slammed down, only just getting his hands in front of him in time.

I pressed my full weight on him and clacked my fangs against his ear. "Who are you? What are you doing lurking in the shadows and watching us?"

He heaved out a breath and tipped his head sideways so he could see me. "You're a big one. You must be joined with a powerful magic user to get so large."

"One of the best. Answer my question, unless you want to experience my venom's sting. You won't recover if you do."

"Relax. I'm doing no harm. I'm working. How did you notice me? I'm usually great at blending in." Considering he was being crushed by a giant venomous spider, this guy was remarkably calm.

"I notice all the trouble in the village. I saw you at the tree lighting ceremony, standing out of the way and watching. And you're back again."

"So I am. For a good reason. I'm Devon Dean."

"Hilda. Familiar to Indigo Ash."

"Nice. You're with an Ash witch. Those witches have skills. Few of them are left alive these days."

"Don't distract me. What are you doing in Witch Haven?"

"If you let me up, I'll tell you everything."

I considered his offer. "Only if you promise not to run."

"Sorry. I didn't mean to. It was a knee-jerk reaction when seeing an enormous spider stalking me. I like spiders. It won't happen again."

I eased off Devon but maintained contact and allowed him to sit.

He took a moment to brush snow off his clothes, briefly rubbed his stomach, then grinned at me. "I'm in Witch Haven because I'm interested in the same thing as you."

"How do you know what I'm interested in?"

"Billy and his gang, right?"

"Go on."

Devon pulled out his wallet and flipped it open. "I'm a private eye. I'm an off-the-\books kind of investigator."

"What does that mean?"

"It means I leave no trail and get paid in cash doing the jobs most other private eyes turn down because they're too dangerous." He rubbed his ink-stained fingers together. "I was hired to track Billy and see what he's up to."

I studied his license. "Why?"

He flipped his wallet closed and slid it into his pocket. "Billy owes someone money."

"You're here to get it back?"

"Nothing so strong arm. I was told to find Billy and watch him for a few days. The guy he owes wants to see if he's got any of that money left. If he doesn't get his money back, then it'll be payback time." Devon raised his hands. "I've seen you around the village, asking questions about one of Billy's gang members. If you're still looking for Grinder, I know where he is. Why don't we help each other?"

The offer wasn't unreasonable, and it could save me some time. "Where is Grinder?"

His smile widened. "Right here. Billy's been giving you the runaround. He loves to mess with the Magic Council. You know what these biker guys are like. They see a figure of authority and have to play with them."

I clacked my fangs in frustration. I shouldn't have been so trusting. "Since you've been watching Billy, have you seen him with Spike Buchanan?"

"The guy found dead? Sure. They bashed heads a few times. But if you're asking me if Billy had anything to do with Spike's death, I couldn't tell you."

"You aren't running surveillance on Billy around the clock?"

"They don't pay me enough to do that. My client wants to know where his money is, rather than all of Billy's movements. I clocked up my hours for that day and then went back to the B&B I'm staying in. I wasn't around when Spike died."

"Is Grinder at the cabin with the others?"

"You got it. We can go there together. I need to check in to see what Billy's up to, so I'm headed that way."

Another ally could be useful, and I always appreciated an extra pair of eyes, even though I had plenty of my own. "Let's go. And I'll remind Billy why lying is a terrible trait."

Devon chuckled. "I expect you could get information out of anyone. If I didn't like spiders so much, I'd have told you all my family secrets. Probably all my paying clients' secrets, too. You're impressive to look at. Some might say beautiful."

"There's no need for flattery." I blushed as I stepped back so Devon could stand. He grimaced for a second and gripped his stomach. I touched his leg. "So you can hear me, I'll have to stay in contact with you. Do you have a problem with that?"

"No. I've got several pet tarantulas at home. I'm happy to let them walk all over me. It kind of tickles. Although you may need to shrink down, so you're easier to carry. Hand?"

"Shoulder will do." I shrunk down, then hopped onto his shoulder. "And let's be clear. I'm no one's pet, so don't think about taking me home and introducing me to your spider cage."

"I don't doubt that for a second. You're your own spider. I expect you'd eat my little guys as snacks." Devon set a brisk pace as he marched to the woods.

I grimaced. "That's cannibalism, so I'll pass. How long have you been watching Billy?"

"Five days. I'm due to pack up any time and report my findings."

"And then what?"

"Then the guy who wants his money makes a decision. I doubt it'll be a fun decision for Billy if he doesn't give back the money he owes."

I lifted a leg. "Can you hear raised voices?"

Devon sped up. "That sounds like Billy yelling." He broke into a jog, almost shaking me off his shoulder.

As the voices grew louder, Devon slowed. He ducked behind a tree and peeked around it. "It's Billy and some girl."

I looked around the tree trunk with him. "I know her! Well, I don't know anything about her, but that mistletoe witch attended the tree lighting ceremony."

Billy grabbed the tiny witch by the tops of her arms and shook her. She squeaked and punched out at him.

Two other bikers strolled over, their eyes narrowed as they watched the fight. More swiftly joined them.

"We need to help her," I whispered.

Devon shook his head. He was taking pictures. "This fight has nothing to do with me, and there's no way I'm tangling with Billy and his gang over a girl."

"It's one witch against six bikers. That's not a fair fight."

"My job is to observe and report back. That's it. If you want to do anything else, you're on your own."

I scowled at Devon, then hopped off his shoulder as he backed away and landed on the tree. So much for having an ally. What a coward.

My attention was fixed on the bikers and the witch. It was time to kick biker butt.

# Chapter 9

While Devon hightailed it out of there, I crept toward the fight. The mistletoe witch was tiny, but magic sparkled off her, and her glare was so fierce, it made me flinch.

I'd reached the last tree I could conceal myself behind, then climbed up so I had a good view and a jumping off point if things got nasty.

"Is it true? Spike is dead because of you?" The witch's voice was shrill as she swayed in Billy's forceful grip.

"Of course not. I wouldn't kill the guy. Maybe I should have, though."

"You're disgusting. And you're a liar. Let me go!"

Billy kept hold of the witch. "You go when I say."

"I'm here to find out what happened to Spike. That's all."

Billy loomed over her and bared his teeth. "Maybe you don't deserve to be alive for much longer, either."

She raised her chin. "You don't scare me. You did something bad to Spike, and I'll find the proof. Then you'll be sorry."

"Woman, you're insane. And I have limits. You slammed past those a long time ago. Now, I'm done being nice to you."

"I know you've hurt people before you went after Spike. I know all about your shady past."

"Is that so?" Billy shoved his face close to the witch's. "Then you should know to be more respectful. I don't make threats and not follow through on them. You won't be so sparkly once I'm done with you."

She glanced at the watching bikers, her stance defiant despite the terrible odds of winning this fight. "I suppose you'll make me disappear?"

"If that's what it takes. You claim I'm bad, but there's nothing good about you. You're only here to cause problems." Billy shoved her away. "Get out of here, before I do something I'll regret."

"I'll tell everyone you killed Spike. I'll go to the Magic Council and say I saw you kill him."

Billy snarled and raised his hand.

I leaped off the tree, landed on his knuckles, and sank my fangs into the fleshy part of his palm.

He yelped and flapped his arm. "Get off me! What are you doing?"

The mistletoe witch stared at us with wide eyes before she burst into laughter. "You're getting what you deserve. I should have bitten you. That would have taught you not to lay hands on me."

His gang advanced, Billy still hopping and flapping his arm to shake me loose, but my fangs were sunk in deep, although I held back my venom.

"It hurts! It hurts! Stop! I wouldn't have hit her. I just wanted to teach her a lesson."

I eased my fangs from his flesh, then wrapped webbing around his palm, so I had a secure base. "You never raise your hand to anyone. That behavior is despicable."

"It's adorable you're looking out for me, spider, but I can handle myself," the mistletoe witch said.

"You, be quiet," Billy snapped. "It's your fault this thing is biting me."

"That thing is a magnificent, magical spider, and you should show her more respect. Then she wouldn't have bitten you." The mistletoe witch winked at me.

I was surprised she could hear me, let alone figure out my gender. Most people couldn't just by looking at me. But mistletoe witches had an affinity with the natural world, which must extend to creatures who lived in it.

Billy gingerly raised his hand and stared at the holes I'd made. "I don't deserve this." His rage was fading, and he looked like a scolded schoolboy rather than a rough, tough biker.

"I'm glad I came back again," I said. "Although helping this witch wasn't the reason for my return visit."

Billy grunted. "Come to hassle us some more, I suppose? You don't give up, do you?"

"You lied about Grinder's location. You said he'd left Witch Haven, but he's been here this whole time, hasn't he?"

Billy shrugged as he continued to inspect his hand. "That'll teach you not to disturb my sleep and toss around accusations."

I lifted my fangs, and he flinched. "It gave you an opportunity to coach Grinder, so he'd say what you needed him to when the Magic Council asked for your alibi."

"The Magic Council thinks you killed Spike, too?" The witch crossed her arms over her chest, one small, sparkly pink slipper tapping on the snow.

Billy growled. "That has nothing to do with me. Now, I already said to get out of here, or I'll make you sorry."

She glowered at him for a second, then turned and stomped off.

"Who was that witch?" I said to Billy.

"My business, not yours." He tried to shake me off once more, then reached into his pocket, pulled out a knife, and aimed it at my torso.

I leaped away at the last second and landed on his shoulder. The blade stabbed straight into his palm.

Billy howled and fell to his knees, clutching his bleeding hand, the knife abandoned on the ground.

"You deserved that," I said. "Bringing a knife to a venom fight is cheating."

Billy glared at me, his eyes narrowed. "Get off me! You're not welcome here."

"I'll go as soon as I've spoken to your alibi."

He got off his knees, magic pulsing between his hands as he healed the self-inflicted stab wound.

I looked around the cautious, watching group. "Which one of them is Grinder?"

"Him." Billy spoke through gritted teeth as he pointed to the smallest member of the group. He was an average-sized guy, dressed in dark, grubby denim and a black leather jacket.

"Boss?" Grinder stepped forward.

"This freaky spider needs a word."

I scuttled to Grinder and leaped on his hand. "I need Billy's alibi for the night of Spike's death. Where was he between midnight and three in the morning?"

Grinder rubbed the back of his neck. "We hung out together. Did nothing much. Drank a few beers, then headed out to do business."

"Where did that business take place?"

Grinder glanced at Billy. "Here and there. We rode around and spoke to a few people."

Billy smirked at me. "You see. I have an alibi."

It was a lousy alibi as far as I was concerned. "Thank you, Grinder." I coiled and leaped onto Billy's head, making him squeak. "I need to know who you spoke to. That alibi won't hold up in court."

"I'm not going to no stinkin' court for what happened to Spike. And it'll take more than threats from you to make me talk. If I had a newspaper, I'd squash you."

"Try it. Maybe another bite would get your lips flapping." I was tempted to test that theory, but I wanted to speak to the mistletoe witch before she got away. She was here because of Spike, and I needed to know why. "If I find out Grinder lied to me, you'll be in trouble."

"You're the only one in trouble."

I leaped onto the snow.

"Get going, you ugly critter." Billy swung his foot in my direction.

After shaking my fangs at him, I raced away. I wasn't done with Billy and his gang of motley fools, and I'd be happy to return and show him exactly how scary I could be if he continued to cause trouble.

I heard the mistletoe witch before I saw her. She was talking to herself and flailing her arms around, still angry from her encounter with Billy and his gang.

I skittered around her, increasing my size so there'd be no way she'd miss me. "Don't scream. I come in peace."

She froze and stared at me, her eyes wide. Then she smiled. "You again! You're adorable."

"Thank you. Few people call me that."

"I love all creatures. Big, small, scaly or hairy. What's your name?" She crouched in front of me and held out her hand.

I approached and allowed her to pet my back. "I'm Hilda. And you?"

"Jasmine Silverdale."

"I saw you at the tree lighting ceremony with your friends."

"That was a fun evening." She glanced over her shoulder and scowled. "Things have gone downhill since then. Thanks for biting Billy."

"I couldn't help but overhear your argument. I was worried he might get the rest of his gang involved if things got any more heated."

"He would! Too much of a wimp to stand up to me on his own. And I know he hurt Spike." Jasmine stood from her crouched position, her pretty, sparkly dark lips pressed together in a thin line.

"You mind if I walk with you? I'm helping the Magic Council with the investigation into what happened to Spike."

Her eyebrows flashed up. "No kidding. They're working with spider shifters now?"

"I'm not a shifter, but I'm bonded to a powerful witch who lives in the village. She has connections to the Magic Council."

"Oh! You sound like someone important. Should I curtesy?" She giggled and mock curtseyed in front of me.

"I'm just trying to do the right thing."

"Well, then, that means we must be friends. But let's get out of these woods. I half expect Billy and his creepy gang to follow. It would be just the sneaky, mean thing he'd do. You wanna ride?"

"That's most welcome." I shrank to a normal size.

Jasmine placed me on her shoulder. "Comfy?"

"This is an ideal spot. Billy's not popular around here. How do you know him?"

"I don't. I'm here because of Spike." Her mouth tugged down at the corners. "I'm his sister."

"Sister? But you're a mistletoe witch."

A tinkling laugh slid from her sparkling lips as she marched along. "What gave me away?"

"Your unique coloring. Those beautiful dark lips. The strands of white berries sown through your hair."

Jasmine grinned. "I'm a walking cliché, but I don't feel right without my berries."

"How were you related to Spike? He was a warlock."

"We were adopted, so we're not related by blood. He was still my brother, though, and I must find out what happened to him." She shook her head, her eyes hazy with tears. "Spike was so hopeful when he moved here, where people didn't know about his past and didn't judge him. He was done with the violence and law breaking. I was so proud of him. But then this..." She swiped tears off her cheeks. "So unfair."

"I'm sorry for your loss. I didn't know Spike well, but he was always respectful."

"He was. I keep hearing conflicting information when I ask around. Do you know what happened to him?"

"I know some of the facts. Have you been in touch with the Magic Council?"

"Sure. They weren't helpful. I got passed around to various departments before someone told me the basics, but they said it's still ongoing, and I had to prove who I was before they could give me any more details."

"It's true they don't know everything. An autopsy and tests are being conducted to see what the cause of death was."

Jasmine's forehead furrowed. "I'm confused. I was in the café getting coffee, and someone said a spider killed Spike, and not Billy. Why do they think that?"

"It's the reason I'm involved. A young spider shifter is a suspect. I'm certain he's innocent, so I need to find the killer."

"Just like I plan to." She strode in silence, occasionally slowing to inspect some berries. "This spider shifter is young?"

"Barely sixteen. He's a headstrong young man, but no killer."

She sighed. "I feel sorry for the kid. To be in the middle of a messy investigation must be scary. I'm overwhelmed, too. Neither me nor Spike had great starts, but he was finally getting himself sorted. Just when he was on the right track, his past comes back and bites him."

"Was that what your argument with Billy was about?"

"Billy has to be involved. Other people told me about his gang and the problems he caused in the village. I know what these biker types are like. They love causing trouble with rival gangs. I was always telling Spike to be careful. I was thrilled when he got out. It took a lot of nagging, though. But I'm persistent when I want something." Jasmine flashed me a tear-tinged smile.

"Then Billy arrives, and everything goes wrong," I said.

"That's why I had to confront him. I thought I'd get the truth out of him. I hoped there'd be a slither of kindness in there, or guilt over what he'd done."

"You didn't find it?"

"The man's a monster." Jasmine glanced at me. "I can usually find good in everyone, but not Billy."

"How long have you been in Witch Haven?"

"I arrived three days before the tree lighting ceremony. Spike invited me, and I brought some girlfriends, too, and we all hung out together. I asked Spike to spend time with us at the event, but I think he found us loud, so he made his excuses and left." Her laughter was bittersweet.

I smiled. I'd found the giggling and shrieking annoying, so I understood why Spike had stayed away from the gaggle of mistletoe witches.

"I wish I'd insisted he stay with us. He could still be here. That guy was an idiot, but I loved him." More tears flowed.

"Where did you stay after the tree lighting ceremony ended?"

"I've got a room in a shared house. It's along Shadowvale Way. You know the place?"

"The little cottage with the white door?" Pippin Jaggers often rented her spare room to travelers to make extra cash.

"That's it. It's all done up for Christmas. It's adorable." Her sunny expression dimmed. "I can't stop thinking about Spike. I'm determined to get to the truth."

"So am I."

She walked along, the crunch of snow and the soft rasp of her long white skirt the only sounds. "I know we don't know each other, but can you help me? It was dumb to confront Billy, but I need answers."

I gently patted her cheek, dabbing away tears. "Of course. I plan on finding Spike's killer, and if that brings you comfort, then so much the better."

Jasmine briefly leaned her head down, giving me a gentle squeeze between her cheek and shoulder. "Thanks, Hilda. Billy has to be involved. Everyone says he's trouble. And when I spoke to the owner of the inn, the one with the eyepatch, she said Billy was hanging around Spike. That's suspicious." We reached the edge of the woods, and she stopped and blew out a breath. "I need time to cool off and figure out what to do next."

"Maybe don't try confronting angry bikers on your own as your next move."

She grinned. "That's sweet of you to say, but I have skills. If they'd gotten too feisty, I'd have fought back. I'm sticking around, so please let me know what you find out about my brother."

"Of course." We said our goodbyes, and Jasmine walked away.

The more I saw and heard about Billy, the more I was convinced he was involved in Spike's murder. He was happy to rough up a lone mistletoe witch rather than help her during this tragedy. The man had no soul.

"Hey. How did it go?" Devon appeared from behind a tree.

I was tempted to snub him, but I had manners. I sidled over and into his waiting hand. "Smoothly, no thanks to you. I thought you'd fled?"

Devon lifted his phone. "I changed my mind. Wanted to make sure you didn't get injured, and I thought a few more pictures wouldn't hurt. I also followed you while you had your friendly chat with that witch."

"Why do that?"

"To see what she told you." He waggled his eyebrows. "And she lied. That witch wasn't Spike's sister. She was his girlfriend."

I gave Devon my full attention before leaping onto his shoulder. "She told me they were adopted."

"Not true." He strolled toward the village. "And she's also dating Billy. I guess he found out she was seeing Spike."

"How do you know all this?"

"I've seen them together. She told you her name's Jasmine?"

"Yes. Is that also a lie?"

"No, I think that's true. Jasmine would hang out with Billy, then leave and meet Spike. She took risks and wasn't discreet while she was here. Anyone would think she wanted to get caught, so they'd fight over her." Devon smirked. "Some women are like that."

"Not the ones I know. Why is Jasmine here?"

"To see Billy?"

"But they were fighting when we saw them together. He wasn't happy. Neither was she."

"Jasmine must be angry because she's lost one of her regular guys. And she wanted to know if Billy had done it. Maybe she was excited by the thought he'd killed for her."

"That's dark," I said. "And I didn't get that vibe. Jasmine was genuinely sad about Spike's death."

"Crocodile tears. That woman is here to patch up her messy love life and make sure all her men are happy."

"You're cynical. Does she have more boyfriends living here?"

"I've only seen her with Billy and Spike, but who knows? You always need to watch the pretty ones. They rob you blind and crush your heart."

I was stumped. Jasmine deceived me. She'd been sweet and obliging when asking for help, but it was a front. "Thanks for the information. Are you sticking around? The Magic Council will be interested in this information, so they may want to talk to you."

"Sure. I'm staying at the B&B on the edge of the village. Happy to share with them if you think it'll be useful. But I must be discreet. I don't need my customers knowing I talk to the authorities." He held a hand against his stomach.

"Did you get injured when I jumped you?"

"Oh, no! I've got a case of gut rot. Must have eaten something dodgy at the tree lighting ceremony."

"There's something going around. I didn't feel too good that night, either. Several others have also been unwell."

"It'll pass. It has to. My current client isn't the kind of guy to let you take a sick day. If I do, that sickness might become terminal."

"Got you. I'll speak to my contact at the Magic Council straightaway. Since she lied to me, Jasmine has to be a suspect in this murder."

"That's what I figured. And what else is she lying about?" Devon lifted me off his shoulder. "I'll see you soon." He set me down in the snow and strode away.

I dashed to Olympus's office and slid under the gap at the bottom of the door. He was on the phone, Monty snoozing in his huge leopard bed in one corner. I hopped onto the desk and tapped on the back of Olympus's hand.

He jumped, then smiled, raising a finger. "Thanks. I'll call you back with that information." He set down the phone. "I was wondering where you were. I got the preliminary autopsy report and initial test results on Spike's body."

"What did they show?"

"A spider bite didn't kill him."

I tap-danced on his hand. "I'm happy to hear it. I knew it wasn't young Dylan. So, what killed Spike?"

"Mistletoe and dark magic."

# Chapter 10

"Mistletoe!" I skittered back and forth. "When I found Spike's body, I thought his lips had changed color because of frostbite. The discoloration was a sign of mistletoe poisoning?"

Olympus nodded.

I kept scuttling across his desk as I put the puzzle pieces together, then landed back on his hand. "What about the bite marks on Spike's neck?"

"There's no doubt about it. A spider made them, but the bites didn't kill him. We found no spider venom in his system."

"Dylan's ill!" My heart lurched. "What if he found Spike already dead and bit him? He'd have ingested the poison and magic."

Olympus grimaced. "Why would he bite a corpse?"

"He's a young, curious spider. We like to know what certain foods taste like."

"Hilda! Spiders don't eat people."

"Well, we do. We enjoy skin flakes, and never turn down the opportunity to have a tasty, warm blood sample." Given how shocked Olympus looked, I decided not to tell him about the flesh-eating spiders on the island of Whistling Skulls. It would turn his hair white.

He raised his hand until we were at eye level. "You don't ever drink from me when I'm asleep, do you?"

"I never drink from family. Drinking is only done by mutual agreement." I bobbed up and down to reassure him. "Dylan is at that age when he's curious about everything, even if he pretends not to be. He's testing his boundaries and finding what he likes."

"You think he found Spike dead, poisoned by mistletoe and dark magic, and what? He sank his fangs in and feasted?"

"Yes! And when he did, he ingested some of the poison meant for Spike. That's why Dylan's been feeling so unwell. He could even have bitten the spot where the mistletoe was injected."

"Covering evidence that someone gave the toxic concoction to Spike." Olympus scrubbed a hand across his face. "It makes sense."

"We must contact Ginger. Dylan won't get better until he's been treated. Do you know what dark magic was used?"

"It was a necrotic spell. It would have leached through Spike and made him feel lousy before he died." Olympus already had the phone lifted and was dialing a number. "Let me speak to Ginger."

He put the phone on loudspeaker as the call connected. "Ginger. It's Olympus Duke."

"What do you want?" Ginger's tone was cold.

"And Hilda. We have news. We know why Dylan is sick."

"So do I. It's a stomach bug."

"It's not. Is he available to talk? This is urgent. His life is at risk."

There was a pause. "He's most likely asleep. He's barely left his room since your visit."

I glanced up at Olympus. We had no time to waste. "We need to know if Dylan bit Spike."

A sigh rattled down the line. "How many times do we have to tell you? Dylan didn't kill anybody."

"We know. We just got the autopsy results. Spike was poisoned, and we think Dylan bit him after he died. Which means he's also been poisoned."

There was silence on the line for several heartbeats. "I'll go get him."

I waited impatiently until there was a rustle on the line.

"He's here. So is Ana Maria," Ginger said.

I quickly recapped the information. "Dylan, it's crucial you tell us the truth. We know you didn't kill Spike, but did you find his body and want to know what he tasted like?"

"No!"

"Be honest, Dylan," Ginger said. "We can't make you better unless we know what's wrong with you."

There was a grumbling sigh. "I bit him. But like you said, he was dead. I did nothing wrong. My bite didn't kill him."

"Dylan! You should have been in bed, fast asleep." Ana Maria's tone scolded as Dylan grumbled and groused.

"I wasn't tired. I snuck out my window and went for a walk. I wandered to the tree and saw this dead guy lying underneath it. I went to take a look. Then ... I bit him."

"What time was that?" Olympus said.

"About two in the morning." Dylan shushed Ana Maria as she told him off for being out so late. "I didn't know what to do, but he was dead. I prodded him and walked all over him. Nothing. He'd been gone a while, because he was cold."

"So you took a nibble?" I said. "No judgment if you did. We all like to explore when we're young."

"I heard from some of the others it's an intense sensation when you drink blood. I've never been allowed to do it, though. And I didn't get much from the dead guy. It was gross and sludgy."

"You're too young to drink blood," Ana Maria said. "It's important you can control your urges before you drink the red nectar. Otherwise, you risk becoming dangerous."

"Yeah, yeah, whatever," Dylan said. "Anyway, there was already a hole in his neck, so I stuck in a fang. Then both."

"That was the injection site," I said. "Dylan, you're sick because you received the same toxic combination of mistletoe and dark magic as Spike. You don't have a stomach bug."

"Am I gonna die?" He no longer sounded like a surly teen, but a terrified boy.

"No. We can treat you, now we know what's wrong with you. You'll make a full recovery."

"Oh! Thank you for finding out what's wrong with my son." Ana Maria's throat sounded clogged with tears. "I've been so worried. Nothing I tried worked. No spell held for long. I was panicking."

"That's because there's something deadly swirling around Dylan's system. If we hadn't discovered how Spike died, Dylan wouldn't have recovered," Olympus said. "And we'd have found out quicker if Dylan hadn't concealed things from us."

"Of course. And he's sorry. Aren't you, Dylan?"

There was more grumbling and possibly a muttered yeah.

"Tell me what to do," Ana Maria said. "I'll mix the antidote."

I spent a few minutes explaining the antidote ingredients. "He'll need several doses over the next twelve hours, but he'll be fine."

Ana Maria thanked me profusely, and I even got a grumbling thank you from Dylan before they disappeared off the line.

Ginger huffed out a breath. "I want to thank you both, too. I knew Dylan was innocent. Well, he's not exactly innocent, since he interfered with a crime scene."

I overlooked the fact that Ginger had done the same by moving Spike's body. "We're happy to help. I'm glad Dylan's in the clear."

"Do you know who did it?"

"Yes, I think I do," I said.

Olympus raised his eyebrows at me.

"If we can help in any way, we're at your disposal. You saved Dylan's life, and I'll be forever grateful. Ana Maria will be, too."

After saying goodbye to Ginger, Olympus placed the phone in its cradle. "You've got something you need to tell me?"

"It's been a busy day." I settled on the back of his hand. "I ran into a private eye, Devon Dean, who's been watching Billy and his gang. I'd noticed Devon around the village so went to see what he was up to."

Olympus smiled. "I suspect there's more to that story than you're revealing."

"Perhaps, but it's not relevant at the moment. Devon told me Billy lied about Grinder leaving Witch Haven this morning. He was at the cabin the whole time."

"Billy has been messing with us." Olympus shook his head. "I'm hardly surprised."

"I visited Billy and his gang again with Devon. When we got there, we discovered a mistletoe witch, Jasmine Silverdale, accusing Billy of murdering Spike."

Olympus leaned back in his seat. "Why would she think that? Did she see what happened?"

"No. You haven't heard the best bit. When I spoke to Jasmine, she told me she was Spike's sister, and the same family adopted them. Devon told me another story. Apparently, Jasmine dated Spike and Billy at the same time. He's seen her with them while tailing Billy."

"Jasmine is using a cover story because she had something to do with Spike's murder?"

"I think so. Billy's alibi isn't perfect, but I met Grinder, and he said they were out of the village doing business together, but Jasmine lied to cover her tracks. We need to bring her in and find out why."

"We need to do more than that," Olympus said. "She's a mistletoe witch, so she has access to the berries that killed Spike. Do you know where she's staying? I'll rush through a search warrant, see if we can find anything to implicate her."

"Pippin Jaggers rented her a room."

While Olympus got to work on the warrant, I paced the desk, then hopped off and walked over to Monty, who'd been listening with one eye open.

"Mistletoe witches are cute," he said. "Do you really think she could take down a huge guy like Spike?"

"Enough poison and dark magic will kill anyone," I said. "Maybe Spike wanted to end the relationship, so she got revenge."

"Or Spike wouldn't let her go." Olympus glanced up as he waited on hold. "Both are solid motives for getting rid of him."

"It's always the cute ones you need to watch out for," Monty said. "I forget to have my guard up when I'm around them because I get so dazzled by how sweet they are."

"Do you have your guard up around hairy things that scuttle and bite?" I tapped him repeatedly on the nose.

Monty ducked his head. "You're scary in a good way. We always need a scary friend to have our backs."

I accepted the compliment and snuggled in his bed for a quick snooze. Things always took time when the rusty wheels of Magic Council bureaucracy groaned to life.

An hour later, and after Olympus called in a few favors to get the search warrant through before the end of the day, we were headed to Jasmine's rented room on Shadowvale Way.

The tiny cottage she stayed in sparkled with fairy lights, and a bundle of mistletoe was pinned on the door.

I sat on Olympus's shoulder, Monty beside him, doing his best not to leap around and kick snow in our faces. He mostly succeeded.

Olympus stopped at the cottage and knocked on the door.

Jasmine opened it. Her gaze landed on me. "Hilda! Have you got news about Spike?"

"Yes. And we have questions for you. This is Olympus Duke and Monty from the Magic Council. May we come in?"

"Of course. Anything I can do to help with the investigation, just ask." Jasmine stepped back and allowed us inside. The house smelled of cinnamon and chocolate, and nearly every surface sparkled with decorations. "Pippin is out doing last-minute gift shopping. I've just made cookies if you're interested." She led us into a tidy living room.

"This isn't a social visit," Olympus said. "You're now a person of interest in Spike Buchanan's murder."

Her jaw dropped, and a flash of magic sparked in her eyes for a second. "I'd never kill Spike. I loved him. Why would I hurt him?"

"Jasmine, you lied to me about your relationship," I said. "You weren't his sister, you were his girlfriend."

Her hands slid together, and she circled her thumbs around each other. "I... How did you find out?"

"You haven't been discreet when dating," I said. "You were seen with Spike and Billy."

"Oh! I didn't think anyone would care what I did here. Nobody knows me in Witch Haven."

"We care," Olympus said. "Especially since a murder's been committed. And because you're a suspect, I have a search warrant. I need to look around."

Jasmine took the warrant he held out and studied it before shrugging. "Help yourself. I have nothing to hide. Sure, I hid my connection to Spike, but I was being careful. I don't want to upset my other male friends. Some of them can be sensitive flowers." She scratched her nails through Monty's thick fur.

Monty purred and leaned against Jasmine.

"Monty, we're working. With me. Mind if we start in the room you're renting?"

"No. There's not much up there, though. I only brought a few things with me. I'll come up with you, show you where it is."

We headed up a steep wooden staircase and into a single bedroom. Olympus and Monty started the search while I stayed by Jasmine.

"Was it Billy who told you?" Jasmine said to me.

"No, someone else. The source is reliable," I said. "It was a risky move, dating two guys while you were here. Witch Haven is small, and everyone loves to gossip."

"I was more serious about Spike than Billy. I planned on visiting Spike after he told me he was moving here and retiring from the gang." Jasmine perched on the edge of a chair. "I wasn't sure how I felt about it. I've always loved the bad boys."

"Is that why you were drawn to Billy?"

She sighed. "He's gorgeous, but more trouble than he's worth. He's so possessive. It's usually easy to date multiple guys, since they rarely ask me questions about myself. The arrogant ones never do. But Billy found a message Spike left me and got jealous. We argued, and he ditched me. Not that we were officially a thing, but he said it was over."

"When you found out Billy was in Witch Haven and then Spike was killed, you assumed the worst had happened?" I said.

"I did. I was confronting him when you found us. I'm still impressed by the way you bit him. You were fearless."

Olympus looked up at me.

I waggled a leg at him to carry on the search. "Billy deserved it. He was intimidating you."

"He was trying his best to intimidate." She twirled a strand of silky hair around one finger. "When he's not being a jerk, he can be sweet. But it would never have worked between us long term. I have so much love to give, and there are so many delicious men to enjoy. I can never resist. Especially when they come with a leather jacket and a motorbike. Dating an honest, decent guy is boring. I tried it and stuck it out for two months before losing interest. Nice guys are dull."

"Billy wanted you to change your ways and be exclusive with him?"

She snorted a tiny laugh through her button nose. "He didn't want me exclusively, but he didn't want anyone else to have me. Typical guy. Wants it all."

"Where were you when Spike was killed?" I said. "He died between midnight and three in the morning after the tree lighting event."

"Um ... I ... don't be angry. I was with someone."

"Billy?"

She dropped her gaze. "Yes."

"But you accused him of murder! How could Billy have killed Spike if he was with you?"

Olympus had stopped his search and also waited for an answer.

"I didn't know what time Spike had died! I just put the clues together and figured out it had to be Billy. I confronted him when I learned what happened." Her bottom lip jutted out. "Sorry for lying to you, but people can be judgy and make assumptions about the kind of person I am when they learn I'm into free love."

"I'm not judging you for that, but I am judging you about this." Olympus lifted a gloved hand. He held a small blowpipe.

Jasmine tilted her head. "What's that?"

I scuttled over and inspected Olympus's find. "The tool you used to kill Spike."

She rushed over, but Olympus held up his hand before she touched the blowpipe. "Is this yours?"

Jasmine shook her head, her hair whooshing around her. "No! I have no idea how that got there. What do you mean, that was how Spike was killed?"

"He was injected with mistletoe and dark magic," I said. "We were wondering how it got into his system. Then we discovered an injection mark on his neck. Did you lure Spike to the tree for a romantic liaison and then kill him?"

Tears flooded Jasmine's eyes, and her hand covered her mouth. "No! I loved him. I love all my men. Even when they turn on me like Billy. I didn't do it. I'd never hurt someone I care about."

Olympus shook his head and bagged the evidence. "Jasmine Silverdale, you're under arrest for murder."

# Chapter 11

The next morning, it felt like Christmas Day had arrived early.

Spike's killer was found. Dylan was in the clear, and I was ready to relax and celebrate with my friends and family.

And I wasn't alone. Nugget, Russell, and Indigo were settled around the breakfast table. Indigo was enjoying a stack of cinnamon-dusted pancakes drenched in maple syrup. I had a bowl of candied flies, while Russell and Nugget fought playfully over a hunk of ham hock. It was the perfect start to an ideal day.

"Olympus should be back soon," Indigo said around a mouthful of pancake. "He had a few loose ends to tie up before stopping for the holidays."

"Jasmine must have confessed by now," I said. "With the evidence we have against her, there's no way she'll get away with this."

Indigo tilted her head from side to side. "It's weird she kept the murder weapon. If I was in her position, I'd have destroyed the blowpipe the second I'd used it."

"Maybe she planned on leaving Witch Haven by now, but her unfinished business with Billy slowed her down."

"Or Billy was her next target." Nugget tore off a wedge of ham and gulped it down. "She's a black widow. Killing all the men who scorned her."

"Real black widows don't do that." Some species ate their mates during intimacy, but not all. And no spider shifter did. "I have friends who are black widow shifters, and they're the sweetest spiders you'll ever meet."

Nugget wrinkled his nose. "If you say so. I'll pass on any black widow get togethers, though."

"They'd never want to eat you," Indigo said. "You're too tough to make a decent meal."

The front door opened, and Olympus brought in frigid air and snowflakes on his thick winter coat. Monty bounded in behind him and shook snow off his fur.

Olympus kicked off his boots, removed his outdoor gear, and joined us at the table. "Any left for me?"

Indigo grabbed him a plate of warm pancakes from the griddle. "You're lucky. Russell has been eyeing these for ages."

Russell flapped his wings and then chased Nugget for more ham. Monty joined in.

Olympus poured himself a coffee and settled in a seat. "The test results are back on the blowpipe. There were traces of mistletoe and dark magic on it."

"Can you match it to Jasmine's magic?" I said.

"Not yet. And it's possible she bought the magic from someone, then mixed it with the mistletoe and stuck it in a dart."

I tapped my legs on the table. "Yes. A dart."

"Is Jasmine talking?" Indigo said.

"She's refusing to confess, despite us finding the murder weapon in her things. She keeps saying she'll fight and is prepared to go to trial." Olympus rolled his shoulders. "I was hoping this would be over quickly, but unless she changes her plea, it'll drag out for weeks, potentially months, with the holidays getting in the way."

"She'll only make things worse for herself by taking this to court."

I jigged around the table. Why hadn't we found a dart at the crime scene? Maybe Jasmine took it. But why wasn't it found during the search? "Did Jasmine tell you why she did it?"

"No. She keeps saying she has so much love to give, she could never hate anyone enough to kill." Olympus took a huge bite of pancake. "I figured if I left her alone today, she'll experience life in a cell, and it might change her mind. Jasmine doesn't seem like a witch who'd handle being stuck inside. Mistletoe witches love their freedom and being outdoors."

"She must have planned on sneaking out of Witch Haven before you found her connection to Spike," Indigo said. "Fortunately for you, my awesome spider stopped that from happening."

Olympus grinned at me. "I'll be forever grateful to Hilda. But it's weird. Jasmine claims she was staying in the village until Spike's killer was found. She was so convincing. If we hadn't found that evidence, I'd have believed she was innocent."

"Never trust a scorned woman," Nugget said. "They have darkness in their broken hearts."

"So cynical, for someone so cute and fluffy." Indigo leaned over and tickled Nugget's head.

Nugget hissed, but then quietly purred, before going back to the game of tag with the remaining ham hock.

"It's sad what happened to Spike," Indigo said. "He came here for a new start, but his past wouldn't let him go."

"It is unfair," I said. "At least Dylan's in the clear. He's got his future ahead of him. Ana Maria has given him the antidote, so he's on the mend. And Ginger has been teaching him it's best not to bite bodies you find lying on the ground."

"Always sensible," Nugget said. "You never know how long they've been lying there, or what they're infected with. You don't want to bite someone who's been nipped by a ghoul. That wouldn't end well."

"We can all agree biting any dead body is bad," Indigo said.

Russell cawed and dived on Monty.

We continued with breakfast, chatting over the case.

Once I was finished, I scuttled to Indigo and settled on the back of her hand. "I'm going to visit Dylan."

"Give him our best," Indigo said.

I checked out the window and was surprised by the heavy snow on the ground. It would be a white Christmas in Witch Haven come tomorrow.

Nugget trotted over as I headed to the door. "You're leaving?"

"To see Dylan."

He sighed. "You're useless."

"Why say that?"

"You've done no sleigh practice."

"The reindeer are still missing? I thought Olympus was looking for them."

"Everyone is. Apart from you. We're getting lumbered with pulling that charity sleigh, and you've done nothing to help."

"I solved a murder! That must count for something."

Nugget looked less than impressed as he washed his face.

"What's wrong with your paw?" The underside of Nugget's paw was fat and pink.

"Not that you care, but I've been working hard to perfect my sleigh technique. I got ice burns."

"Looks painful. Get Indigo to heal it." I felt guilty for not helping. "How about we practice later? Would that work for you?"

Nugget flicked his tail as he walked away. "I'll check my diary."

I shook my head as I left the house. Nugget's schedule involved eating, sleeping, grousing, and grooming.

I was dashing through the snow like an overeager reindeer keen to get to my trough of oats, when a figure staggered into an alleyway behind the café.

It was Devon! He clutched his stomach, using his other hand to prop himself up on the wall.

I changed direction and raced after him. By the time I got into the alleyway, Devon was face down in the muddy snow and unconscious. I scuttled over his face, glad to feel a pulse in his neck, although it was uneven.

Had Billy discovered him snooping and taught him a lesson? Maybe it was the shady loan shark who'd hired him.

I couldn't see if he had injuries on his front, but he'd been holding his stomach. Perhaps he'd been stabbed. There was no sign of blood pooling in the snow, but I couldn't take the risk. If Devon had a serious injury, he'd need help.

I cast a translocation spell, and we arrived inside the small Witch Haven hospital. I ran to the reception desk and jumped on the blonde nurse. "Hello! I need help."

She flinched, then brushed me off, her striking green eyes wide. "What's wrong?"

I jumped back on her hand. "I brought in a patient. He's in the corridor. He's unconscious."

She dashed out from behind the desk and hurried into the corridor, crouching beside Devon. "What happened to him?"

"I just found him like this. He was staggering and seemed in pain. By the time I got to him, he was out cold."

The nurse gently moved Devon until he was on his back. She checked his pulse and looked into his eyes.

I examined his torso for injuries, but there was nothing. No tears in his clothing to suggest someone had used a weapon on him.

"I don't like his color or how fast his pulse is. I need to get him stable. What are those stains on his fingers?" The nurse ran her hands from the top of Devon's head down to his toes. She repeated the movement several times, pale pink magic flickering over his body.

I leaped onto one of her slow-moving hands. "Ink? Is he recovering?"

"I see no improvement. Whatever's wrong with him, it may not be easy to heal. I'll be back in a second." She flicked me onto Devon's stomach, then dashed away, and returned with a colleague and a trolley.

I stepped back as they worked, lifting Devon and pulsing more magic over him, before pushing the trolley away. I hurried along with them.

"Are you a friend of his?" the nurse said.

I jumped onto her shoulder. "We've only just met. He's been helping with an investigation I'm doing with the Magic Council. I'm Hilda. Familiar to Indigo Ash."

She nodded. "Is he here with anyone? Any family in the village?"

"Not that I know of. Devon's here for work." We arrived in a room, and were joined by a doctor, who began a thorough examination after getting a briefing from the green-eyed nurse.

Green Eyes carried me out of the room. "Thanks for bringing him in, but we'll take it from here. He could be with us for a few days, so he'll need his things brought in. And it would be helpful if you could find contact details of his next of kin."

"Of course. I know where he's staying, so I'll see if he's got a diary or a phone with his details in it."

"I'd appreciate that. What's his full name?"

"Devon Dean."

She glanced over her shoulder. "Don't take too long. Something nasty has gotten hold of him. I've seen nothing like it before." The nurse lowered me to the floor, then hurried back into the room.

I dashed out of the hospital and raced to the B&B where Devon was staying. It was easy to sneak in and up the stairs. There were only six bedrooms, and after a quick investigation of three, I found Devon's, recognizing the jacket slung on the bed.

The room was your typical comfortable guesthouse bedroom, with a soft-looking bed, a table and chairs, and a compact bathroom attached.

Devon's clothes were folded on a chair, and there were a few toiletries in the bathroom. I hopped onto the desk and discovered a small pile of notes and an old-style ink pen.

I rifled through the notes, hoping to find a name or a contact I could notify about what was going on, but I found nothing useful.

With some effort, I pulled open the drawers and looked through them. Most were empty, but there was a small pocket diary in one. I hopped into the drawer and flicked through the pages.

I found no useful names or numbers to call, but there was a picture in the back flap of the diary.

It was of Jasmine Silverdale. And her eyes were gouged out.

# Chapter 12

A few hours later, I was back at the hospital with Olympus and Jasmine.

"I'm not changing my story." Jasmine had her arms crossed over her chest. "This is a trap. You're trying to get me to say I killed Spike. I didn't do it."

After I'd discovered the picture of Jasmine in Devon's belongings, I'd hurried back to Olympus, and after some research, we'd discovered Devon wasn't a private eye, and the license he flashed about was fake.

"We know you didn't kill Spike," Olympus said. "And I can't tell you why we brought you here, but we know who did."

The tension drained from Jasmine's shoulders. "How did that blowpipe get into my room? The killer put it there?"

"We believe it was planted," I said. "They wanted you to take the blame for what happened to Spike."

Her eyes widened. "Why would anyone do that to me?"

I tapped a long leg on the floor. "No judgment from me, but perhaps because you've been dating multiple men at the same time, one of them took offence?"

"Oh! Well, I suppose so. I could be more transparent with my dating situation. Not everyone is into open relationships, though. I don't get why. It makes sense to me."

"I'm all for free love if everyone agrees. Shall we solve this murder?" I gestured at the closed hospital door.

Olympus nodded. "Jasmine, I need you to wait here for a few moments. I'm putting my trust in you that you won't go anywhere."

"I want to find out what happened to Spike as much as you. If being here solves that, I'm going nowhere, especially now I know you aren't charging me with murder."

"Make sure you don't move," I said. "If you run, I'll find you. When I do, I won't be my usual friendly self."

Jasmine tickled me under the chin. "You could never scare me. You're too cute."

Olympus opened the hospital door, and I scuttled in, then hopped on his shoulder. He eased the door shut and walked to the bed where Devon lay.

"Still not feeling good?" I tried to sound sympathetic, even though I was angry at being fooled by Devon.

His eyes flickered open. His skin was yellow and his lips black, lines of poison radiating across his cheeks, just like it was on his supposedly ink-stained fingers. "Hey, Hilda. No, not great. I'd be dead if it weren't for you. You saved my life by bringing me here."

"You may not be thanking me in a moment," I said. "Devon, we know it was you. You murdered Spike."

His eyes widened for a second. "I don't know the guy. Why would I do that?"

"Because he had an intimate relationship with Jasmine, and they were getting serious. You couldn't let that happen," Olympus said.

Devon struggled up in the bed. "Jasmine? You mean the mistletoe witch who dated Spike and Billy?"

"It's no use pulling the innocent card," I said. "After I found you sick in the alleyway, the nurse asked me to go to your room and bring in your things. I found a picture of Jasmine with her eyes gouged out. Why do that if you don't know her?"

"I know nothing about that picture." He shifted in the bed and grimaced, his hand going to his stomach.

"You know all about mistletoe and dark magic, though. That's what you used to poison Spike. You must have thought your luck was in when a young spider appeared and concealed the injection site by biting him. Did you see Dylan do it?"

"You've lost me," Devon said. "I'm just here doing a job."

"You're not a private eye. We checked your license, and it's fake," Olympus said. "You made up a cover story so you could snoop on Jasmine and her other boyfriends."

"You've got the wrong guy. Now, I need to rest." Devon's gaze flicked to the door.

If he was thinking of running, he wouldn't get far. "You need to tell the truth if you want to get better. I told the doctor mistletoe and dark magic is in your system. He ran tests and found exactly that. What a coincidence."

Devon's jaw wobbled. "That's ... impossible."

"Not if you inhaled the toxic concoction by mistake before you fired a blow dart at Spike," Olympus said.

Devon gulped. "I wouldn't be that dumb. And I know nothing about blow darts. They're like syringes, aren't they?"

"Not exactly," I said.

"Did you find one on the body?" There was a flicker of smugness in his words.

Devon thought he'd gotten away with it.

Olympus remained calm as he stood by the bed. "No."

"You made your dart with ice," I said. "You mixed mistletoe berry juice and dark magic into water and froze it. You may have only inhaled a tiny drop, but there was so much poison in Spike's system, you must have used a hefty dose. That poison is making you sick. It's the same poison you used to murder your victim, and the same poison that made Dylan unwell after he bit Spike."

Devon played with the edge of the blanket. "It's an interesting theory, but that's not what happened. I am a private eye. Maybe I don't have a license anymore, but I can still investigate."

"The tests don't lie," Olympus said. "There's no other way you got that combination of toxins in your system. It's exactly the same as we found in Spike and Dylan's test results."

I scuttled closer. "I'd never have figured out you used an ice dart, but when I saw ice burns on Nugget's paw, it was the same as the red mark on Spike's neck. Your ice dart left a trace."

Devon ran his tongue across his front teeth several times.

"Did you even know you'd poisoned yourself?" I said. "You must have been under stress before killing Spike. Your hands were sweaty, and the heat melted the ice dart."

"I'm saying nothing. I need legal representation. You're framing me for something I didn't do. And get the doctor in here."

"Perhaps a visitor will change your mind." Olympus opened the door and gestured Jasmine to come in.

She stepped inside, her gaze latched onto Devon, and she gasped. "What are you doing here?"

Devon's cheeks flushed. "Jasmine! It's ... it's not what you think. I'm sick, and these idiots are trying to charge me with something I didn't do. Did you come to see me? Were you worried about me? How did you know I was in here?"

His desperate, longing tone told me everything I needed to know about their relationship. "Do you know this man?" I said to Jasmine.

"Of course. This is Charlie August. He's the good guy I told you about. I tried to get the bad boys out of my system by dating him." She bit her lip. "I was bored out of my mind within five minutes."

"Hey! I was great for you. I looked after you."

"Charlie, you treated me like I was made of glass and I'd break. You were sweet and obliging, and you never told me when I stepped out of line. I need a man who'll keep me on my toes and pull me up when I go too far." Jasmine drew in a sharp breath, and her eyes narrowed. "Wait. Is this why you brought me here? You think Charlie killed Spike?"

"We do. Devon, or rather, Charlie, lied about being a private eye so he could spy on you and your boyfriends. Perhaps he saw you getting too close to Spike and needed to stop things," I said.

"Charlie! Shame on you. I broke things off nicely and told you to find a sensible, ordinary girl who'd appreciate your attentions. I didn't expect this. Murder!"

He hung his head. "I love you, Jasmine. I've never felt this way about anyone. When you ditched me and said you didn't want me, it broke my heart. I had to convince you we were perfect for each other."

"By killing my other boyfriends?" She stuck her hands on her hips. "Who were you going after next?"

"No one! I promise. I thought... I thought you'd need a shoulder to cry on after Spike died. You'd realize dating guys like that only ever led to heartbreak. It would make you come back to me."

Jasmine was quiet for a few seconds. "I don't know whether to be appalled or flattered."

"Be appalled," I said. "Killing someone to get your attention will never end well."

The door to the hospital room slammed open, and Billy appeared.

Jasmine glared at him. "Is he involved, too?"

"When I heard you'd been arrested for Spike's murder, it made me sick. I couldn't stand the thought of you being behind bars." Billy's face was red, and he was sweating. "Babe, you're innocent."

Jasmine tilted her head, then she giggled. "You're so cute. The Magic Council knows it wasn't me. You ran all this way to save me?"

Billy nodded as he strode closer. "Are you sure you're not getting charged?" His gaze cut to Olympus. "Jasmine was with me when Spike was killed. I didn't leave Witch Haven with Grinder that night. I was right here, with my woman."

Jasmine blinked rapidly, then sighed. "Sweetie, you're doing this to protect me?"

"I'm sorry we argued about something so dumb." Billy cupped Jasmine's face. "You get me so hot under the collar when you talk about other guys, but I want nothing bad to happen to you. I love you."

Her expression softened, and she wrapped her arms around Billy's neck. "You're such a sweet thing. I love you, too, in my own way."

Charlie jigged up and down in his bed, bright spots of color on his cheeks. "You see what I have to put up with? One guy is never enough for you. That's why you had to be stopped. You're a hateful creature. I take it back. I don't love you. I hate you!"

Jasmine turned away from Billy. "I'm living my best life, and I have no regrets." She glanced at me. "How did you figure out Charlie killed Spike?"

"This guy is the killer?" The disbelief was clear in Billy's tone.

Jasmine patted his arm. "I'll tell you everything later, sweetie."

"Charlie used an ice dart to deliver the poison. He swallowed some of that poison by mistake," I said.

A snort of surprise shot out of Jasmine. "Revenge medicine doesn't taste so yummy, does it?" She looked at me and Olympus. "Since I'm innocent, can we leave? I want to celebrate with my guy. I'm a free witch."

"You'll be sorry," Charlie said. "I won't forget this."

"That's enough." Olympus placed a restraining hand on Charlie's shoulder as he feebly tried to get out of bed. "Jasmine, Billy, you're free to go."

"What about me?" Charlie sounded pathetic as the love birds vanished. "I'm dying. Help me!"

"The doctor knows why you're sick, and you'll get the appropriate treatment," I said.

Olympus nodded. "And after you've recovered, you'll be charged with murder."

***

I stood at the base of the Christmas tree in the center of Witch Haven. Indigo, Olympus, Monty, all the spider shifters, Dylan included, and Billy and Jasmine were with me.

The day was bright, and fresh snow had fallen on Christmas Eve, making the village look untouched by the tragedy of the recent murder.

As a group, the spider shifters headed to the tree. They danced up it, weaving more webbing. It glowed and sparkled the same deep red as Spike's hair.

I headed to the highest point on the tree and weaved a bright red star to match the one Spike had on his leather jacket.

Jasmine stepped forward and placed a beautiful mistletoe wreath underneath the tree and then grabbed hold of Billy's hand.

"Spike only lived here a short time." I headed down the tree and stood in front of the group. "But he was a decent person. Everyone is welcome in Witch Haven, no matter how troubled their past was, providing they're looking to the future and aiming to be a better person."

Jasmine sniffed. "He was a good man. I cared for him."

"You care for too many people, babe." Billy slung an arm around her shoulders. "That's why that Charlie dude framed you."

"I'm glad the truth came out." Ginger headed down the tree, with Dylan beside him. "We've all learned lessons. I could be better at working with other magic users." He nodded at Olympus. "Dylan's learned a valuable lesson, too."

"To not munch on dead bodies?" Indigo said.

"Well, yes, that was an important lesson, too. But he's learning to be honest. If he'd told the truth from the beginning, this wouldn't have been such a mystery," Ginger said.

"I'm glad we could get this resolved before Christmas, so everyone feels safe in Witch Haven," Olympus said.

We all took a moment to remember Spike, our gazes on the beautiful glowing webbing that was a memorial to our fallen friend.

"I imagine Charlie's Christmas won't be merry and bright," Indigo whispered to Olympus.

"He's feeling better now he's received the antidote, but he'll see plenty of Christmases from behind bars for what he did. Love makes people do strange things."

"You should know." Indigo stood on her tiptoes and kissed his cheek, making him chuckle.

"It's time!" Nugget dashed over. He was followed by Monty and Russell, who pulled the sleigh behind them. It bounced and bobbed along the snow, covered in sparkle, glittering stars, and tinsel.

The group broke up, and Indigo grinned as she headed over to meet Nugget. "I'm so proud of all of you for doing this. Christmas wouldn't be the same if we didn't have the sleigh going door-to-door around the village."

"I'm getting both turkey legs for doing this total humiliation," Nugget grumbled.

"You're welcome to them." Indigo glanced over her shoulder. "Is everybody ready? It's sleigh time."

I joined them, and Indigo took a moment to touch me, Russell, and Nugget to supersize us so we could pull the sleigh with ease. Monty didn't need help in that department.

"Make sure you behave," Olympus said to Monty. "No fooling around. This is for a good cause. The gremlins are relying on donations to keep the reform school going so they can run new classes next year."

"I'll be on my best behavior." Monty puffed out his chest as Olympus checked his harness. "I won't snarl at anyone, I'll wag my tail, and I'll beg for more money if people are being cheap."

"Just be cool." Nugget slipped into his harness. "And make sure we all pull in the right direction. Don't do what you did when we practiced."

"What did Monty do?" I got myself into a harness and waited for Indigo to strap me in.

"If you'd bothered to come to any of the practices, you'd know Monty mixes up his left and right." Nugget dug his paws into the snow. "Everyone ready? The good cause awaits."

After more strap adjustments to make sure we were comfortable, we did a practice trot around the village green. Other than Monty getting confused a few times, and the snow being slippery and clumping under the sleigh, it was smooth going.

"That's as good as it's gonna get. Let's get this over with," Nugget grumbled. "And don't dawdle. The quicker we go, the quicker we get this indignity done."

Everyone stood back as we took off. We started at the village green, did another circuit, then headed along the main street.

Before we'd reached the first house, doors were opening, and people were coming out to see the brightly decorated sleigh.

Mystica Shade stopped us, an oversized Santa hat draped on her head, put a healthy donation in the bucket and then held out a heaped plateful of savory beef nibbles. "I heard you'd all stepped in to help. We're so grateful. These are for you."

"Treats?" Nugget sniffed the food. "These are all for us?"

"Oh, yes. It's a tradition we do every year for the reindeer. Every house they visit, they get fed. Didn't you know?"

Nugget's whiskers twitched. "I approve of this tradition." He scooped up a huge mouthful of the treats.

We quickly joined in, and within seconds, the plate was empty, and we'd moved on, after wishing Mystica happy holidays.

The owner of the next house made a donation and provided another plateful of incredible festive nibbles.

"If someone had told me about the food, I wouldn't have minded doing this," Nugget said around a mouthful of roasted goose pie.

"This is the best day ever." Monty had half a turkey leg sticking out of his mouth.

"Yeah, the reindeer can suck it," Nugget said. "I vote we do this every year."

I chuckled as Russell cawed his joy as more people came out with platefuls of delicious food and donations.

Witch Haven was safe again. Well, as safe as a village full of powerful magic users could be. A killer had been caught, and justice had been parceled up and delivered. My friends and family were happy, and my belly was full.

This village was such a magical place, but when you added in the kindness of Christmas, people's generosity, and the love of friends and family, this truly was the most magical time of year.

# Yuletide of the Witch

K.E. O'Connor

# Chapter 1

"Promise me Cloven Hoof won't have been burned to the ground by the time Christmas is over." Tempest Crypt wandered in front of me, inspecting the shelves full of last-minute gifts.

"How can you even think that would happen?" I trotted behind her, sniffing the lower shelves as I hunted for perfect presents for my pups.

Tempest turned and arched an eyebrow. "Wiggles, the last time they got excited, I had to replace two couches in the club, all the scatter cushions, and throw out a new duvet after they burned a hole through it. You've got to be tougher on them. They set light to everything."

I shrugged. "They're young and testing boundaries. You were the same at that age."

"My boundaries didn't include blasting fire every time I got agitated or overexcited. Well, not most of the time." Tempest turned over a snow globe and shook it.

I sniffed at a fake candy cane. I'd been Tempest's sort of familiar all my life. I'd started out as a regular mutt with no special abilities, trotting around and sniffing everything, barking at joggers, and hunting for treats under every chair. Then a literal run-in with a car and a blast of magic from Tempest and her equally powerful sister, Aurora Crypt, turned me into a unique hellhound.

I didn't object to the change, and it made life more interesting. Although being a father to four hellhound-poodle cross pups had never featured in my plans. Neither had being hit by a car, but that turned out better than fine. I was just sniffing my way through parental responsibilities slowly.

Tempest rested her hands on her hips. "I could spray everything I value with fire retardant. Would that stop them?"

I sauntered to the display of squeaky Christmas pudding dog toys and tried a few out. "That has no effect on hellhound fire. I'll make sure they behave."

"As much as I love the pups, Christmas will get crispy if you don't keep them under a firm paw."

"The only thing that'll be crispy is the turkey at the family dinner. Focus on that. And figuring out what you're getting Rhett for Christmas."

Tempest groaned. "He's so hard to buy for. Still, we've got time."

"Have you checked the calendar? It's the twenty-first of December. We've officially entered the zone of last-minute panic gift buying. How about a voucher and underwear?"

"Boring. We're not an old married couple."

"Don't all men like underwear as gifts?" I'd seen plenty of present buyers tossing packs of festive smalls into their shopping carts.

"Only because guys can't be bothered to buy underwear for themselves. It's such a boring thing to get someone, and we're not at the boring relationship stage yet. Hopefully, we never will be." Tempest flicked through a couple of festive spell books.

"You'd better figure out something fast, or he'll open an empty wrapped box come the big day." I chewed on another Christmas pudding toy. "And what about Aurora?"

Tempest yanked the toy away and stuffed it in her basket. "That's your gift sorted. And please stop. You're stressing me out by telling me how much I have to do. The club is wall-to-wall parties every night, so I have little time to shop."

"Then we need to focus while we're here." I considered getting my pups their own squeaky Christmas pudding toys, but dismissed the idea. I'd get a headache if they squeaked those things for hours. Although, they were kinda fun.

We continued browsing. Willow Tree Falls was only small, but we did Christmas in style. Three temporary Christmas stores had set up, selling everything from turkey tinsel to snow globe explosions. But I'd yet to find the perfect gifts for my pups.

And, if I was being honest, I was still adjusting to becoming a father. And before anyone raises a paw and tells me I should have been more responsible if I didn't want to be a parent, these things happen. Precautions fail, and I haven't regretted a second of welcoming my adorable pups into my life.

And since coparenting wasn't an issue, since my poodle princess had dumped the pups on me and left, I had free rein on how to raise them. Everything would work out.

If the worst happened during the festivities, and the club accidentally burned to the ground because of my pups' inability to control their powers, we were insured. I was certain of it. You could insure against acts of puppy hellhound misbehavior, couldn't you?

"How about this for Aurora?" Tempest held out a glittering pink shawl.

"She'll love anything you get her."

She dumped down the shawl. "That's the trouble with my sister. She never says what she really wants."

"Aurora wants everyone to be happy and have a good time. So long as we do that on Christmas Day, she won't care what she unwraps from under the tree." I wandered to the end of the aisle and lifted my ear as Puddles Lavern's shrill voice carried toward me.

"I'm telling you, they're all here."

"They can't be! They'll be too busy to take a break in the village." That was the store owner, Judi Bloomburg.

"I've seen him. He introduced himself. Such a charming man."

"It was someone dressed up to look like him. They all come out this time of year, putting on their cheap red suits and fake white beards. If you ask me, it's distasteful."

"This was the real deal. Santa Claus is in Willow Tree Falls! And he's not alone. The Christmas Fairy is here, too."

My ear flicked up. The big guy was visiting our little corner of magical paradise?

"Why? What brings him and the Christmas Fairy here?" Judi said.

I wandered closer, my interest piqued. I always turned into a big pup around Christmas. Maybe it was the delicious food that got me excited, but there was something magical about this time of year. And if Santa Claus and the Christmas Fairy were hanging out here, I'd fix a meeting and take my pups with me. They'd love to see them.

"Whatever they're doing, it must be something big. Maybe a new deal on a Christmas range? You know Santa Claus. His face gets everywhere. And he just got that huge sponsorship deal with Delightful Diamonds. Have you seen the ads?" Puddles said.

"I'm not a fan of those sponsorships," Judi said. "Besides, isn't it the Christmas Fairy's job to make everything sparkle? She should have gotten the diamond deal."

"Why can't they both do it?" Puddles said. "He's got such a wonderful smile. When we met, he told me to call him Sandy. He's such a handsome man."

"If you like beards."

Puddles sniffed. "There's nothing wrong with a decently groomed beard."

"Hey! Who are you listening to?" Tempest had tiptoed up behind me.

"Puddles and Judi reckon Santa Claus and the Christmas Fairy are here," I said.

"Yeah, right. Why come here?" Tempest grabbed a tree star off the shelf and looked it over.

"Beats me. I intend to find out if they are here, though. I could get an exclusive meeting with Santa Claus and take the pups. They could sit on his knee and tell him what they want for Christmas. I'll listen in, then know what to get them to make Christmas Day perfect."

"They'd run around causing chaos and singe his beard. Keep them away from Santa. He's got enough on his plate without hellhound-poodle pups lighting up the sleigh."

"They'll behave. I've already told them the Yuletide Witch will be after them if they're not on their best behavior until Christmas."

"How's that working out?"

"Have you had anything catch fire today?"

"Not so far, but there's still time. You should have extended that warning to the New Year, then we could all get some peace and goodwill." Tempest scratched between my ears. As much as she complained about my pups, she loved them as much as I did.

"I miss the old ways," I said. "Like Celebrating Gyrla."

"And her cat?"

"Not the cat. Cats have been worshipped for far too long. But Gyrla could give me tips on dealing with pups."

"Wiggles! She took the bad kids and tossed them into her cauldron. You want that to happen to the pups?"

I huffed out a smoky breath. "Okay, maybe we won't celebrate her or her dumb cat. How about the goblin offerings? You know, the warty guys who sneak around plotting the end of the world if they don't get enough festive treats. We should do something special for them."

"Should it be something food related?"

"That's the perfect idea. We should buy extra food for the goblins."

"And if they don't show, you'll eat it?"

I shrugged. "You wouldn't want it to go to waste."

Tempest laughed. "It always comes down to treats with you. You only want people to leave out goblin offerings, so you get to steal them."

"Not steal! Never steal. Just taste for quality, so the goblins don't get angry and destroy the world." I wandered along the aisle, losing interest in Puddles and Judi as their gossip shifted to another villager. "And we must celebrate the Winter Werewolf, so he doesn't stalk us next year."

"Yep. We can't have that happening."

I glanced up at her. "You don't believe in the old ways?"

"I didn't say that. The old traditions ground people so they don't get lost in all this tinsel and glitter." Tempest twanged a piece of tinsel. "It's easy to forget Christmas has a dark side. But so long as the traditions involve a feast, I'll celebrate anything."

"Happy to go along with that. And I intend to enjoy everything on offer." That was one thing I had no problem with during this season. All the treats. Everywhere I went, people left delicious mince pies, roast meat sandwiches, puffed pastry delights, and cinnamon sugar cookies unattended. It was rude not to sample the goodies.

Tempest glanced out the window. "It's snowing again. Come on. This is a lost cause. Let's get out of here. I've got three parties at the club tonight, so I need to make sure everything is on track."

"It will be. Merrie will have everything in hand." I inspected some small, brightly colored toy parrots on a shelf. "What do these do?"

"Dunderheaded dog. What do these do?" A parrot mimicked back at me.

Tempest crouched and grinned. "They must have a recording device in them." She tapped a parrot on the head.

"They must have a recording device in them," the parrot said. "Of course we do, idiot witch."

"Huh! They're rude recording parrots," I said.

"Huh! They're rude recording parrots. Have you got a brain inside that fur?"

Tempest stood and took a step back. "Let's leave them here. We don't need parrots cussing the customers."

I shook my head. "The pups will love them. I'm getting them one each. They'll have so much fun being rude to each other."

Tempest rolled her eyes to the ceiling. "They need no more encouragement to be sassy."

"It'll be good for them to get sassed back. I'm getting them. Is there anything you want?"

Tempest held out a basket for me to sweep four parrots into. "I'm shopped out. I'll try again tomorrow."

"What about that sparkling shawl for Aurora?" We walked to the counter and queued to pay.

"It's on the maybe list. Not that she needs more clothes."

Once Tempest paid for my presents, after all, I had no pockets so never carried money, we headed into the early evening gloom. There was a light layer of snow on the ground, and more flakes gently drifted in the frigid air.

Tempest flipped up her collar. "They said it would be a white Christmas."

I blasted a jet of flames to melt the snow. "It doesn't bother me."

"It does me. Let's hustle back to the club before I freeze."

We'd only gone a few steps before two familiar, white fluffy shapes shot past, holding an angel tree topper decoration between them.

"Err... Wiggles, shouldn't that be on the Angel Force tree?" Tempest watched my pups slip and slide through the snow as they yanked apart a once beautiful tree topper that had graced the glorious tree outside the front of Angel Force.

I tossed the bag containing the parrots at her. "Look after these. I need to deal with my misbehaving infants."

Tempest laughed as I dashed after my pups. She'd seen me in this situation plenty of times. My pups tested the limits every day, often blasting through the boundaries I set. But they were young and full of curiosity, so I never scolded them too much.

I skidded around the corner. "Shade! Ghost! Stop that this instant. You should be inside, putting paw prints on Christmas cards. What are you doing with that angel topper?"

Shade turned, wagged his adorable stubby tail at me, then tossed the tree topper in the air.

Ghost blasted out flames, and the angel exploded in a sparkle of orange.

I cringed at the brightness. My pups were awesomely powerful, but they often directed that power into the wrong missions.

If I couldn't get them under control and conceal this misbehavior from the angels, I'd spend Christmas at the cells, visiting them.

# Chapter 2

"Is that our tree topper?" Dazielle, head of the local branch of Angel Force, strode over as I appeared in her open-plan office the next morning with evidence of my pups misbehavior in my mouth.

I spat out the burned tree topper. "I can explain."

She glowered down at me. Dazielle was an enormous angel, standing at over seven feet tall and with a much larger wingspan. And most of those powerful wings were extended to display her displeasure.

"That tree topper is over a hundred years old. It was an antique. Why did you set fire to it?"

"I... It was an accident. I'll replace it."

"Antiques can't be replaced." Her wings fluttered behind her, then she sighed. "But I have more important things to worry about. Christmas is a crazy time. As much as it brings out the best in people, everyone else loses their mind. The cells are full to bursting, and we've been getting messages all morning about infractions of the law."

"I'll just leave that there and go. Don't want to get in the way." I inched backward toward the exit.

Dazielle pursed her lips. "This is too much, Wiggles. I'm disappointed in you."

"I'm disappointed in myself." Better she thought I'd done this than my pups, or they'd go on her naughty list.

After reprimanding my pups for stealing the tree topper over a breakfast of maple bacon and mince pies, then setting them the task of finishing their family Christmas cards, I'd needed to reveal what happened to the tree topper. Ghost and Shade hadn't been discreet with their snatch, tear, and explode mission, so I had to minimize the damage.

Dazielle waved a hand at me. "Get out of here. I'll deal with you later, when I can think of a suitable punishment." She turned and strode away to a group of anxious angels waiting for their instructions.

Dominic, my favorite, half-witted handsome angel, dashed over, scooped up the charred tree topper, and ushered me out of the office. "I thought I'd get you out quickly, in case Dazielle changes her mind and charges you with tree topper destruction."

"What's up with her?" I snagged a lone cinnamon pecan cookie off a plate as I hurried along. "She seems distracted."

"You had a lucky break this morning." Dominic eased open the main doors, and we stepped into freshly fallen snow. "She's dealing with the big Christmas honchos coming to Willow Tree Falls. It's so exciting!"

"I heard Santa Claus and the Christmas Fairy were in the village. What are they doing here?" I licked cookie crumbs off my whiskers.

Dominic briefly inspected the tree topper angel and then placed her in the nearest trash container. "No clue, but it's making Dazielle tense. I reckon it's something top secret. They're using a room here for their meetings. And it's not just them. The Grinch, the Yuletide Witch, and the Winter Werewolf have been stopping by."

"Huh! Must be something important. We should go find them, see what they have to tell us."

"Not me. I've got a pile of cases to investigate. Everyone's gone Christmas crazy. I've already been out to break up a fight between a dozen old ladies who wanted the last ham. Blood got spilled, and clothes were torn. One of them even jumped me when I asked her to stop cussing. She tugged my wing. It's still sore."

"I'd fight anyone for the last ham, too. I'll go take a peek at the meeting if they're here, see if I can get an audience with Santa."

"Wiggles, don't poke around. The Yuletide Witch is spikier than holly. She's one scary lady." Dominic fished in his pockets and brought out a paper bag of Christmas candy. He offered me one, which I happily took. "Christmas is a balancing act to ensure the old and new traditions don't overwhelm each other."

"Is that what they're here for? Something is out of balance?"

He shrugged. "Maybe. I'm not kept in the loop on the important stuff. I just deal with the salty old ladies."

"I want my pups to have an audience with the big guy. They'll love him."

Dominic grinned. "I expect they have their stockings hung, waiting for all their gifts."

"They've been up since the first day of December. Every morning, they look in them to see if anything has arrived. It's adorable."

"I love the Christmas festivities. You'll have so much fun with your pups."

"So long as they behave, which seems unlikely. We're going to the Crypt household for lunch, and then having party games in the cemetery. Nothing beats Christmas games over the demon prison. They hate to hear anyone having fun."

The Crypt witches had been in charge of the largest demon prison since time began, but no one would know there were thousands of imprisoned demons under my paws unless I told them.

Dominic stubbed the toe of his white boot in the snow. "Sounds amazing. Will you be doing any old Christmas traditions?"

"Always. We're having a tree lighting ceremony, singing carols, assigning the lady of misrule, and of course, it'll be nonstop feasting. It's the perfect chance to overindulge. Well, any time is the perfect time, but no one will complain if I eat until I have to be rolled home."

He gently sighed. "I'm having a quiet Christmas. Just me."

My tail stiffened. "No other angels? Won't that be boring?"

Dominic shrugged and looked away. "I don't mind. Work's busy, so I'll be grateful for a quiet day. Just me, a meal for one, and Christmas music. Maybe I'll take a walk in the snow. Throw snowballs at a wall. That kind of thing."

Dominic was an adorably dumb angel and often helped me and Tempest when we freelanced for Angel Force. "If you want company, we can squeeze another chair around the table."

His head shot up, and his brilliant blue eyes sparkled. "You want me to spend Christmas Day with you?"

"Sure. If you can handle a bunch of noisy, cackling witches. But watch out for Granny Dottie. When she's had a few deluxe cauldron schnapps, always homemade and triple strength, she'll insist you dance with her. And she'll want a few kisses under the mistletoe."

Dominic's cheeks flushed. "I'd love to join you."

"And fair warning, my pups will be there. You could get your wings singed."

"I don't mind. And your pups are cute. Shall I bring something? I could make Christmas Angel Delight. It's my specialty. I add plum jelly and mulled spiced apples."

"Bring what you like. The more food, the merrier."

"I should get gifts for everyone, too." Dominic paced through the snow, a smile on his face.

"Don't worry about gifts. Just bring your charming self and a few bottles of something strong."

Dominic drew in a breath just as the main door opened, and Dazielle appeared. "What are you doing out here? And why are you still here?" She jabbed a finger at me.

"We're making plans for Christmas," Dominic said. "Remember, I told you I was on my own this year? Well, the Crypt witches want me to spend the whole day with them."

"Lunch. You can come for lunch." Dominic's perpetual chirpiness might rub people the wrong way if he overstayed his welcome. All the Crypt witches had an edge. Even smiley, blonde Aurora.

"I'll come all day. I can help with the food. Whatever you like. I can't wait."

"Get inside! These cases won't solve themselves. And you! Stop loitering, or I'll sling you in a cell," Dazielle said.

"There's no room. The cells are overflowing. You told me that."

Dazielle shooed me away. "I can find space for an irritating, smelly hound. Leave. Dominic, you're with me." She turned and strode away.

Dominic hurried after her. "I'll have a think about what to bring."

I turned and ambled away, chuckling to myself. Nothing said Christmas more than a stressed-out angel.

※※※※※ ※※※※※

It was the early hours of the next morning, December twenty-second, for those of you worrying about

242

Tempest's lack of gift-buying focus, and Cloven Hoof was emptying of Christmas revelers. Everyone was drunk, happy, and had sore feet from dancing too much.

Tempest was firmly waving away people who tried to embrace her and wish her a Merry Christmas. My witch wasn't a hugger. I stood by her side, being the perfect hellhound guard dog.

Not that Tempest needed me to guard her. If anyone got out of hand, our faithful bouncer, Suki, the enormous wood nymph, stood on the other side of the door, a stern expression on her face. It was all an act. Suki was the sweetest, softest wood nymph I'd met, so long as you didn't wrong her or her friends. And the silver tinsel wrapped around her neck offset the sternness.

"I'll take a final look around, make sure no one has passed out in a snow drift, then check on the pups," I said.

Tempest nodded, her attention on a group of tipsy witches who staggered past a little too close for comfort.

I wandered into the snow, looking for somewhere suitable to do my business for the night. I was sniffing behind a pile of logs, when a flash lit the darkness, and a wave of warm magic flooded over me, rippling through the snow and shaking the trees.

With one paw in the air, I lifted my nose. That didn't feel like an early gift from Santa Claus. The magic had an icky vibe and made my eyes roll back in my head.

"What was that?" Tempest stood by the door, staring into the night.

"No idea." I wasn't certain where the magic had come from, but it seemed focused by the Christmas tree outside the Angel Force building.

As I trotted toward the tree, four worryingly familiar shapes appeared out of the darkness. My pups stood around a hole in front of the tree.

I raced toward them. "What are you doing out here? You should be in bed. Did you cause that magic?"

"No, papa. We were here when it happened, though." Arcane turned his red-rimmed eyes to me.

I shook my head. They were always sneaking out. "Get home, instantly. It's not safe out here."

Nightmare shook his head. "But papa—"

"No arguing. The Christmas monsters are out at this time of night. If they spot four misbehaving hellhound pups, there'll be no Christmas gifts for any of you."

"We didn't do it, though. It was someone else," Shade yipped.

"We'll be talking about what you did and didn't do back home. Now, move."

"But ... the body." Ghost raised a paw.

"What body?" I attempted to hustle my pups away from the hole, but none of them would budge.

"The one down there." He jabbed his paw at the hole.

I squinted in the darkness, then huffed out a surprised breath as the outline of two legs appeared, surrounded by shards of glass. "Move away! Move away!" I finally got my pups back a few steps. "What happened? Who do those legs belong to?"

"We don't know. We just followed him. He picked up a glowing ball, and it went boom," Arcane said.

"Tempest!" I yelled. "Get over here."

She was already making her way toward the tree, but broke into a jog when she heard the panic in my voice. "What's the matter? What are the pups doing here?"

"Take a look." I shielded the gruesome view from the pups, even though it was too late and they'd already seen the body.

Tempest jumped into the hole and crouched. "I don't recognize him."

"He must have something to do with Christmas. Look at his sparkly clothes," Ghost said. "Auntie Tempest, what happened? Did a demon get him?"

"Tempest, I need you to take the pups home. They can't be here," I said.

She glanced up at me, then nodded. "Sure. Come on, you four."

"We want to stay with the body!" Arcane danced out of her reach.

"No arguing. Let's move." Tempest hopped out of the hole, grabbed them in a squirming bundle of smoke and fur, and puffed out a breath. "I'll let the angels know. They must have felt the magic blast, too, so they're probably figuring things out."

"We want to stay," Nightmare whined.

Shade almost got free from Tempest's arms. "Don't take us home."

"Go with Auntie Tempest," I said. "She has truffle bones with a pig's fat glaze in the fridge."

The pups stopped complaining at the mention of treats. They were just like me. Big appetites, big hearts, and a naughty streak.

I waited until Tempest had successfully removed my pups from the scene, and then clambered into the hole. There was no mistaking the red and green suit worn by the winter elf. He was small, and his clothing was threaded with sparkles that glistened in the moonlight.

I knew better than to touch the body, but I sniffed around. There were no signs of life. I inspected the shards of glass. There weren't many, so they could have come from a glass bauble from the tree.

What caused the explosion? Whatever it was, it must have been powerful magic to kill this elf. If this was one of Santa Claus's helpers, they'd have been an advanced magic user. Hard to kill.

The ground shook as Dazielle and Dominic landed in the snow and strode toward me.

"Tempest said there'd been an incident?" Dominic's gaze flashed around the scene, and his eyebrows rose.

"That's Figgy Jigglejoy!" Dazielle stared at the body. "He was Santa Claus's right-hand elf."

"You know him?" I said.

"We've been introduced." Dazielle fluttered her wings. "What happened? Tempest had your pups with her when we saw her. They'd better not be involved."

"I guarantee they're not. But they found him. Look at the shards of glass. Maybe an enchanted bauble got him." I didn't want Dazielle to get any dumb ideas and think my innocent pups were involved.

Dominic hunted around the scene, his face wrinkled as he concentrated. "Something powerful exploded. We felt it in Angel Force. There was a light, then a wave of magic hit."

"That's what I felt, too," I said. "I was outside the club with Tempest when it happened."

Dazielle strode around, shaking her head and muttering. "Dominic, secure the scene. Wiggles, I'll speak to you later."

I was happy not to hang around. I wanted to get back to my pups and make sure they were okay.

I dashed back to the apartment to find Tempest unsuccessfully getting the pups into their baskets.

She turned as I hurried in. "They want to talk to you."

"Are you all okay? You didn't get hurt in the explosion?"

"No! And it was amazing. We were following the sparkly elf when he picked up a glowing bauble." Shade wriggled around, his curly tan and white fur all fluffy.

"Let me tell!" Arcane barged into Shade and tumbled him out of his basket. "That's when everything got bright and went boom!"

"Then he was dead," Nightmare said. "He fell over and grunted."

"It was like bonfire night with all the whizzes, bangs, and spinners." Ghost bounded over and licked my nose.

Tempest exchanged a worried look with me. "Did you see who left the bauble the elf picked up?"

"It was already there when he grabbed it."

"His name was Figgy," I said.

"He saw it and wanted to play with it." Shade did a zoomie around the room. "I did, too."

I shuddered. My pups had been too close to danger. If any of them had touched that bauble...

"Figgy picked up the bauble?" I grabbed Shade and pinned him in the basket to calm him.

"Grabbed it right up." Shade submitted to me. "As soon as he touched it, that's when it went bang."

I sniffed my pups to reassure myself they weren't hurt, then gave them all a tongue bath. "You've had an exciting night. But we'll be having words in the morning about you sneaking out."

"If we hadn't snuck out, we'd never have seen the explosion," Arcane said. "Best night."

I kept debating with my pups about not sneaking off, but they were too excited to pay attention. After half an hour of grooming and reading them bedtime stories, they finally settled.

I eased the bedroom door shut and joined Tempest in the living room. She sat on the couch with a mug of coffee in her hand.

"What do Angel Force think happened?" she said as I joined her.

"They weren't thinking much. Dazielle was stressing, and Dominic was pacing and trying to work things out. Dazielle identified the victim as Figgy Jigglejoy. Apparently, he was Santa's right-hand elf."

"Any clue what happened?"

"Nope. It's weird. Why would someone want to blow up Santa's helper?"

She shook her head. "Santa's helper? No clue. At least your pups are more excited than scared about finding a body."

"It's rattled them more than they're letting on. They forgot to ask about Santa Claus before going to sleep."

Tempest glanced at me. "Why would they do that?"

"It's all they've been doing since October. Every morning, they ask when he's coming, if they can write him another letter, and how many presents he'll leave. They were even worried about us moving back here while Rhett gets the new kitchen installed. They figured Santa wouldn't find them while we stayed above the club."

Tempest sipped her coffee. "I'm just glad I kept this place as a base. I love living with Rhett, and the extra room is great now we have the pups, but when he grinds metal, or announces he's re-fitting a bathroom, I'm outta there."

"Same here. And where you go, I go." I glanced at the closed bedroom door. "I reassured the pups Santa and his reindeer would know where to come when it was time for all the gifts."

"Your pups are cute, but they're even weirder than you."

"They take after their mother."

"They must." Tempest glanced around the apartment, a puzzled look on her face as she took in the small, glowing tree in the corner and the stockings hung over the fireplace. "I need to clean this place up. I'll do it in the morning."

The apartment was its usual comfortable, chaotic self, with added sparkle to make it feel homey. "You can clean if you like. Tomorrow, I need to see if the angels have figured out what happened to Figgy."

Then I could focus on getting Christmas back on track so my pups and my extended witch family would have a perfect day.

# Chapter 3

After checking to make sure my misbehaving pups were still asleep, I moseyed into the kitchen and hunted for breakfast. Tempest usually left something out for me when she wasn't around because I was always hungry when I woke. But my bowl was empty. And there was no sign of her.

I nosed open the door and wandered down the stairs and into the club.

"We need to get that tree out of here. And the rest of the stuff needs to go, too." Tempest stood in her orange and black pumpkin print pajamas, her hands on her hips as she instructed her bleary-eyed staff to take down the Christmas decorations.

"What's going on?" I said. "Why is everyone here so early?"

"I called them in. Don't worry, they're getting double time for their trouble. I need to fix things up for tonight." Tempest crouched and scratched my belly as I rolled on the floor beside her. "It looks weird in here. It'll put off the customers."

"Where are you putting the tree? It goes perfectly in the corner. No one can bump into it while they're dancing."

"None of this stuff fits. And it'll only get dusty if it stays up any longer. It's time for a change."

I exposed more of my belly to be rubbed. "Whatever you say. It's your club. We're getting more decorations, though, aren't we?"

"Why bother? I was thinking this place needed freshening up, so we need to get rid of anything nonessential."

"Not until the New Year, though. You've been saying for weeks how busy you are. Do the refreshing then."

"When is this place not busy?" Tempest grinned. "I guess it's a compliment. I may even close next week to get it sorted."

She had to be joking. Christmas and New Year were our busiest times. I rolled onto my paws and shook out my fur. "That won't look good for the bottom line."

Tempest arched an eyebrow at me. "Since when have you been my business accountant?"

I tilted my head. "It must be the lack of breakfast in my bowl making me say weird things. I always get light headed when hungry."

"Sorry, I got distracted. I keep thinking about plans for this place. Let's go up and get you fed, shall we?"

Before we headed up the stairs, my pups bounded down them, fighting playfully with each other and yipping.

"Do we get to see more fireworks today?" Shade said.

"No. Last night was a one-off," I said. "Get back upstairs. You're all grounded."

After some more bungling around, the pups hightailed it up the stairs. They knew they wouldn't get away with breaking curfew.

"What happened last night must be playing on their minds," Tempest whispered. "They're tough little guys, though. Just be gentle with them for a few days."

"Of course." I was glad my pups didn't seem badly affected by what they'd discovered. But I'd do the responsible thing and talk to them. Even I remembered finding my first dead body, and that was years ago. It always stayed with you.

Once Tempest had brewed coffee, bowls were emptied of delicious meaty treats, and she'd eaten a croissant, we all sat on the couch.

Tempest leaned back, mug in hand, and let me do my parental duties.

"Did you all sleep well?" I said. "No nightmares?"

"Yeah. Although I had loads of dreams about fireworks." Arcane scratched behind one ear.

Nightmare puffed smoke at him. "Me too. My dreams were better than yours."

"Were not! Mine had Catherine wheels."

"Mine had enormous rockets that blew everything up."

I thumped my tail on the couch to get their attention. "You all saw something unpleasant last night. If you feel upset or anxious, you can talk to me or Auntie Tempest. We're here for you."

My pups wriggled around. None of them looked concerned.

"We didn't really see him," Shade finally said.

Ghost nodded. "I mean, he grabbed that exploding thing, but it happened super fast."

"Yeah. Then he fell into the tree, and slid into the hole the ball made when it went boom," Arcane said.

Shade wagged his tail. "It was a huge boom! So bright!"

I grimaced. "Still, that wasn't a nice thing to see."

"I'm telling everyone!" Nightmare hopped up and bounced on his paws.

"Maybe don't gossip about the dead person," Tempest said. "The angels won't be happy if they hear you've been talking about an active investigation."

Shade poked out his tongue. "The angels can suck it."

"Angel Force do their best," I said. "There's no need to be mean about them."

"You and Auntie Tempest say they're useless. You always complain about them."

"Because we're grown-ups, and we're allowed to complain." I glanced at Tempest. We needed to be more discreet when cussing Angel Force's incompetence.

"Can't we at least tell Great Granny Dottie?" Arcane raised a paw and whined. "She'd love to hear all about it."

"You can tell her on the big day, when we're all together," I said.

"When's that happening?" Shade cocked his head, his cute little white ears pricked.

"Soon. You must all be excited."

The pups barged into each other, and a rapid bout of play fighting and snarling ensued.

Tempest grabbed the cushions as tiny fireballs shot out of my pups' mouths. "Wiggles! Get them under control. I'm not shelling out for more throws and pillows."

I pulled apart my pups. "Behave, or you know what happens."

Ghost blew a smoke ring. "Naughty step?"

"No squeaky balls?" Arcane whacked Ghost with one paw.

"The Winter Werewolf will come for you. He targets badly behaved puppies this time of year."

"Winter Werewolf?" Nightmare looked confused. "Who's that?"

I'd been telling them about the creepy, supernatural Christmas Werewolf almost every night to get them to behave. It occasionally worked.

"I'd forgotten I'd put stuff up in here, too." Tempest placed her mug down and grabbed a strand of tinsel. "I don't know what I was thinking."

"You're not taking it all down, are you?" I said. "When you said you wanted to freshen up the club, I didn't think you meant the apartment, too."

"Why not? Get it all over and done with." She stood and yanked down more tinsel.

The pups joined in, thinking it was a game, and within a few minutes, there was a bundle of tinsel on the floor, along with their discarded stockings.

I was surprised they were so eager to get rid of their stockings. But they seemed more interested in the exploding bauble and telling everyone about seeing a body than the upcoming festivities. It took little to distract my boys.

Since the conversation was over, I left the pups with Tempest, who seemed determined to take down anything Christmas related, left the apartment, and headed to Angel Force.

Dominic stood by the front door as I arrived. "Morning, Wiggles. No Tempest?"

"She's on pup-sitting duty. And focused on revamping the club. She's taking down the decorations. Not sure what's gotten into her."

"Maybe it's because the New Year is almost here. People like to make changes and reinvent themselves. Not that Tempest needs to do that. She's perfect."

Even after all these years, and countless rejections, Dominic still held a tiny flame for my witch. "I guess. Although she's done nothing like this before. Tempest isn't a fan of change."

"We all change. Have you eaten?"

I was about to say yes, but then shook my head. "Not had the time."

"Come inside. It was my turn to get the breakfast pastries." He tapped a large white box he'd set on the ground.

I was always happy to have a second breakfast, especially when it involved pastries.

Dominic led me into the kitchen and set the bakery box on the table. Within seconds, angels had dashed in and stolen half the contents.

"Any news on Figgy?" I hopped onto a seat and grabbed three pastries before more greedy angels arrived.

Dominic hurried over, a coffee for himself and a bowl of water for me, which he set on the table. "I was here late doing a background check on him. Figgy Jigglejoy had a colorful past."

"Go on," I said around a mouthful of sticky maple bun.

"Figgy was a criminal. He'd served time, gotten arrested when he was eleven, and got caught almost every year doing something he shouldn't."

"You think someone from his past got revenge? Someone he'd wronged? Or another criminal who didn't want Figgy getting in his way?"

"They're all possibilities," Dominic said. "I've got a meeting scheduled with his probation worker in half an hour. She should give us leads on people who had problems with Figgy."

"What about family?"

"No family. They're dead. Figgy spent his life committing crime, then suddenly turned over a new leaf. After his last stretch inside, he got involved with a prison reform program. It seems he went through a big change, too."

"Sure. I've seen you guys ferrying criminals around as part of that scheme. Getting them working on community projects."

"It can be effective if they want to change. It worked for Figgy." Dominic leaned back in his seat as he ate a croissant. "He signed up to the program, got a support partner, and everything improved. Since then, he got his degree, volunteered at a refuge for homeless imps, and then landed a job working with Sandy."

"You mean Santa Claus?"

"Um... Sure. When I spoke to him, he said everyone calls him Sandy. He's dropping by soon. I thought he'd have useful information about Figgy. Maybe give us a few leads on who'd want him dead."

"Don't discount Sandy as a suspect. Maybe they argued," I said. "Jolly old Sandy decided he didn't want to reform a criminal anymore. Could Figgy have concealed his past from Sandy, and he got found out?"

"No. Sandy is a fan of the reform program. He often takes in successful candidates and helps them progress their careers."

"It could be Figgy's old habits returned. Maybe he took something he shouldn't from Sandy. He got found out, and this was the result."

"I don't think Sandy has anything to do with this," Dominic said. "He's a decent guy."

"Even Mr. Christmas has an off day."

"Um ... that's not his surname," Dominic said.

The kitchen door opened, and an angel poked her head around the side. "There's someone here to see you. He says his name is Sandy. And he's wearing a wonderful red suit."

"Thanks. Take him into interview room one, please." Dominic quickly finished his croissant and coffee. "Let's see what we can find out about Figgy."

"Mind if I sit in?"

"Fine by me. I figured you'd be interested since your pups were at the scene. How are they doing?" Dominic headed out of the kitchen, and I followed him.

"They're resilient. They keep talking about the explosion and how it reminded them of fireworks."

"That's good. I wouldn't want them traumatized. What were they doing out so late?"

"Testing boundaries, as usual. Dazielle's not thinking they could be involved, is she?"

"No! Such adorable babies wouldn't have anything to do with this." Dominic glanced down at me. "Right?"

"One hundred percent right. My pups may have the occasional bout of misbehavior, but they'd never kill a winter elf. Or any elf. Or anything."

We headed into the interview room to discover Santa Claus sitting at a small table. His designer suit had a faint sparkle on the fabric, and his white beard was neatly trimmed and glistened. He was the Hollywood version of Santa Claus, all perfect lines and clever tailoring. And there wasn't a wobbly belly in sight. Santa Claus did things stylishly these days.

Personally, I preferred old school Santa, with the straggly beard, wonky hat, and fondness for mince pies. Still, as Dominic said, things change.

Dominic shook Santa Claus's hand. "I appreciate you coming in at such short notice. This is Wiggles. He's sort of my partner in this case."

I greeted Santa Claus. "I doubt you have a minute to spare this time of year."

"I always make time for important things." His voice was warm and deep. "And Figgy was important to me. Almost like a son."

Dominic settled in a seat, and I hopped into the chair next to him. He ran through a few formalities, taking down Santa Claus's details, although he insisted we call him Sandy, and then we got started.

"I've been looking into Figgy's background," Dominic said. "He had a colorful past."

"Ah! He did. He had fascinating stories about that past, too."

"You were aware of everything he'd done?" I said.

"I insist on honesty with all members of my team. And, of course, I recruited Figgy from the prison reform program, so I had full details of his criminal activities."

"That must be tricky to balance with your work," I said.

Sandy tilted his head. "Why do you say that?"

"Maybe some households you visit don't want a criminal involved with their children."

Sandy's mouth turned down. "Perhaps not. But everyone deserves a second chance. They always get that with me. Even naughty children can become good."

"When was the last time you saw Figgy alive?" Dominic said.

Sandy pursed his lips. "Yesterday evening. We'd finished for the day, and everyone went off to do their own thing. That was around eight o'clock."

"What was he doing out so late?" I said. "It was the early hours of the morning."

"I couldn't tell you. My team is free to come and go as they please. Some of them are night owls."

"Was Figgy?" Dominic said.

"Not usually. He liked to get up early."

"You don't know why he went to the tree?"

"No. Maybe he couldn't sleep, so he went for a walk. We haven't been here long, and it always takes me a few days to adjust to a new place. Every bed feels different. Although Figgy hadn't said he was having trouble sleeping."

"If you don't mind me asking, where were you when you heard the news?" Dominic said.

"Of course not. I was in my room. It had been a long day."

"With Mrs. Claus?" I said.

"Mrs. ... no. I was alone." Sandy shifted in his seat. "Keep this between us, but I've been divorced for years. We just haven't updated the promotional material. Everyone likes to see me happy and with the love of my life. I can't risk falling out of favor with the public because my marriage failed."

"Of course. Sorry to hear that," Dominic said.

"Thank you. These things happen. People change. My work keeps me busy, so I'm not innocent in the failure."

"And what about your meetings with the rest of the winter superstars? How is that going?" I was curious to know why Santa Claus was in Willow Tree Falls.

His white eyebrows flashed up. "You know about that?"

"I've heard rumors. It's hardly a surprise when Santa Claus, the Christmas Fairy, the Yuletide Witch, the Grinch, and the Winter Werewolf show up in the same place. I hope there aren't any problems."

Sandy looked puzzled. "No, no problems. I often meet my colleagues to discuss future plans. It just so happened we chose Willow Tree Falls this year. I've been hearing such wonderful things about the place. And they're all true. I visited your stone circle and had a wonderful time. I'm going to the thermal spa next. I heard if you cover yourself in mud, it takes ten years off you."

Dominic chuckled. "It does. But you don't need help there."

Sandy preened under his praise. "You're kind. I must admit, I wonder if the white beard and hair are aging, though. I was considering dying them."

"No! They're your trademark. Along with the red suit, everyone knows who you are." Santa with a black beard, felt wrong, like he was going to the dark side.

"Hmmm. Perhaps you're right. We must consider brand recognition. I'll get my office to run a poll, see how the customers respond."

"Can you think of anyone who had a problem with Figgy?" Dominic said. "Anyone who wanted him dead?"

Sandy blinked several times. "This is a murder investigation?"

"Most likely. What did you think happened to him?" I said.

He stroked his pristine beard. "I assumed the magic went wrong, and Figgy touched something he shouldn't. Everyone knows Willow Tree Falls is a powerful place."

"It is. But someone put a nasty spell inside the bauble that killed Figgy. Why would they do that?" I said.

"I... I couldn't tell you. Some bad magic user showed up and caused trouble? The gremlins can be difficult this time of year, but I've never heard of them doing something so cruel." Sandy dabbed at his top lip. "Figgy was really killed?"

"It's early days in the investigation." Dominic glanced at me. "But it seems foul play was involved. Unless you know of any problem Figgy had with his magic. Could he have made a mistake?"

"Unlikely, but anything is possible." Sandy puffed out a breath. "I'm stunned. I can't think of anyone who'd want to hurt him. Ask everybody, and they'll tell you how amazing Figgy was. It was how he rose up the ranks so quickly. Normally, the recruits I take from the reform program remain at a lower level, but I spotted Figgy's potential. He worked with me for three years, and every year he got a promotion. I'll be lost without him. He was my go to elf. No, someone can't have done this to him."

"I think someone did," I said.

"Most likely, someone did," Dominic said.

I puffed out a smoky breath. "Sure. Most likely. And we intend to find out who."

"I'll have a think, but I can honestly say Figgy was popular and adored. You won't hear anyone say anything bad about him." Sandy sank back in his seat, color draining from his face. "I feel faint after this news."

Dominic sprang to his feet. "Do you need anything? Water? Fresh air?"

Sandy waved away his offers. "No, but thank you. I just need a minute to wrap my head around this."

Dominic returned to his seat, and we sat in silence while Sandy closed his eyes and breathed deeply. He had seemed shocked after discovering Figgy's death was no accident.

He finally opened his eyes. "I'm sorry, but I should go. Unless you need anything else from me. I need to tell the team what's going on. You will keep me informed? It makes me sick to my stomach to think someone would hurt my friend."

"Of course. And if you think of anyone who may have had a problem with Figgy, let us know. Anything could help," Dominic said.

"I will. But I'm not sure any information I have will be useful. As I said, everyone loved Figgy." Sandy nodded at me as he stood.

Dominic showed Santa Claus out and then returned to the room. "I didn't expect that. Sandy was shocked by the news Figgy could have been murdered. He almost fainted."

I puffed out another breath. "He's very smooth."

Dominic's eyebrows slowly rose. "You think Sandy's hiding something?"

"Maybe. We need to ask around. Find out what everyone else thought of Figgy. Everyone has enemies."

# Chapter 4

Three hours later, and after a conversation with Figgy's probation officer, and speaking to numerous people involved in Santa Claus's retinue, everyone told us the same thing. Figgy had been loved by all. He'd never hidden his criminal past, and willingly talked openly about it to anyone who was interested. He was a reformed character, and no one spoke a bad word about him.

Which was odd. Because nobody was perfect. Not even jolly old Santa Claus. But it seemed everyone thought Figgy was the ideal Christmas treat. They were sad he was gone, and shocked at the idea someone did this to him.

My stomach growled, so I did a circuit of the office, snaffling a few thoughtlessly abandoned sandwiches. I didn't spot any Christmas treats, though. Yesterday, there'd been icing-dusted pies, little chocolate yule logs, and I'd even grabbed a couple of turkey legs. The angels were hiding the best treats from me. Greedy angels.

Dominic appeared from the kitchen. "I don't know about you, but it feels like we've hit a dead end."

"There's something weird going on here." I looked around the office, still sniffing for Christmas food.

"Murder is always weird," Dominic said. "Although I'm wondering if Sandy had a point. Maybe this was a case of magic gone wrong."

"Figgy must have been a powerful magic user to become Sandy's right-hand elf. He'd know not to mess with something dangerous."

"Perhaps. I need to see if anything useful showed up from the initial examination of his body. You want to come with me?"

I lowered my nose. Dead bodies were never fun. "I should check on Tempest and the pups, make sure they haven't blown up the club. I'll catch up with you later." I headed outside, considering lunch options, when a shadow shifted in an alleyway close to the Angel Force building.

I sniffed the air and got a hint of wood smoke and coal. The shadow shifted again, and tattered black lace drifted in the frigid air. Long, gnarled fingers clutched the wall, and a thin witch with jet black hair inched out.

My eyes widened as I caught a whiff of ancient power. That must be the Yuletide Witch. Why was she lurking in the gloom? She was acting furtive, as if she didn't want to be seen. When someone behaved like that, it always caught my attention.

After a moment of skulking, she slid from the shadows and headed toward the woods. I followed.

She shuffled along, shoulders hunched, and her head down. But she moved fast, and it only took a few minutes to get to the edge of the trees.

She glanced over her shoulder, and I ducked out of her line of sight. Everyone knew the dark tales of the Yuletide Witch, and you didn't want her to pay you attention. Still, I was curious to know what she was up to.

I stepped into the icy gloom of the woods and looked around. She was almost out of sight, hurrying along as if she had a deadline to meet. I hung back, but made sure I could see where she headed.

The trees shivered as she moved past them, gently shaking snow off their bare branches. Every living thing was cautious of this witch. She represented the most primal side of Christmas, and her beliefs revolved around sacrifice and blood magic, taking life to bring forth something darker and twisted. There were few who celebrated her version of Christmas anymore. That was no bad thing. No one wanted bloodletting or bone worshipping ceremonies over the Christmas turkey and crackers.

A dry branch snapped under my paw. I froze at the same time as the Yuletide Witch, then ducked behind a tree. She didn't pause for long. She must have assumed it was a woodland creature scurrying away from her energy.

I hurried after her. Wherever she was going, it was deep in the woods, to a place where she wouldn't be seen. Few people were brave enough to venture into Willow Tree Falls woods alone. There were creatures that lived here who ate you first and asked no questions.

I blinked and looked around. She was gone. The shadows were deep in this part of the woods, but she couldn't have snuck off without me seeing which way she went.

A chill wrapped around my tail and flipped me over. The Yuletide Witch stood above me, her sharp teeth bared and her clawed hands pressed against a delicate part of my belly. "What creature dares to follow me?"

I puffed out smoke, not appreciating the icy chill sneaking up my tail and around my spine. "Hey. I'm Wiggles. I'm following you because you're sneaky. What are you doing?"

"Wiggles. Why the interest, tiny creature?" Her jagged nails raked my skin.

"In case you haven't heard, one of Santa Claus's helpers died last night. I'm helping Angel Force figure out who did it. Any comment?"

She clacked her pointed teeth. "Santa Claus?"

"Yeah, you know, jolly guy who gives presents to the well-behaved children on Christmas Eve. Ring any bells?"

Her forehead wrinkled. "I follow the old ways." She leaned down and sniffed me. "How tasty would you be?"

"I'd taste terrible. My smell reveals where my power comes from, and I didn't get here thanks to the angels. So, unless you're into rotten eggs, you wouldn't enjoy me, even if I was deep fried in butter and marinated in spices."

After a short pause, she chuckled. "You have no fear of me. Interesting. Is that because you're smart or foolish?"

"You get over the fear thing when it's almost impossible to die. I guess you must feel the same. How many centuries have you been around?" The cold seeped through me, but I'd be able to warm myself soon enough.

She hissed at me. "Long enough to know I deserve respect."

I was done being her plaything. I shook off her magic, flipped over, and growled. "You have to earn my respect. What do you know about Figgy Jigglejoy's murder?"

She flicked a hand, and ice shot out and surrounded me.

I blasted out flames to melt her magic. "I could do this all day. How about you?"

Her eyes widened. She tipped back her head and cackled. "Wonderful! It's so rare I meet an equal. I get bored with everyone cowering on their knees and begging me to save them."

"I only beg for treats. Have you got any of those?"

She cackled again. "What did you say your name was, remarkable creature?"

"Wiggles. I'm sort of familiar to Tempest Crypt. She's one of the witches who looks after the demon prison."

"Of course, you would be associated with the most powerful witch family within a thousand-mile radius. It makes sense you'd be her guardian."

"I'm kind of her guardian. It's a long story. But I'm looking into another story right now." I cocked my head. "Do you have a name, other than Yuletide Witch? It's kinda formal. It's like calling me Hellhound Pup."

"You may call me Quantum." She traced a finger through the air. "You want to know about the troubles facing the end of the year?"

"Maybe. If those troubles have anything to do with Figgy being killed."

She leaned forward, her icy breath gliding over me. "I'll let you in on a secret. This time of year is in serious trouble. Would you like to know why?"

"Sure. I mean, so long as it's not a long story. I was about to get lunch, I still have gifts to buy, and I need to check on my pups. If you want to give me the highlights, though, that would be great."

"May I tempt you with gingerbread and spiced hot chocolate? It comes with a twist." She tapped her overly long fingernails together and licked her lips.

"Sounds good. Do you have a place around here?"

Quantum snitched her nose. "You're impossible to scare. I love it. I'm using a cabin in the woods. This way." She turned and strode off, leaving behind a trail of ice, which I melted with my fire.

A few minutes later, we arrived at a tiny, moss-covered cabin. It didn't look like it had been used for years.

"A word of warning." She paused by the door. "Once you enter, you'll never see the world in quite the same way."

"Oh, I don't see it in the same way as most people. Did you know dogs only see certain colors? It's weird. I used to be an average dog, but magic turned me into a hellhound, so my vision is super screwy."

She huffed out a breath. "Then enter and enjoy."

I walked into an icy cold room. The only signs of Christmas decorations were dry twigs placed in bundles around the room and a holly sprig resting on a shelf.

"Mind if I light a fire?" I headed to the stacked fireplace and breathed on the wood until flames flickered high up the small chimney.

"Since you're my guest, I'll permit that, but I'm not a fan of heat." Quantum grimaced at the fire and inched away.

"Sure. You're all about the deep midwinter. I get it. It might cheer the place up a bit, though. You should add some tinsel, too."

"Tinsel? How interesting." She settled on a small wooden stool, clicked her fingers, and a plate of iced gingerbread appeared, along with a steaming mug of hot chocolate covered in squirty cream and chocolate sprinkles. "Help yourself. You'll find the effects enchanting."

"Thanks." I grabbed a chunk of gingerbread and swallowed it in one gulp. "You're not having any?"

She tilted her head from side to side. "I rarely eat. How do you feel?"

"It's not touched the sides. Mind if I have another?"

"Have as much as you need." Her smile was sharp as she watched me eat. "You have questions about Figgy?"

"Since meeting you, I've got loads of questions. Let's start with the dead elf, though. What can you tell me about him?"

"I knew him. Not well, but he supported Sandy's work."

"He was his right-hand elf. What did you think about Figgy?"

"He was rarely a concern of mine. He always seemed obedient to Sandy and happy to serve."

"You never argued with him?"

"I barely spoke to him."

"Did you see Figgy have problems with anyone?"

Quantum's gaze lifted to the ceiling as she considered my question. "From what I saw, everyone liked him. He seemed ... nice. The perfect companion for Sandy, I suppose. Sandy hates friction. But without it, life gets blunt."

"It makes sense Sandy wanted his chief assistant to be an asset and help ensure Christmas ran smoothly."

"Christmas?"

"Yeah. Isn't that why you're all here? You're involved in these hush-hush meetings being held at Angel Force."

"Eat more gingerbread."

I didn't argue with that command. After I'd eaten three chunks of gingerbread under Quantum's scrutiny, she sank into her seat. "Since you're still alive, I consider you worthy of knowing what's going on."

"Why wouldn't I be alive?"

Her gaze settled on the gingerbread, and she shrugged. "There is trouble in winter paradise. The big names are revolting. In both senses of the word. They've gotten greedy."

I eyed the empty plate. "Sandy and the others are taking a cut from Christmas?"

"Hmmm ... that I can't say. But they've lost their way. Sandy and the fairy are the worst." She sighed. "Big change is coming, and that saddens me. I love the sparkle and glitter around this time of year, and it brings me joy to see children happy. There's nothing more appealing than a chubby cheek to squeeze."

She probably squeezed them before tossing them into a cauldron to slow boil until tender. I glanced around Quantum's sparse rental. She hadn't bothered to bring the sparkle and glitter here. "Hey! I've got one of those. Well, four of them. I bought them for my pups as gifts."

Quantum glanced at the gaudy green and red parrot perched almost out of sight on a shelf. "It looked entertaining. I had to take out its magic pack, though. Too noisy and rude."

"They're great, aren't they? My pups love anything like that. Did you get it for your kid?"

"No, I have no children." She twirled her bony fingers in the air. "Although, I consider all children my own in a way. I value teaching them the true magic of winter."

"And the consequences of not following those values?" I snuffled crumbs off the plate.

"Every action has consequences."

"Including Sandy and his crew? You don't approve of the changes they're making?"

"I don't mind what they do, so long as it doesn't interfere with my traditions. More gingerbread?"

"Maybe one more slice." Another plate of treats appeared. "I don't want Christmas to change. And this year must be perfect for my pups. They're growing so fast. It won't be long before they consider themselves too old to unwrap gifts under the tree."

"You adorable little creature. There's no such thing as a perfect winter celebration. I've seen all too often this time of year brings fights, resentment, disappointment, and always gluttony." Her gaze rested on the plate.

"Well, I guess it does in some families. But I want my pups to be happy."

"I'm sure they will be. And don't get me wrong, I adore this time of year." Quantum clicked her long nails together. "I love extremes of anything, and enjoy absorbing the heightened emotions when things don't go to plan. It buoys me up. I can hibernate peacefully, knowing there'll be more of that energy the following year."

"You feed off people's negativity?"

"Everyone needs a food source, whether it's gingerbread or pain. You can't blame me. It's my role. There have to be checks and balances. Sandy and fairy bring the over-the-top enthusiasm, and I level things out with a little reality, much like the Grinch."

"I guess. We all have different shades of magic."

"And yours is wonderfully murky. Your power is intriguing. And immune to my ... talents."

"Thanks. It's pretty awesome. I have Tempest and her sister to thank for that."

"Don't underestimate yourself. If you didn't have the inner strength to evolve, you wouldn't have lived through those trials. You see, tough times improve us. Getting a lump of coal in your stocking forms character."

"Are the meetings tough? The ones about the Christmas crisis?"

She exposed sharp teeth. "So persistent. I'll answer, since I don't dislike you. I'd hoped they'd have solved their issues by now. But since a death has occurred, it seems someone stepped into violence. I'm curious whether it was Sandy or the fairy."

"You think one of them killed Figgy? His murder has to do with your meetings?"

"Who else? Figgy worked closely with Sandy, but he'd been speaking with the fairy over future plans. Twisted alliances form at pivotal moments of change."

"What about the Grinch or the wolf? Or you? Maybe you created a deal with Figgy that got him killed."

"Grinchy and the wolf are minor players in this situation." Quantum raised her eyebrows. "You could simply ask for my alibi if you consider me involved."

"I'll take it. Figgy died just after three in the morning. Where were you?"

"I work by the night clock, so I was awake. But I was with our negotiator, Gwendolyn Drach. We were at Angel Force, going over the details of the last meeting."

"You have a negotiator. Sounds serious."

"It is. Life-changing plans are forming. Check with Gwendolyn. She'll prove my innocence."

"I'll do that. And I'll pass the information to Angel Force so they can check everything out."

"Gwendolyn had to leave on a family emergency, but she'll be back in a day or so." Quantum pursed her blackened lips. "I'm pleased you're working with the angels. They're incredible to look at, although their brightness hurts my eyes. I wonder what happened to their brains, though? Perhaps they were absorbed into all that beauty. So pretty, but so dumb. It's often the way the world works. Why form opinions when you have looks to enchant others with?"

"They have their dumb moments, but they figure things out in the end. And they have big hearts. Even Dazielle, who hides her kindness under paperwork and stress."

"My fragrant new friend, with you on their side, this mystery will be solved in no time." She arose like a shady phoenix from a pile of ash. "Now, if you'll excuse me, I have tasks to attend to. And I need rest. Daylight displeases me. You know where I am if you have more questions."

My gaze flicked to the remaining gingerbread and hot chocolate. I hated food going to waste.

She cackled. "Take it for the road. You must report back if you have any symptoms."

I wagged my tail. I never turned down free food. With several pieces of gingerbread jammed into my mouth, and after lifting a paw in farewell, I headed out.

Quantum was as creepy as they came, but she had an alibi. It needed checking, but I didn't get a sense she wanted Figgy dead. Now, if he'd been a chubby-cheeked cherub complaining about his Christmas gifts, she'd be getting out butter and seasoning and setting the cauldron to simmer, but Figgy wasn't a target for the Yuletide Witch.

Still, the angels needed to know about this angle and the problems taking place behind closed doors in the Christmas community.

And since Quantum had suggested Sandy and the Christmas Fairy should be suspects, they were my next targets.

# Chapter 5

"You're sure that's what Quantum said?" Dazielle paced in front of me in her office.

"Yep. She thinks the holiday season is in trouble, and Figgy's murder could be connected." I hadn't been able to meet Dazielle or Dominic after visiting Quantum, so had to wait until late afternoon to update them.

I almost regretted it. Dazielle was deeply suspicious of my valuable input. She didn't trust me because I occasionally borrowed a cookie off her desk. I always intended to replenish her stock, but it was too easy to get distracted by more food, the pups, or Tempest's demon-hunting missions.

She shook her head, her large white wings fluttering behind her. "I can't imagine why Sandy or the fairy would want Figgy dead. Dominic, you interviewed Sandy. You told me Figgy's loss devastated him."

"I wouldn't say devastated," I said. "He seemed glum, though. I guess he didn't want to cry and get snot on his beard. He wouldn't want that kind of picture making the front pages of the gossip mags. It would impact on his fan base."

"Maybe I embellished." Dominic looked at anything but Dazielle. "But Sandy was shocked to learn Figgy's death wasn't an accident."

"I imagine he was. Sandy has goodness running through him. He sees kindness in everyone, even the children on his naughty list." Dazielle glanced at me. "And the naughty hellhounds."

"Sandy doesn't give me gifts. That's the Winter Werewolf's domain. He fixed me up with an awesome rawhide chew last year. Took me a week to chew through that sucker."

Dazielle grunted. "You said their negotiations aren't going well?"

"They don't sound good. And with Christmas less than a week away, they'll need to hurry if they plan on making a deal."

"You're saying that word wrong."

My ears flipped. "What am I saying wrong?"

"That Christmas word." Dazielle almost couldn't say it, and it came out more like Chris-Tmas.

"What do you call it? Do the angels have a special word for this time of year? Is it something politically correct? Do you call it Christine-mas so the ladies don't get offended? Is Christmas too malecentric?"

"Stop being ridiculous. It just sounds wrong to my ears." She waved a hand around. "And you mumble every time you say it."

"Wiggles is right." Dominic lifted the calendar from Dazielle's desk. "It's only a few days to go until Christmas." He also stumbled over the word.

Dazielle grabbed the calendar and stared at it. "That must be a printing error. It feels wrong."

"These things creep up on you." The stress was clearly getting to Dazielle if she'd forgotten Christmas was almost here. "Five minutes ago, I was baking under the sun. Now, I'm slipping in the snow and figuring out what to get Tempest as the perfect gift."

Dazielle paid me no attention as she tapped her fingers against her biceps. "I don't want to do this, but we should bring Sandy and the fairy in for questioning."

"Maybe Quantum, the Grinch, and the Winter Werewolf, too," I said. "Anyone here who's associated with Christmas."

Dazielle turned and wrinkled her nose. "I wish you'd stop saying that. It sounds almost obscene."

"Fine. Christine-mas. Whatever you call it, I'm looking forward to it. I can't wait to see the look on my pups faces as they open their gifts. I got them rude repeating parrots."

Dazielle squinted at me as if figuring out if I was real or a figment of her imagination. "We must be discreet. These are high-ranking individuals, and we don't want them taking offence."

"You're worried you'll be put on the naughty list?" I said.

She tutted at me. "Of course not. I'm too old for all that silliness."

"No one is too old for fun. And I couldn't care less if they get offended. If one of them killed Figgy, they need to pay for it."

"Of course. But I can't picture either of them being involved. And I'm tempted to leave Sandy off the list since you've already interviewed him."

"It wasn't a thorough interview," I said. "Sandy got sick and left. Maybe he faked being ill because we got close to the truth."

Dazielle strode into my personal space. "Did you make him unwell? Why am I only just hearing about this?"

"It was the shock," Dominic said. "Wiggles did nothing to Sandy."

She shook her head and stepped back. "If you must interview him again, don't make it obvious we consider him a suspect. Such a charming man wouldn't have done such a dreadful thing."

"Serial killers can be charming," I said. "The psychopathic ones. They fake being nice to manipulate people and get their victims where they want them, and then stab, stab, stab, or bludgeon, drown, suffocate—"

"Don't suggest anyone involved in this case is a serial killer." Dazielle's cheeks flushed, and her wings sagged. "Wiggles, stay out of this. You're not a trained investigator."

"I'm pivotal to the case. I was almost first on the scene. And you're overstretched and under-angeled. I'm being helpful. You need me." I followed Dazielle as she continued pacing.

She turned and almost tripped over me. "Will you behave?"

"Not usually. Something is playing on my mind." I dodged out of her way. "Why kill Figgy? Sure, he had a criminal past, but he was reformed. Everyone Dominic spoke to only said good things about him, and Sandy adored him. Even Quantum said he was obedient and hard working. So, what's the motive for wanting him dead?"

"It's what we're looking into," Dazielle said. "That's how investigations work. Figgy must have done something wrong."

"I'm with Wiggles on this," Dominic said. "Figgy was an all-round, amazing guy."

"Which got me thinking," I said. "Figgy wasn't the target. He found a bauble left for somebody else."

"Who?" Dazielle said.

"We have the key Christmas players in the village. And according to Quantum, they're dealing with a crisis. What if one of them planted the bauble for the other to find?"

"Shush! You can't go around saying Sandy or the fairy are trying to kill each other? They're influential public figures."

I chuckled. "I knew you were worried about what you'd get in your Santa stocking."

"Stop talking nonsense! There's no such thing as this Santa creature you keep on about."

"It's tragic. You're too adult to believe. But what if this deal they're negotiating is going wrong? One of them felt they were losing and got desperate. It's a motive for murder."

"If we're following that train of thought, Figgy worked for Sandy," Dominic said. "Do you think Sandy got a message about the bauble and sent Figgy to pick it up, not knowing the deadly surprise it contained?"

"Which means the fairy planted it," I said.

"It means no such thing," Dazielle said. "Quantum has a dark streak to her traditions. And since the other key winter players are around, what's to say one of them didn't do it?"

"Sparkling baubles aren't Quantum's thing," I said. "You should see the place she's staying in. It was bare of decoration. Sparkles and glitter are the Christmas Fairy's calling card."

"I prefer the term Winter Fairy," Dazielle said. "It's more inclusive than this Chris you keep going on about."

"Fine! Winter, Christmas, it's all the same to me."

"This theory stays between us," Dazielle said after a moment of contemplation. "Word can't get out that Sandy or the fairy are vulnerable to another attempt on their lives, or that either of them could be involved in killing Figgy."

"We've got to tell them," I said. "They're at risk if the killer tries again. And Christmas will be canceled if Santa Claus dies. My pups will never forgive me."

Dazielle and Dominic looked confused, although I couldn't figure out why. I hadn't used any complicated words. They must know if there was no Santa Claus, there'd be no Christmas.

I sat in front of Dazielle. "We have to get them off the streets and keep them informed. What if another bauble gets planted? Or the killer attempts a different type of attack? You don't want a key winter figure killed in Willow Tree Falls, do you? Think what it'll do to your key performance indicators come review time."

Dazielle bared her teeth. I'd just hit her weak spot. "Dominic, get Sandy and the Winter Fairy in here. See what they have to say. And you," she jabbed a finger at me. "Behave."

***

It took several hours of wrangling and the promise of a free dinner before Sandy and the Winter Fairy agreed to meet with us.

We'd started with them, since they were pivotal to what happened at Christmastime. If needed, we'd bring in the other festive players if a dead end presented itself.

I stood at the main door with Dominic, my ears lifted. "You told them to be discreet when they came here, right?"

"Of course. We don't want the rumor mill starting, and we don't want everyone knowing we're questioning them about a murder. Dazielle is worried we'll get sued by Sandy's legal team if word gets out."

"It's just that the ground is shaking. And I can hear an engine."

Dominic tilted his head. "An engine?"

The day had grown dark quickly, but the full beam lights from the enormous red limousine that stopped beside us meant you'd have to be blindfolded and locked in a darkened room not to notice Santa Claus's splendid arrival.

The limo driver climbed out and opened the back door. Sandy slid out, wearing an immaculate red suit, and smoothed his white hair down with one hand.

His smile was almost as dazzling as the headlights when he saw us waiting. "What an unexpected treat to receive a dinner invitation from the angels."

Dazielle pushed past us and shook his hand. "We received your rider, and everything you requested has been provided."

"Rider?" I muttered to Dominic.

"It's common with celebrities. They have a list of things they need before an event. Sometimes, it's food or drink, exercise equipment, particular types of towels, flowers. Anything really to help their creative muse."

"I thought we were just giving them dinner and talking murder?"

"That, too."

"Here she is. She's always trying to upstage me." The smile on Sandy's face didn't reach his eyes. His gaze was fixed on the enormous glittering carriage pulled by four white horses with plumes of feathers attached to their harnesses.

"That must be the Winter Fairy," I said. "We need to teach them what discretion means."

"I did my best," Dominic said. "But they're not used to being discreet. They love to be seen."

"If they get seen too much, they may not survive the night."

Dominic hurried over and opened a sparkling door, extending a hand to the Winter Fairy.

She slid out and alighted on the snow. She wore an ivory gown that would have looked like a wedding dress, if it weren't for the glittering cape and slit that exposed her shimmering stockings.

She commenced with a round of air-kissing, stopping when she got to me. "I didn't put an adorable puppy on my rider. What a delight. Do you do tricks?"

I shuffled back as she tried to kiss my head. "I'm working with Angel Force. And since I'm mostly hellhound, I've got a fragrance that takes a while to get used to. Lay off the kissing until we know each other better. It's for your benefit, not mine."

Her button nose wrinkled, but she still smiled, her lip gloss and eye make-up as sparkly as her cape. "I would love to eat you up. Yum, yum, yum. You've got an adorable pot belly. I'll be squeezing that later."

She wouldn't. This winter babe gave me the creeps. There was something fake about all that sparkle. Was she hiding a secret? A secret that involved killing Figgy.

"Please, come inside," Dazielle said. "Everything is laid out as per your requests."

"I was intrigued when I got the invitation," the Winter Fairy said. "And since I had nothing better to do, I decided to let the angels entertain me. And, of course, you." She booped me on the end of my nose with an icy finger.

Dominic held out his arm to the fairy, while Dazielle escorted Sandy inside. I led from the rear, not sure what to make of them. From Sandy's reaction to the fairy's arrival, he thought little of her. And although she oozed sparkly feminine charm, there was something sharp about that fairy that had me on my guard.

I stopped when we got inside. The office had been transformed, the desks moved back, and a table sat in the center. And on that table, boy oh boy, was a banquet. There were half a dozen meats, roasted vegetables and potatoes, and various winter salads. No turkey, though. The angels must have decided a turkey feast would be tiresome for our guests. They must get sick of the sight of that bird.

Dazielle had instructed some of her angels to serve, and they hovered nearby, waiting to provide first-class service with a beautiful smile.

Once everyone was settled at the table, small talk completed, and our plates were full, mine included, Dazielle cleared her throat. "This is just an informal conversation. We'd welcome your input on a sensitive case."

"Go ahead," Sandy said. "You mentioned this gathering had to do with Figgy."

"Yes. In a way." Dazielle toyed with her silver fork. "We're worried about your safety."

Sandy paused as he was about to take a sip of his white wine, the glass hovering by his lips. "Why do you think we're at risk? Have you received a threat? They happen this time of year. We have people who deal with that sort of thing, though. Please, pass any information on to them. I'm sure it's nothing to worry about."

"What are we being threatened by?" the Winter Fairy said.

Dazielle glanced at me. "We're working on a theory regarding Figgy's untimely death."

"Yes. So sad," Sandy said. "I keep expecting to see him. I've even called out to him a few times, and then realized he was gone. No one made a chai latte as good as Figgy."

The Winter Fairy patted his hand. "You poor thing. Have a drink. It always makes you feel better."

Sandy moved his hand away. "You're so thoughtful."

Dazielle drew in a breath. "It's possible Figgy wasn't the target for the exploding bauble."

"Did you receive a message about a bauble delivery?" I said to Sandy. "Since it was so late, perhaps you sent your right-hand elf to get it."

"No, I'd have remembered that. The first I heard about the bauble was after it was connected to Figgy's death. And Figgy would have told me if he'd received a message about a parcel. He was a reliable assistant."

"What about you?" I turned to the Winter Fairy. "Were you close to Figgy? Did you receive information about a surprise under the tree and ask him to collect it for you?"

"He didn't work for me, so I'd never do that. And I received no information about a bauble."

There was a moment of silence while everyone sipped their wine. I stuck to water. Alcohol and fire were a heady mix.

"We're struggling to find a motive for Figgy's death," Dazielle said. "That's why we're pursuing this new line of investigation."

"Perhaps it was an accident," the Winter Fairy said after a few seconds of silence. "As extremely powerful beings, we know magic is tricksy. It has a mind of its own."

"Not if you know how to control it," I said.

"You adorable little smoosh ball. No one has complete control over magic." Her smile was bright, but her blue eyes looked like they held ice shards.

I was tempted to argue with her, but I'd had a few occasions when my magic had backfired.

"We don't want you to be at any risk," Dazielle said. "I'd like to assign you both with angel protectors until this mystery is resolved."

"It's endearing you're concerned for our safety," the Winter Fairy said. "There's no need to worry, though. We have our own protection."

"You haven't received any threats or been concerned about anyone bothering you?" I said.

They shook their heads as they took delicate bites of food.

282

"We run well-oiled machines," Sandy said. "And everyone who works for us is vetted, so there are never problems with our teams."

"Although you will insist on helping criminals." The Winter Fairy tinkled out a laugh. "Perhaps that's the root of this problem."

Sandy set down his glass. "You shouldn't judge a person based on their past. It's how they behave in the present that matters."

"You always love to see the good in people."

"I do. Even you," he muttered.

"Perhaps if we knew more about the reason for your stay in Willow Tree Falls, it could provide another avenue for this investigation," Dazielle said.

Sandy and the fairy shared a look. "We're here for work, just as we told you when we arranged to use your office space. Every business needs to monitor their bottom line."

"And we picked this cute village because we love sharing ourselves around," the Winter Fairy said. "The bigger towns and cities often get our attention, and twee places like this get overlooked."

"It's kind of you to think of us," Dazielle simpered. "You're so right. Willow Tree Falls is often forgotten about."

"Not true. We get tourists year round, visiting the stone circle and messing about in our thermal spas. We're always busy. And some of the most powerful magic users I know put down roots here because of the magic this place contains," I said. "The Crypt witches wouldn't call this village home if it didn't hold power."

"Not now, Wiggles," Dazielle muttered. "We're all grateful you're spending time here. It must be nice to plan for the future together."

"Oh, it's a hoot," the Winter Fairy said. "I look forward to seeing Sandy and the others every year."

"As do I, my dear. I count the days until this meeting." Sandy smiled broadly, showing too many teeth. "What could be better than coming together with my oldest companions to figure out how to make everything merry and bright?"

The Winter Fairy's grin turned feral. "Seeing you is joyful."

I chewed on a hunk of roast beef. They were lying. They hated each other.

"You can't think of anything that's been concerning you?" Dominic said. "We're here to help, but we can only do that if we have all the information."

"And while we appreciate that, you're wasting your time," the Winter Fairy said. "We've been looking after ourselves forever. We're not vulnerable. Now, shall we feast? Let's not talk about death anymore. It's so gloomy."

Dominic looked at me and shrugged.

These two weren't planning on spilling the festive beans. They were happy to play nice and act like there wasn't a problem, but I didn't buy it.

"You may not care about Figgy's murder, but we're not having an unsolved death on our paws." I stamped on the table. "Stop roadblocking and be honest with us."

"Wiggles!" Dazielle hissed. "Manners!"

"Murder trumps manners. We don't want this village known as the place Santa Claus was slaughtered. That's what could happen if we don't find the killer and they move on to a new target."

"Santa ... Clause?" the Winter Fairy said.

"Or you. You could be the next victim. We know you're hiding things. You're here to negotiate Christmas being in crisis. Why? Is that the reason Figgy is dead?"

# Chapter 6

"Hmmm ... you are a curious creature. Although I lost half of what you said in translation," the Winter Fairy said after a momentary pause.

"Ignore Wiggles. He doesn't work for Angel Force, and he's overstayed his welcome." Dazielle glared at me. "It's time you left."

"I may not work here, but I'm a part of this village, and I care what happens. We must know the truth. Your meetings have to do with Christmas," I said. "What are you trying to change? What does it have to do with Figgy?"

"You're cute and feisty. I adore you! Ask your questions, my adorable bundle of yumminess," the Winter Fairy said. "We have nothing to hide."

I ignored the stink eye coming from Dazielle. "Thank you. Sandy, you said you were in your room when Figgy was killed."

"That's right. I was on my own. But I have a night watch assistant, Martino. He's excellent. He sits outside my room to ensure no one bothers me. When you get to my age, you need all the beauty sleep you can get."

"And you?" I turned to the Winter Fairy.

"Much the same, my fluffy angel of perfection. At our level of celebrity status, we need to protect our downtime. I was asleep, but my assistant works through the night to make sure I'm not disturbed and I don't have a pile of problems to deal with when waking. Stress ages the skin. Lily is wonderful. She deals with it all, so I barely have to lift a finger."

"Hard work is nothing to be ashamed of," Sandy said.

"Remind me again how many assistants you have?"

"We need Martino and Lily to confirm this," I said to Dazielle.

She bristled under my order, but focused on Sandy and the fairy. "If neither of you have any objections, speaking to your assistants would help us eliminate you from our inquiries."

"I have no secrets," Sandy said. "Ask away. Martino usually gets up around this time, and he'll be happy to talk to you."

"So will Lily," the Winter Fairy said. "And of course, I understand, you're only doing your job. You must find out what happened to Figgy. A death in the ranks looks badly for poor Sandy. His popularity numbers are already on the wane, so when this news is leaked—"

"Who would leak it? Surely, not one of my oldest friends?"

A sharp laugh tinkled out. "As if, sweets. But you know how these things happen. I'm only pointing out the obvious."

Sandy's eyes narrowed for a second before the overly bright smile returned. "My supporters will stand by me. They'll know I had nothing to do with this tragedy."

"Of course they will, my dear. I so hate to think of you worrying, though. Seeing such an old friend in distress when he's already struggling is never comfortable."

"Why are you struggling?" I said to Sandy.

"It's this job. It isn't easy. When you're at the top, somebody always wants a piece of you." Sandy's gaze was on the fairy.

She ripped grapes off their stems and ground them between her tiny white teeth.

"Let's take a break," Dazielle said. "Dominic, arrange for Martino and Lily to be brought in immediately."

He looked at his food and sighed. "Of course. I'll get on it."

While Dominic hustled away to make the arrangements, we enjoyed stilted small talk and more food. I kept a close eye on our guests. Although the fairy kept laughing and patting Sandy's arm, neither of their smiles were genuine, and they kept making little digs at each other, wrapped in blankets of insincerity.

After my third plate of food, I excused myself and headed to the reception area to wait with Dominic. I was unhappy to see the usual plate of Christmas cookies was absent. Those gluttonous angels were definitely hiding food from me.

"They'll be here any minute." Dominic leaned on the desk, his head propped on his hands.

"How did they sound when you contacted them?"

"Happy to help. Eager to please their bosses."

"Guess that's part of the job description. What do you think of those two back there?" I hopped onto the desk and snuffled for snacks.

"They're civil enough with each other, but there's tension."

"They're hiding something," I said. "Let's hope the assistants are more honest, or we could hit another dead end."

Martino and Lily appeared at the same time. Martino was a neatly turned out winter elf dressed in a dark green suit. His black hair was slicked off his face, and he wore a woody cinnamon cologne. Lily was all sparkles and blonde hair. She was a curvy fairy with a smile that lit the room.

"We came as soon as we could," Lily said.

"We appreciate that. This won't take long," Dominic said. "We just have a few questions."

"Whatever we can do to help, name it," Martino said.

Once they were settled in interview rooms, we tackled Martino first. Dazielle joined us, leaving Sandy and the Winter Fairy to finish the food. Let's hope they didn't kill each other while our backs were turned.

"Thank you for coming in so quickly." Dazielle started the interview and ran through the formalities. "Martino, could you tell us where you were between the hours of two and four this morning?"

"The same as always. I'm Sandy's night watch assistant. He goes to bed around midnight, and I sit outside his room and work."

"All night?" I said. "You never take a break?"

"If I do, someone takes over. But I was there during those hours."

"What were you doing?" I said before Dazielle could ask more questions.

"Finalizing the calendar for the New Year. Sandy has big plans, and we need to make sure nothing is missed."

"Did Sandy leave his room at any point?" Dazielle shot me a glare out of the corner of her eye.

"No, he always sleeps soundly and rarely leaves his room. He was in there all night. He woke at seven, and that was when I broke the bad news about Figgy."

"How did he respond?" I said.

"He was sad. We all were. We both had a little cry."

After asking a few more questions and getting nowhere, we left Martino with a mug of coffee and his thoughts, and headed into the next interview room. Lily sat neatly in the chair, her hands folded in her lap.

"I so admire Angel Force. Catching the bad guys sounds terribly scary." Her smile was so dazzling, I needed shades.

"It is. And we need to catch the bad guy who killed Figgy," I said. "It's why you were asked here."

"Oh! Me! I mean, I didn't do it. You don't think that, do you?" Tears flooded her eyes.

"Please, relax. No one is accusing you of murder." Dazielle made the introductions and then ran through the formalities. "We need to know where you were between the hours of two and four this morning."

Lily sniffed. "I promise, it wasn't me."

"We're establishing timelines, so any information could be useful," Dazielle said.

"Of course. Sorry. Your furry friend got me flustered." Lily smoothed her hands over her sparkles. "I look after the Winter Fairy at night. I'm a night owl and never sleep before dawn breaks. I was outside her room, working."

"What were you working on?" I said.

"The calendar for the New Year. She has so much going on, I wanted to make sure nothing was missed."

I tilted my head. That sounded almost the same as Martino's statement.

"Did she leave her room at any point that evening?" I said.

"No. She's a sound sleeper and rarely wakes for anything. And I never let anyone disturb her."

"You didn't wake her to tell her about Figgy?"

"Oh, no. I heard about it just before my shift ended, so I broke the bad news when she came out."

"And how did the Winter Fairy react to the news?" Dazielle said.

"She was sad. We all were. Figgy was a great guy. We both had a little cry over his death."

It sounded like Lily and Martino had been given scripts to recite. Who came up with that bright idea? The killer?

"There was no way the Winter Fairy could have snuck out without you seeing?" I said. "Perhaps you left your post at some point."

"No! Not possible. And if I leave my post, someone takes over. But I was there during those hours."

I wasn't surprised to hear her repeat that to me.

After a few more questions, we left Lily alone. If she'd been coached to give specific answers, this was a waste of time.

"Did anyone else think that was suspicious?" I said, once we were in Dazielle's office and she'd checked to make sure Sandy and the Winter Fairy were still happily munching through their feast and hadn't throttled each other.

"There was similarity to their answers." Dazielle sank into her seat. "Could they be hiding a connection to the murder? Maybe they blew up Figgy."

"If they did, they were only following orders. It's what they do." I paced the room for a moment. "We should bring in Quantum. Maybe her presence will rattle Sandy and the fairy. She tipped me off about there being a problem between them, and since they're unwilling to share what it is, they may have no choice when she reveals what they've been discussing."

"Very well. But let me handle this. Sandy and the Winter Fairy are A-listers. I can't have this coming back and biting the angels where it hurts."

"Dazielle, justice first. We always fight for good, don't we? Even if it means your derrieres get nibbled on."

"Get out of my way, you irritating mutt." She stood, stomped out of the room, and we headed back to the dining table.

Sandy and the Winter Fairy weren't looking at each other, and tension simmered like a pot of cranberry punch perched over a cauldron.

Sandy turned his brilliant smile on us. "Is everything sorted? As much as I enjoy my companion's company, I have a lot to do."

"Unfortunately, we still have questions," Dazielle said. "It appears your assistants have been coached."

A snort shot out of the Winter Fairy, while Sandy's mouth dropped open.

The Winter Fairy recovered first. "Who would do such a thing?"

Sandy glanced at her. "This must be a coincidence."

"It's not," I said. "You're still concealing things. And a source informed me Christmas is in crisis. Since you won't tell us what that crisis is, we'll bring in Quantum, the Grinch, and the Winter Werewolf to sort this. If you're not being honest, perhaps they will be. Hopefully, they'll help us uncover which one of you killed Figgy."

Neither of them spoke, although they exchanged furious glances.

The Winter Fairy smacked her empty wine glass on the table. "You may as well know what's going on. But it had nothing to do with Figgy being murdered."

"Am I right about Christmas being in crisis?" I said.

She gave me a flat stare. "We are in crisis. And it's Sandy's fault."

"My fault?" He shoved back his seat and stood. "You're the one roadblocking. I've offered you a fair deal, but you're greedy."

"You'd know all about greed." She flew from her seat, her hands in fists. "I know about the deal you made with Snow White Soap. They wanted to work with both of us, but you told them I was unreliable!"

"I'm the face of this season. You can't muscle in. And you only complicated things by bringing in the others to fight your battle. We could have made a deal between us. But no, you flapped your lips at Quantum, the Winter Werewolf, and the Grinch, and now they have their hands out, too. You're losing out because you're a gossipy harpy who complains to anyone who'll listen."

The Winter Fairy shrieked. She lunged at Sandy, grabbed his beard, and yanked it. "I know this is a fake! Give it to me. I'll show the world what a phony you are."

He yelped and caught her by the wrists. They staggered about the room as the Winter Fairy alternated between yanking on Sandy's beard and thumping his arm.

"I hate you! You're so smug."

"Everyone loves me more than you." Sandy pried at the Winter Fairy's fingers to get them free from his beard.

"I bring the glitz and glamor to a tired season. This time of year, people are too lazy to even get out of bed. If it weren't for me, the world would hibernate."

"Shouldn't we do something?" Dominic whispered.

Dazielle stood with her wings extended. "There's no need to fight. We can figure things out."

"That's what we've been trying to do," the Winter Fairy snarled. "But this overly stuffed sack of corporate greed won't take his sticky fingers off the cookie jar and let the rest of us take a bite. He wants it all." She landed a solid thump on Sandy's belly, and he gasped and doubled over.

Dominic strode over with Dazielle, and they pulled them apart before the violence escalated beyond thumps and beard pulling.

"Put them in separate cells," Dazielle said. "Since neither of you can behave, you need a time-out."

Although they protested, Dazielle stood firm, and they were led away. I was impressed. People in authority usually dazzled her.

Dominic returned a moment later, minus our warring Christmas characters.

"I knew they were hiding something," I said. "They're determined to ruin Christmas, and we're still no closer to figuring out which one of them killed Figgy."

Dazielle sighed and leaned against a desk. "Why do you keep going on about Christmas, Wiggles?"

"It has to be the reason they're fighting. It sounds like the Winter Fairy wants a cut of Santa Claus's corporate deals. Although I'm not sure about having his face on a bar of soap while I'm cleaning my unmentionable bits."

"That Santa Claus name sounds wrong," she said.

"Whatever you call the big guy is fine by me. He's the one who's been in charge of Christmas for thousands of years. Sandy must rake in billions with the deals and exclusive contracts, so the others feel sidelined. That's why they're here." I shook my head. "I understand them being sniffy about it, though. Christmas has gotten too commercial."

Dazielle rubbed her forehead. "Just because those two are fighting doesn't mean either of them killed Figgy. Why would they?"

"He could have gotten in the middle of an argument, maybe said something he shouldn't, and the bauble was a way of getting revenge."

She tipped her head back and stared at the ceiling. "Go home, Wiggles. Don't you have pups to look after?"

"Sure. But that's what Auntie Tempest is for. She's watching them so I can focus on this murder."

"This murder is a mess, and you're making it worse by insinuating the key seasonal figures are involved. It'll be a PR nightmare if you're wrong."

"And if I'm right? They're involved. I know you believe that, too. Otherwise, you wouldn't have put them in the cells."

Dominic hovered between us as we glared at each other. "Let's work together. We all want answers to this mystery."

I huffed out smoke. He was right. And as I'd just witnessed, arguing could lead to the murder of innocent bystanders.

Dominic crouched in front of me. "It is getting late, though. You must want to go home and see to your family. We'll start again in the morning. Maybe a night in the cells will convince Sandy and the Winter Fairy to talk to us."

I wanted this solved, but I couldn't neglect my parental duties. I grudgingly said goodbye, getting ignored by Dazielle, and left the office, heading into the wintry gloom.

I was so focused on figuring out whether it was Sandy or the Winter Fairy who'd killed Figgy, it took me several minutes to notice no one had their Christmas lights on.

Usually, the streets were ablaze with twinkling lights, sparkles, and candles. But no one had lit up. Maybe it was a show of respect because of Figgy's murder.

A glance over my shoulder revealed the tree outside Angel Force had gone, too. That seemed extreme. Maybe they'd taken it down after my pups stole the tree topper.

I hustled into the club, which was just getting going for the night. After greeting the servers, I dashed up to the apartment.

Tempest lounged on the couch with my pups slumbering beside her. She pressed a finger to her lips. "Keep it down. I've only just got them off."

I trotted to the bowl in the kitchen, had a snack, then hurried back. "We've not made much progress finding Figgy's killer. I'm sure it was Santa Claus or the Winter Fairy, though."

"Uh-huh." Tempest gently stroked each pup.

I slumped against her feet and heaved out a sigh. "No decorations up yet? Don't you want people in the festive mood?"

"Decorations?"

"The Christmas tinsel and sparkle."

"Christmas? Never heard of it. Is it some trend that's passed me by?"

I stood and stared at her. "Christmas. You know, December twenty-fifth. All the presents, feasts, and merriment. The thing you've been complaining about because you're so busy."

"You didn't get a bump on your head when you were out, did you? Or are you coming down with something? I heard there's a gross flu doing the rounds."

I looked around the sparkle-free apartment. Tempest was talking as if she'd forgotten Christmas existed. "I'll be back soon."

I dashed down the stairs and outside, ignoring her protests that she needed to work and couldn't pup-sit for much longer, and raced to Quantum's cabin.

The Yuletide Witch had been around since the dawn of time. She'd know why people were losing interest in Christmas.

Without knocking, I barged into her cabin and found her lounging on a seat, studying an old spell book.

She looked up and bared her teeth. "More enchanted gingerbread?"

"We need to discuss Christmas."

Her eyebrows drew together. "What's Christmas?"

# Chapter 7

After speaking to Quantum, who'd been adamant Christmas wasn't real, I'd spent a restless night walking around Willow Tree Falls, hunting for signs this magical time of year still existed.

But my worst fears were confirmed. Anyone I asked about Christmas denied knowing what it was. The houses were bare of decorations, there was no festive food on display in the store windows, and I found no sign of the tree that had been outside Angel Force.

Christmas couldn't be gone. If there was no Christmas, there'd be no presents, feasting, or fun.

I had to get it back. I was determined to give my pups the perfect day, but how could I do that, if Christmas no longer existed?

With aching paws and tired eyes, I trudged up the stairs to the apartment. I was happy to find my pups slumbering, and Tempest just shuffling out of her bedroom, bleary-eyed.

"I didn't agree to look after the pups all night." She stumbled to the kitchen and switched on the kettle. "If this is going to be a long-term thing, you'll need to pay someone to look after them. I love those little guys, but I also love my business. And I love sleep. Those four never rest."

"Sorry. It was an emergency." I waited for her to fill my bowl and emptied it in thirty seconds. "Have you got your memory back about Christmas?"

"It's too early to make up nonsense words. Where did you go last night?"

"I was looking into a problem. And I'm not sure how far it goes. Maybe the world has forgotten about Christmas. What does that leave us with?" I checked my bowl again, but it hadn't magically refilled.

"Please, no problems. Not before coffee." She nodded at the counter. "Someone left you a card."

I hopped onto a stool and saw a white envelope on the counter with my name on it. "Who left this?"

Tempest shrugged. "No idea. It had been pushed under the door."

I pulled the card out with my teeth. There was a winter scene on the front, with the words Merry Christmas in an arc at the top. "You see! Someone still believes in Christmas."

She looked at the card, her expression puzzled. "I don't see it catching on. This is just winter. We've celebrated the solstice, so now it's time to go into hibernation mode. I'm even considering closing this place for a week or so and decorating. People won't mind if I don't open for a couple of weeks, will they?"

"The calendar is full of Christmas parties. And New Year's Eve is always huge." I stared at the card. This was proof I wasn't the only one who still believed.

"Yeah, I guess I'll keep New Year's Eve going, but I've had loads of cancelations. People don't see the point of celebrating this time of year."

"Everyone is canceling their Christmas parties?" I flipped open the card with my nose.

"Maybe they're saving. I don't know. But whatever this weird Christmas thing is you're going on about, it's got nothing to do with it."

I stared at the handwritten words inside the card: *Don't use Figgy as the centerpiece for the holidays.*

Tempest inspected the card. "What does that mean?"

I reread the words. "It's a message about what happened to Figgy. He's not the centerpiece? Does that mean he's not important?"

"Don't say that. The guy is dead."

I flipped the card over, but there was no information on the back to help me figure out who'd delivered it. "You sure you didn't see who brought this up?"

"No clue. I need a shower, then I'm figuring out if it's worth opening anymore this year. You okay with the pups?"

"Sure. Aurora is having them today. They can play with her familiars."

"Poor kitties. The last time they spent the day together, they got charred fur." Tempest ambled into the bedroom.

After a quick breakfast with my pups, making them presentable for Auntie Aurora, and then dropping them at her store, I headed back to Angel Force with my Christmas card and its elusive message.

I trotted to Dominic's desk, happy to drop the card and accept half a cream cheese bagel he held out for me.

"Dominic, when I say the word Christmas, what does it mean to you?"

His forehead wrinkled. "It's that new word you used yesterday. And I don't know what it means. What does it mean to you?"

I sighed. It was official. Christmas had been forgotten. "It means we're in trouble. And I'd place good kibble on Sandy and the Winter Fairy being involved with making the magic of Christmas disappear. Have either of them talked overnight?"

He shook his head. "They've said nothing useful. Although they're no longer hiding how much they dislike each other. I always thought those two were the best of friends."

"Shall we get them together and talk all things Christmas?"

"I'm not sure using your made-up word will help," Dominic said. "And you need to be on your best behavior. Dazielle is in a super grump. And she said some less than angel things about you last night after you left."

"No doubt. She's worried about bad publicity, isn't she?" I trotted after him as we headed to the cells.

"Well, we do have the official face of winter locked in a cell as a murder suspect. If we get this wrong, Dazielle will never forgive you."

"All I'm doing is getting to the bottom of a murder she can't solve."

"And, unfortunately, you're giving her a headache while doing it." He patted me on the head. "Don't worry. I've got your back."

Dominic lifted me so I could look through the viewing hole to see Sandy. He looked remarkably well put together, his suit barely crumpled after a night in a cell.

Sandy walked to the door. "Sorry I got angry with the fairy, but she presses my buttons. And you saw her attack me first. She's fortunate I'm a benevolent soul, or I'd press charges." He touched his beard.

"You're entitled to," Dominic said. "We would like to talk to you both again, though. See if we can get to the bottom of this."

"Of course. And I'll be civil. I've learned over many years of dealing with that uptight fairy, that she loves drama. Yesterday, I didn't have my guard up. It won't happen again."

Dominic let Sandy out, and then we went to see the Winter Fairy.

She looked a little less sparkly, but still gave us a beautiful, over-the-top smile. "If I say sorry again, will you let me out? I didn't mean to lose my temper. I don't really hate Sandy. Well, he is a jerk, but I'm used to it. I know better."

"I'm standing right out here," Sandy said.

"Oops! My bad. Sorry, sweets. I love you, really." She made kissy noises and winked at me.

"We would like to speak to you both together," Dominic said.

The Winter Fairy held up her hands. "I'm ready to talk. Sandy was the one who wanted everything kept a secret."

"That's not true," he muttered.

"You see what I have to work with," she said. "He's so difficult. And he always has to be right. And have the last word."

"Do not."

"Enough," I said. "You both want to find out what happened to Figgy, don't you?"

"Of course," Sandy said. "That's my focus."

The Winter Fairy grumbled under her breath before nodding.

Five minutes later, we were sitting around a table. Sandy and the Winter Fairy had been fed and had coffee, and then Dazielle joined us.

She glanced at me. "You're like a bad penny. You keep showing up."

"I'm sticking with this until Christmas returns."

"Wiggles," Dominic muttered. "That's not why we're here."

"It is." I clambered onto the table, resisting the urge to grab the Winter Fairy's half-eaten croissant. "I need to talk to you both about Christmas. What does it mean to you?"

The Winter Fairy blinked several times. "Is it a foreign word? It doesn't sound French. Maybe Italian?"

I looked at Sandy. "Everyone knows you as Santa Claus, Father Christmas, Kris Kringle, Papa Noel, and all the fancy foreign names I can't pronounce. You must remember what people call you. All those eager faces watch for your arrival on Christmas Eve with their gifts on your sleigh."

He shook his head. "People call me Sandy. I insist on it. It helps them relax. People get anxious when meeting a celebrity."

The Winter Fairy rolled her eyes. "You like to make out you're the key figure for this season, but we all play a part."

"You bring the decoration," Sandy said. "The Grinch brings the pessimism. The Winter Wolf shakes things up with a little fear. And the Yuletide Witch, well, she reminds people what happens if they're truly bad. You all complement me, but I'm the face of this season. You must accept that and move on."

"Without us, you'd be nothing! And don't think we won't follow through with what was said. If you don't give us a fair cut, we're not doing this anymore. See how long you last on your own."

"You want some of the money Sandy makes over Christmas?" I said.

"I know nothing about this Christmas, but we were negotiating over his extortionate ad revenue income and the deals he's secured," the Winter Fairy said. "We're part of that. We make this season what it is."

"You think you do," Sandy said. "But I manage fine without Quantum's warped values, or the Grinch's grumpiness. And no one will miss your tacky sparkle."

The Winter Fairy glowered at him. "If I wasn't here to make everything shine, you'd be seen for the dull donkey you really are."

"Let's refrain from name-calling," Dazielle said. "And we'll put aside this strange Christmas idea Wiggles keeps referring to. It's true you're here to negotiate because you're unhappy with the way things are being run?"

"I'm perfectly happy," Sandy said.

"Because you get all the money," the Winter Fairy said. "Your face is everywhere this time of year. What do I get? A few poorly paid commercials. I deserve more. I work hard."

"You get what you deserve. The others are the same. You get paid according to the contribution you make. That's the deal."

"The deal must change. We're sick of you getting the glory."

"So you came together to figure out what you can get out of Christmas?" I said.

"Wiggles, you're confusing things by making up something that isn't real," Dazielle snapped. "We now know why Sandy and the Winter Fairy are here. Focus on that."

Sandy leaned forward. "I assure you, these negotiations had nothing to do with Figgy. I don't know why he was killed, but not because of the talks we were holding."

I thumped my paws on the table. "It has to be. That bauble exploded, and everyone forgot Christmas. This is all connected."

Dazielle pointed to the door. "I had little patience before this day began. You just stole the last of it. Leave."

I could have argued, but Dazielle had that stubborn look on her face that meant I'd be barking down a dark alley with no hope of the lights coming on.

But I was right, and that panicked me. The exploding bauble was behind Christmas vanishing. And whoever was behind that bauble killed Figgy.

I jumped off the table. "Figgy was an innocent bystander. I have proof."

"Wiggles!" Dazielle stood, her wings out.

"I got a clue delivered to my home. Figgy shouldn't be the focus of this investigation. He wasn't the target. He was an unfortunate victim of a bigger conspiracy. The conspiracy to wipe out Christmas!"

She swooped her wings around me, and all I could smell was warm angel cinnamon stink.

"Get off! You need to know this." I squirmed in her crushing embrace as she dog-handled me out of the room, through the office, and dumped me in the snow.

I rolled over and lay on my back, winded by the unwanted angel attention.

Dazielle loomed over me. "I've told you we must tread carefully, but you don't listen! You yell crazy theories, make up clues, and this Christmas thing is bizarre." She fluttered her wings back into place. "I'm putting your unacceptable behavior down to stress. But don't test me, or I'll arrest you."

"What for? Saving Christmas?"

"Being a smelly thorn in my side and stopping me from doing my job." She turned and marched away.

"You need no help to do that."

The door slammed, and the lock was turned.

I stood and shook snow off my fur. I was getting Christmas back and finding out who killed Figgy. And if I had no angel help, I'd do it on my own.

# Chapter 8

Later that same day, I found myself in the same room as Santa Claus, the Winter Fairy, their assistants, Martino and Lily, Quantum, the Winter Werewolf, and the Grinch.

"I don't know how you did it, but I owe you," I whispered to Dominic, who sat beside me.

"I told you I had your back. Dazielle just needed to calm down. But don't talk. I assured her you'd only listen to the conversation."

I stared at him. "If she keeps asking dumb questions—"

"And don't call her dumb!" He petted my head. "Dazielle is tense because her reputation is on the line. That makes her snappy."

"You mean, she's proud. Isn't that a sin? Angels don't sin."

He tickled me under the chin. "Hush! If you can keep quiet for two minutes, I'll buy you a steak."

"How big we talking?"

"Bigger than my head."

"I want bigger."

He chuckled. "Just behave. Please. I worked on Dazielle for an hour to convince her you should be here. Focus on our guests."

"Suspects."

"Please!"

"I'll do my best." Any other time, I'd have been excited to meet all the Christmas characters, share entertaining tales, and learn about plans for the holidays, but as I looked around the group, I felt no joy. We were here to talk murder and bringing back Christmas. At least, I wanted to talk about Christmas.

I checked the wall clock. I could manage two minutes of silence. Then I was leaping in and saying my piece.

The meeting room door opened, and a woman I vaguely recognized dashed in. She had a neat blonde bob and wore a practical pants suit in a pleasing shade of crimson. "So sorry I'm late. My family matter took longer to deal with than I anticipated."

"No problem," Sandy said. "We're grateful you had time to come back."

"Gwendolyn Drach?" Dazielle rose and shook the woman's hand.

She nodded and looked around the group before being introduced to Dominic and me.

"I've seen you around the village," Dominic said.

"I've been here almost a week." Gwendolyn sat in the empty seat pointed out to her. "Whenever I visit a new place, I make the most of my spare time and visit all the tourist hot spots."

"Gwendolyn's been helping us tiptoe through these negotiations," Sandy said. "We needed someone with experience, given how difficult the players are." He looked at the Winter Fairy.

She rolled her eyes. "You're the only one throwing hissy fits every time I suggest a compromise. If you weren't so greedy—"

"Now, we agreed not to use disparaging words during this negotiation," Gwendolyn said. "We're here to get the best outcome for everyone. And remember the children. They make this time of year special."

I checked the clock. Two minutes hadn't passed yet. I bit my tongue.

"Could you start by summarizing how these negotiations are going?" Dazielle said. "Since Figgy was involved, any information could be useful."

"Of course. I'm happy to help. And having spoken to everyone here, they agreed full disclosure is the best thing," Gwendolyn said.

"I didn't say that," the Winter Wolf said, his broad shoulders tight against his ears. "I'm only here for the cash. The fairy said this would be worth our while to stick it out and get a deal done."

"That's not true." Gwendolyn smiled at him. "You want what's best for the children. Same as everyone."

"Sandy only wants a bigger bottom line," the Winter Fairy muttered.

After more grumbling around the table, everyone settled. They all looked at Gwendolyn.

She nodded her approval once the room was quiet. "Thank you all for giving me your attention." Gwendolyn focused on Dazielle. "We've been here seven days. I received an urgent communication from Sandy. He was concerned about demands being placed upon him, and needed a neutral support to resolve things calmly."

"Those demands, as he calls them, are reasonable," the Winter Fairy said.

"Depends whose point of view you're looking through," Sandy said. "My business was fine until you all stuck your hands out and demanded a cut."

"Sandy, you know why everyone has grievances. They've expressed them clearly," Gwendolyn said.

"They can express them how they like. If it weren't for my hard work, none of these deals would be in place. Why should I share when they had nothing to do with setting things up?"

"You're a liar," the Winter Fairy said. "You don't own this time of year. You didn't create it."

"Yeah, yeah. You've told me so many times how you had a key part to play. It's boring."

"Everyone has a role and a purpose," Gwendolyn said. "We've explored your roles during this important time of year. Everyone agreed they add value."

"Christmas!" I blurted out as the second hand moved into the third minute. "I get it! Sandy is the public face of Christmas. He's the figurehead. The Winter Fairy is the sparkle and joy. And the rest of you mix in fear and pessimism to ensure people don't float away on a wave of Christmas cheer, and get themselves in debt after the big day."

"That's kind of what I do," the Grinch said. "I don't know that word, though. What is it?"

"Wiggles has a theory. It's an incorrect theory," Dazielle said. "Pay him no attention. He's only here as an observer, and he knows the terms of staying involved. Dominic explained them, didn't you?"

Dominic nodded, his expression pleading as he caught my eye.

I growled, but kept my mouth shut. We needed to get through everyone's alibi and figure out which one of these Christmas clowns killed Figgy. Then I was going after them and shaking them until they told me what they'd done to Christmas.

"Please, go on," Dazielle said to Gwendolyn. "You were telling us about the negotiations."

"As I said, we've been here a week. We all want to find a common path. Something we can agree on."

"Were you finding that common path?" Dazielle said.

Gwendolyn tucked her hands under her thighs. "It was proving tricky."

"Because Sandy won't give anything up," the Winter Fairy said. "I know how much money he rakes in every day. He's worth a fortune. He should share."

As they bickered, it was easy to see why the negotiations had gotten nowhere. It was time to move past their selfish needs. "Someone in this room murdered Figgy, and they killed Christmas. Which one of you did it?"

"Wiggles!" Dazielle said.

"I'm done shuffling around and being pleasant because these people are public figures. They could be rulers of all magical beings, but if they've done something wrong, they pay for it."

"I accept that." The Grinch rubbed his snub nose. "But I didn't kill the elf. And I've never met this Christmas guy you keep going on about. Is it a guy? Has someone else died?"

"No! Christmas isn't real. Wiggles is making it up." Dazielle's fingers danced on the table. "We're focused on Figgy's murder. Only Figgy."

"I didn't kill Figgy either," the Winter Werewolf said. "I liked him. He always had time to talk."

No one seemed sure what to say next. So, I took over. I was coming for Christmas, and nothing could stop me. Not even Dazielle.

"If you can prove you weren't at the scene of the crime, and didn't plant that exploding bauble, you're both free to go," I said to the Winter Werewolf and the Grinch.

"Stop doing my job," Dazielle muttered.

I shrugged. She wasn't doing it, so somebody had to.

Dazielle adjusted her wings. "It would be helpful if we had your alibis. We've already spoken to Sandy and the Winter Fairy, and they've provided information about where they were."

Fake information. Which made me think one of them did it, but I didn't blurt out that thought.

"You already know our alibis," the Grinch said. "One of your angels caught us."

"What were you doing?" Dazielle said.

"Nothing. Hanging out."

"Hanging out and breaking the rules?" I wagged my tail.

The Winter Werewolf chuffed out a laugh. "I got bored with the negotiations. Sure, I want a cut of what greedy old Sandy has stuffed in his pockets, but every time we challenged him, he came up with some smooth line. He blocked every suggestion. I needed a break. We'd been cooped up late into the night, and I had to blow off steam. So, I nudged the Grinch into action, and we went out."

"Did the angel who found you write you up for your transgression?" Dazielle said.

"Oh, sure. She was an official gal. We tried to talk her around with some charm, but she was having none of it. She even fined us."

"You haven't told us what you did?" I said.

"Just a little running through the village. We may have borrowed a few gnomes and left them somewhere." The Grinch giggled behind his hand.

"You stole property?" Dazielle scowled at him.

"We did no harm. And the gnomes looked better on your mayor's roof. We figured he'd find it funny."

"Dominic, check the files for this report." Dazielle gestured at the Winter Werewolf and the Grinch. "We don't encourage lawbreaking in Willow Tree Falls. People need to know they're safe."

"They're safe from us," the Winter Werewolf said. "We were tired of the pointless negotiations. Sandy's not budging."

"He'll budge if I kick him hard enough." The Winter Fairy looked at Quantum. "You're quiet. You want a percentage of what Sandy has, too."

Quantum yawned. "All this talking in circles is tedious. Sandy has this time of year wrapped up. I don't mind what he does. It's nice to see everyone happy and getting what they deserve."

The Winter Fairy thumped a small fist on the table. "You're all pathetic! I won't give up. I'll make sure everyone knows Sandy isn't the smiling, kindhearted figure his PR company present him as. He's a moneygrubbing, deceitful jerk who's only focused on the bottom line. No one will like him when they realize the only reason he sticks around is because of the money. He doesn't care about happy families or children opening gifts."

"I do, so long as those gifts come from a company I own," Sandy said. "Times have changed. You need to move with them, or you'll become irrelevant."

Dominic returned with a piece of paper. "This confirms it. Jophiel wrote up the Winter Werewolf and the Grinch at just gone midnight on the night of Figgy's murder."

"That proves nothing," the Winter Fairy said. "It still gave them time to kill Figgy."

"The angel who fined them followed them for half an hour. They went nowhere near the tree with a bauble. There's also a report of them being uncooperative, so Jophiel put them in the cells. We didn't release them until dawn."

"They're not involved," Sandy said. "I'll vouch for the wolf and the Grinch. Before they went on their rampage, we were here, negotiating. We didn't break until just before midnight."

"That's right." Gwendolyn looked up from her diary. "I note the times and days we meet. We had an extralong session that day."

"Which means we're innocent," the Grinch said. "And I'm done. I only hung around because sparkle wings said she'd get Sandy to change his mind. It's not happening. If I don't need to be here, I'm leaving. I've got pessimism and broken dreams to spread."

Dazielle looked at the report. "Given the information we have, you're free to go. You too." She nodded at the Winter Werewolf.

"Perfect. And I'm out of these negotiations. I don't need the money. I've been setting up a sideline of automotive repairs. There's money to be made in fixing things."

"You can't give up on Christmas," I said.

"Whatever you say, little dude. Let's go." He clapped the Grinch on the shoulder, and they left.

The Winter Fairy huffed out a breath. "I knew those two were weak. We've only been negotiating for a short time, and they've given up."

"Take that as a sign." Sandy leaned back in his seat and cupped his hands behind his head.

"What about you, Quantum?" I said. "You're giving up on Christmas, too?"

She pointed a bony finger at me. "I know what this is. A side effect from my enchanted gingerbread. I knew my magic would affect you. It's giving you false memories."

"Christmas is real, and I'm getting it back," I said. "And since Gwendolyn's here, we can check where you were. If you pass, you can leave, too." Even though Quantum was deeply creepy, I kind of liked her. I hoped she wasn't involved.

"We were together that evening," Gwendolyn said. "Once the negotiations ended, we took a brief break. Then Quantum wanted to discuss ideas to help things move forward. We stayed in the meeting room for several hours after the others left."

"It wasn't the most pleasurable evening, but I wanted to contribute," Quantum said.

"I can vouch for them being here," Dazielle said. "They stayed in the meeting room, and I passed by several times and heard them. They didn't leave until after three."

"That only leaves us with Sandy and the Winter Fairy." I'd been right all this time. "Which one of you did it?"

"Absolutely not," Sandy said.

"It wasn't me!" the Winter Fairy squeaked. "I'm shocked you'd think that. I'm the good fairy."

"So am I. Well, a good Sandy. I mean, I'm a good person."

"Santa Claus! You're Santa! Everyone knows you're the symbol of hope, kindness, and charity at Christmas."

"That's nice of you to say." Sandy smoothed down his hair. "Although I'm not sure about this Santa Claus title. Just call me Sandy. Everyone does."

"Neither of you live up to the nice theme all that well. We know Martino and Lily lied for you," I said.

Dazielle's nostrils flared. "Before I put you in the cells, I wanted to question you about your alibis. We suspect you coached your assistants to say you were in your bedrooms. They used almost word for word the same alibi when questioned."

Martino cringed in his seat, while Lily's eyes widened.

"Does no one want to say anything?" I said. "You faked your alibis. What were you really doing?"

"It's none of your business," the Winter Fairy snapped. "I didn't kill that elf."

Sandy sighed. "We may as well tell them, or this hound will keep digging until he finds the unpleasant truth."

She covered her face with her hands. "No! It was a horrible mistake. I refuse to admit to it."

312

I looked from Sandy to the Winter Fairy. Her cheeks were flushed, while he looked mildly smug. "You were together?"

"Stop talking," the Winter Fairy said. "It makes me feel sick to think about it."

"I didn't hear you complain at the time," Sandy said.

"I'd had too much champagne. We all make mistakes. This is one I deeply regret."

Dazielle looked appalled, while Dominic grinned, and I shook my head.

Quantum grimaced, although amusement gleamed in her dark eyes. "I should have known. You hate each other so passionately that naturally it spilled into the bedroom. What will the media think of this sordid liaison? It'll tarnish your reputations. And Sandy! Aren't you still pretending to have a happy marriage?"

"They can't find out! Quantum, please. I have a reputation to keep."

She slid her arm out of Sandy's grip. "A fake one."

"You got your assistants to lie so you could have a fling?" I said.

"It wasn't a fling. It was a drunken fumble that should never have happened," the Winter Fairy said. "I was lonely and tipsy, and Sandy wasn't being as repugnant as usual."

"You've had the hots for me for decades," he said.

She plugged her fingers into her ears.

Dazielle gestured for her to stop. "You were together when Figgy died?"

Sandy nodded. "We spent the night together. We told our assistants to cover for us. This is a private matter, and we can't allow for it to get into the public domain."

The assistants nodded, looking pale and more than a little worried they might be about to lose their jobs.

"Which means neither of you did it," Dazielle said on a sigh. "The Winter Werewolf and the Grinch were in the cells, and Gwendolyn and Quantum were here. That leaves us with..."

"No one!" I couldn't believe it. They all had alibis. What had I gotten wrong?

"We're all sad Figgy is dead," Gwendolyn said. "But he was playful and inquisitive. I wonder if he messed with magic and something went wrong. It's the only thing I can think of."

Dazielle stared at the notes she'd made on a piece of paper. "It's something to look into."

"Someone is lying," I said.

She ignored me. "I'm sorry to have wasted your time. You're all free to go."

"We're not done. What about Christmas?" I hopped up and down on the table. "Find who stole Christmas, and we find Figgy's killer."

"It's not missing," Dazielle said. "It doesn't exist. Christmas has never existed. Dominic, find Wiggles something to eat. That'll keep him quiet. I'll show our guests out."

I stared at her, open-mouthed. She was letting the suspects go!

Quantum paused to pet my head. "I'm intrigued by how my magic has affected you. Be well, Wiggles. I hope you survive, but you did eat two plates of enchanted food. You should be much sicker than this. Well, you should be dead. Remarkable creature."

I grumbled a goodbye as she left with the others.

One of them had to be the killer. Dazielle didn't believe me, Dominic thought I was talking nonsense, and no one in the village remembered Christmas.

A decent elf was dead. The magic of Christmas was destroyed, and I had no idea why it happened, who did it, or how to make this better.

# Chapter 9

I needed a break after that washed-out excuse for an interrogation. I stomped out of Angel Force, ordered dinner to be delivered to the pups, and then strode back to Cloven Hoof.

I had a head full of questions and no answers.

The Winter Werewolf and the Grinch had cast-iron alibis. Sandy and the fairy had been playing hide the Christmas yule log rather than killing Figgy. And the angels had overheard Quantum and Gwendolyn talking at the time of the murder. So, who did that leave?

The more I dug, the more I felt Figgy had never been the target for the exploding bauble.

The Christmas card clue ran through my thoughts. Don't make Figgy the centerpiece. This mystery wasn't about him, but he'd been caught in it and had lost his life.

I slowed as I reached Aurora's store. Despite it being late, the place was crowded and lights blazed from the windows.

She spotted me and waved, then pointed at my pups who snoozed on her counter. Rather than disturb them, I left them in Auntie Aurora's capable hands and headed home. I'd be terrible company, and would only grouch at my pups because of the killer problem I had on my paws. That wasn't fair to them.

I headed into Cloven Hoof and looked around. There were a few members of the team getting the club together for the evening, but other than that, it was quiet, and there was no sign of Tempest.

"Hey, Wiggles," Merrie Noble said from behind the bar. "Tempest is out. This is the last night we're opening, so she needed to get a few things."

I wandered over, taking my time to check for snacks that had rolled under the furniture. "She's definitely closing?"

"Yep. She said we could help with the redecoration if we wanted, but I'm not great with a paintbrush. I was thinking of going somewhere warm for a few weeks."

"You can't leave. It's almost Christmas."

"What's that?"

I puffed out smoke. "Never mind. Tell her I stopped by. I ordered the pups dinner, so it'll be here soon. She just has to heat it up."

"Before you go, someone left a card for you." Merrie held up a white envelope.

I dashed over, leaped onto a stool, and grabbed it out of her hand. I yanked the card out with my teeth. I flipped it open and read the words inside. *All that glitters is not good.*

"You got a secret admirer?" Merrie said.

"Not an admirer, but someone is telling me something. What do you make of this?"

Merrie read the note. "I'm not a fan of glitter. It gets everywhere. You always find it in places you shouldn't weeks after you've used it."

"I don't think it means that kind of glitter. Could it be the Winter Fairy? Is my secret clue leaver pointing me in the fairy's direction as the killer?" I shook my head. "But she has an alibi. And there's no way Santa Claus would cover for her. Despite them having a messy fumble, they can't stand the sight of each other."

"Wiggles, you've lost me." Merrie placed a bowl of fresh bar nuts out for me. "I get it, though. Parenthood is stressful."

"Yeah. It'll be chaos over Christmas."

"Is that a hellhound thing? You do something special this time of year?"

"Sure. We eat, drink, open gifts, and spend time with loved ones. You should try it." I tucked the card behind the counter, said goodbye to Merrie, and headed outside.

I was rounding the corner, deep in thought about where Christmas was hiding, who'd murdered Figgy, and what those cards meant, when a small gasp followed by a squeak reached my ears.

I looked around. Two legs flailed in the snow.

"Help! I'm stuck."

"Gwendolyn?" I trotted over and peered into the hole. She was partially covered by snow, and papers lay scattered around her. "Need a paw up?"

"Oh! Wiggles! Please. I wasn't looking where I was going. Someone dug an enormous hole in the snow. Can you believe it?"

"Huh! Can't imagine why anyone would do that." I had to help, since I'd planted this accidental booby-trap. It was fun to dig through the snow. Add a little fire, and it was easy to make a deep hole. A hole people could fall in and hurt themselves.

I hopped down, grabbed the back of Gwendolyn's thick winter coat, and pulled.

She squeaked again, but after a second, dug in her heels, and between us, we got out.

She brushed snow off her coat and took a minute to make herself presentable. "We should fill this in, so no one else has an accident. I was lucky not to break a bone."

317

"Yeah. Great idea. Let me." I bounded around, kicking snow and flattening it with a gentle wave of heat. As I worked, Gwendolyn gathered her fallen papers and put them in order. "Tah-dah! You wouldn't even know it had been here."

She smiled down at me, her gaze shifting around. "Have you seen my mobile snow globe? I dropped it when I fell."

I sniffed about and pulled it from the snow. There were several unread messages from someone called *Baby Bro*.

"Thanks." She checked the messages, sighed, and dropped the globe into her purse. "Sorry the meeting didn't go as planned. You seemed angry when you left."

"Not angry. Frustrated. And not at you. But the situation is twisty, and I don't know which way to turn."

She gestured for me to walk with her. "It's nice you want to find out what happened. Did you know Figgy?"

I trotted beside her. "No. But my pups found his body, so I'm duty bound to figure this out and get Christmas back on track."

"That must have been tough for them."

"They're strong, but I'm monitoring them. Well, their aunties are. They're great with them."

She nodded. "It's nice to have family to help."

"Sure is. I suppose this wasn't the Christmas you hoped for. Stuck with a bunch of squabbling A-listers while the angels blunder about. You'd prefer to be with loved ones?"

"I work any time of year. It doesn't matter to me. If someone needs my services, I'm there for them," she said. "People just need a safe space to talk, and a nonjudgmental ear to listen. It helps them work through their issues."

"You've been doing this gig long?"

"Most of my life. My parents are negotiators, too. They've worked with some impressive people. Leaders of countries, pack alphas, celebrities. Of course, we sign privacy agreements, so I can't name names, but ... I've met some characters."

"And now you're working with Santa Claus and the Winter Fairy. Must be an experience."

Gwendolyn studied me with her calm gaze as a chunk of snow slid down the sleeve of her soaked coat. "You seem troubled. If you want a coffee and a chat, we could talk. No charge."

"Nah, you're good. I don't need therapy."

"Which is perfect, since I'm not a therapist."

After a second of consideration, I nodded. It would be good to talk this through with a professional and get another opinion.

"I make no assumptions, but sometimes, when a person is close to a subject, they struggle to see the bigger picture. They miss things, or misinterpret things." She lifted a hand. "I'm not saying that's what you're doing, but a listening ear could help. I can ask questions you haven't even thought of. It's what I do. And, not wanting to toot my own horn, I'm good at it."

"Sure. I'd like that."

"Great. But not out here. I'm freezing, and my coat is soggy."

"Then I'm buying you a coffee. It's my way of saying sorry."

"Sorry for what?"

"Oh, you know. Holes in the snow that appear out of nowhere."

She glanced over her shoulder and smiled. "Well, then, I'll have a coffee and a cookie."

"This way. Sprinkles should still be open."

"Mind if we get takeout and go back to my rental? I need to change before I catch a cold."

"Sure."

We trudged through the snow. A quick look around showed no Christmas decorations in any windows.

"You're worried about something," Gwendolyn said. "I promise I won't judge. Whatever you tell me will be in confidence."

"I get all that because I'm shouting you a coffee and a cookie?"

"No, but not only am I a negotiator, I'm an empath. Your fears echo through me. I want to help. I feel better by making other people feel better."

"Works for me."

Patti Kays was just flipping the sign to Closed as we got to her door.

I barged into the shop. "We won't be long. I owe this lady."

Patti rolled her eyes. "Make it quick."

Five minutes later, Gwendolyn carried a large mug of takeout coffee, and I carried the bag of cookies. I did my best not to drool over them.

"This way. I'm renting a cute place a few minutes from here. It has an open fire."

We arrived at a hobbit-style house, and I got the fire going in the living room hearth, while Gwendolyn changed.

When she returned, she wore loose black harem pants and a chunky red sweater. She curled into a chair, took a cookie from the plate, and lifted her mug. She took a sip. "Heavenly. Now, where do you want to start?"

I finished the last bite of cookie I'd been munching, took a breath, and the words poured out. I told her my fears over Christmas vanishing, my concerns over everyone forgetting the magic of this time of year, why Figgy's death was a puzzle, and what I'd do to make sure Christmas was perfect for my pups.

As I blurted my thoughts, Gwendolyn listened and nodded. She didn't ask a single question, just kept focused on me. She barely touched the cookie she'd picked up.

I blew out a breath. "What do you think? Am I crazy? Parenting four pups is the most intense, incredible, frustrating experience I've been through. Has it sent me over the edge? Am I not meant to be a father?"

"No, you're not crazy, but I understand your concerns. I'm sure you make an excellent parent. The fact you're questioning your ability to raise them shows you care." She paused. "You have a deep belief in this thing called Christmas, and no one else does. That must frustrate you."

"I'm not the only one who remembers. Someone is sending me clues in Christmas cards. They want me to figure out why Figgy died."

"It's good to have an ally. Do you know who's helping you?"

"No idea. They keep slipping the cards under the door."

Gwendolyn sat in silence for a moment. "I wish I could help. I feel your pain. This really bothers you." She rubbed her chest.

"Unless you can figure out how to bring back Christmas, there's not much you can do. Although it is good to talk. I feel better." I ate another cookie.

"And I'm always happy to listen. A good negotiator needs her mouth closed and her ears open. Sometimes, that's all people need. They talk through their problem and find the solution themselves."

"It hasn't happened in my case, but I appreciate it, anyway." I hoovered crumbs off the floor. "You must get sick of hearing everyone's complaints."

"I focus on finding solutions. Although I can't find a solution to your Christmas problem."

I sniffed the empty plate. Neither could I.

"Do you want more to eat?" Gwendolyn was already out of her seat and headed to the kitchen.

I'd been eyeing a bowl of foil-wrapped chocolate coins on the sideboard. "We could crack these open."

She turned and looked in the direction my nose was pointed. "Oh, no! They're only for decoration."

"Decoration? You must have bought them when you still believed in Christmas. I planned to put coins in my pups' stockings. Hellhound friendly, of course." I huffed out a breath. "I won't do that now. Tempest took down the decorations, and the stockings have been banished to the basement."

Gwendolyn walked to the bowl. "Why do you put coins in stockings?"

"It's a Christmas tradition. It's hard to explain if you don't believe."

"Wiggles, I want to believe. Christmas sounds fun. Maybe you could make it a thing. Have your own Christmas. Just you and your pups."

"I guess. It wouldn't be the same, though." I hopped up and headed for the bowl. "Eating these will make me feel better. I'm happy to share."

She lifted the bowl out of my reach. "You shouldn't eat these."

"Are you saving them for a special occasion?"

"Isn't chocolate bad for dogs?"

I lifted a paw. "Tempest is always saying that. But I'm a hellhound, so I'm basically impossible to kill. I'll just have a few. You won't even notice them gone."

She shook her head and placed the bowl on a high shelf. "No coins for you, just in case. If they made you sick, I'd feel terrible."

I scowled at the bowl. Now that I'd seen those chocolate coins, they were all I wanted to eat. Gwendolyn was keeping them so she could gorge on them later. I could understand. We all liked to overindulge on our own now and again.

"Can I get you anything else? Or would you like to talk some more?" She politely hid a yawn behind one hand.

"No, I should get going. It's almost Christmas Day, and I have presents to wrap. Although I'm not sure I'll bother. It seems like a waste of time, since no one remembers what Christmas Day means."

"When is Christmas Day?" Gwendolyn stumbled over the word as she led me to the door.

"Two more sleeps to go. I've got my pups loads of gifts. I was looking forward to them opening the presents under the tree and then eating turkey. They were getting one each. Now, there's no tree, no presents, no Christmas, and no turkeys."

Gwendolyn tentatively petted my head. "I hope you figure things out."

I said goodbye and trudged outside.

Failure lodged in my gut like a stale rock bun. There was nowhere else to turn. The suspects had alibis, and Christmas was gone, so there was nothing to celebrate with my pups. All the amazing festive food I'd been dreaming about for weeks had vanished. Even Santa Claus wouldn't deliver gifts to delight everyone.

I blasted flames to melt the snow as I stomped to the apartment. This Christmas sucked, or whatever I was supposed to call it.

It was time to do the only thing I could think of. Bury myself under a mountain of food and forget about helping.

# Chapter 10

I rolled over and came face-to-face with a snoring Tempest. A quick glance through the gap in the curtain showed it was getting light out.

I'd spent yesterday hiding, overeating, and feeling sorry for myself. And my mood was no brighter as Not-Christmas morning arrived.

After rolling off the bed, I did a full body stretch and shook out my fur. My overindulgences had left me unsatisfied and with a food hangover.

If it had been a real Christmas Day, my pups would have woken us by bouncing in at three in the morning and insisting they open gifts. Tempest would have complained while secretly laughing, and I'd have told them to go back to bed, then allowed them one gift and one treat.

But my pups slumbered in the corner of the bedroom. There was no sign of Christmas joy. It was time to forget it existed.

I slipped out of the bedroom and headed down to the club. I shouldn't have wasted my time, but I'd snuck gifts downstairs. It didn't matter if the pups found them because they wouldn't understand their significance, but there was a tiny part of me that was still determined to find Christmas.

I wandered into the kitchen and nosed open the cupboard door where I'd stashed the gifts. Four green and red talking parrots stared back at me. "I should return you. You're no good to anyone."

"I should return you. You're no good to anyone. We know you're no good to anyone. Can't even solve a murder."

I growled at the cheeky parrot.

It growled back.

I wandered into the club and ambled around. It looked unloved without the tinsel and sparkle. What if this wasn't temporary? What if everyone in Willow Tree Falls had forgotten Christmas existed for good?

No, I couldn't accept that. My stomach turned over. What if this wasn't confined to the village? What if the world had forgotten Christmas?

I stared at something white poking out from under the main door leading into the club. I hurried over and pulled it free. It was another envelope with my name on it.

After tearing it open, I read the words inside. *What else should we celebrate?*

I bounded upstairs, collected the other cards, brought them down, and lined them up. I read each sentence in turn.

*Don't make Figgy the centerpiece.*

*All that glitters isn't good.*

*What else shall we celebrate?*

"I don't know," I muttered.

One parrot quietly mimicked me from the kitchen.

"Figgy, glitter, and an alternative celebration." I slumped on my belly and stared at the cards.

I closed my eyes. Maybe Christmas was lost, but it didn't need to be a washout. I could still have fun with my pups. We could play in the snow, and then I could give them their gifts and tell them it was because they'd been so good. Well, they weren't good. They were fluffy, fire-breathing devils, but they did their best.

My gaze tracked across the cards. All that glitters isn't good. There was so much glitter and sparkle at Christmas, but if I took it literally, it meant I should focus on the Christmas characters who came with glitz and glamor. The Winter Fairy sprang to mind. She was over the top with her sparkles, and even her lip gloss glittered. But then the Yuletide Witch shimmered, too, although it was a dark glitter, mingled with gold.

And Even Santa Claus occasionally sparkled!

"What else shall we celebrate?" I wasn't that up to date on Christmas history, but everyone knew we hadn't always celebrated this way. There were traditions involving freaky horse skull parades, and even the occasional blood sacrifice if you went back far enough.

Quantum would know about the old ways. There was even a time when yuletide was the preferred date to celebrate, starting on December twenty-first. But it couldn't be her. Gwendolyn had confirmed they were together, and the angels had overheard them. Angels don't lie. Or if they did, they exploded. Well, that's what I always imagined happened.

"I'm missing something," I muttered.

"I'm missing something. Most likely your brain," a parrot grumbled.

I stared at the cards, then raced into the kitchen and looked at the parrots. "How long do you record for?"

"How long do you record for? Wouldn't you like to know?"

"This is serious." I kicked a parrot over and looked at its base.

"Squawk! This is serious. Kick me again, and you'll regret it."

I rolled the annoying bird under my paw. "I got it! I know who killed Figgy."

"Figgy! Figgy! Figgy!"

The parrots mocked me as I raced out of the club, skidding across the snow in my haste to get to the woods and speak to Quantum.

It made sense. She loved the old ways. Sure, she said she liked the sparkle and fun, but visiting her rental had shown the opposite was true.

I slowed as I got near her cabin. Quantum stood at the door. She had a coat on and a bag in her hand.

"You're leaving?"

Her head shot up. "Wiggles! What brings you here so early?"

"It's Christmas Day, and I'm looking for answers. I think you have them."

She busied herself with the lock. "Answers about what?"

"You own a talking parrot."

Quantum glanced at me. "I do. I thought it was cute. Why the interest?"

"You didn't think it was cute," I said. "You thought it would give you an alibi."

She turned and stared down at me as I stopped at the bottom of the porch. "An alibi for what?"

"Getting away with killing Figgy."

Quantum was silent for a second, then laughed. "Come inside. Let's talk. I have more gingerbread." She unlocked the door and strode in.

I didn't hesitate, and hurried to the shelf where I'd seen the parrot. It was gone. "What have you done with it?"

She shrugged off her black, tattered lace-covered coat. "Done with what?"

"The parrot! You tampered with it so it would record a fake conversation you had with Gwendolyn."

Quantum rested her hands on her hips. "Why would I do that?"

"To get away with murder." I sniffed around the room, but there was no sign of the parrot. "It was never Figgy you intended to kill, though, was it? You always planned to kill Christmas."

Her gaze drifted around the sparse room. "My enchanted gingerbread has done more harm than I realized. You're remembering a celebration that never existed."

"You still remember. And you hate Christmas. You want to bring back the old celebrations. That way, everyone will worship you like they do Santa Claus and the fairy. The Christmas Fairy, not the Winter Fairy. That's her real name."

"You adorable little thing. You need help."

"No, I need your confession."

"I confess to nothing. Now, leave." Quantum stepped toward me, her black, glittering magic sparking between her hands.

"Tell me what you did with the parrot?" If she'd destroyed it, the evidence was gone.

"Why does it matter? Maybe I gave it away. It was irritating."

"It's proof you laid a trap. But it went wrong, didn't it?"

"Enough! Get out of here." She marched to the door.

"I'm going nowhere. Not until—" my spine arched as ancient, icy power wrapped around me.

Quantum dragged me toward the door as the air exploded out of my lungs, and I couldn't draw in another breath. "I gave you fair warning, tiny creature." She flexed her hand and squeezed her fingers into a fist.

Pain exploded around my heart. "If you kill me, it'll show you're guilty. Tempest will hunt you and destroy you."

"I don't fear a Crypt witch. And I'll be long gone before your chubby little corpse is discovered. I'll bury you out back with that dumb parrot."

I struggled against her power, but I couldn't draw enough breath to blast a flame. Intense pain wracked my bones, and my vision grew fuzzy.

"Succumb to my ways, puppy. Everyone will soon learn the yuletide celebrations are the most important. And if anyone remembers that ridiculous freak show known as Christmas, they'll feel what you're feeling. That'll make them forget the over-the-top sparkle and fake jolliness." She jerked her hands together. "This time of year needs to welcome the darkness, the cold, even the pain. It's how it should be. It was how it was for a long time, and I'm demanding that return. Santa Claus and that ridiculous fairy have had things their way for too long."

"It was you," I wheezed out.

"It was. But you're the only one who knows." Quantum crouched until we were at eye level. "You're a remarkable creature. It's almost a shame to destroy you. But you won't keep my secret, so I have no choice." A laugh growled out as she raised her hand.

I'd always assumed I was impossible to kill, but this ancient witch had the edge over my hellhound skills.

As the last of my breath left my body, voices flickered through my head. Was this the flashing before your eyes moment everyone got before they died? It sounded like Tempest, but there were other voices, too. And footsteps. Footsteps crunching through the snow.

The agonizing pain around my heart faded just as there was a knock on the cabin door.

"Don't say a word," Quantum hissed at me. "If you want your witch to live, you'll stay silent."

I couldn't get to my paws, but I could breathe again. I drew in a breath to yell Tempest's name, but Quantum's skeletal fingers clamped my muzzle shut.

"I warned you. I will kill her."

Foolish witch. She'd obviously never gone up against a Crypt witch, or she wouldn't be so blasé about the awesome power she was about to face.

There was another knock on the door. "Hey, Wiggles. Get your butt out here and help with your pups. They just jumped me in the shower. The curtain is burned to a crisp, and I lost an eyebrow. Again."

My eyes widened. Did Tempest have my pups with her? They weren't safe around Quantum. They were amazing little fluffballs, but had years of training before they could control their magic.

There was more thumping. "Open up. I can see you."

That wasn't Tempest's voice. Santa Claus had his face pressed against the obscured glass, his hands cupped on either side of his cheeks.

Quantum grated out a sigh. "I have more loose ends to tidy up than I realized. Not a word, or your family gets fried." She released my muzzle, strode to the door, and opened it.

Standing outside was Santa Claus, the Winter Fairy, their assistants, Gwendolyn, and Tempest, who held my squirming pups.

Tempest's eyes narrowed as she studied Quantum. "Is Wiggles here?"

"You must be the great Tempest Crypt. Wiggles has barely stopped talking about you."

"Sure. That's me. Is he here?"

"He is. We formed a friendship since my arrival, and he came to wish me well before I left." Quantum's words were silky, but her hands flexed behind her back, trickles of black magic dripping off her nails.

I had to stop her, but my legs shook, and my power was wonky. I needed a minute to recharge.

Tempest looked past Quantum. "Wiggles, you okay?"

Quantum whirled from the door. "He's not himself. I've been worried about him. How did you know he was here?"

"A location spell." Tempest set down the pups, and they darted off and played in the snow. "Wiggles, you're never this quiet. What's going on?"

"I offered him an herbal tincture to see if it would help." Quantum stepped into Tempest's path. "Why not let him sleep it off here? I can return him to you later."

Wrong move. The worst possible move to stop my witch from getting what she wanted.

Tempest's fingers twitched, and she sucked in air.

Santa Claus cleared his throat. "We met Tempest on our way here. We're leaving today, too, so we wanted to wish you well."

"The angels are happy for you to go?" Quantum said smoothly, her glare on Tempest, daring her to shove past.

"We all have alibis, so no one needs to stay." Santa Claus's gaze landed on her bag. "It looks like we caught you just in time."

Quantum shrugged. "Wolfie and the Grinch left last night, so there's no point in sticking around. Especially since the negotiations failed."

"It was her," I forced out through my teeth. "Quantum killed Figgy. And she stole Christmas."

"Oh, dear. Tempest, your pup is unwell. He seems obsessed with this thing called Christmas." Quantum turned to me, the smile on her face not concealing the hatred in her eyes.

"Get Angel Force here." My words sounded broken. "Quantum is behind this."

"Me? Behind what? I can't imagine what he means."

Tempest scowled at Quantum. "Wiggles doesn't lie. Well, he sometimes conceals stealing food, but never lies about anything important. Why does he think you killed Figgy?"

"He was delirious when he got here. I was about to get help when you arrived. He's running a fever."

"He always runs hot. Why didn't you open the door when Sandy knocked? What don't you want us to see?" Tempest barged past Quantum, crouched beside me, and ran her hands over me. "You are running hotter than usual. Has this witch done something to you?"

"Quantum didn't answer because she was busy trying to kill me." I felt better with Tempest beside me. "And she faked an alibi with Gwendolyn."

Everyone looked at Gwendolyn.

"Ignore him," Quantum said.

"Let's get you out of here." Tempest lifted me into her arms. "I'm taking you to the vet."

I struggled to get away, but was weaker than a new born unicorn. "No! Anything but that. Besides, the vets don't open on Christmas Day."

"You see, he's delusional about Christmas," Quantum said. "I hope you can heal him. I've grown fond of Wiggles since I've been here."

"Pups, you're with me." Tempest strode out of the cabin with me in her arms.

Quantum followed us onto the porch and stood with a smug smile on her lips.

"Well, we'll get going, too." Santa Claus adjusted the lapels of his red suit. "Sorry things didn't work out for you. Maybe next year?"

Quantum's smug expression deepened. "You can guarantee, I'll be all people will talk about." Her gaze cut to me. "I wish you well, Wiggles. Have a Merry Christmas."

My head shot up, and I stared at her.

Quantum froze to the spot, her smile tight.

I feebly wagged my tail. "Got you."

# Chapter 11

Tempest kept me in her arms as she turned to Quantum. "What did you say?"

Quantum's laugh grated out of her. "I thought it would help. Wiggles is obsessed by this imaginary Christmas."

"You sounded like you meant it." Tempest set me down. "Do you also believe in Christmas?"

I dived into the snow to cool off, then checked on my pups. "The parrots tipped me off. I went downstairs to figure out what to do with the pups' Christmas gifts, and found another card clue. It was what I needed to figure this out and realize Quantum killed Figgy."

"You should get him emergency treatment right away." Quantum spoke through gritted teeth. "I don't think he's got much longer."

There was no indecision on Tempest's face as she crossed her arms over her chest. "If Wiggles says this Christmas thing exists, then it does."

"Err ... perhaps we should leave." Santa Claus caught hold of the Christmas Fairy's elbow.

"You stay," I said. "This involves you."

"Don't accuse us of killing Figgy as well." The Christmas Fairy pointedly moved away from Santa Claus.

"You didn't kill him. You're both innocent. Well, Santa Claus, you're greedy and have forgotten how to share, but you're no killer." I lapped up snow to remove the last of Quantum's foul feeling magic from my system.

He spluttered out a few noises, but a glare from Tempest kept him quiet.

"Go on, Wiggles. How did you figure out Quantum killed Figgy?" she said.

"I'm intrigued to learn that, too, since I didn't do it." Quantum wasn't looking at me as she spoke, but Gwendolyn.

Gwendolyn looked at the ground, her shoulders tight around her ears and her expression grim.

"When Figgy was found, we focused on the wrong thing. We assumed he'd been killed because of his past," I said. "But no one said anything bad about him. According to the angels, even his probation officer loved him. Figgy was never the target. He wasn't supposed to die."

"Who was?" the Christmas Fairy said.

"Sandy. Or rather, Santa Claus."

His mouth dropped open. "Impossible! Who'd want me dead? Why?"

I looked at Quantum. "You got in the way of ancient traditions. And a mimicking parrot tipped me off that Quantum planned to change that."

Her smirk looked frozen. "What use would I have for a child's toy when committing murder?"

"Those parrots are smart. I should know since I own four. And I'm sure, with tinkering, they could record longer conversations. Such as the conversation you allegedly had with Gwendolyn when Figgy was being blown apart."

"Tinkering with a parrot?" Quantum shook her head. "This is ridiculous. I need to leave. So does everybody else. This pup is wasting our time with his deranged ramblings."

"We should let him ramble," Tempest said. "Wiggles is on to something."

Santa Claus and the Christmas Fairy looked uncertain, but remained where they were. Gwendolyn continued to look unhappy, while the assistants waited for orders.

I nodded at Tempest. She always had my back, even though she had no clue what Christmas was. "I started getting Christmas cards delivered. They were anonymous, but contained clues. Clues about the killer."

"What's a Christmas card?" Santa Claus said.

"No one knows," Quantum said. "Because he's making it up. How much more proof do you need?"

"I've seen the cards," Tempest said. "And there was a new one downstairs when I got up. Something about different celebrations?"

"Yes. I received three cards. The first clued me in to the fact Figgy was never meant to die. The second told me someone with glittering magic wasn't as good as they appeared to be."

"Not me," the Christmas Fairy said. "I provide goodness at this time of year. The joy and happiness. I can't use my magic to do bad things. It makes me sick."

"You're not the only one who glitters," I said. "It was the final clue that made me realize someone wanted to bring back the old ways. They were done with everyone celebrating the commercialized version of Christmas."

"So you assumed the worst about me? Pick on someone else. The Winter Werewolf is almost as old as me," Quantum said. "Chase him and make those wild accusations. Or are you afraid of his bite?"

"He has a cast-iron alibi. Although his teeth are sharp, so I wouldn't want a nip from him."

She tapped her bony fingers on her biceps. "This is guesswork. Bad guesswork."

"There's one last thing. Gwendolyn has a huge pile of chocolate gold coins at her rental. At least, I assumed they were chocolate. But she didn't want me to eat them. When I tried, she took them away."

"Chocolate is bad for dogs," Gwendolyn whispered.

"Those coins are actual gold. And they were payment from Quantum. All that glitters isn't good. That clue wasn't about magic, it was about gold. The person leaving me clues wanted me to know something was going on."

"Why would I pay Gwendolyn?" Quantum said.

"Maybe it was a bribe. You paid her to plant the enchanted bauble, but then things went wrong. That bauble was meant for Santa Claus. Did Figgy find the note you left, Gwendolyn? He was such a good little helper that he went to collect the bauble as a surprise for Sandy, who was too busy plotting his next ad campaign to get it himself."

Gwendolyn remained quiet and hunched.

"Stop bothering her," Quantum said. "She works for us, not you."

"Why would you bribe Gwendolyn to kill me?" Santa Claus fretted with his beard as he stepped behind his assistant.

"I didn't! The hound is making it up. If he were mine, I'd have had him put down a long time ago."

I growled at the same time as Tempest.

"Try it. See how far you get." Sparks of red magic flickered around Tempest. "Pups! First one to find an angel and bring them here gets a bone and doesn't have to bathe for a week."

Quantum sucked in a breath as the pups yipped with glee and raced away. She raised a hand, but Tempest grabbed her wrist. "Don't even think about making a move on them."

"There's an easy way to test this theory," the Christmas Fairy said. "Let's see the coins. If they're chocolate, there was no bribe."

"I'll send Martino for them. Where are they?" Santa Claus said.

"No!" Gwendolyn worried her bottom lip with her teeth. "They're ... they're gone. I ate them."

"You couldn't have eaten that bowlful on your own," I said. "It was enormous. Even I'd have struggled. Where have you hidden the bribe?"

"There was no bribe. There is no Christmas. And there is no conspiracy to kill," Quantum said. "Figgy made a mistake with his magic. It happens. He was under a lot of pressure working with Sandy."

"Don't pin this on me," Santa Claus said. "Figgy was well paid and had plenty of breaks. And he'd never make a mistake like that. Did you do this, Quantum? You want me dead, so people worship you instead?"

"Of course not."

Santa Claus kept stroking his beard. "There are rumors you were involved in that assassination attempt three years ago."

She inspected her fingernails and sniffed. "You should never listen to gossip."

"Gwendolyn, did you send me the clues?" I said. "You must feel terrible that Figgy died. You wanted to confess, but knew if you did, you'd be arrested, too."

"Don't say a word," Quantum said. "The hound is trying to trick you."

Gwendolyn remained quiet, her gaze on the ground. "I'm sorry."

"What have you got to be sorry for?" Santa Claus said. "You're excellent at your job."

"She's an empath. She's feeling sorry about this bizarre situation and stressed because she's hoovering up everyone's anxiety."

Quantum made a move toward Gwendolyn, but Tempest blocked her. "I don't think so. Let Gwendolyn tell us what happened."

Quantum waved a hand in the air. "She has nothing to say!"

I bounded to Gwendolyn and rested my front paws on her leg. "Why accept the bribe to kill Santa Claus? You must have known how terrible you'd feel ending someone's life."

Her teary gaze went to Quantum. "I... I needed the money to pay off my brother's debt. The debt collector threatened to kill him if he didn't pay by the end of the year. Quantum found me crying about it and offered me a solution."

"You mean she discovered you were in need and exploited you," I said. "That's what the messages were about on your mobile snow globe? Your baby bro needed you, and you couldn't let him down."

"Don't say another word." Quantum glared at Gwendolyn.

Gwendolyn's head remained lowered. "I really am sorry."

"Silence!" Quantum shrieked.

When Gwendolyn lifted her head, tears trickled down her cheeks. "You said the bauble wouldn't kill. It was only supposed to scare Sandy and make him think twice before taking all the money."

The Christmas Fairy gasped. "What a terrible thing to do."

I paid her no attention. She'd have been thrilled if Santa Claus had exploded.

Gwendolyn sighed. "My thoughts are so confusing. Something happened when that bauble exploded, and I can't hold on to my memories. And every time you say the word Christmas, I get brain freeze. I know what you're saying makes sense, but then I don't."

"Quantum's magic affected everyone when that bauble went boom," I said. "Maybe she didn't tell you the bauble would kill, but she also didn't tell you the magic inside it wiped memories. She wanted Santa Claus out of the way and for people to forget Christmas. It was a risky move, putting so much power into a single object."

Quantum shrugged. "As a powerful being, you'll understand it's possible. Not that I would. I'm simply saying we know our limits."

"You didn't know your limits when it came to murder," I said.

A cold glaze filtered across Quantum's face. "It's not my fault Gwendolyn wanted Sandy dead. She's behind this."

Gwendolyn raised a hand and stepped back. "I'm not taking the blame. You said the explosion wouldn't injure anyone. You promised me."

Quantum's foot tapped rapidly. "I'm not responsible for your actions."

"You might have gotten away with pinning the blame on Gwendolyn," I said, "but you just wished me a Merry Christmas. Why say that if you have no idea what Christmas means?"

She pursed her blackened lips. "I was humoring you. Hoping it would make you feel better."

"You remember Christmas."

"So do you! Perhaps you planted the bauble."

"I wouldn't want anyone to forget Christmas. I've been planning how to keep my pups entertained for months."

"That's not enough evidence to arrest me." Quantum turned to grab her bag. "I'm leaving before this hound says something he can't take back."

"The parrot!" I said. "You told me you buried it, and you'd do the same to me. We dig up the parrot and play the recording of your made up conversation with Gwendolyn. That's proof."

"Good luck finding it." Quantum's gaze danced to the window, her surety she'd get away with it looking shaken.

"Or one of you can confess," I said. "Angel Force may go easier on you if you tell the truth and save them all that work. After all, it is Christmas Day. Everyone should be celebrating, not digging through the frozen dirt to get evidence to show you're behind this."

Quantum pressed her lips together. She wouldn't break.

However, Gwendolyn's jaw wobbled, and tears continued to fall. "I feel terrible."

"Don't do it," Quantum said. "Everyone can walk away the victor."

"Not Figgy," Santa Claus said.

The Christmas Fairy pressed her glittery-nailed hand to her chest. "Quantum! You did do it. You killed Figgy. Did you destroy this made-up Christmas thing, too? What's so special about it?"

Quantum smirked. "It amuses me to hear you say that. But you're right. No one believes in your version of Christmas anymore."

"I do," I said. "And soon, everyone else will, too. I'm bringing Christmas back."

There was a whoosh of warm air over our heads. Dazielle and Dominic landed. They each carried two of my pups.

As soon as the pups saw me, they squirmed out of the angels' arms and bounded over.

"Did we do good, Papa? We got the right angels? I got mine first. I bit his ankle and made him squeak," Shade said.

"So did I! I grabbed her fat wing and chewed on it. She ran around yipping like someone had squashed her tail," Nightmare said.

"Then I jumped on her." Ghost circled Dazielle and growled.

"And I sat on the dumb one's face." Arcane danced through the snow, wagging his adorable little tail.

Dazielle brushed a hand down her wing. "I didn't yip. I was surprised when a pup flew through the air and bit me, that's all."

"You're all good boys. Well done." I looked up at Dazielle and Dominic. "Did they tell you what's going on?"

Dazielle strode over with Dominic beside her. "I understood some of their garbled yapping. This had better not be a joke."

"No joke. Quantum paid Gwendolyn in gold coins to plant an enchanted bauble under the Christmas tree to kill Sandy." I raised a paw. "And before you say Christmas doesn't exist, hear me out. The bauble wasn't meant for Figgy. He must have collected it and was killed by the magic that exploded out when he touched it. Gwendolyn will tell you the rest."

Quantum was creeping back, her narrow gaze on the angels, but a sharp glare from Dazielle stopped her.

Gwendolyn's shoulders sagged, and more tears dripped onto the snow. "I wish I'd never gotten involved in these negotiations. I used to adore this time of year."

"You can say the word Christmas," I said. "It doesn't bite. That's what you love so much."

She sighed. "Maybe. If I hadn't taken the job, I'd never have learned how materialistic Sandy and the Winter Fairy are, and I'd never have been persuaded by Quantum there was a way to protect my brother."

"You were desperate to help him," I said. "And once Quantum got you, you were in too deep. But you tried to help by leaving me clues."

"I was confused. I knew something important had been lost, but that bauble magic was so strong it wiped out my memories. I kept getting flashbacks involving sparkling trees and presents, but none of it made sense. Then I found some strange cards in my bag.

I didn't understand the Christmas word, but it meant something."

"Is this true?" Dazielle said to Quantum. "You hired Gwendolyn to kill Sandy?"

Quantum remained silent.

"Quantum also remembers Christmas," I said. "You'll need a shovel to dig up the rude mimicking parrot she used to record a conversation with Gwendolyn. It's how they faked their alibis. And check Gwendolyn's things for gold coins."

"How are you able to remember Christmas?" Quantum snarled. "I'm stronger than you. Better than you."

"That's just been proven wrong. Wiggles is awesome," Tempest said. "Angels, make the arrest."

Dazielle and Dominic looked puzzled, but they understood Quantum was in the murky middle of this mystery.

Dazielle's wings extended, and she grabbed Quantum before she could fling out magic. "Dominic, go get a shovel. We have evidence to find."

***

"It's Christmas! It's Christmas! Where are my presents? Where's the food? Papa, can we play in the snow?"

I was knocked off my paws as my pups surrounded me, barking out questions, demanding licks, tummy rubs, and snuffles. Then more presents and food.

After Quantum reluctantly revealed what magic she'd concealed in the bauble, we could undo its effects with a tailored reversal spell. Christmas was back. People's memories were restored. And the fun was just getting started.

"Leave your father alone." Tempest emerged from the bedroom. She wore a startling red sweater with an enormous snowflake on the front.

"A gift from Aurora?" I gently nudged my pups off me and rolled to my paws.

Tempest tugged at the sweater and shrugged. "She does it every year. How many ugly Christmas sweaters do I need?"

"You can never have too many. The color suits you."

"She got you a sparkling bowtie, too. The pups have festive onesies. We'll have fun putting those on them."

"Papa! Can we open one present? Just one?" Nightmare raised a paw and whined.

I gathered my overenthusiastic pups in front of me and waited for almost silence. "If you go downstairs quietly, you'll each find a gift under the tree. Wait for me and Auntie Tempest to join you before opening them. No peeking, or you won't get any more gifts."

That was all the prompting they needed. They bundled and fought to be the first out the door and down the stairs.

Tempest wandered over, laughing. "There's no way we're surviving this Christmas."

"I can think of worse fates." I leaned against her leg. "Quantum almost got me, you know."

Tempest crouched and clipped my new bowtie around my neck. "Yeah, that was a close call. You should have asked for my help."

"You didn't believe in Christmas. I had no choice but to work this mystery alone."

"I'll believe you from now on. Whatever you say."

"I read somewhere hellhounds need a third breakfast." She smirked. "Uh-huh!"

"You said you'd believe me."

"So long as it's not food related." Tempest tweaked the red bowtie. "Let's go see what carnage the pups have engaged in."

"We'll be fine once we're at your parents' house. There'll be all the aunties, uncles, and grandparents needed to keep them under control."

She wandered down the stairs with me. "I still can't believe everyone forgot Christmas."

"It took me a while to realize what was really going on. Figgy's death concealed something so much bigger than a simple murder."

"Quantum really thought she could get away with obliterating Christmas and returning her traditions for people to worship?"

"She's powerful. Almost as powerful as me." Maybe even stronger, but I didn't want Tempest to worry when this was a day of celebration and happiness.

The second we entered the club, my pups took it as a cue to tear into their gifts. Of course, I'd wrapped up their talking parrots.

"Knock, knock." Dominic's head appeared around the main door of the club. "I didn't know whether to go straight to your parents' house or come meet you first."

"Um ... that depends on what you need," Tempest said.

"I forgot to tell you. He's joining us for Christmas," I said.

Dominic brought in two gigantic bags of gifts. He wore a white sweater with red bobbles on. "If it's still okay. It is okay, isn't it?"

Tempest walked over and uncharacteristically hugged him. "It's more than okay. You're always welcome. Merry Christmas, Dominic."

He grinned. "Merry Christmas to you all, too. That's something I wasn't saying a few hours ago."

"Quantum is talking?" I said.

"Grudgingly. Gwendolyn's being more cooperative. She's just relieved to get everything off her chest. She feels dreadful about what happened. She thought she could help her brother, make Christmas more meaningful, and solve the issue between the bickering Christmas alphas."

"Even if Gwendolyn's sorry and didn't come up with the plan to destroy Christmas and kill Santa Claus, she's still involved," Tempest said. "She can't get away with it."

"She won't. They're negotiating a deal. As for Quantum," Dominic nodded at me, "we found the parrot behind the cabin."

"It revealed their recorded conversation?"

"It did. We also found the gold in Gwendolyn's case when we searched it and traced it back to Quantum's personal supply."

"Quantum wanted the old ways back that badly?" Tempest said.

I sniffed at the gifts Dominic had brought in. There were food treats for me buried somewhere in a bag. "Some people aren't glitter fans."

Tempest tweaked her sweater. "I'm not a glitter fan, but I still wouldn't destroy Christmas."

"Neither would I." Dominic dodged two rampaging pups as they bounced past with parrots hanging out of their mouths. "Maybe we need a better balance, though. Sometimes, people forget what Christmas is all about. Quantum wanted to change that, but she went too far."

"We can have balance," I said. "So long as it doesn't end in murder."

"Food. It needs to end in food and lots of it," Tempest said. "Round up the pups. Let's get out of here."

After corralling, promising, and warning the pups to behave, we were out the door and heading to the Crypt witch house for festive feasting and fun.

My tongue lolled out, and I wagged my tail. All the Christmas sparkle was back. Every house glittered, lights gleamed in windows, and trees twinkled by doorways.

"It's good to have you back," I said. "Merry Christmas, Willow Tree Falls. Merry Christmas, everyone. Now, where's that turkey I've been dreaming about?"

# About Author

K.E. O'Connor (Karen) is a mystery author living in the beautiful British countryside. She loves all things mystery, animals, and cake.

If you want to practice spells, solve a few murders, and spend time with amazing witches and their talking familiars, join her weekly newsletter.

Sign up today.

**Newsletter:**
https://BookHip.com/GXDVFRA

**Website:**
www.keoconnor.com

**Facebook:**
www.facebook.com/keoconnorauthor

# Afterword

Thank you for spending time with the wonderful talking familiars from my magical worlds. They had a blast telling you their festive tales.

Each familiar appears in a different series.

Juno is the main character in the **Magical Misfits Mysteries series**.

Hilda is a supportive familiar in the first three books of the **Witch Haven series** (told through the viewpoint of her much loved witch, Indigo Ash.)

Wiggles is the (usually) faithful talking sidekick in the **Crypt Witch series**. He helps his witch, Tempest, solve crimes while resisting the allure of brownies!

Witch Haven and the Crypt Witch series are complete if you wish to indulge in these fun stories. At the point of publication, there are six books in the Magical Misfits Mysteries series.

To find out more, keep reading.

If you want to explore more of Hilda's weird and wonderful world, enter Witch Haven.

## Spells and Spooks

I'm back in the last place I want to be. A place where my magic went rogue, and people died. Witch Haven should be a haven, but I messed that up big time. I have no friends to help me. No family left. And not even a witch's familiar to keep me on the right path.

Magic used to flow through me, but now I'm a lone witch, drained of power and hoping I can sneak into Witch Haven, clear up the mess my stepmom left behind, and get out alive.

If the villagers find out I'm here, I'll be hunted. If the Magic Council catch me using anything more powerful than a light spell, I'll go back to jail. And if my guilt doesn't choke me, the gnomes will.

Home sweet home never felt so unwelcoming.

Welcome to this cozy witch paranormal mystery series, full of magic and puzzles to solve. Meet failed witch, Indigo Ash, as she struggles to get over her past and stay alive, along with a cast of quirky, fun characters who'll entertain you.

**Spells and Spooks is available in paperback and e-book.**

**For a complete list of books in this series and their reading order, turn the page.**

# Also By

## WITCH HAVEN

Spells and Spooks
Hexes and Haunts
Curses and Corpses
Muffins and Moonlight
Cupcakes and Cauldrons
Pancakes and Potions
Hauntings and High Jinx
Hauntings and Havoc
Hauntings and Hoaxes
The Case of the Screaming Skull
The Case of the Poisoned Pumpkin
The Case of the Cursed Candy
Fire Fang
Silvaria

To keep exploring the wonderful world Wiggles lives in, enjoy an adventure in Willow Tree Falls.

## Luck of the Witch

### There's a little bad in every good witch!

When Tempest Crypt's not chasing demons, she's running her bar and avoiding eye contact with the leader of the biker gang.

Things turn dark when her sister, Aurora, is arrested for the murder of Deacon Feathers, a front-runner in the local mayoral election.

Tempest must go head to head with Angel Force, the bumbling group of angels who keep the peace, to save her sister. With too many suspects, too little time, and a troublesome demon of her own to keep in check, she has her back against the wall.

Along with her feisty four-legged sidekick Wiggles - a cake obsessed hound with a difference - Tempest must solve this murder before Aurora goes to jail for a crime she didn't commit.

### Luck of the Witch is available in paperback and e-book.

### For a complete list of books in this series and their reading order, turn the page.

# Also By

## Crypt Witch

Luck of the Witch
Hell of a Witch
Revenge of the Witch
Curse of the Witch
Son of a Witch
Framing of the Witch
Trickery of the Witch
Wishes of the Witch
Harmony of the Witch
Remedy of the Witch
Gift of the Witch
Toil of the Witch
Jinxing of the Witch
Craving of the Witch
Union of the Witch
Chaos of the Witch
Sleighing of the Witch

If you want to spend more time with Juno, enter the world of the magical misfits.

## Every Witch Way but Ghouls

Feisty enchanted hedgehogs with eye-watering gas issues, a half-dragon with an attitude, and a headless corpse aren't the best things to start the day with! But that's what we encounter in our first week working for animal control in Crimson Cove. We'd only come here to find a missing person, but got more than we bargained for. As an enchanted cat, few things phase me, but even I wince when my wonderful witch, Zandra Crypt, finds a body missing its head.

Much like my witch, I have a strong sense of justice, and when the angels are stumped over the killer, we poke around. It doesn't take long before we find a worrying connection to the body, a dangerous gang of magical criminals, and what happened to Zandra's mother (she's the missing person.)

How will a plucky witch and a strikingly beautiful white cat (that's me) beat the gang, find the killer, and locate Zandra's mother?

Care to find out, help me solve a murder, while I share a secret or two with you? Then welcome. The price of entry into this magical witch mystery is one head tickle and some fishy treats for me. Enjoy!

**Every Witch Way but Ghouls is available in paperback and e-book.**

**For a list of books in this series and their reading order, turn the page.**

# Also By

## MAGICAL MISFITS MYSTERIES

Every Witch Way but Ghouls

Every Witch Way but Vamped

Every Witch Way but Bitten

Every Witch Way but Wolf

Every Witch Way but Hidden

Every Witch Way but Demon